ASHES

ASHES

ILSA J. BICK

EGMONT
USA

NEW YORK

EGMONT
We bring stories to life

First published by Egmont USA, 2011
443 Park Avenue South, Suite 806
New York, NY 10016

Copyright © Ilsa J. Bick, 2011
All rights reserved

1 3 5 7 9 8 6 4 2

www.egmontusa.com

Library of Congress Cataloging-in-Publication Data
Bick, Ilsa J.
Ashes / Ilsa J. Bick.
p. cm.
Summary: Alex, a resourceful seventeen-year-old running from her
incurable brain tumor, Tom, who has left the war in Afghanistan, and Ellie,
an angry eight-year-old, join forces after an electromagnetic pulse sweeps
through the sky and kills most of the world's population, turning some of
those who remain into zombies and giving the others superhuman senses.
ISBN 978-1-60684-175-4 (hardcover) —ISBN 978-1-60684-231-7 (electronic book)
[1. Science fiction. 2. Survival—Fiction. 3. Zombies—Fiction.] I. Title.
PZ7.B47234As 2011
[Fic]—dc22   2010051825

Printed in the United States of America

CPSIA tracking label information:
Printed in July 2011 at Berryville Graphics, Berryville, Virginia

FOR DAVID,
NOW AND ALWAYS.

I tell you the past
is a bucket of ashes . . .

CARL SANDBURG

"Where are you?" Aunt Hannah demanded as soon as Alex thumbed TALK. "What do you think you're doing?"

"I just crossed into Michigan," Alex said, choosing the easiest question first. When she'd spotted the WELCOME TO MICHIGAN sign—GREAT LAKES! GREAT TIMES!—she felt a sense of things opening up, expanding, as if she'd been traveling in a perpetual night on a lonely road hemmed by a thick, black forest and was only now getting her first glimpse of the sun. "I had to get gas." Which was really neither here nor there.

"Michigan. What the bloody hell's in Michigan?" Aunt Hannah's second husband had been a Brit. Aunt Hannah wasn't. She was originally from Wisconsin—Sheboygan, which Alex didn't think was a real place until the Everly Brothers mentioned it—and said *bloody* was way better than other swears because all her friends, most of whom were Lutherans, thought she was just being cute: *Oh, that Hannah.* So Aunt Hannah said *bloody* quite often, especially in church.

"Lots of things," Alex said. She stood a few feet away from the gas station's bathrooms in a blush of salmon-colored light from the setting sun. Across the street, a billboard suggesting a visit to Oren in Amish country jockeyed with one exhorting families to bring their elderly to a hospice named Northern Light—GOD'S LIGHT IN DARK TIMES—and another suggested a visit to the Iron Mining Museum north of town. "I just needed some time."

"Time. Time for *what*?" Aunt Hannah's voice was tight. "You think this is a bloody game? We're talking about your *life*, Alexandra."

"I know that. It's just . . ." She toyed with a silver whistle on a sterling chain around her neck. The whistle had been a gift from her father when she was six, on their first overnight hike: *You ever get into trouble out here, honey, you just blow that and I'll be there in a heartbeat.* This was one of her few, clear, precious memories of him. "I need to do this now, while I still can."

"I see. So they're with you?"

Alex knew what—*who*—she meant. "Yes."

"I notice your father's gun is missing, too."

"I've got it."

"I see," Aunt Hannah said again, although her tone suggested she really didn't. "Do you honestly think suicide is the answer?"

"Is that what you think?" From somewhere over her shoulder, Alex heard the bathroom door open, and a moment later two girls, a blonde and a brunette, swished by, each wearing a powder-blue sweatshirt with SOMERVILLE HIGH and a tennis racket stenciled in a blaze of white. "You think I'm going to kill myself?"

She regretted the words as soon as they were out of her mouth.

Glancing at Alex, Ponytail Blonde leaned in to whisper something to Ponytail Brunette, who also threw Alex a look. They both did the whole peek-whisper-giggle routine all the way across the lot to a small, ancient-looking school bus and a harried older guy with glasses and a frizz of Einstein hair.

Cheeks burning, Alex turned away. "It's nothing like that."

Although if she were being truthful, it wasn't like she hadn't downed a couple shots of Jack and taken her dad's gun out a few times for a good hard stare. The thing that stopped her, mainly, was the thought that her hand might jerk and she'd end up giving herself a frontal lobotomy or something, which would be just too pathetic. She could picture the gossip girls—kids like Ponytail Blonde and Ponytail Brunette—at lunch afterward: *Like, gawd, how* lame.

Aunt Hannah said, "Yes, but if you were coming back, you wouldn't have taken them."

"No. All it means is that *they're* not coming back."

"Alexandra, there's no need for you to do this on your own. Your mother was my sister." Aunt Hannah's voice got a little watery. "I know she would never have agreed to this. This was not their *intention*."

"Well, isn't it good they're not around to argue the point?"

Aunt Hannah went from watery to desert-dry in a nanosecond. "Don't use that tone of voice with me, Alexandra. You are only seventeen. You are a very sick young woman, and you are not old enough to know what's best in this situation. Stubbornness and self-pity are not answers."

3

This was getting them nowhere. All Aunt Hannah saw was a seventeen-year-old orphan, with a brain tumor the size of a tennis ball, who'd finally cracked under the strain. "I know, Aunt Hannah. You're right. Feeling sorry for myself and being a pain in the ass are not answers."

"Good. Now we've cleared that up." Her aunt honked into a tissue. "When are you coming back?"

Uh . . . maybe never? "First week in October. Maybe . . . the eighth?"

She could hear her aunt counting under her breath. "Twelve days? Why so long?"

"It takes that long to hike there and back."

"Hike?"

"Well, there aren't any roads."

"But you can't be serious. You're not strong enough."

"Sure I am. It's been three months since the last cycle. I've been running and swimming and lifting, and my weight's up again. I'm plenty strong."

"But what about the *new* treatments? You're due in three days and—"

"I'm not doing any more treatments."

"Dr. Barrett was very clear that this new procedure—" Her aunt broke off as Alex's words registered. "What? What do you mean you're not doing any more treatments? Don't be ridiculous. Of course you are. What are you saying?"

"I'm saying that I'm done, Aunt Hannah."

"But . . . but the experimental drug," her aunt spluttered. "The procedure, the *PEBBLES*—"

4

"You know they're not going to work." Like the new drug, the PEBBLES—Probes Encapsulated By Biologically Localized Embedding—were also experimental: nano-sized beads, full of poison and coated with a special light-sensitive chemical. Once injected into her bloodstream, the PEBBLES made their way to her brain, where they snuggled up to the tumor: a stubborn monster that had, after a dozen rounds of chemo and radiation, refused to die. When activated by an optic probe, the beads were supposed to release their deadly payload. So far, after four tries, hers had not, even though the doctors had reloaded her brain with enough PEBBLES to run a few dozen pinball machines.

"You have to give it time, Alexandra."

That's so easy for you to say. You've got time. "Aunt Hannah, it's been two years since they found the thing. Nothing's worked."

"Granted, but the tumor's growing relatively *slowly.* Dr. Barrett said you *could* go several more years, and by then, there will be new drugs."

"Or there might not be. I just can't do this anymore." She expected an explosion on the other end, but there was only dead air. The silence spun out so long Alex thought their connection had dropped. "Aunt Hannah?"

"I'm here." Pause. "When did you decide?"

"After my appointment with Barrett last week."

"Why now?"

Because my left hand shakes, Alex thought. *Because I can't smell anything. Because I've got a headful of teeny, tiny little rocks that aren't working and that means more regular chemo and radiotherapy and I am so sick of losing my hair and puking my guts out for nothing and doing schoolwork in bed, and I'm not going into some hospice. Because, for once, I'm calling the shots.*

But what she said was, "I don't think there will be a better time. I need to do this while I still can."

More silence. "I imagine the school will ask after you. Dr. Barrett will have a stroke."

Privately, she thought Barrett might be relieved. No more having to look on the bright side. "What are you going to say?"

"I'll think of something inventive. Will you call?"

"When I make it back," she said, unsure if this was a promise she would keep. "To the car, I mean. Once I'm in the Waucamaw, there's no cell coverage."

"And what am I supposed to do? Hang a lantern from a tower? Twiddle my thumbs? Take up knitting?" When Alex didn't reply, her aunt continued, "I've half a mind to call the police and have you dragged back."

"What's the other half say?"

"That you're stubborn. That once you've made up your mind, there's no talking to you." Her aunt paused. "And that I'm not sure I blame you. That is *not* the same as saying that what you're doing is *right*, but I understand."

"Thanks."

"Don't mention it." Her aunt sighed. "Oh, Alex, do be careful, all right? Try to come back in one piece?"

"I'll be okay. It's not like I've never backpacked before."

"It's not your competence I question. Make a fire, live off the land, build a house out of twigs and chewing gum . . . so like your father. If the bloody zombies attack, you're set."

"Thanks," she said against the prick of tears. Crying was not the way she wanted this to end. "I should probably go. I love you, Aunt Hannah."

"Oh, you bloody little fool," her aunt said. "Don't you think I know that?"

They never spoke to each other again.

PART ONE:
THE MOUNTAIN

1

Four days later, Alex perched on a knuckle of bone-cold rock and whittled an alder branch to a toothpick as she waited for her coffee water to boil. A stiff wind gusted in from the northwest, wet and cold. Far below, the Moss River sparkled with sun dazzle, a glittering ribbon that wound through a deep valley of leafless hardwoods, silver-blue spruce, and the darker green of dense hemlock and feathery white pine. The chilly air smelled chilly—which is to say that for Alex, it really smelled like nothing at all. Which Alex was pretty used to, having not smelled anything for well over a year.

The cold was a surprise, but then she'd never hiked the Waucamaw in late September either. The Waucamaw Wilderness had always been a summer adventure with her parents when pesky no-see-ums, bloodsucking mosquitoes, and heat that could melt a person to a sweat puddle were her biggest problems. Now, she was crunching over brittle ice and skidding on frost-covered roots and bare rock every morning. The going was treacherous, each step an invitation to turn an ankle. The farther north and the closer to

Lake Superior she got—still two days in the future and nothing but a hazy purple smear smudging the horizon—the greater the risk of bad weather. She could just make out, to the very far west, beneath a slate layer of clouds, the feathery, blue-gray swirls of rain blowing south. But for her, the way ahead was nothing but blue skies: a day that promised to be crisp and picture-perfect, and something she was pretty sure her parents would've loved.

If only she could remember who they were.

In the beginning, there'd been smoke.

She was fifteen and an orphan by then, which was kind of sucky, although she'd had a year to get over it already. When the smoky stink persisted and there was no fire, her aunt decided Alex was having one of those post-traumatic things and shipped her off to a shrink, a complete gestapo-wannabe who probably wore black stilettos and beat her husband: *Ah zo, ze smoke, zis is a repetition of your parents' crash, yah?* Only the shrink was also pretty smart and promptly shipped Alex off to Barrett, a neurosurgeon, who found the monster.

Of course, the tumor was cancerous and inoperable. So she got chemo and radiation, and her hair and eyebrows fell out. The upside: her legs and pits never needed shaving. The downside was that the antinausea drugs didn't work—*so* just her luck—and she puked about every five minutes, driving the bulimics at school a little nuts because she was, like, this total pro. In between treatments, she stopped puking and her hair, rich and red as blood, grew back. A chronic headache muttered in her temples, but like

Barrett said, no one ever died from pain. True, but some days you didn't much enjoy living either. Eventually, the smell of smoke went away—but so did the smell of everything else, because the monster didn't shrivel up but continued silently growing and munching.

What no one warned her about was that when you had no sense of smell *at all*, a lot of memories fizzled. Like the way the smell of a pine tree conjured a quick brain-snapshot of tinsel and Christmas lights and a glittery angel, or the spice of nutmeg and buttery cinnamon made you flash to a bright kitchen and your mother humming as she pressed pie crust into a glass dish. With no sense of smell, your memories dropped like pennies out of a ripped pocket, until the past was ashes and your parents were blanks: nothing more than the holes in Swiss cheese.

A stuttering beat, something between a lawnmower and a semi-automatic rifle, broke the silence. A moment later, she spotted the plane—a white, single-prop job—buzzing over the valley, heading north and west. Her eyes dropped to her watch: ten minutes to eight. Sucker was right on time. After four days, she decided that it was the same plane that made a twice-daily run, a little before eight every morning and about twenty minutes after four every afternoon. She could pretty much set her watch by the guy.

The buzz of the plane faded and the quiet descended again like a bell jar over the forest. The hollow *thock-thock-thock* of a woodpecker drifted up from the valley far below. A trio of crows grated to one another in the pines, and a hawk carved a lazy spiral against the sky.

She sipped her coffee, heard herself swallow. The coffee smelled and tasted like nothing, just hot and brown. Then, something—a soft, tan blur—moved out of the corner of her eye, off to the right. She tossed a quick glance, not expecting anything more exciting than a squirrel or maybe a chipmunk.

So the dog was, well, kind of a surprise.

2

She froze.

The dog was lean but muscular, with a broad chest, black mask, and sable markings. It looked like a German shepherd but was much smaller, so maybe not fullgrown? A bright blue pack was snapped around the dog's middle, and a length of choke chain winked around its neck.

From somewhere down the trail came the faint scuffle of leaves. The dog's ears swiveled, though its dark eyes never left Alex. Then a man's voice drifted over the rise: "Mina? You got something, girl?"

The dog let out a low whine but didn't budge.

"Hello?" Her throat was very dry, and the word came out more like a croak. She slicked her lips, tried swallowing past a tongue suddenly as rough as sandpaper. "Um . . . could you call your dog?"

The man's voice came again. "Oh my God, I'm sorry. Don't worry, she won't hurt you. . . . Mina, down, girl."

The dog—Mina—instantly obeyed, sinking to its belly. That was encouraging. The dog didn't look half as ferocious lying down.

"She down?" the man called.

And if she wasn't? Then *what?* "Uh-huh."

"Excellent. Hang on, we're almost . . ." A moment later, a weedy man with a thatch of white hair labored over the rise, a walking stick in his right hand. He was dressed like a lumberjack, right down to the black turtleneck beneath a red flannel shirt. A sheathed hatchet dangled from a carry loop attached to the frame of his pack.

The girl—a kid with blonde pigtails—was a step or two behind. A pink Hello Kitty daypack was strapped to her back, and she wore both a matching pink parka and a scowl. A pair of white earbuds was screwed into her ears, the volume so loud that Alex caught the faintest thump of bass.

"Hey there," the old guy said. He nodded at Alex's coffee press. "Smelled that halfway down the trail and decided to follow my nose, only Mina beat me to it." He stuck out a hand. "Jack Cranford. This is my granddaughter, Ellie. Ellie, say hello."

"Hi," said the girl, colorlessly. Alex thought she was maybe eight or nine and already had way too much 'tude. The kid's head bobbed the tiniest bit with the throb of her music.

"Hey," Alex said. She didn't make a move to take the old guy's hand, not only because this guy, with his hatchet and dog and sullen granddaughter, was a complete stranger, but because the way the dog stared made her think that *it* would be just as happy to take her hand first.

The old guy waited, his smile wobbling a bit and a question growing in his eyes. When Alex didn't volunteer anything else, he shrugged, took his hand back, and said, genially, "That's okay. If I were in your shoes, I wouldn't trust me either. And I'm sorry about Mina. I keep forgetting there are a couple packs of wild dogs in the Waucamaw. Must've scared the bejesus out of you."

"That's okay," she lied, and thought, *Wild dogs?*

The silence stretched. The kid bobbed and looked bored. The dog began to pant, its tongue unfurling in a moist pink streamer. Alex saw the old guy's eyes flick from her to her tent and back. He said, "You always talk so much?"

"Oh. Well . . ." How come adults got away with saying things that would sound rude coming out of *her* mouth? She groped for something neutral. "I don't know you."

"Fair enough. Like I said, I'm Jack. That's Ellie and that's Mina. And you are . . . ?"

"Alex." Pause. "Adair." She wanted to kick herself. Answering had been a reflex, the way you didn't ignore a teacher.

"Pleased to meet you, Alex. Should've known you had a wee bit of the Irish with those leprechaun eyes and that red mane. Don't run into many Irish in these parts."

"I live in Evanston." Like that answered something. "Uh . . . but my dad was from New York." What was she *doing*?

The old guy's left eyebrow arched. "I see. So, you by yourself up here?"

She decided not to answer that one. "I didn't hear your dog."

"Oh, well, I'm not surprised. That's her training kicking in, I'm afraid. Actually, she's not mine. Technically, she belongs to Ellie here."

"Grandpaaaaa . . ." The kid did the eye-roll.

"Now, Ellie, you should be proud," Jack said. To Alex: "Mina's a Malinois, actually . . . Belgian shepherd. She's a WMD, working military dog. Used to work bomb-detection, but she's retired now." He tried on a regretful smile that didn't quite make it to his eyes. "She belonged to my son, Danny . . . Ellie's dad. KIA. Iraq, about a year ago."

The girl's lips drew down and an edge of color flirted with the angle of her jaw, but she said nothing. Alex felt a little ping of sympathy for the kid. "Oh. Well, she's a really nice dog." Which, as soon as she heard the words leaving her mouth, made her cringe. She knew how awkward people got when they found out you'd *lost* a parent. Even the word made it feel like, somehow, it was your fault.

The girl's eyes, pallid and silver, slid from Alex's face to the ground. "She's just a stupid *dog*."

"Ellie," Jack began, then bit back whatever else he'd been about to say. "Please take out your earplugs now. You're being rude. Besides, it's too loud. You're going to ruin your hearing."

Again with the eye-roll, but the kid uncorked her ears and let the buds dangle around her neck. Another awkward silence and then Alex said, impulsively, "Look, I just made coffee. Would you guys like some?"

The girl gave her a *duh, hello, I'm a kid* look, but Jack said, "I'd love a cup, Alex. We can even make a contribution." Jack winked. "You won't believe this, but I packed in some Krispy Kremes."

"*Grandpaaaaa*," the girl said. "We were *saving* them."

"That's okay," Alex put in quickly. "I just had break—"

"We are *having* doughnuts." Jack's tone took on an edge, and Alex heard the ghosts of a lot of old arguments.

"Sure, that would be great," Alex chirped, so cheerily she sounded like Alvin on speed. "I love doughnuts."

"They're probably stale," said Ellie.

3

The Krispy Kremes *were* stale—she still got texture—but dunked fine. To Alex, they tasted like wet paste.

"I used to take a French press, only this one time I forgot to grind the beans beforehand." Jack dumped powdered creamer into his mug and stirred. "Ended up smashing the beans with my ax."

Ellie broke off another bite of a chocolate-dipped with sprinkles, flipping the morsel expertly to the dog, who snapped it up in midair. "Isn't that, like, being totally addicted?"

Jack colored. Alex felt sorry for the old guy and said, "I'd have done the same thing."

Ellie gave her a withering look, but Jack only chuckled. "Well, I wouldn't recommend it. That coffee was so strong, my teeth curled . . . Ellie, honey, that doughnut's going to make Mina sick. Chocolate's not good for dogs."

"She's fine," Ellie said, and flipped more doughnut to the dog.

Alex changed the subject. "So where are you guys from?"

"Minneapolis," Jack said. "I used to be a reporter—foreign

correspondent for the Trib. Haven't been able to write a lick since Danny died. My editor's tearing his hair out. Seeing as how he's already bald, that's kind of a challenge, but he's a good guy."

Ellie snorted. "Is that why you call him a jerk every time you get off the phone?"

What was *with* this kid? "My English teacher said that a writer is the worst judge of his own work," said Alex.

"Maybe. Mostly, I don't much believe in my writing anymore. People don't care. Most have the attention span of gnats and can't be bothered. Like that baloney about combat operations in Iraq being over? What a crock. It's political. What they don't tell you is that for the guys still over there, the rules of engagement are the same, and there's plenty of shooting—" Breaking off, Jack sighed, then ran a hand through a swirl of snowy-white cowlick. "Sorry. That makes me sound angry and bitter. I'm not. It's just . . ."

"Well, you ought to be mad," Ellie said, with sudden heat. "My dad's dead, but no one's going to jail. He gets blown up, and all I get is a stupid dog. How come that is?"

"Now, Ellie, we've talked about this. In a war—"

"A war? What kind of answer is *that*?" The girl hurled the rest of her doughnut at the dog. Surprised, the dog retreated a few steps and darted an anxious look at Jack.

Alex couldn't help herself. "You ought to be nicer to your grandfather. He isn't doing anything to you."

"Who *cares* what you think? You're not my mother. I don't know you!" Ellie kicked at Alex's WindPro. The tiny stove overturned and the coffee press tumbled to the rocks in a spray of glass and hot liquid. The dog danced out of the way with a startled yip. "No one *asked* you!"

"Ellie!" Jack made a grab for his granddaughter. "That's *enough!*"

"I hate this." Ellie slithered out of reach. "I hate this, I hate you, I hate these woods, I hate *everybody*! Just leave me *alone!*"

"Cool off!" Jack rapped, his patience finally snapping. "Go for a walk. Get control of yourself, you understand me?"

"Fine!" Ellie spat. She jammed in her earbuds and stalked in the direction of the trail Alex had traveled the day before. The dog began to trot after, but the girl hurled a command over her shoulder: "Stay!" The dog faltered, then took another uncertain step after the girl. Ellie fetched up a stick and cocked it like a baseball bat. "Stay, you dumb dog, *stay!*"

"Ellie!" Jack roared. "Don't you dare hit that dog! Mina, *come!*" As the dog sprinted back, Jack said to the girl, "Sweetheart, honey, why do you have to be so hateful?"

"Why *not?*" Ellie said. "It's not like being good ever got me anywhere." Then she whirled on her heel and flung herself into the woods.

"It's been a very hard year. With her mother gone God-knows-where and my Mary passed on, it's just me," Jack said. He cupped a handful of jagged glass. "Look, I'll be happy to pay for this."

"No, no, it's okay. I understand," Alex said, but she was pissed. Jack was nice enough, but she had her own problems and, now, no coffee press. Thank God she'd packed instant. She inspected her WindPro and almost groaned. Two of the struts were bent, and she didn't like the way the fuel hose was kinked. With her luck, she'd have to take a rock to the metal, maybe bash it straight. "Careful you don't cut yourself, Jack."

"Oh, I'm pretty tough for an old bird. Well, all except my ticker. Got me this new pacer about six months ago." Jack dumped glass into the empty Krispy Kreme bag. "It's Ellie got me worried. She's a little time bomb. I was hoping if I could get away with her awhile, maybe do some fishing . . . People mean well, but there's just so much sympathy a little girl can take."

Alex could definitely relate. Everyone was always *so sorry* when, really, *sorry* was just a word you said because it was more polite than *whoa, better you than me.* "Where's her mom?"

Jack grunted. "Hell if I know. She took off a year after Ellie was born. Said she needed *time* to get her head on straight, needed to *find* herself. Get herself *lost* is more like it. Haven't seen her since. You know the world's screwed up when they make you get a license if you want a dog but let any fool have a kid." He sighed. "A lot of this is my fault."

"How do you figure that?"

Jack waved a hand at the dog, which sprawled on its belly in a doze. "Mina was my idea. Once the dogs are retired—if they're too banged up to work or just plain old—the military lets handlers' families adopt, if they want. Mina was wounded in the same blast that killed Danny, so I thought having her would make Ellie feel better, like having a little bit of her father still around. He loved that dog, but Ellie hates it. She's really not a bad kid. Most of the time she's about as cooperative as you can expect a sad, really angry eight-year-old girl to be."

"That doesn't sound so great."

"You get used to it. I thought it would do her good to unplug and get out in the fresh air, spend some time with Mina . . ." Jack waved away the rest. "Enough of that. So what's your story?"

"Me?" Alex gave up trying to force the WindPro's bent struts. "I'm just figuring things out."

"Where you headed?"

"Mirror Point."

"On Superior? That's pretty damn far. I wouldn't want my daughter out here alone. No telling what might happen."

She knew Jack meant well, but one of the perks of being terminally ill was you got to break all kinds of rules. So she pushed back. "Jack, I don't need your permission, and I didn't ask for your opinion."

"Doesn't mean I'm not going to give it. You kids think you're invulnerable, but there are wild dogs in these woods and all kinds of nuts."

Not to mention old guys poking their noses in other people's business. But that would be too snarky, and she had a feeling that Jack was hassling *her* because he couldn't fix Ellie. So she focused on dismantling her WindPro and let the silence go. After a moment, Jack reached down to squeeze her shoulder. "Sorry. I know I'm just being an old fart."

"Jack," she said, exasperated both with her stove and the conversation. "I appreciate your concern, but it's really none of your—"

All of a sudden, Jack's hand clamped down hard enough to hurt. Surprised, she looked up and then whatever she'd been about to say evaporated on her tongue when she got a good look at his face.

"I . . ." Jack's face twisted in a sudden spasm, and he pressed the heels of both hands to his temples. "I . . . wait, wait . . ."

"Jack!" Alarmed, she reached for him—and then she saw the dog. Mina was completely rigid, her muscles quivering, the hackles along her spine as stiff as a Mohawk. The dog's black lips curled back to reveal two glistening rows of very sharp, very white teeth, and a growl began somewhere in the dog's chest.

Alex felt a stab of fear. "Jack, Mina's—"

Jack gagged, a deep, harshly liquid sound. An instant later, a sudden jet of bright red blood boiled from his mouth to splatter onto the icy rocks. Alex screamed just as Mina let out a sudden high yelp—

And a second later, the pain had Alex, too.

4

The pain was fire, a laser that scorched her brain. A sudden metallic chattering bubbled in her ears, and her vision sheeted first red and then glare-white, and then she was stumbling, her feet tangling, and she fell. Something wet and hot spurted from her throat and dribbled down her chin.

Jack was in just as much trouble, maybe worse. His skin was so chalky that his blood looked fake, like something for Halloween. His legs folded and he began to sag, one hand digging at his chest, and then he simply dropped like a puppet whose strings had been cut. He hit hard, his head bouncing off the rock and his glasses jumping away, the lenses sparking in the sun.

Stunned, she could only sprawl there like a broken doll. Blood pooled in her throat and she began to cough as her vision spun like water swirling down a drain. That weird metallic screech was still very loud, splashing down from the sky. What *was* that? Dizzy, a drill-bit of pain coring into her brain, she dragged her head up, struggling to focus. At first, she thought she must be passing out, because the sky was getting blacker and blacker—but then she realized the blackness was *moving*.

Birds. There were birds. Not just a few or a flock, but hundreds and hundreds, *thousands*. All kinds, all shapes, all sizes. And the birds were everywhere, in the sky above and exploding up from the valley below in a spiraling, screaming funnel cloud. They weren't organized, not following the way a flock does, but smashing into one another, either because there were so many or the pain that had her in its iron grip had them, too.

Something thudded against her legs. Shrieking, she flinched away as a dying crow tumbled to the rock. One massive wing was bent all the way back, and its black beak had snapped clean off, like lead in a pencil. All around, dead and dying birds began to shower from the sky.

There came a loud, inhuman scream. Cringing, Alex darted a look over her shoulder just in time to see a trio of deer crashing up the hill. They hit the ridge and then reared, driving their hooves into the rock with a sound like jackhammers. One—a large doe—let out a harsh, wet, coughing bray, and then blood burst from its mouth in a crimson halo. The doe reared again, its front legs pedaling, and the other two answered, slicing the air with their hooves. Then the deer surged forward, as if pulled toward the edge by an unseen hand.

No, no, no. Alex's thoughts came in jagged splinters. *No, you're not . . . you're not seeing this. They're not going to . . . they* can't . . .

But they did.

The deer catapulted off the ridge and over the cliff into empty space.

For an instant, they hung, suspended between the bird-choked sky and the darker maw of the valley, and Alex thought of flying reindeer . . .

But then the real world took over again. Gravity closed its fist.

The deer fell, their screams tailing after like spent comets, and they were gone.

5

A split second later something snapped in her head, an almost physical lurch as whatever had her by the scruff of the neck let go. The vise around her skull eased. Her stomach instantly rebelled and she vomited onto the rock. Even when she was sure there was nothing left to bring up, she hung there on all fours, exhausted, a sparkling sensation of pins and needles coursing through her veins and prickling her skin as if her entire body had fallen asleep and her brain had only now figured out how to reconnect. Her heart was hammering. The inside of her head felt slushy and bruised, like someone had stuck in a spoon and given a good stir. She was shaky, as if a good walloping dose of chemo had flooded through her veins. A slow ooze wormed down the right side of her neck, and when she swiped at her skin, her fingers came away bloody.

Oh my God. She closed her eyes against a lunge of sharp-nailed panic clawing its way out of her chest and into her throat. *Take it easy, take it—*

"Graaaandpaaaa?"

★ ★ ★

Ellie groveled on hands and knees at the forest's verge. A slick of blood painted her upper lip. "Grandpaaa?" Her voice hitched and rose a notch. *"Grandpaaaaaa?"*

"Ellie." Alex pushed to a sit, but too fast. The world went off-kilter in a woozy tilt, and she had to fight against another wave of nausea as her stomach crammed into the back of her throat.

"Where's my—" Ellie's gaze shifted to a point beyond Alex, and then the girl's eyes went buggy, the whites showing around motes of silver-blue iris. "Grandpa?"

Alex followed the girl's gaze. Jack was motionless, facedown on the rock, a lake of blood widening around his body in a red corona.

"Grandpa." Ellie began to crawl. Her arm brushed against a dead bird and she pulled back with a yelp, a gluey frill of bloody feathers matted to the back of her hand. Shuddering, she batted at the mess, her words coming in gasps. "Do something, d-do something . . ."

Do something? Do *what*? Alex knew CPR; her doctor-mother had made sure of that. But Jack looked pretty dead, and besides, he was *old* and had a pacemaker, and doing CPR on a real person who'd vomited *blood* . . . Her stomach did another tidal heave. And what if she brought him back to life, or he *had* a pulse—what then? She couldn't call for help, and she was *days* out from her car.

Come on, get a grip. Just check and get it over with.

Touching Jack made her skin crawl, and she winced at the squelching, sucking sound Jack's body made as she rolled him onto his back. Blood painted his face in a slick mask still warm enough to steam. His front teeth, bottom and top, had snapped on impact against the rock into a scatter of smeary, squarish bits that looked like Chiclets. Steeling herself, she pressed her fingers to Jack's neck to check for a pulse. His blood was sticky, and she clamped back on a whimper. *Come on, you can do this. Don't lose it. . . .*

"Do something," Ellie said. Her hand hooked on to Alex's arm. *"Please."*

She caught a quick butterfly-flutter beneath her fingers and almost said something incredibly stupid before realizing that was *her* pulse, not Jack's. She forced herself to give it another few moments to make sure, but she knew Jack was dead. She ought to be sad, but all she felt was relief for the excuse to take back her hand.

"I'm sorry, Ellie," she said. Smears of drying gore and darker red crescents rimed her nails, and she was suddenly desperate for a shower, a bath—anything to wash away the creepy-crawly feel of Jack's blood. And shouldn't she look for something to cover him up? Maybe something in his pack. "I think your grandpa's dead."

"No." Ellie snuffled blood. Her teeth were orange, and the crotch of her jeans was splotchy and dark. "No, no, you're lying!"

"No, I'm not." God, all she wanted was to get off this crazy mountain and back to her car. What had happened anyway? Or—a clutch of fear grabbed her chest—what if it happened again?

I've got to get out, she thought. The stink of Jack's blood, wet and coppery, bloomed in her nose, and she could smell Ellie now, too—the harsh bite of ammonia—and knew the little girl had peed herself. There was a ranker odor frothing from the girl's skin, too, like she'd forgotten to brush her teeth. *Get out, get to my car, and maybe the ranger at the entrance will—*

And then Alex thought, suddenly, *Wait . . . what?*

6

She went absolutely still.

No.

She was wrong. She had to be.

She couldn't smell. The tumor had gobbled that up.

But.

But there was blood. She smelled Jack's blood. Ellie had peed herself, and she smelled *that*. Just now, just this very *second*.

That couldn't be. It must be her imagination, the pain or the shock or . . . or *something*.

But what if it wasn't?

She was almost afraid to try again. But she did; she had to *know*. As awful as the moment was, she leaned over Jack and pulled in a long, slow, deliberate breath, still thinking, *You watch; it's a hallucination—just one of those phantom brain-things.*

But it wasn't nothing. There it was again, the scent so nearly physical she felt it feathering her nose. She smelled something and it was . . . she groped after the comparison . . . yes, it was the scent of wet pennies.

A split second later, a tiny flashbulb popped in the meat of her brain, and she suddenly saw her little red wagon, the one she'd left out in the rain, as clear as day. She was so startled, she actually flinched. That wagon . . . how old had she been? Six? No, no, *seven*, because now there came a series of quicksilver bursts, like the twinkle of fireworks: a brick patio, white roses climbing a trellis, the lazy drone of bees, and then there was her mother, her mother, her own beautiful mother, standing next to her dad and her dad was saying, *I guess we thought you being seven was old enough for you to know how to take care of your things.*

Dad. Alex pulled in a quick gasp. Air rushed into her mouth and over her tongue, and then she registered sour . . . and sharp char and . . . and *sweet.* Coffee—that was the taste of *coffee* and . . . and the *doughnut.* She'd vomited it all back, and now she *tasted*; she could *smell.*

And Alex thought, *Oh. My.* God.

Barrett had talked about The End: the loss of this function, the death of that ability, and, maybe, the need for *pain management*, which was doctor-speak for doping you up until you quietly slept to death.

But Barrett wasn't sure even about that, because The End might be very quick. The tumor would keep getting bigger and bigger, and there was only so much room up there. Build up enough pressure in that contained space and then her brain would squirt from the base of her skull like toothpaste out of the tube. Then it would be lights-out as everything that kept her ticking—heart, lungs—simply stopped.

Mind you, Barrett wasn't *positive* about anything, because

everyone was different. He couldn't tell her what to expect because, well, he'd never died. Fair enough. But she was absolutely positive: Barrett had never, *ever* said anything about how, at The End, she might actually get back what she'd lost.

Like her sense of smell.

Like taste.

Like her dad. Her mom.

Now, she *smelled* Jack's blood. There had been those forgotten memories of her wagon and white roses and her mother. She'd heard her father's *voice*. She could taste the raw edge of vomit in her mouth, and she was awake; she wasn't dreaming.

Maybe this was what people meant when they said your life passed before your eyes when you died. She didn't know. She'd never specifically asked Barrett about that. To be honest, she hadn't been sure she wanted to know. She'd heard of near-death experiences, of course. She'd seen *Ghost*, and she knew the stories: how all your loved ones who'd passed on before hung out waiting for you to walk into the light. But that was dumb. It was what people hoped would happen, not what *really* did. She knew enough science and had plenty of her own experiences. The brain was one funky organ. Kill your sense of smell, chew up your ability to taste, and a lot of your memories got swallowed, too. So, cut off the brain's blood supply, starve the cells of oxygen—and maybe white light was what you saw when you croaked. Who knew? She sure didn't. She had no idea what to expect at The End.

Unless this was it.

Unless this was *her* end, and she was living it.

7

The dog groaned.

"Look." Ellie's voice was stuffy and clogged. A smear of bloody snot glistened above her upper lip. "By your tent."

No, no, go away, just leave me alone. A needle of fear pierced her heart. If she didn't pay attention, would everything—the smells and memories—slip away? All she wanted was to hunker down alone somewhere quiet, focus on what was happening to her.

"What?" she said, but now she spotted the dog struggling to its feet and had to suppress a groan. The animal looked bad, dazed. Blood dribbled like thick syrup from a gash on its scalp. Panting, the dog tottered toward Jack's body, wading through a scatter of dead birds, inking the rock with bloody paw prints. Wary, Alex tensed as Mina began to sniff Jack's body. She had no experience with dogs. Didn't some refuse to leave once their owners were dead? God, what would she do if Mina—

The dog began to bark, furiously and very loudly. Startled, Alex jumped.

"Shut up, you dumb dog!" Ellie clapped her gory hands over her ears. "Shut up, shut up!"

"Shh, shh, Mina, shh," Alex said. The barks were unbearable, like gunshots. She started forward, with no clear idea of what she meant to do; she just wanted the dog to be quiet. She reached for the animal. "Mina, hey."

With a snarl, the dog whipped its head around, teeth bared. Alex snatched her hand back with a small cry, and then, in the very next second, she caught the odor of dank fur—and something else, feral and thick and wild.

What *was* that? Alex felt the tiny hairs bristle along the nape of her neck. The smell was overpowering, rolling off the animal in waves. Alex was dead certain she'd *never* smelled anything like that before in her life.

"Okay," Alex said, her pulse thumping in her neck. "Okay, girl, it's okay." Without looking around, she eased back, felt the soft give, and then heard the *crunch-crackle-pop* as her boot flattened a bird. An instant later, the reek from the animal's smashed guts coiled into her nostrils, and a little whimper of disgust tried to push itself between her teeth.

Leave the dog; let Ellie deal with it. Despite the chill, sweat oozed down her neck, and her mouth filled with a metallic tang that cut through the taste of curdled vomit. She reeked of warm salt and cold fear. *Just get your gear, get the kid, and get off this mountain while you still can.*

No matter what she said or how loudly she said it, Ellie wouldn't budge. Frustrated, her patience fraying, Alex finally grabbed the girl by the wrists. "Ellie, *listen* to me. We've got to leave."

"*No.*" The girl jerked free and slapped her hands to her ears again. The kid was insanely strong. "I'm not going *anywhere* with you!"

"You can't stay here."

"Yes, I can. Don't you tell me what to do."

"Ellie, I'm sorry about your grandpa, but he's dead and we have to get out of here. We have to tell someone what's happened." An inspiration: "Your grandpa would want you to be safe."

"I'm not leaving."

Did this kid do *anything* she was asked? Alex wanted to shake the girl until her teeth rattled. "I can't leave you here."

"Why not? I can take care of myself. I know how to camp."

While she doubted that, Alex decided to try something she'd read about in psychology. "Look, I'll need your help on the trail. It'll be a long, hard hike, and I need someone to come with me."

The girl cracked one eye in a narrow squint. "Where?"

"Hang on, I'll show you." Digging through her pack, she riffled the contents until she found the map she wanted. "You ever seen a topographic map?"

A sparrow of curiosity flitted over the girl's face. "What's that?"

"It's a really detailed map. A good topo shows just about every-thing—streams, rivers, old quarries, railroad tracks, how high the mountains are, how steep. Red lines are roads. Solid green means forest and . . ." She ran her finger over the map until she found a black, blocky silhouette of a house with a flag at its peak. "This is what we want."

"What is it?"

"That's the ranger station. They'll know what to do. They can radio for help."

Ellie considered. "It looks far away and kind of high up."

The station *was* pretty far—a good twenty-five miles east—and a lot higher, adjacent to a fire lookout tower situated atop steep bluffs hemming a small lima bean of a lake. But going there was a better plan than backtracking four days. If they pushed their pace, they might make the station in a day and a half, maybe sooner. "It's nothing you can't handle."

Face darkening into a by-now very familiar scowl, Ellie said, "Well, it *looks* hard. Grandpa and I only did six miles a day."

Whoa. Alex felt a prick of disquiet. Six miles a *day*? What did they do, *crawl*? At that speed, she and Ellie would have much bigger problems, like running out of food. *Okay, don't panic yet; Jack must have supplies.* Aloud, she said, "I'll bet you can do way more. You look pretty strong."

Ellie threw her a look that practically screamed she knew bullshit when she heard it. Her eyes flicked over the map, and then she jabbed at a tiny symbol in the far left corner: ⟨

"What's that?" she asked.

"Maybe an old mine southwest of here. Or a cave."

"There are mines? There are *caves*?"

"Well, sure. This is old mining country, and there are abandoned shafts and caves, but—"

"Are there bears?"

"In the caves? Not yet. They won't den until it gets really cold, but black bears won't bother us so long as we're careful. So don't worry about—"

"What about wolves?"

Okay, they were on a roll. "Yeah, they're around. You can hear them at night, right? So that's another reason to get away from here. All these dead birds'll attract animals—coyotes, raccoons, wolves, and . . ." Too late, she read Ellie's stricken face and realized what she'd said.

"You're going to let the wolves get *Grandpa*?"

"No, no, I meant—"

"They'll *eat* him!" Tears splashed Ellie's cheeks. "They'll *get* him!"

"Ellie—"

"No!" Fists balling, Ellie kicked at the map, the toe of her boot catching a crease. The map made a sound like worn cloth torn in two. "I won't, I won't, I won't!"

"Ellie!" Alex dove for the map. "Stop! We *need* this."

"Well, I don't need *you*!" Ellie was stumbling back, slipping on dead birds and a slick of Jack's blood. "I'm not going anywhere with you!"

"Fine! Then you and your stupid dog can *stay* here. But it's getting late." Pushing to her feet, she pulled back her sleeve to glance at her watch. "I've got a lot of ground to cover, and I don't have *time* to ar—"

She broke off as her brain stutter-stepped.

Wait. She stared at her watch. *That's not right.*

8

Her watch was an older-model Casio IronMan, the only watch she wore when she hiked because the watch was rugged and waterproof and cheap. She'd had it about ten years, maybe replaced the battery twice in that time. The watch had never failed her, or given her a millisecond of trouble.

Now, however, the gray screen was blank.

Had she fallen that hard? She inspected the watch, saw that the face had only the dings and scratches she remembered. No, she was sure the watch had been working just fine. In fact, she remembered checking the time.

Well . . . okay, so her watch had died. A coincidence.

Yes, but so had Jack, and something made those birds go nuts and those deer. Something had sizzled through her brain like an electric shock—no, more like lightning—so bad she'd nearly passed out. Only now she had her sense of smell back.

So . . . maybe not a coincidence.

Her fingers shook as she dug out her iPod. She thumbed it. Then she thumbed it again and then a third time, but the iPod stayed just as dead.

She tried her cell. Nothing. Not just no signal—she expected that out this far—but the cell wouldn't power up.

Neither did her radio. Changing the batteries did nothing. By the time she figured out that her two LED flashlights were also dead, leaving her with just a big Swiss Army clunker her father had bought about a million years ago, she was thoroughly freaked out.

One electronic gizmo crapping out was something that just happened.

Two was bad luck.

But *everything*?

Her gaze crawled to Ellie, and those iPod earbuds still dangling around the kid's neck. "Ellie, is your iPod working?"

"No." Ellie's silver eyes inched up grudgingly. "It got hot."

"What?"

"It got *hot*." Her tone suggested that Alex was clearly as deaf as she was a complete moron. "I was listening to it, and it got hot."

"Hot."

"Like it burned my hand, okay? And then it stopped working and—"

Alex interrupted. "Do you have a flashlight?"

"Of *course*."

"Can I see it?"

Ellie got that pouty look again. "No."

Alex knew not to push it. Then her gaze snagged on Ellie's wrist. "What time is it?"

"You've got a watch."

Alex wanted to pitch the kid off the cliff. "Can you just tell me?"

Ellie heaved a deep sigh. "Nine and . . . eleven."

Alex was confused, then thought maybe an eight-year-old kid might not know how to tell time, and she sure wasn't going to get into *that*. So, 9:11 would be 9:55, and that seemed right. Which meant that *Ellie's* watch . . . "Your watch still works?"

Ellie nearly sneered. "Of course. It's Mickey Mouse. It used to be my daddy's. I wind it every day like Grandpa taught me."

A wind-up. So are we talking just the batteries? No, Dad's Swiss Army flashlight works. It's got to be something else. Even with all that blood, she made out the watch on Jack's right wrist, but she was too far away to be certain. She didn't want to touch Jack again. Mina might not let her get close anyway. "Does your grandpa's watch still work?"

"I don't know. Why are you asking all these questions?"

"Ellie, could you check, please? I don't think Mina will let me—"

"I don't want to touch him," Ellie blurted.

"Oh." She understood that. "Well, can you hold Mina? I don't want her to freak out, but I have to check something." For a moment, she thought Ellie might refuse, but then the girl's hand snaked around Mina's collar.

Alex slid forward, one eye on the dog, the other on Jack's watch. The Seiko's hour hand was locked on nine. The minute hand said it was three minutes after the hour, and the second sweep hand was notched between twenty and a hash mark—and it wasn't moving. Alex stared at that watch face so hard that if she'd been Cyclops, she could've burned a hole right through it. She stared so long, her eyes watered. But that second hand didn't budge.

Her watch and Jack's, the iPods, the radio, and her LEDs—all dead, and Jack . . . Her gaze drifted up to his face. Something he'd said was important: *I'm a tough old bird, all except my ticker.*

Of *course.* Jack had a pacer. That was the only explanation for why Jack was dead and they weren't. She knew pacers had tiny computer chips that synchronized the heartbeat to what a body required at any given moment. Jack's pacer had shorted out and that's what killed him. But how? What could reach inside Jack's chest, fry his pacer, kill *all* their electronics—and grab *them?* They'd all felt it: Ellie, with her nosebleed and headache; the dog, which had yowled in pain; and the birds and the deer, which had all gone insane.

And *she* could smell again—things like blood and the tang of resin from the evergreens and her sweat. She smelled the dog, too: not just its fur but something nameless steaming from somewhere deep inside the animal.

Yet Ellie was back to normal, which for her seemed to be somewhere between whiny and nasty. The dog . . . well, who knew? It wasn't attacking her, at least. She threw a quick look into the sky, eyed a hawk floating by on an updraft and then, still higher, a trio of turkey vultures turning a slow, looping spiral. The birds seemed back to normal, too.

So, if her sense of smell didn't evaporate, then only *her* brain had altered in some way. Out of all of them, only she had changed.

But how? And was she done changing? Was that the end of it?

Or was this just the beginning?

9

The good news was that Ellie cooperated just long enough to dig out a blue rain poncho that Alex used to cover up Jack. The bad news was that Ellie decided she was done being helpful and Mina wouldn't let Alex anywhere near Jack's pack. Every time she got close, the dog's teeth showed, and finally, Alex gave it up. They'd just have to leave whatever food and water Jack had. That was okay. Ellie could have most of her food. If she could get the kid to lay down some distance, they wouldn't be on the trail more than two days. Three, if they were really unlucky. She'd get by.

As she broke down her tent, she again flirted with the idea of going back to her car. With the electronics on the fritz, would her car start? She knew as much about cars as she did Chinese—like, *nothing*—but most cars had complex electronics, and a computer chip or two. So maybe not.

She buckled her lumbar pack around her waist. The pack was heavier than usual because, along with her emergency survival gear, she'd also wedged a black, soft-sided case she hadn't unzipped for nearly three years, since the week after her parents died. The case was weighty, almost twelve pounds, and was sort of hers and sort of not. Aunt Hannah had never made the contents a secret; had told Alex she should feel free to look inside any time she wanted. *It might do you some good* was how her aunt put it, though she never explained what that good might be and Alex sure didn't know.

There were memories in this case. At first, they'd been memories too painful to want to think about, much less remember. For the first year, she'd had no control over those memories at all. The triggers could be almost anything: a snatch of song, the sudden warble of a police cruiser, a stranger with hair so exactly like her mother's that the sight stole her breath. Every memory brought pain that was sharp and sudden and so fierce it was like someone had slipped a knife between her ribs and given a good twist. Then, as the monster grew and her sense of smell died, the triggers seemed fewer and her memories harder to get at, as if she were trying to recover files from a corrupted hard drive. In a way, she'd been okay with that. What she never told Aunt Hannah was that, sometimes, having a monster squatting in her brain—eating away at her memories, crunching them to dust—had been, almost, a relief. Her brain wasn't exactly hers anymore, but at least her thoughts weren't out of control.

It also occurred to her now that she'd stolen the case from her aunt for nothing. No way she'd reach Mirror Point now. Her reasons for coming to the Waucamaw to begin with had just gone up in those proverbial flames.

Which was pretty ironic, considering what was in the case.

★ ★ ★

"I'm leaving now," Alex said. "I think you better come with me."

"No. I hate you."

Yeah, yeah. "Okay, listen: I'm taking the shorter trail, the one I showed you on the map that goes straight down into the valley. When you decide to come—"

"I'm never coming."

"Don't forget your pack, and don't forget to strap on Mina's pack . . ."

Ellie stoppered her ears. "I'm not listening to you."

". . . because I don't have dog food. If you could go through your grandpa's pack and bring along some—"

"La-la-la-la," Ellie sang. "La-la-la-la."

"— some more food and water for us, that would be good, too." Honestly, she didn't want the kid or her dog to come along, but Ellie was only eight. Alex didn't even remember what it was like to *be* that young.

Slipping her father's Glock from her pack, she slotted in a full magazine, pulled back on the slide, and jacked a round into the chamber. A standard Glock didn't have an external safety. It was one of the reasons her cop dad had liked the weapon. Just point and shoot. When she'd inherited the gun, though, she'd installed a cross-trigger safety. No really good reason—this was well before the monster sent up smoke signals—but maybe her subconscious was on the ball even then. Considering how often she and the Glock had gotten cozy in her aunt's basement, the time it took to jab that little button and release the keeper bar probably accounted for why she was still ticking. A millisecond was just long enough for a person to change her mind.

Now, after double-checking the safety, she reseated the gun, then clipped the paddle holster to her right hip.

Ellie had stopped singing. "Why are you wearing that?"

Because Jack's dead and our electronics are toast and I smell you, Ellie. I smell blood. I smell the dog. "You can never be too careful."

"Whose is it?"

"My dad's. Mine, now."

"My grandpa says guns kill people."

She wasn't going there. "Don't wait too long. It gets dark fast."

"So go." Ellie screwed in her earbuds. "I don't care."

She wanted to point out that the iPod was dead but thought that was mean. "You will if you're caught on the mountain in the dark."

"I'm not coming."

"I'll see you later."

"No, you won't."

"Okay then." She set off and didn't look back. But she felt Ellie's eyes for a long time just the same.

10

The trail was much worse than she'd imagined. The drop was steep, slippery with dead birds, scaly rock, and soft, splintery gray limestone. Centuries of erosion from rain and snowmelt had left the mountain scored with steep chutes and funnels where debris— loose rock, fallen trees—emptied before being swept down into the valley. After an hour, her thighs and knees were screaming; her face was oily with sweat, her mouth gummy, and her shirt glued to her shoulder blades. Stopping for a water break, she stripped down to her sweatshirt, tying her parka to her pack, then dragged off her cap to let the air's cold fingers glide over her scalp. Tugging free one of two Nalgene bottles from her fanny pack, she splashed water onto her face, sucking in a breath against the chill. The water was a luxury. Normally, she'd conserve, but there was a stream where she planned to camp overnight, and she had a good filter with a seventy-ounce capacity, so she could afford to splurge. She'd need the extra water, too. After the stream, there wouldn't be any more opportunities to replenish her supply until she intersected the river fifteen miles on, and then nothing until she hit the station.

From habit, she held her water bottle in her right hand, the one that didn't shake. Now she paused, and then—before she could chicken out—she shifted the bottle, grabbing it with her left with all the force she could muster.

Her left hand was rocksteady. No shakes. She'd built up muscle mass the last few months with all that lifting, but that had done nothing for her shakes. Now, though, the shakes were gone, and she felt stronger. Powerful. Like she could grab hold and *really* hang on.

This is so crazy. She was still freaked out, but her getting *better* didn't jibe with her idea of what happened when a person died. Or—wait—did it? Weren't there stories about how people came out of comas just long enough to say good-bye? Like the brain was on its last legs and kind of let go all at once, all the juices flowing so that everything clicked one last time? Well, maybe she ought to enjoy this for as long as she could.

She brought the bottle to her nose. She still didn't trust her sense of smell; kept expecting it to vanish. But the water had a scent that was clean and very cold, and she had another of those flashbulb moments: her dad hoisting her onto his shoulders, his strong hands wrapped around her ankles as he waded into Lake Superior, singing, *Old Dan and I, with throats burned dry, and souls that cry for water . . . cool, clear water.*

She let the water roll over her tongue and moaned, savoring the taste of every molecule, every wonderful atom, every precious particle of memory.

She thought, *Well, at least it's wet.*

And that made her cry a little bit more, because her dad always said that, too.

She looked back up the way she'd come, swept her eyes first left and then, slowly, right. A wink of sun dazzle caught her attention. Was that Ellie? Had she been wearing a frame? No, Ellie's Hello Kitty pack had been very small. Probably just room enough for some clothes, her toothbrush. Maybe a book, though, honestly, Ellie didn't strike her as the bookish sort. With Ellie, they were talking Nintendo DS, and it would be a brick just like the kid's iPod. A moment later, Alex saw that the dazzle had resolved to glare bouncing off rock. No Ellie.

She sighed. What had happened? She'd turned the morning over in her mind a dozen times. She ought to be able to figure this out. God knows, she had the time. Physics wasn't her thing, but she'd gotten an A in bio and she knew that the brain—most of the body, for that matter—effectively ran on electricity.

So, this morning, her brain had gone haywire. The electronics— anything that was solid-state—got toasted, as had the deer, the birds, the dog. The birds were really important, too—something about the way they navigated . . . Magnetic?

Now, her hand didn't shake. She was stronger. After that bolt of white-hot pain, her headache—always a low growl—was gone. Her memories were starting to pop to life again because her sense of smell had returned, and, with it, her sense of taste.

Only it wasn't just regular smell, was it? She'd had time to think about this, rewinding to that moment she'd approached Mina and how Mina had looked: teeth bared, ears flat. Going by looks alone, you'd think that Mina had been angry.

But then there'd been that weirdly feral stink, and the word that popped to the front of her brain now was *fear.* She'd smelled the dog—and how the dog *felt.* Mina had been scared to death.

And what about Ellie? There'd been the ammonia reek of urine and the coppery stink of blood—and another sourer scent, riding just beneath. That cross between morning breath and curdled milk—was that the odor of Ellie's fear?

So what did all that have to do with anything? How did it fit?

After another few seconds, she gave it up. All she had were a bunch of facts, a few theories, and much bigger problems—like getting the hell off this mountain and down to water before dusk.

How much daylight did she have left anyway? She threw a critical eye at the sun. There was a way you could tell time if you knew true north, but damned if she remembered how at the moment. Something else about time was important, too. What? She nudged the feeling the way she used to worry a loose tooth when she was a little kid, hoping to make the tooth pop out of its socket. Something really important about time . . .

The faint scent of char whisked up from the valley. A fire? No, something was wrong with that smell. Not wood being burned, but something artificial, almost sweet. She knew that smell. What was it?

There was a flicker of movement out of the corner of her left eye. Something above her. She flicked a quick peek back up the mountain, and then her gaze sharpened on a flash of pink.

Finally.

*   ★   ★

The best thing was to slow down, take another water break soon, let the kid close the gap without tipping her to the fact that Alex was actually waiting. Better Ellie should think this was her idea.

After another half hour, give or take, Alex had slowed to a baby crawl, but Ellie was close. Alex could hear the slip and slide of the kid's boots on all that scree. From the sound, she thought the kid was going a little too fast. A slithery stream of tiny rocks trickled down the slope to her left with a sound like the chatter of seashells sucked and dragged by a retreating wave. Veering into the chute, the rocks picked up speed and sluiced in a rush down the mountain. That was bad. If the kid made a misstep and slipped, she'd pick up speed pretty fast, get herself banged up for sure.

Time for a water break. With a casual, practiced shrug, Alex unseated her pack, then slung it to the ground in front of her boots. Tugging a water bottle from her fanny pack, she uncapped it, tipped the bottle to her mouth, and let her eyes crawl back up the mountain.

Still a good fifty yards above Alex, Ellie was coming down fast. The space between them was clotted with brush and gnarly pines jutting at weird angles. Alex could see much more clearly now where debris from higher up the slope funneled toward the chute which was now on her right as she faced into the mountain. This part of the trail wound in a rough, looping curlicue back and forth and well away from the chute, so safe enough. But Ellie was taking shortcuts, shaving off corners and sending down a continual shower of debris.

And the kid was alone.

Unbelievable. It was one thing for Alex to back off—she liked all her fingers, thanks—but what kind of kid left her *dog*? "Hey, take it easy," she called, annoyed. "I'll wait."

She was too far away to see Ellie's face, but Alex heard the scowl. "I'm fine," Ellie shot back. "I'm not tired."

"That's not what I'm worried about. You're kicking up a lot of rocks, and in case you haven't noticed, *I'm* below you. I'd like to avoid getting brained, thanks."

Ellie said nothing. If anything, she went faster. Alex turned aside with a snort. Man oh man. Still clutching her water bottle in her left hand, she fished up her pack in a one-handed grab and hefted it onto her right shoulder. This kid was really cruising for a bruis—

The shots were sharp, sudden, and utterly unmistakable: *pop-pop-pop-pop-pop!*

Gunshots? Someone was *shooting*? Her mind blanked and then she was crouching down fast, her frantic eyes scouring the valley. More shots—different, crisper, bigger—and she thought, *Rifle.* What the *hell*?

Ellie was so close, she heard the girl's airy gasp of alarm and then the slither-crunch of Ellie's boots sliding over rock. Alex saw the girl sway, arms windmilling, her boots stuttering back on the mountain. Alex ducked as a spray of rocks rained down around her head and shoulders. "Ellie," she called, "don't fight it. Sit *down*, sit—"

Too late. Ellie's center of gravity, already precarious, shifted.

"No!" Without thinking, Alex straightened—exactly the wrong move. Her water bottle flew from her hand, the water spraying in a wide corona, and then the bottle ricocheted off stone and out of sight. Balanced only on the hump of her shoulder, her unsecured pack caromed down her right arm like a luger on sheer ice and shot off her wrist. *No, no!* She made a wild snatching grab—another wrong move that pulled her out of the fall line and did no good anyway. Hurtling down the slope, the pack tumbled end over end, following the natural lie of the funnel before sliding into the chute. There it picked up speed, dragging an avalanche of loose stones in its wake before bouncing out of sight.

Gone.

She just had time to think, *Oh shit.* But that was all because she was off balance, too, shifting on the mountain, swaying as her boots skidded and slipped on loose rock. With a wild shriek, she threw herself into the slope, her scrabbling fingers sliding over rock. Sharp stone sliced her fingers, cut into her palms. She thumped heavily to her butt, left leg crimped, nearly horizontal, like the blade of a jackknife she couldn't quite close. Her knee bellowed with sudden pain, but she stopped falling.

A scream. Alex's eyes jerked up in time to see Ellie's left boot kick up and away from the mountain, an exaggerated slapstick version of slipping on a banana peel. Still screaming, Ellie tumbled onto her side, sliding directly for the chute.

"Ellie!" Alex shouted. "Roll over, Ellie! Roll onto your stomach, roll over!" She thought the girl tried; saw the girl's parka bunched in pink pillows as friction drove the material up the girl's chest. Ellie slowed, but she did not stop.

Move, move, move! Alex's boots slid over loose rock as she side-stepped to her right. The chute was forty, fifty feet farther on, but there was a scrub pine corkscrewing out of the mountain only twenty feet away; she could grab that. Ellie would have to slide past before she reached the chute, and if Alex got there in time . . .

A slurry of dirt and scree skittered down the slope, breaking over Alex's head. She heard the rattle of more rocks as they slalomed into the funnel; saw a spray of them slam and then pinball against bigger rocks and into thin air. Ellie was turtled on her back now, arms nearly vertical as the pack rode up the girl's shoulders.

Kicking the toes of her boots into the mountain, Alex dug in with her knees, then hooked on to the pine with her left hand. Her hand screamed as the bark's scales knifed into her already bloodied palm. "Ellie!" she shouted. "Over here! Give me your hand, give me your *hand!*"

She surged for the girl, and then Ellie's hand clamped around her wrist. There was a mighty jerk that nearly tore Alex's shoulder out of its socket, and *would've* pulled her off and sent them both crashing toward the chute if the slope had been any steeper.

Ellie slid, slowed . . . and stopped falling.

Gulping, Alex closed her eyes. Over the boom of her heart, she heard Ellie crying and shouting: "I *told* you this was a stupid idea!"

★　★　★

In a little under two minutes, she'd saved a kid who hated her guts and, in the process, lost her pack, her gear, her parka, her *food*.

And, oh, yes, some maniac was shooting out there.

They were so completely screwed.

11

Four power bars.

Five packets of instant Jell-O: two lime, one orange, one lemon, one cherry.

A space blanket.

A small brown bottle of ancient iodine tablets.

One bottle of water. Her car keys with a working mini-flashlight. A spare magazine of 9mm bullets for the Glock.

An airline travel pack that contained a sliver of soap, a folding toothbrush, and a teeny, tiny tube of toothpaste she must've squirreled away after a flight somewhere.

In the Altoids tin she always carried in her fanny pack, she hit real pay dirt: fishing line and weights, a cable saw, waterproof matches, a couple Band-Aids, two small X-Acto blades, a couple safety pins, a tiny baggy of cotton balls, a mini-tube of Vaseline, and four foil packets of alcohol wipes. A miniature compass.

That, along with the Glock and her knife, was the sum total of their gear, everything she had left. Of course, Ellie hadn't brought a thing down the mountain other than her little Hello Kitty daypack. Except for a collapsible fishing rod, a small box of lures, and an ancient Black & Decker flashlight—working, thank God—the pack was crammed with kid stuff: a handful of toiletries, wads of clothes, a water bottle with three gulps left. A patched, grimy Gund bear that was more thread than anything else.

Okay, so maybe they weren't completely screwed. The basic four for survival were warmth, shelter, water, and food. Well, Alex could start a fire, which she would need because all she had were the clothes on her back. She could build a debris shelter easily enough. Her filter had been in the frame pack, so that sucked, but she still had the one full bottle, and she knew where to find more water. She had the compass and the sun, and she knew roughly where they had to go, how far away they were, and that she'd have made it on her own without too much trouble.

Food was kind of a problem. There was the Glock, but aside from the spare magazine, the rest of her ammunition—an entire brick—was gone, along with the rest of her gear. Not that she knew the first thing about hunting with a pistol, or was about to waste bullets figuring it out. She might set a snare. Deadfalls were relatively easy, but using any kind of trap meant setting several and staying put, and no way was she interested in that. They could certainly fish; they were heading for the river, and the rangers were only a couple days away, max. She could make it on half a power bar a day, if she had to.

"What's the Jell-O for?"

She glanced over at Ellie huddling against a fallen, lichen-encrusted tree trunk. The valley floor was dense with a carpet of dead leaves and a logjam of dead and blasted trees, their trunks broken into jagged, splintery toothpicks and coated with cool slicks of moss. Alex spied a few withered, knobby platters of fungus on one tree. Chicken of the woods, if she was right, which was a shame because that was an edible mushroom she actually knew, but it was way too late in the year now: too late, too cold, everything remotely edible—ferns, chokecherries, cattails, duck potatoes—either dead or too hard to get at. She might find nuts: hickory or beechnuts. Acorns were a better bet, but you had to soak them, didn't you? For days, if she remembered right. Probably a reason the Ojibwe thought of them as famine food, something you ate as a last resort. Well, they weren't there, yet.

"The Jell-O's for quick energy," she said. "You mix it with water and then drink it before it sets."

Ellie made a face. "Yuck."

"You won't say that when you're hungry." She drew in a deep breath and let it go with a sigh. Now that the day was going, the air was very cold, but it was still edged with that strange charry stink. "You smell that? It smells like burned rubber or something."

"No." Ellie nibbled on her lower lip. Her iPod earbuds were draped around her neck. She looked small and miserable, and only smelled like piss and sweat now. "You know, I didn't *mean* to fall."

Which, Alex considered, was about as much apology as she was going to get out of Ellie. "No one's blaming you," she said, a complete lie, but no point arguing about it. "It could've happened to anybody."

Ellie gave her a long look, and then seemed to consider the subject closed, because she said, "Why are they shooting at us?"

"I don't think they were," she said absently, thinking that maybe she ought to follow the base of the mountain, see if she could find her pack. There was no way she could follow the pack's exact line of descent, but if she could pinpoint as closely as possible just where she'd been on the mountain, there was an outside chance she'd find it. "The first couple of shots were from a handgun and then the others were from a rifle. Anyone with a rifle probably has a scope, and if they were shooting at us, we'd have known it."

"Then what were they shooting at?"

"Beats me." Rifles usually meant hunters. Dogs, too. Did they use dogs for deer? She didn't think so, but deer season hadn't officially begun and most hunters didn't use pistols. Now that she really thought about it, those first shots—there had been more than three, maybe as many as five—had come rapid-fire. So, probably not a hunter calmly bagging a deer, but someone freaked out enough to squeeze off a *lot* of rounds.

Just what we need: some crazy hunters.

Ellie was okay with that pink parka—there was no way she could be mistaken for a deer—but *her* sweatshirt was black. She might as well be wearing a target, like the deer in that Gary Larson cartoon.

"How come you know so much about guns?"

"My dad taught me."

"How come?"

"He wanted me to be prepared, I guess."

"Is that why he gave you that gun?"

"Mmm." She didn't want to get into it. She began repacking her emergency gear. "Look, I'm just going to bushwhack along the base of the mountain a little ways, see how bad it is. If the going's not too rough, it might be worth it to see if we can find my g—" Her voice choked off.

Ellie had the black case in her hands. "Wow, this is really heavy." Her fingers fumbled with the zipper. "Maybe there's food—"

"No!" Alex snatched the case from the startled girl. "It's . . . it's not food."

"Jeez, spaz much?"

"I'm . . ." Alex snugged the case into her fanny pack and then zipped the pack. "It's private."

"Whatever. I'm staying here."

"No, you should come."

"I don't want to."

"Well, I—" Something spirited out of the corner of her eye, and her head jerked right, scanning the woods. She caught the tiniest stir of leaves, nearly behind them now, and she spun around in time to catch the slink of something dark threading through underbrush—and then the stink, more feral than Mina's fear and even wilder, hit her. An animal, but what? There were coyotes in the woods, and wolves. She just didn't know. She worried about the odor, turning it over in her mind, trying to place it.

How am I able to do this? A person's not like a wolf or dog, but I think I'm getting things regular people don't smell. Ellie doesn't smell that sweet, burnt stink—and I'll bet she doesn't smell this.

As if on cue, Ellie tossed a dispirited look over her shoulder, then back at Alex. "What is it?"

"Nothing." No, she didn't know the smell, couldn't even find the right words. If not for the odor, she'd have believed what she'd seen was a trick of the light. "I thought I saw something, that's all."

"I don't see anything."

"It's gone. It's probably nothing, but I don't know if you should stay alone."

"I don't care what you think." Ellie's face was grimy. One knee of her jeans had ripped, and the knee was scraped raw. Her pink parka had torn, the artificial fill boiling out in white gobbets. "I'm tired, I don't like you, and I'm not going anywhere right now."

Well, that did seem to cover it. "Fine. Just holler if you need anything."

"I don't need you."

"I won't be but fifteen minutes."

Ellie screwed in her earbuds. "I don't care if you never come back."

After twenty minutes of clawing her way through briary hummocks of brush and jumbled heaps of splintery branches, she was huffing. The forest pressed in with claws and fangs, snatching at her hair, whipping her face, tugging at her ankles. She paused, arming sweat from her forehead, sorting through the problem like a geometry proof.

a) If she had a lot of time . . .

b) If she did not have to worry about a kid . . .

c) She might have a decent chance of finding her gear.

d) However, judging from the rubble she'd found so far, her pack was more than likely torn to shreds, its contents spilled over the mountain like debris from a plane crash.

e) So, hello, her pack was gone.

She retraced her steps, trying to dredge up what she remembered from the map. They could maybe squeeze out another four or five miles before dark, if they hustled. That would put them at the campground where she'd planned to stay overnight, wouldn't it? The campground was maybe a quarter mile off the main trail and probably had a ready-made fire pit, so that was good. They might luck out and find a shelter, too.

She spied a puff of smudgy pink through the trees. Ellie had her back to Alex, and she was looking down at something. Then Alex spotted her emergency gear piled to one side. What? She'd repacked her gear; she remembered that. She'd left her pack behind because she was going to be right back, so what was Ellie—

"Hey!" She thrashed through the brush. "What are you doing?"

At the sound of Alex's voice, Ellie jumped, threw a startled look over her shoulder, and then must've decided that she did not like what she saw, because she was already up, backing away, her hands up as Alex crashed out of the woods. "I was just looking!"

Alex's eyes dropped, and then her heart fell.

The case was open.

12

"I wasn't going to steal anything," Ellie said. Her voice was a little gluey, her breath edged with a nip of cinnamon. "I was just trying to help."

"Help?" Alex's voice came out hoarse and ragged with rage. "You ate a whole power bar."

"I was hungry." Ellie tried a defiant glare, which, somehow, made her look even more pathetic. A pearl of a tear glistened on one cheek.

She wanted to strangle the kid. It wasn't just about the power bar. "You ate a day's worth of food—"

"It was *one* bar—"

"*And* you wanted to know what was in the case! *That's* the real reason you went into my things."

"Well, so *what?*" Ellie shouted. She stamped her foot. Her eyes blazed. "It was no big deal! It's just a Bible and a couple of baggies. Why are you carrying around crap like that anyway?"

"It's not crap." Aunt Hannah's Bible lay on the ground. The Bible wasn't strictly part of the game plan but was sturdy enough to cushion the two, heavy-gauge plastic bags.

Ellie had teased out the letter as well. *Alexandra Bethany* was scrolled in funky purple ink across the envelope, and the paper smelled, very faintly, of lavender and spice. Alex had slid the letter into the Bible at random, not really with any particular passage in mind. She'd never been sold on the Bible as Ouija board, but somehow, the letter had found its way to Job: *Wherefore I abhor myself, and repent in dust and ashes.*

"Is that you?" Ellie asked.

Alex didn't reply. Turning the envelope over in her hand, she saw that the back flap was intact. She slid the letter back to its place in Job and squared the Bible into the bottom of the case. Then she gingerly cupped the larger of the plastic bags in both hands. The bag was heavy, maybe eight pounds, and might easily split, but her careful eyes spotted no rips or tears. The contents were lumpy and gray and sifted in her hands like sand, and she almost allowed herself to think that it *was* only dust.

"Why," asked Ellie, "are you carrying around dirt?"

13

"Are we going to stop soon?" When Alex didn't reply, Ellie tried again. "It's getting dark. Are we going to stop—"

"Yes," Alex said. She did not turn around. They'd been walking steadily for what Alex judged had been about two hours, and in virtual silence. The sun was just skimming the trees immediately behind, and the light was fading as the afternoon began slipping into night. It had gotten even colder, the canopy of high, dense pines trapping the chill. A thick carpet of pine needles muffled their steps as effectively as heavy snow.

Ahead, she picked out a dilapidated trailmarker tacked to an oak, the sign listing to the left on a single rusted nail head:

MOSS KNOB 9.7 MI

←

FIRE MOUNTAIN 13.7 MI

⟶

LUNA LAKE 32 MI

↑

Alex's stomach cramped. Over *thirty* miles to the lake? That was farther than she'd estimated. If only she had her gear—and especially her *maps*—she might be able to figure out a shorter route.

Yeah, but you don't, so stop driving yourself crazy. Just stay calm; you can deal with this.

Another arrow, canted at a forty-five-degree angle and pointing northwest, helpfully noted that in a little less than a quarter mile they could put up at the Spruce Valley campsite. Okay, that was good.

"Another fifteen minutes or so and we'll hit the campsite," Alex said. "We'll stay there overnight."

"Outside?"

"There might be a shelter."

"But there's no water; there's, like, *nothing*."

"There'll be water. The map said there was a stream."

"A stream? But . . . how will I go to the bathroom? We haven't even got a tent. I don't want to stay in the woods. It's spooky in the woods."

Had *she* ever been such a major pain in the ass when she was a kid? "Look, Ellie, this is the way it is. We sleep in the woods. We drink what we can purify. We *share* the food." She paused a little—yeah, she was rubbing it in—and then went on. "If we're very lucky, we'll get to the rangers in a couple of days. Now this isn't exactly my idea of fun either, but it's what we've got. Whine all you want, but it won't change anything, all right?"

"No, it's not all right." Again with the footstomping, only this time it was more like a thud because of the pine needles. If the kid had felt bad about, oh, stealing food, that had sure worn off fast. "I don't want to stay here. I don't want to sleep in the woods. I don't even have my sleeping bag."

"I'll show you how to make—"

"I want a bath. I want a shower. I want to wash my hair."

"Ellie." She had to clench her fists to keep from screaming. "You're in the middle of the woods. You wouldn't have had a shower anyway. If I had my gear, we could've washed—"

"But I *smell* him!" Ellie grabbed her hair in both hands. "I've got Grandpa all *over* me! I've got his bl-blood under my nails and in my h-hair . . ." She began to sob.

Alex's anger evaporated. At that moment, she saw Ellie for what she was: bloodspattered, rumpled, exhausted. And very, very young. Of course Ellie was scared. In less than twelve hours, she'd lost her grandfather, left behind her dead father's dog, nearly fallen off a mountain, and now was stuck with some stranger who was just about as scared as she was. Who'd gone ballistic over, yeah, a bunch of dirt and a letter from a dead woman.

"Hey, I'm really sorry. I wasn't thinking." Alex reached for the girl's shoulder, meaning to give a reassuring squeeze. "We'll figure out some way to—"

"No!" Ellie ducked away. "Don't touch me! I *hate* you! Just leave me *alone!*"

"Ellie," Alex called, but the girl had turned and was thudding down the trail. Sighing, Alex trudged after. Ellie was headed in the right direction and wouldn't go far. *Just like a little kid who runs away and ends up sitting on the basement steps.* Despite everything, her mouth moved in a grin. Hadn't she once—

She pulled up suddenly, her nose wrinkling. Weird. That strange, charred smell was back, and stronger now, and strangely sweet. Perhaps it had been stronger for some time, but she'd been too preoccupied to notice, or had simply gotten used to the stink. Only now she sensed—smelled—something else. She dragged in a deep, full breath and then flinched at the slap of some horrible, almost alien odor.

Oh my God, what is that?

The stink was gutchurning: dead, stagnant, and gassy, like days-old roadkill stewing beneath an insanely hot sun. The reek was so strong it pillowed and balled in her mouth. She spat, but the taste clung, furring her tongue.

Just ahead, she spotted Ellie's pink parka crouching behind a very thick snarl of underbrush. She very nearly called out, but one look at Ellie and the words jammed behind her teeth at the same moment she realized something else.

She could smell Ellie again, and over a distance of, what, twenty yards? Thirty? The smell was strong, too—not enough to overpower that roadkill stink, but it was the same complex aroma she'd smelled once before, on the mountain: a reek of curdled milk and sour breath.

Fear. Ellie was scared. No, Ellie was *terrified.* The air was a welter of odors: Ellie's fear, that charry, sweet stench; her own peculiar perfume of sweat and anxiety; and that dead-meat stink that billowed through the woods like ashy, gray smoke.

Ellie did not look around. She'd clapped her hands over her mouth, and her eyes bulged as she stared at something beyond a dense veil of branches.

What was Ellie looking at? Something told Alex she *really* didn't want to know. The lizard part of her brain was screaming for her to run, run, *run!* But she couldn't leave Ellie behind, not like this; that wouldn't be right.

Slowly, carefully, Alex dropped to her knees, the cold earth biting through her hiking pants. Ellie didn't move a muscle. Wordlessly, Alex followed the girl's horrified gaze—and then her blood turned to slush.

No, she thought. *No, please, God, I'm not seeing this.*

14

The tent had burned and melted at the same time. What was left clung in cold, hard, black ash clots to scorched aluminum poles, like petrified meat on the fossilized ribs of a prehistoric dinosaur. An overturned cookpot vomited a coagulated brown spew that had slopped over the stones ringing the fire pit and seeped into the dirt. A murder of crows hopped around a scatter of their fallen kind, and as Alex watched, one leaned over, stabbed with a very black beak at a dead woodpecker, and came up with something blue and stringy that it tossed back into its maw with a snap.

Next to the cold fire pit were two people: a girl and a boy. The girl was blonde and wore a powder-blue sweatshirt with the words SOMERVILLE HIGH and a tennis racket stenciled in white.

Oh my God. She *knew* this girl. Where? Yes, when she'd stopped to gas up and call Aunt Hannah.

The girl was Ponytail Blonde.

She didn't recognize the boy, although he'd probably been on the same bus. He was reedy, mostly legs with a platform for a head. His sweatshirt, also light blue with the same lettering, featured a basketball.

In another life, they might have been a couple, having a picnic.

Except these kids weren't munching sandwiches.

There was also a woman, a grandmotherly sort who lay flat on the ground, head thrown back, mouth unhinged. A pair of eyeglasses on a keeper chain dragged in the dirt. Judging from the dried rills of blood on her right cheek, that eye was gone.

So was her throat.

The skin was ripped, the knobby tube of her windpipe slopping out like a fleshy tapeworm. The blood—and there had been a lot of it—had dried to rust in a wide bib over the woman's chest. From the way her hands were clawed, Alex thought she'd been clutching her belly when she died. Hadn't done the woman any good either, judging from the way her guts boiled out in a dusky, desiccated tangle, like limp spaghetti.

The boy and girl were eating. Stuffing their faces, actually. Splashes of blood smeared their mouths and dripped over their chins like runny clown's makeup. With a grunt, the boy plunged his fist into the woman's abdomen and rooted around before coming back up with a drippy fistful of something liverish and soft enough that Alex could hear the squelch as the meaty thing oozed between his fists.

Oh. My. God. Alex felt the low moan begin in her chest and clapped a hand to her mouth to stopper it back up. Her vision bloomed with black roses, and she felt her head going a little swimmy.

Squealing, Ponytail Blonde made a grab for her companion's

tasty treat, but Basketball Boy let out a warning grunt and batted her hands away. Pouting—*yes*, Alex thought crazily, *she's pissed*—Ponytail Blonde tossed her head hard enough to make her filthy hair dance. Then, turning away from the boy, the girl jabbed with two stiff fingers and gouged out the woman's left eye. She gave the slick, bloody globe a triumphant wave, as if taunting her basketball-playing boyfriend, but he paid no attention and kept chowing down on whatever it was he'd pulled out. With another toss of her head, Ponytail Blonde popped the eye into her mouth like a grape.

At that, Ellie let out a very tiny—but very distinct—squeak.

Alex's heart tried to blast right out of her chest. *Ellie, no, shut up, shu—*

The boy and the girl went still.

No, no, no . . . Alex watched in a kind of sick free fall of terror as Ponytail Blonde stiffened and then lifted her nose and sniffed. Testing the air, checking for intruders, trying to catch a scent—Alex understood that at once. After all, *she* smelled *them*, the dead woman, the burned tent, Ellie's fear.

She and Ellie needed to get out of here, maybe make a run for it. There was enough light to see the trail. If she just flat-out dug in and *ran*, she might outdistance them. Alex had endurance; she was still shaky from this morning, but thank God, she was months out from chemo and strong enough. Except these kids were once athletes and they were acting like, well, animals. *Real* animals. So they were probably pretty fast, and even if Alex could get away, she didn't think Ellie could.

She realized then that her hand had strayed to her Glock and thumbed away the retaining strap without her being aware at all. Could she do that? She'd only shot at targets, never anything alive, and her conscious mind balked: *No, they're kids; they're my age. There's no way I can just shoot them.*

In the end, she never had to find out.

A crow saved them. Emboldened by the lack of reaction to its presence, the crow—very large and very stupid—decided to try its luck. It hopped up to Basketball Boy, hesitated, and then snatched at a stray lump of the liverish meat that had tumbled to the dirt.

Quick as a snake, the boy seized the crow by the neck. The crow let out a huge squawk of surprise. At the sound, the rest of the crows—the entire murder—lifted into the air in a squalling black mass. Distracted, Ponytail Blonde whirled around as the boy wrestled with the struggling crow. The crow was very strong, and it twisted, slashing at the boy's face with its claws. Gargling in pain, Basketball Boy let go. The crow tumbled from his fists in a cloud of torn feathers. One wing was crooked, but the crow was moving fast, hopping away and pulling at the air with its one good wing.

It almost got away.

Spinning on her heel, Ponytail Blonde lunged as if sprinting for a crosscourt volley. She was, Alex saw now, wicked fast.

The bird began to scream in huge, raucous squawks. Ponytail Blonde bawled with excitement.

"Go," Alex said to Ellie in a low, urgent whisper. "Don't look back; just go, go, go for the trail and keep running!"

Without a word, Ellie scurried away, crashing through the

underbrush so loudly that Alex cringed. Hand still on her Glock, she shot an anxious look over her shoulder, but either the crow's shrieks drowned out the sound of Ellie's flight or Ponytail Blonde was having way too much fun.

The girl clamped her hands around the animal's neck and gave a savage twist. The crow's neck snapped with a crisp, crackling sound like a Thanksgiving wishbone, and then Ponytail Blonde corkscrewed the crow's head from its body with a gleeful squall.

Alex didn't wait to see any more. She turned and fled.

15

"Alex?"

"Mmm?"

"Are we going to be okay?"

"Sure." Alex hugged the girl closer, not out of affection but expediency. The less space between them, the warmer they'd be. Beneath them, their nest of leaves and debris crackled with a sound like dry cellophane. The debris shelter was warm, almost toasty from their body heat—captured as it was in a thick, three-foot mound of leaf litter. "We'll be fine. Couple more days and we'll be at the rangers. They'll know what to do."

They'd run as the sky fired with a startling, blood-red sunset, one that made Alex think of that really famous painting where the guy was standing on a bridge and screaming. They'd kept on running as that weird light faded, and then they'd run some more, stumbling on by flashlight until the only scents Alex picked up were of the forest and themselves. By then, with the moon not yet risen, the woods were black, and the going too treacherous for them to continue.

Ellie hadn't wanted to eat. Really, Alex didn't much blame her; she was pretty queasy, too—almost chemo-queasy—and wrung-out from the accumulated horrors of this terrible day. Clutching her useless iPod, Ellie watched as Alex threw together a debris shelter using pine boughs and deadfall. Somewhere along the way, the girl had vomited, and Alex used her shirt to get rid of the worst of the muck on Ellie's face and parka. She managed to coax the kid into chewing the moist inner bark of a thin twig of white pine: *It tastes like a sugar lemon drop, Ellie. Honest.* Pines were famine food, too; the Ojibwa used to pound the dried pulp into flour, and Alex briefly considered then abandoned the idea. They were so not sticking around any longer than they had to.

But they *would* be in a world of hurt if Alex couldn't find water, and soon. The stream was back the way they'd come, but there was no way she was retracing her steps, not with those kids out there. They just had to hope another stream intersected the trail, because, at this rate, the river was still three days out. Not good.

Now, Ellie asked, "What about food?"

"We've got Jell-O and the power bars."

"But I ate one."

"It's okay, Ellie. You were hungry, it's fine."

"I *stole* it."

She decided on a different tack. "When we get to the river, we'll fill up our water bottles and catch a couple fish."

"But you said fishing would slow us down."

"Well, not necessarily. If we're stronger, we'll move faster. You've got the rod and lures, right?"

"Uh-huh." Ellie's voice was so drained of color it sounded transparent as glass.

"So we're set."

"What if they're not biting?"

"They'll bite." Then she thought of something. "Your grandpa took you out of school to go hiking, right? So when were you supposed to go back?"

"To school? Um . . . Tuesday."

Today was Saturday. "Which means you'd have to get back on Monday, latest. So, is there anyone at your house?"

"Just Mrs. Pierce. She lives next door and takes in the mail and does stuff with the lights."

"So there you go. If you guys don't show up by Monday, Mrs. Pierce will get worried. She'll probably phone the rangers at the park entrance or maybe the station. I wouldn't be surprised if the rangers know all about you by the time we get there."

"Won't anyone worry about you?"

"Sure, but not for a while." It occurred to her then that without her watch, she might easily lose track of the days. One more thing to worry about. Maybe notch a stick . . .

"What if Mrs. Pierce doesn't worry? What if it takes her a couple days?"

"Well, you worrying about her not worrying won't help. Don't sweat it. Come on, try to get some sleep."

"I can't." A rustle as Ellie squirmed. "These leaves are itchy."

"Try."

"But what if . . . what if that girl . . . what if they . . . ?"

"They won't. It'll be okay."

"But how do you know?"

"Because we ran a long time and they didn't come after us and now it's dark. If they were going to chase us, they'd have done that already."

Pause. "Why were they doing that? Why were they—"

"I don't know." Maybe the brain-zap made the kids go crazy, like the deer and the birds. But the birds were back to normal and so was Ellie, and *eating* people was way, *way* out there. Just thinking about it stroked gooseflesh from her skin and set her teeth. Had those kids *killed* that woman? They must have. She looked pretty old, like fifty or sixty, so between the two of them, taking her down, might have been easy. Alex could almost see the movie in her mind, like one of those Animal Planet videos: the kids attacking, pouncing, swarming over the woman, tearing open her belly, ripping out her throat with their teeth.

God, just like animals. She shuddered at the thought. And what was with that *stink?* It smelled like . . . she didn't know . . . roadkill, yeah, but it was a really *old* smell, too. No, *old* wasn't the right word either.

The kids smelled . . . *wild.* They *were* wild. They were like zombies—only alive instead of coming *back* to life. Or maybe they *had* died and then . . . ? No, no, that couldn't be right. Could it? God, she didn't know. All she knew was *their* electronics had fried and so had their brains. The brain-zap hit them all: the animals and these kids and her and Ellie. Until now, she'd thought that she was the only one who'd changed—a stupid assumption, but she just hadn't had anything to go on. Hell, she'd never stopped to consider that the zap might cover a big area: not just the mountain but the valley, too. The mountain was, what, five miles back? So, if the zap was a circle, say, with a radius of five miles, square that and times pi and . . .

Oh my God. Her breath caught. Eighty square *miles?* The Waucamaw was huge, almost four hundred square miles. If she was right, that zap hit a fifth of the wilderness—a lot of land. And how many people? This far north, the fall colors were past peak by a good week, which meant that tons of tourists already had come and gone.

And what was with those kids? They'd *changed* in a way that was different from her.

Or maybe not. She remembered how Ponytail Blonde had tested the air. *What if their sense of smell sharpened, too? What if that's the first step?*

Her restless mind strayed back to those gunshots. For the first time, she considered that maybe the question wasn't *what* those guys had been shooting at, but *who.*

Was that going to happen to her? God, she'd put a bullet in her head first. But what if she didn't notice until it was too late? Worse, what if she didn't *want* to stop the change? What if she didn't care?

"Alex?" Ellie's voice floated out of the dark. "Is what happened to those kids going to happen to us?"

Hearing her thoughts come out of Ellie's mouth thoroughly creeped her out. "No," Alex said automatically. "It's been too long. It would've happened already."

Liar. The voice was small, only an inner whisper misting through her mind. *You don't know anything for sure. You've changed, and you're still changing. You're smelling things—and you're smelling meanings. That zap was only this morning, and look how far you've come since then. Look how fast those kids changed. Maybe what happened to them hasn't caught up to you yet.*

Go away, you. She couldn't worry about this now. She didn't want to worry about it ever. All she wanted was to close her eyes and not dream at all; to wake up in her own bed and see that this was all a really bad nightmare or something.

"Come on," she said, "go to sleep. We have a long day ahead of us tomorrow."

"But I'm scared to go to sleep," Ellie said. "What if I don't wake up like *me?*"

"We'll be okay."

"How do you know? Maybe we're going to die."

"No, we're not. Not today." It was another automatic response, a little bit of the gallows humor—or reality—she'd adopted over the past two years. "And not tomorrow either."

A pause. "I'm sorry about Mina. She wouldn't leave. I couldn't get her to come."

"You did the best you could," Alex said, though she doubted this was the case. The kid hated that dog.

"Do you think she'll be okay?"

"I don't know, Ellie. She seems like a pretty smart dog."

"Maybe she'll go wild."

"Maybe. I don't know how fast dogs go wild." *If they're*

starving, maybe very fast. But that was her voice now, not this other whisper.

"Grandpa said there are lots of wild dogs in the Waucamaw already. He says that people leave them here because they think they're doing the dogs some big favor by setting them free, only a lot starve and the ones who don't go wild."

"I don't think worrying about Mina will help."

"Oh." Silence. "I wish I could do it all over again."

"Do what?"

"Everything. I wish I had been nicer to Grandpa," Ellie whispered miserably. "I wish I'd been nicer to Mina. Maybe if I'd been better, my mommy wouldn't have gone away."

She wasn't exactly sure what to say. "Your grandpa said your mom went away when you were really little. It couldn't have been anything you did. You were just a baby."

"Maybe. Daddy had some pictures, but he didn't like looking at them because they made him sad." Ellie was quiet a moment. "I don't even remember what Daddy looks like anymore. He's all blurry. He made me mad, too."

"How come?"

"Because he went away when I told him not to. He said he had to because it was his job."

Alex knew what this was like. "Sometimes when you're sad, it's easier to be angry."

"Do you get mad at your parents?" asked Ellie.

Alex's throat balled. "All the time," she said.

* * *

Ellie fell asleep not long after, but tired as she was, Alex couldn't relax. Her mind churned, and she was restless, jumpy, her legs a little herky-jerky. The feeling reminded her of the time Barrett tried a med that was supposed to make her not puke during chemo—Reglan, was it? She couldn't remember; she'd been through enough drugs over the past couple of years to keep a small army of pharmacists in business. The problem with meds was that even the ones that were supposed to take care of side effects *had* side effects. Like the way Reglan made her all twitchy, with a horrible, total-body sensation of ants swarming over her skin. So she'd been a total spaz *and* nauseous, which sucked.

The distant cry of a coyote came then, a sound like the squeal of a rusty hinge. Maybe she should keep watch. There were animals, after all, and those two brain-zapped cannibal kids. Who knew what—who—*they* might have in mind for dessert. Yeah, maybe a quick turn around their camp. Better than lying here, ready to jump out of her skin. Reaching for her Glock, which she'd taken off along with her fanny pack before bedding down, she winced at the sharp, harsh crackle of leaves, but Ellie didn't stir.

She cradled the gun. Its solidity was reassuring, and so was its scent: gun oil, the faint metallic char of burnt powder. The holster smelled like comfortable shoes mingling with just the tiniest whisper of sweat—a scent that was not hers; she knew that.

Oh, Dad, tell me what to do. Her throat tightened. Would he understand if she had to use the gun? Would her mother? Because if Alex changed even more—if she got like those kids—she'd have to take control, *do* something before it was too late. Anyway, it wasn't like she'd never thought of suicide. Call her crazy, but suicide was a way of taking charge and fighting the monster, an alien invader she'd never thought of as remotely belonging to her in any way. Killing herself before *it* could finish its work was sticking her thumb in its eye, a way of depriving the monster of its final victory. Now, though, she and the monster might be inseparable, one and the same, and that changed everything.

I'll be the monster. If I use the gun, I won't be taking it out. I'll be killing me.

Then she had another, even more horrible thought. What if she was all right, but *Ellie* changed? Could she shoot a little kid?

God, this was all so messed *up*! She burrowed out of the shelter fast, winking against the burn of tears. After the warmth of the shelter, the slap of the chilly forest air set her teeth, and she stood a few moments, shivering in the dark, her throat working. The rasp of her breaths seemed very loud, and she clapped a hand to her trembling lips to catch a sob. *Stop this, stop this!* She had to get ahold of herself. She had to deal. She was the only one who could. Ellie was just a little kid, so it was up to Alex to get them out of this. She just didn't have *time* to feel sorry for herself—

She gasped.

Time. The airplane. The *plane. That's* what had been bothering her all day: that feeling like a toothache, that thing about *time.* The airplane hadn't come back, and it *always* came back at the same time, every day.

She hadn't heard the airplane on its return trip.

She ticked through the possibilities. Maybe the plane had crapped out and could no longer fly. Or maybe she'd just missed it. There'd been a lot going on. Maybe the plane's engines wouldn't carry into the valley, or it had altered its flight path. Maybe it didn't fly back to its home field on Saturday nights. Maybe it came back on Sundays.

Or what if the plane had been airborne when the zap happened? Would the plane crash? She thought back over the time frame of that morning. The plane passed overhead at 7:50. The zap happened at 9:20, ninety minutes later, give or take. Where would the plane be then? That depended on its speed, right? It might've landed before the zap. Or maybe not. If the plane crashed, would she hear it? She thought not.

But assuming she *could* hear it and the plane a) hadn't crashed and b) flew a regular Saturday afternoon route, then either she'd missed it in all the excitement—*or* the plane could *not* fly, and if *that* was true, then this thing was way bigger than eighty square miles.

There were two ways to figure this out. She could wait for morning, get herself oriented, and listen for the plane. If it flew over or near the valley, she would hear it. If she didn't hear it, that didn't necessarily mean anything bad, but she'd still have a lot of questions.

Or . . .

One thing about being really far away from other people and cities: no light pollution. Even with a moon, she should be able to spot planes even high overhead. First, she had to find a break in the trees. Now that her eyes had adjusted, she could make out her immediate surroundings: a murky patchwork of moth-eaten splotches of gray at her feet, the blacker forms of trees rearing up from the forest floor, glimmers of moonlight that shone through gaps in the forest canopy as dull, silver coins. The moonlight was a little off. Not as bright as she expected. Too gray. Weird. In the four days she'd been on the trails, the moon had been waxing. The last time she'd noticed, the moon was, what, three-quarters full? Well, maybe the moon was setting.

A splash of silver-gray light glimmered off to her right, which meant a large break in the trees, and she moved that way, slowly, one hand in front of her eyes to ward off low-lying branches, pausing every few paces to listen, wincing at the rustle and stir of the forest with every step. Twice, feeling a little foolish, she even sniffed, registering cold leaf rot and soggy wood but no roadkill reek—nothing that translated as *wild* or *dangerous*. So that was good.

The gap in the trees was as big around as a house, and she stood in the center, her head back and her left hand raised to block out the indirect light of the moon leaking from behind a veil of pine. The stars were a little off: not hard and glassy the way stars were in fall and winter, but hazier, like summer stars. Well, that was strange. Stars always seemed brighter this time of year, not only because the view was different but because cold air held less moisture and the Earth was turning from the Milky Way. With fewer visible stars in the sky, the ones that were left were easier to see and appeared brighter. But *this* sky looked fuzzy, the stars not glassy but gauzy silver burrs.

Now why should that be? The rusty cry of a coyote sounded again, though she barely heard. Instead, frowning, she turned a slow circle, her eyes gliding over the night sky and those strange stars—and then the moon.

No. Her heart jerked in a sudden, painful lurch, and her mouth fell open. She was so stunned, she forgot to breathe. *No, it can't be.*

But it was.

The moon was blue.

PART TWO: TOM

16

By Tuesday afternoon, three days after what Alex had come to think of as "the Zap," she had not heard or seen any planes, the moon was a deep, dark blue, and they were down to two packets of instant Jell-O and half a power bar. Alex's head thumped from hunger and caffeine withdrawal, her stomach had shriveled to the size of a raisin, and her thoughts were starting to get muddy, sluggish, and thick. On the thin side to begin with, she'd definitely lost more weight. She kept hitching up her hiking pants, and she'd jabbed another hole in Ellie's belt to keep the girl's jeans from puddling around her ankles.

When they stopped to rest, Ellie only sat and stared until Alex coaxed her into moving on again. Despite rationing themselves a half cup of water a day, there were only two swallows left in her bottle. The river was still miles in their future, and Alex knew they were in big trouble.

Because they'd hit the damn fork in the road.

Alex stood there a few seconds, absolutely stupid with amazement. The valley trail was marked with blue blazes so faded that the bark had bled through and turned them gray. Yet other than that first dilapidated sign, they'd not run across a single marker. And now this: a fork and faded blue blazes on *both* trails, each of which was thick with weeds. Neither trail looked as if anyone had taken it in quite a while.

"Which way do we go?" Ellie finally asked.

Something her father always said bubbled up from memory. "When you come to a fork in the road, take it."

"What does *that* mean?"

"It's a joke," Alex said. The memory gave her an idea, though.

Ellie said, "What are you doing?"

"Just . . . hang on." Closing her eyes, Alex inhaled again. She smelled herself, big surprise. Successive days of stewing in her own sweat had left an itchy rime on her skin; her cheeks were puckery with dried salt, her mouth gummy, and her tongue so swollen she could barely choke back the instant Jell-O she'd swallowed dry to save on water. There was Ellie's distinctive scent, and there was also the forest itself and its welter of aromas: the sharp turpentine of pine and the dry spice of dead leaves. Then she caught it: just the faintest whisper of wet.

She opened her eyes. "This way," she said, and pointed to the left fork.

"Are you sure?"

"As sure as I can be. The station's northeast and the sun's behind us on the left. If we go to the right, we'll be heading south, and that's wrong."

They walked as the day died and the sunset fired the sky with that weird, blood-red light. The wet smell got stronger, or maybe that was wishful thinking. Alex would've kept going, except that by dark Ellie was stumble-down exhausted, and the last thing they needed was for the girl to turn an ankle or break a leg.

Unbuckling her fanny pack, Alex handed over the water bottle. "Go ahead. I'll put the shelter together."

Ellie shook her head. "I'm not thirsty."

"Drink it, Ellie." Alex raked up leaves. "We'll hit the river tomorrow. We're really close."

"But there won't be any left for you."

"I'll be okay," Alex said, though it was more of a vocal tic than something she really thought about. Arms full, she pushed to her feet, then gasped at a sudden swirl of vertigo.

"Alex?"

"It's nothing." Well, that was bull; she was dehydrated and running on fumes. Her face was clammy, and her entire body felt shivery and weak. She waited until she was sure she wasn't going to pass out and then made her way to the frame of boughs she'd constructed at the base of a white pine. Dumping the leaves, she began pushing them into the shelter. "I'm just tired. Come on, drink up."

Ellie looked doubtful but tipped the last of their water into her mouth. The sight and that lovely, liquid sound and the *smell* set off an aching so strong, Alex could feel it in her bones. Turning away, she pushed into their shelter, busying herself with their bed of leaves.

There'll be water tomorrow, she thought furiously. *You just focus on . . .*

A soft sob from outside the shelter, and Alex frowned. "Ellie?"

"I'm . . . ," the girl choked. "I'm . . ."

Alarmed, Alex scuttled out of the shelter. "What's wrong?"

"I-I'm *sorry*. I'm s-sorry about *everything*." Ellie's face knotted, but she was too dehydrated for tears. "This is al-all m-my f-f-fault."

"It's nobody's fault. We're both doing the best we can."

"But *I'm* not! I st-stole your f-food and you're giv-giving me your water. I don't know anything important. You make the f-fires and tell us wh-which way to g-go. You know how to do *everything*!"

She surprised herself. "Well, then, we have to change that. Come on, I'm going to teach you how to start a fire from scratch."

Startled, Ellie looked up, gulping back tears, "Really?"

"Yeah. Really." What had Aunt Hannah said? *It's not your competence I question.* Being competent was Alex's best line of defense against the monster. Maybe all it gave her was an illusion of strength, but she would take that over feeling helpless any day. She gave the girl a little poke. "Come on, we need to get fuel."

Ellie scrambled up to comply. She was so eager, she hauled back a small dead pine—*the whole bloody tree*, as Aunt Hannah would've said. The tree was too newly dead, too green to be useful, but Alex stifled an impulse to point out to the girl what she'd done wrong. Instead, she showed Ellie how to take from the tree what they *could* use—dead needles, the thinner branches—and then had the girl segregate and mound the fuel.

"The foundation's really important. If you don't build it right, you've wasted your time. Now, this is the best part." Tearing open an alcohol swab, nose twitching against the sharp chemical alcohol sting, Alex pinched out the wet gauze square most of the way, then had Ellie hold on to the foil as she lit one of their waterproof matches. "Okay, hang on to the foil," she said, then passed the flame beneath the swab. The swab caught with a very small *whup*. A tiny, liquid-like flame sprouted, bright and blue.

Ellie gasped. "Wow."

"Yeah, wow. It's cool because it lasts a lot longer than the match, but now you've got to use it to light the tinder." She watched as Ellie touched off the tinder, saw the yellow-orange bloom as the tinder caught and then almost died. "Here, look," she said, and gently blew on the guttering tinder, which then brightened as hot and blood-red as those fiery sunsets. "Come on, blow—just not too hard."

The fire went out twice: once when Ellie blew too hard and again when she didn't blow hard enough. On the third try, the fire caught and held. "I did it!" Ellie whooped. Alex started to laugh as Ellie jumped up and did a little dance, pumping her fist in the air. "I did it, I did it!"

"Yes, you did," said Alex, giving the girl a hug. "You totally rock."

They sat up for the next few hours, feeding the fire, basking in the warmth. Ellie didn't want to let the fire die down, but Alex finally insisted that they had to sleep.

"But it'll go out," Ellie said. "It'll die."

"Not if we bank it. Here." Using a long, stout branch, Alex showed Ellie how to position the burning wood to restrict airflow. "This is where the ashes get really important," she said, and began carefully scooping out handfuls of cool ash which she drizzled over the flames. "The ashes are like a blanket. They protect the embers during the night. Tomorrow morning, all we have to do is give the embers some air and fuel, and we'll have fire."

"But if we stay to restart it"—Ellie's face creased with worry—"won't that slow us down?"

"No, it'll be good practice. We'll be fine."

By the time they crawled into their shelter, Alex felt better than she had in several days. She was still very hungry, but she could stand this. They were close to water, and soon they would be at the ranger station. They would be okay. If they absolutely had to, they could stay put for a day, maybe near the river. Maybe that would be smart. Getting to the rangers sooner wouldn't help Jack and there was Ellie to think of. Maybe, she thought drowsily, they should hang out at the river, catch some fish . . .

"Alex?"

She crawled back toward consciousness. "Mmm?"

"Thanks."

"Mmm," she said again, and yawned. "No problem."

"No, I mean, not just for the fire. Thanks for not leaving me."

That made her wake up. Wasn't a lot of this her fault? Not Jack, of course, but if she'd not gotten so freaked, had a bit more patience, they might be in a lot better shape, with food and plenty of water and maps. And here Ellie was *thanking* her.

"I shouldn't have left you," she said. "You weren't ready, and I was too freaked to see that."

"You won't leave me again, will you?"

"No." She meant that.

"Promise?"

"Promise." She crooked her little finger. "Pinky swear."

After a moment's hesitation, Ellie threaded her pinky around Alex's. "You won't forget?"

"Never," Alex said, and thought maybe they'd turned some corner. By tomorrow, when they reached the river and there was water and fish, their worst days would be behind them.

Famous last words.

17

One second she was sound asleep, the next she was vaulting to consciousness, fully alert, certain that something was wrong. The light was gray in the shelter, and Alex could see splinters of white through the roof of pine boughs. From beyond the shelter came the early morning chatter of birds. She'd cinched the hood of her sweatshirt down around her head, but her face was freezing, her nose a lump of ice, and she heard the sough of the wind through the trees and felt it lick her face with its promise of water.

Wait a minute.

She came up on her elbows and then saw why she was so cold. Why there was wind on her face.

The leaves she'd mounded so carefully at the mouth of the shelter were gone. She saw daylight . . . and she was alone. Her fanny pack was there, but Ellie's backpack and the Glock were gone.

She tunneled out of the shelter so fast that the ridgepole came crashing down. She saw, in an instant, that the fire was as they'd left it. So Ellie hadn't tried to start it on her own.

"Ellie?" she called. Louder: *"Ellie?"*

She got what she expected: nothing. But she smelled the wet again and understood that the wind had changed direction. What was more, she knew they'd been much closer to the river than she realized.

Three seconds later, she'd strapped on her fanny pack and set off down the trail at a dead run.

There came the gurgling boil of water over rocks. Another ten feet through a thick stand of aspen, and then she saw the water churning to white froth. The sight of all that water made her nearly crazy. She wanted to run and dunk her face; no, she wanted to dive in and start gulping.

Easy, just take it easy.

She unscrewed her water bottle, filled it, dropped in a purification tablet, then capped the bottle and gave it a good shake. In seven minutes, she would have plenty to drink.

This river was wide—sixty, seventy feet across—with a series of drop-offs and waterfalls that went on for a good fifty yards before tailing into rocky shallows. A tangled trio of aspens had fallen across from her side of the river, where the bank was much steeper and the ground more unstable. The felled trees acted as a dam, forming a single deep pool—not dead center, but to the right, so that water shot left down a natural rock sluiceway. A fourth tree jutted over the water. Almost exactly halfway down its length, the trunk forked into a wide V, and the thicker, stouter end of the fork hung over the pool.

Ellie was there, rod clutched in both hands, her back and

shoulders hunched against the cold. Her feet dangled fifteen feet above the water. The open bait box perched in a tuft of smaller branches to her left. The Glock—in its holster—nestled on her right.

When she spotted Alex, Ellie threw a look that Alex easily read: *Please don't be mad.* To her surprise, Alex wasn't, but she was worried about how she was going to get Ellie to shore without both of them ending up in the drink. Hitching herself out over the water wasn't hard, but the trees were slippery with frost and *freezing* cold. She could feel the muscles of her thighs dancing away from the frigid bark. She wasn't exactly sold on how stable the thing was either. Every bump and jostle, every quiver, set her teeth on edge, and she kept waiting for a huge *CRACK*.

She stopped when she was perhaps five feet from where Ellie perched. "So, you really think they're going to be biting? It's pretty cold."

"Grandpa says fish get hungry, too." As if to prove a point, Ellie twitched her line, reeled it in, inspected a tiny orange nubbin on the hook.

"What is that? It doesn't look like a worm."

"Egg sack," Ellie said.

"Really?" Everything Alex knew about fishing could be written on the back of a matchbook, a definite gap in her backwoods education. "You mean, like sushi?"

She saw Ellie give this some thought. "Sort of. I don't think you'd want to eat it, though." Ellie flashed a look of concern. "I wasn't hoarding it from you or anything."

"I know." She uncapped her water bottle, tipped back a mouthful. The water was so cold, she got brain freeze and then gasped as the water burned all the way down her chest before exploding in her stomach. She had never tasted anything so wonderful in her life, and despite the ache, she took another swallow and then another. She might have kept going if not for Ellie. As it was, handing over the bottle was an act of will. "Drink up," she said to the girl. "We'll fill our bottles before we leave."

"Thanks," Ellie said gratefully. She took two ginormous gulps, nearly draining the bottle, then cast a fearful look at Alex.

"Go ahead," Alex said. "It's okay. There's a whole river, right?"

"Yeah." Ellie drained the bottle. "Thanks."

"No problem," she said. "So, how's it going? You had the bait in your box?"

"Uh-huh. It's going okay."

"How do you know this is a good place?"

"Because Grandpa said so."

"Because it's a pool?"

"Uh-huh. He said you should always cast on the downstream part of cover and not right on top of them . . ." Ellie prattled on, but Alex listened with only half an ear, her mind already leap-frogging ahead, trying to figure out how to bring up the subject of, *oh, next time you decide to go hiking, please tell me, and by the way, don't touch the Glock.*

"And then you eat them," Ellie finished with a flourish.

Eat them. That got her attention. Saliva squirted into Alex's mouth, and her stomach cramped. If Ellie really *could* catch a fish or two . . . She nearly moaned out loud. "Do you know how to cook them?"

"Sure. Don't you? Your dad taught you everything."

"Not this."

"Oh. Well, you scale them. With a knife. And cut open their stomachs to get out all the guts."

"Yuck." She meant that.

"It's not so bad," Ellie said airily. "You save the guts to use for bait."

"You've done that?" She was genuinely impressed.

"Yup." Ellie's expression bordered on the supremely smug. "Then you poke some branches into their mouths and out the other end and roast them over a fire, and then you eat them just like corn on . . . Alex? Are you okay?"

"I—" Alex began, but then the odor came again, a harsh blast that nudged the gooseflesh along her arms.

"Alex, what—" Ellie's gaze drifted to a point over Alex's shoulder, and her eyes went round. "Oh."

Alex knew what the girl saw. Much later, she would think all that talk of food was to blame for what happened next. That if she hadn't been distracted by daydreams of roasted fish on a spit, things might've turned out differently. Maybe.

Her heart pounding, Alex turned, already knowing what she would find.

A dog.

18

A few feet in from the right bank stood a collie that looked ragged, thin, muddy, and miserable. A length of frayed rope hung from a worn collar. When it saw Alex looking, its filthy tail whisked back and forth a few times, and then it whimpered.

"Ohh," Ellie breathed. "It must've chewed through its rope. Or maybe somebody lost it. It's probably really scared and hungry."

Alex thought that was probably true. After all that talk about wild dogs the night before, she'd been startled at first, afraid the collie was feral. But this dog looked about as dangerous as Lassie. "Hey, girl." She had no idea if it was a girl or not, but thought the dog wouldn't be all that choosy. "How are you? Whatcha doing out here?"

The dog's tail fanned the air, and it danced a step forward and then back.

"Oh, Alex, look, she's *hurt*." Alex felt the tree jiggle as Ellie scooted to get a better look. "There's *blood*."

There was. A dried, rust-colored splotch splashed the collie's rump.

"Someone *shot* her." Laying aside her rod, Ellie hitched herself around and started scooching toward Alex. "We have to help her. Here, girl, it's okay, we won't hurt you. It's okay."

It was the smallest of movements, and maybe the image of that brown slink disappearing into the woods four days ago had stayed with Alex, because her eyes shot left to a dense thatch of underbrush just beyond the collie—and then her stomach bottomed out.

Another dog crouched, belly to the ground, behind dense brambles. This dog was dirty brown, with a huge ax-wedge of a head. Some kind of very big mutt. *Really* big.

And the smell she got from it was *danger*.

Maybe the collie saw her eyes shift and sensed something about to go very wrong, because it let out a short, almost playful yelp.

Ellie laughed. "It wants to play."

Now that she knew what she was looking for, Alex's frantic eyes scoured the forest right and left of the collie. She spotted two more dogs in the underbrush: a dusky, speckled hound and a ragged German shepherd, its left ear hanging in crusty tatters.

Four dogs. *Four.* Less than a week since this nightmare began, and none of these dogs looked like they'd ever been anyone's pet.

"What are you doing?" Ellie said as Alex pressed back. She let out a yelp and then Alex heard something splash. "Alex, you made me knock the tackle box—"

"Move back," Alex said, injecting as much urgency as she could without outright screaming. "There are more dogs, Ellie. Move, *move!*"

"What? I don't see . . ." Alex heard Ellie gasp.

"Go." She felt the girl begin to inch away, and she followed, legs still straddling the trunk, palms cupping the icy bark, eyes never leaving the dogs. She watched as the other three slid from the tangle of brush and briars. The collie was no longer wagging its tail, and the playful look on its face had been replaced by what almost looked like rage. The dogs were rigid, ears pricked, nostrils flaring as they sampled the air. Sampled *them*.

"Go away." Her voice shook and Alex thought, *God, I sound like dinner.* She tried again, putting some steel in it. "Go on! Get out of here, *go!*"

The dogs did not go. Instead, they tossed looks at one another. Alex could almost hear them debating; felt the air go alive with thoughts. Then four pairs of glittering eyes swiveled back, and the hound and the very big mutt began nosing along the bank.

"What are they doing?" Ellie said in a high voice. "Are they going away?"

"No. They're looking for a way across."

"Why?"

"So they can come at us from both sides." The mutt and the hound were picking their way down the bank, slithering on wet leaves. She kept hoping they'd take a tumble, maybe break a leg, maybe get so wet and discouraged they'd just give up, but they didn't look like the kind of dogs that gave up. Then she remembered the dried blood on the collie and she thought, *Gun.*

"Ellie." She craned her head over the hump of her shoulder. The girl's face was bleached of color, and she was crying, silently, huge tears rolling down her cheeks. "Ellie. The Glock. Get it."

Ellie's eyes went even wider, but she nodded—a quick jerk like a puppet. She started backing away in little hip-hops, up and down, like a kid hitching along a balance beam. Every bounce knocked a gasp from Alex's chest, and she hissed, "Not so fast. We've got some time, be *careful*."

"Almost there!" Ellie wailed. She'd made it back to the V butt-first, but instead of turning, she swept her right hand back to reach for the Glock nestled in its thick cradle of branches—

Alex saw it right before it happened. "Ellie, no, *stop!*"

Too late.

Ellie's hand knocked the gun, a good solid hit that sent the pistol sailing. Ellie let out a shrill *no!* She tried to snatch at the gun, but then her body shifted, and she screamed again, throwing herself forward this time and wrapping her arms around the tree. Alex watched in a kind of dumb horror as the gun tumbled butt over bore, once, twice, three times, and then hit the water with a dull, wet *thawunk*, a sound Alex had heard countless times as a kid dropping rocks into a pond from a tire swing. She watched, helpless and sick, as the water swallowed the gun. Swallowed her dad.

"I'm sorry." Ellie's teeth showed in a tight, terrified rictus grin. She hugged the tree with both arms. "I'm sorry, I lost my balance. I'm sorry, I'm—"

There had to be something else she could use as a weapon. Alex's eyes raked the tree, looking for something, *anything*. She saw that the dogs were fording the river now, carefully crossing over rocks, keeping one eye on them and the other on where they were going. She had to *hurry*.

"What about your knife?" Ellie's voice was breathless with terror. "Can you use your knife?"

"Not enough reach." The blade wasn't long and all a dog had to do was dodge and grab her wrist, and then it was over.

Drop into the river? Alex was a good swimmer. She eyed the water, saw the gush. That current was pretty fast. The rocks were slippery and the water deep and, probably incredibly cold. She might make it, but she didn't think Ellie would, not with boots and a parka and clothes to drag her down. And dogs could swim, too; she knew that. Even if Alex got her feet under her, one slip and those dogs would swarm in and she'd be done.

Groping beneath the tree trunk, she wrapped her hand around a branch as thick around as her wrist and pulled. The branch bent, squealed, and Alex tugged harder, heard a snap and then a splintery sound, and gasped as the branch gave so quickly that she slipped. Still clutching the branch, she squeezed her thighs around the trunk; felt her chin bang wood and then pain, red and hot as a brand, as her teeth drove into her tongue.

"Alex!"

"I'm okay," Alex said, swallowing a ball of blood. Her mouth sang with pain. Her fingers knotted around the stick in a death grip. "Go back the way you came. Down that great big branch, the one you were fishing from. *Hurry.*" Alex waited until Ellie had shimmied off the main trunk and begun inching onto the branch before following. She listened to the crackle of branches, holding her breath each time. *Please, God, just get us down there.*

"Alex, how . . . how much farther do you want me to go?"

Alex flicked a glance. The branch was thick and stout, as big around as Ellie, and she was at the midway point. The branch bowed in a slight, gentle curve, but Ellie wasn't swaying and Alex thought it was strong enough. "That's good. Stay right there. I'm coming."

"But what are you doing? What are we going to *do*?"

Alex didn't answer. She wouldn't need to go far, just enough so the dogs had only one way of getting at them. *A funnel leading to a chute, like the rocks on the mountain.* If she was far enough from the V, the dogs would have to come single file, and that she could defend. She butted against the V, then hugged the tree as she swung her left leg up and around. There was a solid *thunk* as the side of her boot knocked wood, and then she was hitching up her hips, thinking, *I never was any good at balance beam.*

"You're almost there," Ellie said. "Scooch up your butt."

Alex did, dropping onto the branch hard enough that she felt the bang ripple up her spine. Beneath her legs, the branch groaned and bent, like an archer's bow being drawn, and Alex held her breath, waiting for the break, the crack, the sharp razor of a rock slicing the back of her head . . .

The limb swayed, creaked like a step in a haunted house, but did not break.

She felt the tiniest squeak of relief. "Ellie, can you give me some more room?"

"Yes." The wood shuddered in Alex's arms as Ellie scooted back, and then Alex saw the bark ripple and buckle. This time, the limb protested with a loud squall that reminded Alex of forcing open a wooden door, swollen with humidity, on a hot summer day.

"That's far enough." Maybe too far, but at least she had some maneuvering room now. She looked left, saw that the very big mutt was already across and eyeing the trunk. Then her head swiveled right, and she saw with a sudden, sickening jolt that the hound was already halfway to the V—just twenty feet away. "Hang on, Ellie—really, really tight."

"Alex? What are you going to do?"

She did not answer. Wrapping both legs around the branch, she hooked her ankles together. She hugged the tree with her left arm but let her right fall, choking up only a little on her makeshift club.

Ten feet away, at the fork, the hound hesitated. It was close enough that Alex saw that its eyes were muddy brown, the whites red. Its black lips curled in a yellow snarl. Then it crept forward one step and then another and another . . .

Alex swung.

Her club cut the air with a whistle. The hound saw it coming, tried twisting to snatch the branch with its teeth, but it was off-balance and too late. The splintery knob smacked the hound's ribs hard enough to make their perch bob, and then the dog was yelping, its nails scoring bark as it skittered over the slick wood. Still yowling, the dog tumbled from the tree and, unlike a cat, smacked the water with a mighty splash that sent up a geyser of water in an icy coronet.

Yes! Elation thrilled through her like blood. Twisting to peer over her shoulder, Alex saw the hound's black head, sleek as oilskin, bob to the surface, but the current was swift and the dog was a good twenty feet downstream and still picking up speed. Beyond her feet, Ellie was dripping. "You okay?"

"Yes." Ellie's face reflected both mingled hope and mortal terror. "Is it dead? Will it drown?"

"No." Alex watched as the hound battled for shore and then, ten seconds later, clambered into shallows on the right. Water streamed from its flanks and then sprayed in a wide halo as the dog shook itself. In another moment, it was bounding back up the bank toward level ground. "It's coming ba—"

"Alex! On your left! Look!"

The shepherd was working its way onto the tree as the collie watched from the safety of solid ground. Then she saw movement to her right, and there was the very big mutt. The animal put a tentative paw on the wood, and then the dog took a step, and then another.

No. The dogs were coming at them from both sides, and she knew she couldn't do this forever. If only Ellie hadn't lost the Glock, she might have—

Something rocketed from the woods, something very fast, charging so quickly that Alex caught only a brown blur, and then she saw, with a start, that it was another dog.

No, no, not another one. And then she caught its scent and thought, *Wait. Isn't that—*

"Mina!" Ellie crowed. *"Mina!"*

19

The hound sensed something wrong. It began to turn, but it was already too late.

Mina slammed into the other dog, a solid body blow that lifted the hound, upending it completely. Squealing, the hound turned an awkward somersault, coming down on its back, legs thrashing, neck exposed. Mina's head darted quick as a snake, and the hound's squeal cut out as Mina's jaws clamped around its throat. With its windpipe cut off, the hound made no sound at all. Its legs thrashed and pedaled air, and then, with a single violent twist, Mina ripped out its throat. An enormous fountain of blood erupted from the hound's neck—

"Alex, look out!" Ellie shrieked.

Startled, Alex whipped around just as a monstrous black shadow loomed. The mutt surged forward, jaws wide, and if Alex hadn't had just enough time to bring up her right arm, the dog would have had her. As it was, the dog caught the club between its teeth, ground down, and gave the club a vicious twist.

Gasping, Alex let go and felt herself slip, and then the world tilted on its axis. Frantic, she made a last grab for the trunk—heard Ellie shout again—but she wasn't fast enough.

She crashed into the water, the blow hammering the air from her lungs in a sickening whoosh. The roaring water, so cold her skin burned, closed over her head, and then a white jag flashed across her eyes as her head struck against unyielding rock. Shocked, dazed, she opened her mouth in a huge, involuntary, reflexive gasp. A torrent of frigid water poured into her mouth, rushing down her throat. In a swirl of horror, Alex felt the muscles of her throat seize, close off, and clamp down, and then the flow of water into her lungs shut off like a spigot twisted shut. The water was gone, and she wasn't choking anymore.

Instead, she was suffocating.

A deep red bled across her vision. Disoriented, her lungs on fire, she churned water in a wild, frothing panic, and then she was lunging for a distant glimmer, what she thought might be the surface, kicking desperately even as the water fisted her heavy boots, greedily fingered her clothes, and tried to pull her back.

She shattered through the water, felt the slash of air knife her face. Coughing, Alex threw her head back, her mouth wide open, and inhaled a single, shrieking gasp. Her blood roared, but her vision cleared, and then she realized that she was turned around, facing downstream, and still moving, the river carrying her in a dizzying sweep. A monstrous tumble of rocks and debris loomed directly in her path, rushing for her face. Too late to flip onto her back, too late!

The river flung her against stone. She felt the impact as an explosion in her left shoulder that scorched a sizzle of electric shocks all the way to her fingertips, but that was also when she realized two things at the same time.

Jammed up against the rocks, almost horizontal, she felt the water's suck and grab, but saw that she was in the shallows, in less than a foot of water, and that she was staring up at the sky—

And the mutt.

20

Water streamed from the mutt's flanks. Blood bubbled from a slash on its shoulder where it had struck a rock or snagged a branch. But it was there and it was alive, and now the animal went for her face with a flash of fangs, white and deadly.

Screaming, Alex pressed back against the rock, her only working arm—the right—flying up to protect her face. It was instinct, pure and simple—and saved her life. Crabbed on her back, unable to get to her feet, she felt the dog batten down, waited in a slow-motion dread for the jaws to grind and for her bones to break . . . Or maybe it would go for her throat next, or even push her under the water, hold her there until she drowned. But then her arm did not break, and she realized the dog had misjudged and that all it had was a very big mouthful of sopping wet sweatshirt. The pressure around her arm lessened for an instant as the dog let up and shifted its jaws, trying for a better grip—

Mina sailed across her vision. In an instant, the mutt had let go of Alex and whirled, incredibly fast for such a large dog. The dogs crashed against one another, fangs clashing against fangs, a snarling ball of fur and muscle.

Move, get up, get up, get up! Alex broke from her paralysis and scrambled on hands and knees over slippery rock, trying to get her footing. She made it to one knee, pushed to her feet, and very nearly fell again. There was blood in her mouth, her head clanged with pain; her left arm felt dead. The foaming water grabbed at her legs and tried to pull her back in.

Ellie let out a piercing, terrified scream. Sick with horror, and still dazed from the fall, Alex saw that the shepherd had reached the V. As Alex watched, the animal took a cautious step and then another. On the third step, it slipped, its tail pinwheeling as it struggled to keep its balance.

Fall, Alex thought fiercely. *Fall!* But the animal did not fall. In a second, it had righted itself, and Alex knew she would never make it to Ellie in time.

She looked back at the dogs just as they broke apart. Mina was panting, the dog's chest going like a bellows. Blood flowed from a rip in her neck, and as Mina danced back, Alex saw that the dog was limping, favoring her left flank. The mutt was also bloodied, but it was a bigger, more muscular dog, and Alex thought this was a fight Mina would lose.

Then Ellie screamed again, and for a precious, fatal second, Mina's attention wavered. The dog's head snapped around to search out her mistress—

And the mutt saw its chance.

Lowering its head, it rammed Mina, driving its shoulder into the smaller dog's chest, knocking Mina head over heels. Writhing, vainly trying to twist in midair, Mina landed with a mighty splash flat on her back. Before she could right herself, the mutt was there, its fangs curving like the slash of scimitars. At the last second, Mina flailed upright, but the mutt adjusted the arc of its attack. Its jaws closed around Mina's left foreleg. There was a loud, grinding crunch, and Mina let go of a high, eerily human shriek, and then she was on three legs, struggling to keep to her feet.

"No!" Alex shouted. Her paralysis fell away, and she closed her fingers around a rock the size of her fist and then let it fly.

The rock struck the dog in the ribs. With a small yip—the dog was more surprised than hurt—the mutt whirled to face this new attacker.

Oh God. Alex felt her insides turn to jelly. She reached to grope for another rock, not daring to take her eyes off the mutt. *If it charges, if I miss—*

In the next instant, the stench that filled her nostrils was so intense, so surprising, Alex gasped. Across the stream, she saw the mutt pull up with a start, its hammer-like head swinging up and then back upstream, and she knew that the mutt smelled it, too. She watched as its ears drew down tight on its skull and its tail tucked between its haunches. The mutt backed up a step, then another, and then it was splashing across the shallows and spurting up the right bank.

Alex couldn't move. Balanced on three legs, Mina was rigid, the hackles bristling along her back, and then the dog was looking left, her lips peeling back in a snarl.

I know this smell, Alex thought—and then horror bloomed in her chest. *Oh God, I* know *this.*

The stench was like summer, hot and torrid: a stink of tarry asphalt and roadkill bloated with decay. The reek was thick as fog, a plague of rotted flesh and squashed guts, so bad it balled in her mouth and coated her tongue.

Her eyes inched left.

And that's when she saw the man.

21

He stood in the trees at nearly the same spot where the dogs had appeared. His hair was very short, a military buzz cut, and he was filthy: his clothes ragged, his skin smeary with dirt and blood. He reeked of death and decay.

The wild dogs were terrified. She smelled their fear. The mutt had darted into the woods, but the collie was still there on the high bank, only twenty feet away from the man. Head low, teeth bared, the dog had shrunk back toward the river but could retreat no farther. On the tree and only ten feet from Ellie, the shepherd had turned to stone.

Ellie spoke first. "Help us! Please, help us!"

The man opened his mouth, and for a crazy second, Alex thought they might actually be all right—a hope that fizzled fast.

What came from the man's mouth was a formless bellow, something so primitive it raised the hairs on Alex's neck. And then he was moving, *charging*, arms out, hands fixed into claws, that wild roar going on and on.

Alex had just enough time to think, *God, no, Ellie!*

The man charged straight at the collie. He was insanely fast and as agile as a panther. The collie immediately sprang to its right, but it was too close to the edge. One back paw swung out over the drop, and the collie skidded. In the next second, the man's hand shot out and grabbed a handful of the collie's matted fur. The dog let out a high, bloodcurdling yelp as its feet left the ground, and then the man was swinging it, spinning the helpless animal around, using the collie's weight the way an athlete built speed to throw a shot put.

He smashed the collie against a tree. There was a sickening *thunk*, and then the dog let out an abortive *ungh!*, dropping in a loose heap like a sack of wheat. Foaming, the crazy man loomed for a moment over the stunned dog. Then he reached down, hooked a hand on either jaw, and gave a vicious yank, scissoring the collie's jaws apart.

There was a snap of bone, a ripping sound like cloth being torn in two. The collie let out a deep, guttural shriek as its mouth split.

Ellie screamed.

Alex watched, a cold fist of horror where her heart had been, as the man bent over the dazed, bleeding animal. For an insane moment, Alex thought he was going to kiss it. Instead, he wrapped up the dog in a gigantic bear hug—literally clasped the dog to his chest—and squeezed.

There came a series of popping, splintering sounds as the dog's ribs broke. Huge bubbles of crimson blood boiled from the dog's mouth, but the collie made not a sound, not even a whimper, because it couldn't. The man was crushing the life out of it, driving the air from its ruined lungs.

Incredibly, the man laughed. The sound was gleeful and crazy and drove spiders scurrying up and down Alex's back. Still laughing, the man reached into the collie's mouth and tore out the animal's tongue.

"Alex?" Ellie quavered. She tried twisting around on her perch. *"Allleeeex?"*

She couldn't answer—didn't dare. Pressed against her side, Mina was trembling. Alex watched as the man bit into the thick, still-dripping flap of muscle, tore off a chunk, and chewed—and then, just as quickly, spat it out.

Ellie let out a screech of revulsion and terror, and Alex thought, *No, no, honey, be* quiet.

On the tree above Ellie, the shepherd came alive. It tried backing down the limb, but the animal was panicked, moving too quickly. Alex heard the loud skittering of its nails on the wood, and then the shepherd slipped sideways. It bulleted for the water, bouncing off the hump of a nearby boulder before doing a spectacular belly flop. An instant later, the dog's head bobbed to the surface, and then it was pulling furiously for the far shore even as the river swept it downstream toward Alex and Mina.

The sound of the splash made the crazy man look up. His chest was a fan of blood. His smeary chin glistened. Alex didn't move; she finally understood why rabbits went so still. *Don't see me, don't notice me.* She saw him glance downstream at the shepherd, which had made the shore now, less than ten feet from Alex. By her side, Mina let out a warning growl, and Alex felt a spike of alarm. But the shepherd was interested only in getting away, and it ignored them, lunging up the bank and out of sight.

Alex's eyes shifted back—and then she felt the day crash down. The man was on his feet now. Still clinging to the tree, Ellie seemed to have finally gotten the message. She had gone small and pink and still, but it was no use. The crazy man knew she was there, and Alex saw, in a flash, that he meant to have her.

She would never scale the bank in time. He was too far away for a rock. So she did the only thing she could.

"Hey!" Splashing across the shallows, she hit the left bank at a run and plowed up the incline. "Hey, over here, *hey*!"

It worked. The man rounded, his mad eyes swimming with hemorrhage, and that dead, hot summer stink washed over Alex again. His face twisted, and then he was starting for her, mouth open, clots of gore and stringy flesh hanging from his teeth.

Mina raced past, faster than Alex would've thought possible for a dog with only three good legs, there and then gone in a flash. The dog sprang, battening down on the man's right arm. Bawling, the man jerked Mina, not a small dog, clean off her feet. Still howling, the man twisted first one way and then the other, but Mina hung on, her body whipping back and forth like a flag in a stiff breeze. With a roar, the man drew back his left fist in a wild roundhouse punch. He was aiming for Mina's head, but the dog saw the blow coming and let go of the man's right arm. As soon as her hind legs hit the ground, Mina launched herself in one nearly seamless movement, her jaws wide, making the switch from right arm to left. Catching the man's wrist, the dog ground down with an audible, grinding crunch.

The crazy man let go of a high, gargling scream and began

backpedaling, crashing against a tree, twisting and turning, spinning in a wild, jittery dance.

In the next instant, Alex heard the unmistakable sound of a bolt
being thrown and then a commanding rap: "Call off your dog!"

Across the river, Alex saw another man pushing from the
woods, rifle held high. He was much younger, closer to her age,
and his face was streaked with grime, a slick of brown curls plas-
tered to his forehead. "Call it off! Do it now! *Hurry!*"

"Mina!" Alex shouted, and then, desperately, "Mina, come,
off, *off!*"

Incredibly, it worked. Mina bounded away, lunging for her and
then, spinning around, pressed against Alex as if to stand between
her and the crazy man. Dropping to her knees, Alex threw her
arms around the dog, fisting her hands into the scruff of the dog's
neck. "Good girl, stay, *stay!*"

The crazy man bellowed. His face twisted; his eyes shone from
his bloody face like beacons, unearthly and mad.

"Jim!" shouted the man with the rifle. "Jim, over here, *here!*"

The crazy man—Jim—whipped around to face him. The reek
of death and insanity steamed from his pores, wreathing him in a
thick, choking stink as tangible as smoke. Throwing his head back,
Jim bayed, a weird, eerie howl that spiked her brain: a sound she
would never forget.

"God forgive me," the young man said, and squeezed the
trigger.

The slug drilled Jim between the eyes and exited in a mist of
blood and brain and bone. Jim's arms dropped limp and lifeless

to his sides, as if he were a marionette suddenly without his pup-
peteer, and then his legs folded and he toppled from the bank. His
head struck a boulder and then the current grabbed him, sweeping
him downstream. The water might have carried him to the shallows, but his foot wedged in a rock tumble and held him there. A
few moments later, the water bled in a swirl of burgundy red that
widened to the black maw of a whirlpool as Alex's vision began to
fade and her mind wobbled.

"Alex?" Ellie's voice sounded very far away. "Alex, are you okay?"

No, I don't think so. Alex began to fall as the whirlpool sucked
her down, dragged her under. *I think I'm passing—*

22

When she woke, the light was gone, the darkness was heavy and hot, and her head was splitting. She couldn't move, couldn't see, and she thought, *This is it; I've stroked out and I'm going to die.* She let out a long, low moan.

"Alex?" A metallic snick, a spear of white light, and then she felt the girl's arms thread around her throat. "Alex?"

"Ellie," she breathed in relief. Her own arms were snarled in a tangle of oversize flannel shirt, and she had to work to shuck free of the sleeping bag. The movement made her head ache, but she didn't care. "Hey," she said, hugging the girl close. "You okay?"

"I'm f-fine." Ellie's head moved against her neck and then Alex felt the splash of tears. "I was so . . . so sc-scared that maybe you were d-dead. . . ."

"Hey, it's okay, we're okay." Right about then she realized that other than the shirt and panties, she was naked and her skin was slick with sweat. The dull red eye of a catalytic heater glowed in one corner, and she thought, *Tent. I'm in a tent.*

Everything came back then: the pack of wild dogs, the river, that choking stink of death, Jim, and . . . "Ellie, where are we?"

"In Tom's tent. Don't you remember?"

"No. Well, I remember the guy with the gun—"

"That's Tom."

"Tom."

"Yeah, Tom Eden. He carried you back and fixed up your head. He said in the army, you learn how to do a lot of stuff."

"My—" Her hand crept over her hair to a rough square of gauze bandage, with something prickly beneath: stitches. She must've been really out not to have felt *those*. "How long have I been asleep? What day is it?"

"Thursday. You were asleep for all of yesterday and today."

"Two *days*?"

"Uh-huh. Tom said you had a concussion. He said it was a wonder you hadn't passed out way before you did. He's outside, making dinner. I came in to see if maybe you were awake."

"Where are my clothes?"

"Right here." Ellie aimed the light to the right. The hiking pants and underwear were Alex's, but the rest—a forest green turtleneck, a set of long black underwear, a pair of wool socks draped over her hiking boots—was not. The flannel shirt she wore was probably Tom's, too, which meant a whole bunch of other things—all of them boiling down to his having undressed her, like, completely. Which she just didn't want to think about, much less try to remember.

"Okay," she said. "Tell him I'll be right out."

* * *

Mina spotted her first. Her tail thumped, and then she was heaving to a stand. Her left leg was splinted, but she pranced over to Alex, who dropped to her knees and wrapped the dog up in a hug. "Good girl," she said. "You are such a good girl."

"Welcome back." Alex looked up to see Tom by the fire, poking at something sizzling in a cast-iron skillet. "How are you feeling?"

The questions were in her mouth, but then she caught a whiff of frying meat and sputtering fat that made the words drown as her mouth watered. "Oh my God, that smells great. What is it?"

"Raccoon and white beans, and there's tea."

"Raccoon." She saw Ellie put a hand to her mouth to cover the giggles and then looked back at Tom. "Like, you caught it?"

"Well, it sure didn't get Fed-Exed. Besides, the dog needs the meat . . . Look, sit before you fall down."

"Ellie said you think I have . . . had a concussion. Aren't you not supposed to sleep if you've had a concussion?"

"Well, I guess you had other ideas," he said, and she decided Tom Eden had a very nice smile, especially that dimple on the left. He wasn't that much older either. Maybe . . . nineteen? Twenty? She wondered if there was a graceful way to figure that out, and then wondered why she was wondering.

Tom said, "How *does* your head feel?"

"Like someone bashed it with a brick."

"I'll bet. I've got some ibuprofen, but you should get something in your stomach." He aimed a knife. "Med's in that canvas bag over there, and you can use that jacket. It'll be a little big, but it's better than nothing. Sorry about your sweatshirt, but it was pretty badly ripped and I used it for the dog's splint."

The coat was a *lot* better than nothing: charcoal gray and long enough to fall midway between her butt and knees. The fabric gave off a musky scent that smelled of safety, like being wrapped up in strong arms that you knew would never let go.

Tom held up a mug and an aluminum camp plate heaped high. "I know you're hungry, but take it slow, okay? Be nice if that stayed down."

Ellie was already gobbling and Alex's stomach was screaming with hunger, but she made no move to take the food. "Look, I don't mean to sound ungrateful, and I know you shot that guy . . ."

"That *guy's* name was Jim, he was a really good friend of mine, and you're welcome."

"Oh. I'm sorry. And thank you. For saving us, I mean." She wouldn't back down. "But I don't know you, and I don't remember what happened after you . . . after you shot your friend."

"Well, you passed out. Any closer to the river, and I'd have had to go in after you. After I made sure you were still breathing . . . Ellie, what happened next?"

"You helped me get off the tree, Tom," Ellie said. Her chin glistened with grease. She beamed at Alex. "Tom let me carry his gun."

"Which you did very well," said Tom.

"Because you had to carry Alex and her head was bleeding like stink."

"Which it was." Tom looked back at Alex. "Then I stitched you up and set up camp, got Ellie out of her wet clothes, and then Ellie and I got *you* out of your wet clothes, and then . . . Do you really want me to go on?"

"No . . . yes." She hugged herself. "Are you a, I don't know, a nurse? Or, like, in medical school? How do you know so much?"

"You learn basic battlefield medicine in the army, and then some, if you hang around the medics and care to learn."

"Okay. So, if you're in the army, how come you're here?"

"I'm on leave from Afghanistan. We were camping—me; Jim; his uncle, Stan; and Jim's dad, Earl. Jim was my team leader, and no, I can't tell you exactly where we were, because then I'd have to kill you."

She tried not to smile. "That's not very funny."

"No, I guess it isn't."

"Where is Stan? Where's Earl?"

"Look, I'll be happy to answer all your questions after we eat." When she remained on her feet, he placed the mug and plate on the ground. "At least sit down."

"Why?"

"Because when you pass out again and fall into the fire, I don't want to have to put out your hair, and I'm kind of partial to that turtleneck."

Now she did smile. She lowered herself to a cross-legged sit. "Better?"

"Much." His dimple showed. In the firelight, his skin glowed orange. "Ellie said you were kind of stubborn."

"Oh yeah?" Alex shot Ellie a look of mock outrage. "She say anything about herself?"

"She said you used to think she was a pain."

"Well," said Alex, fishing up her plate, "she was."

"Hello, I'm right here," said Ellie, sounding very pleased.

"I think, given everything that's happened, we're all entitled to a couple bad days," said Tom.

Alex spooned a mouthful of beans and meat. The smell was so good she thought she was going to faint. "Do you know what's going on?"

"Food first," said Tom. "Then we'll talk."

Despite Tom's warning, taking it slow with the food was hard, what with her stomach clawing a hole right through her gut. The raccoon was tough and a little gamey, but she was too starved to care. She shoveled down mouthful after mouthful, chasing the food with gulps of tea until her spoon clicked metal and her mug was empty. To her right, Mina let out a plaintive whine, and Alex put her plate on the ground for the dog to lick clean. "There. Don't say I never gave you anything."

"That dog eats like a horse." Tom refilled her mug. "If you're up to it, we can hit the trail again tomorrow morning. Ellie said you were headed for the ranger station?"

Nodding, she sucked back a mouthful of tea, let it roll around her tongue, tasted the sweetness and an edge of char. *Russian something or other*, she thought. Her mother had been the tea drinker. "It was the only thing I could think of. I mean, other than going back to my car, but I don't think my car will start."

"Yeah, I'd say that's a safe bet."

"Do you know what happened?"

"You mean to Jim, or to everything?"

"Yes?" She tried to make it a joke and then thought there really wasn't anything about the situation that was remotely funny. Ellie came to snuggle, and she hugged the girl close as Mina finished with the plate and came to lie against Alex's left thigh.

She saw Tom's eyes flick to Ellie, as if he were debating what to say. "Look, I only have a couple ideas, and not all of them make sense, especially about . . ." He gestured at his own head. "You know. What happened to Jim or his dad."

In the firelight, his eyes—she suddenly remembered that they were a strange smoky blue in daylight—were black. For a disquieting moment, she thought of the dead woman with her glasses on a keeper chain and nothing but empty sockets. She wanted to ask about Jim, but she had so many questions, she didn't know where to start. "Did you feel it? The Zap?"

"Is that what you're calling it?"

She nodded. "Did it happen down here in the valley?"

"Oh yeah. I thought my head was going to explode."

Okay, that wasn't good. The mountain was about twenty miles away. She pushed through the ache in her head to do the math and then wished she hadn't. Assuming the Zap spread in a circle, that meant it had hit the entire Waucamaw, and beyond. "Are your electronics dead, too?"

"All the solid-state stuff, yeah."

"So what could do that?"

"Well." Tom's eyes dropped to the fire and then rose to meet hers again. "I don't know for sure. I mean, we're in the middle of the woods, and we've got no way of getting information, you know? But I know the military, and we're testing out stuff all the time. So, based on that and some other things I know—just putting it together—I think it was an EMP, an electromagnetic pulse. Probably more than one, too. A single EMP's not supposed to fry people. Actually, I don't think that's supposed to happen if you set off *twenty*. That's the theory, at least. No one's ever tested it out before."

"So, what's an EMP supposed to do?"

"You ever see *Ocean's Eleven*?"

She thought back. "Is that the one with Brad Pitt and Clooney? That's, like, *ancient*."

"My mom likes it. Well, she likes George Clooney. Anyway, this is like that movie. You remember the pinch? What they used to knock out the power?"

Alex recalled Don Cheadle covering his crotch. "I remember something about X-rays."

"Yeah, that's what a real pinch would do: release this big burst of X-rays. It takes a lot more power than what they showed in the movie, and a real pinch is way too big to fit into a van. But the X-rays aren't what caused the blackout they showed in the movie. That was an EMP: electromagnetic pulse."

"You mean, like a big power surge? *That's* what happened to us?"

"I think so. It's the only thing that makes sense. Take a bunch of EMPs, set them off high enough, and let them spread along the earth's magnetic field, and you'd fry anything that relies on solid-state electronics. You'd also kill power grids, communications arrays . . . just *zap*, like you said. People say there are ways to protect their gear, but again, that's all theory. Sort of like building a fallout shelter, hoping that the design will get you through the next nuclear war without ever testing whether that's true."

"Is that what made my iPod get hot?" asked Ellie.

"Probably. That's also why the LEDs don't work but those flashlights with old-fashioned bulbs do. Even if we could find an old tube radio—or a vintage truck or car with a radio—I'll bet there's no one broadcasting, at least not around here. If it was a bunch of EMPs, there's no power, and all the computers would be fried anyway. Low-orbit satellites might get toasted, too."

"Wait a minute, wait a minute." Alex pressed a finger to the drillbit of an ache in her right temple. "Why does it have to be everything? Maybe it's like you said: just over the Waucamaw. That's still a lot of territory, but—"

"Have you seen any airplanes since this"—Tom waved a hand—"this Zap?"

Alex's jaw tightened. "No. That doesn't mean anything." A lie: the Waucamaw was isolated, but she'd seen plenty of lacy, white contrails stitched against blue sky from high-altitude planes before the Zap.

"You remember 9/11?"

"Not me," said Ellie. She sounded subdued and a little shaky, and Alex hugged the girl a little closer. "I wasn't born yet."

"I wasn't much older than Ellie is now. All I remember is what we saw on TV and the principal calling a special assembly," Alex said.

"I was ten, and that's about all I remember, too," Tom said. "But my dad was overseas when it happened. Right after, all the airplanes in the U.S. were grounded. No planes from anywhere were allowed to enter our airspace for days. My dad was stuck. He didn't make it home for another week."

"So?"

"So, what I'm saying is that we haven't seen any planes. The Zap happened six days ago. Either no one's *allowed* to fly, or the planes *can't* fly."

"So we got *attacked*?" Alex's thoughts jumped to Aunt Hannah, all by herself in their condo off Lake Michigan. *Hold on, if it only happened here, she's fine.* "Like 9/11?"

Tom nodded. "Or some big accident. The military tests weapons systems all the time. Those are the only things I can think of."

"Is that how come the moon's blue?" asked Ellie. "Alex said the sky doesn't look right. Is that why?"

Tom's eyebrows rose with interest. "What have you noticed?"

"Just that the stars are a little hazy." She wished Ellie hadn't brought that up. Wrapping her head around what Tom was suggesting was hard enough. She gave a hurried explanation and then added, reluctantly, "The sunsets are weird. They're *too* red. Would a bunch of EMPs do that?"

Tom raised his hands in a helpless gesture. "Your guess is as good as mine. Some stuff fits. Other stuff doesn't. For example, the sunsets? In Iraq and Afghanistan, they're also very red, but that's because of all the dust and sand."

Would dust account for the haziness of the stars, too? That

made sense. But what could kick up that much dirt? For her, 9/11 was more of an impression than something she really *remembered*. She'd been young, so the attack didn't make much of a dent. Images of crumbling towers and pillars of smoky ash were about all she could recall. *Ash and smoke* . . . All of a sudden, she wished she could boot up a computer and search for *sunset* and *smoke* and *red*. Aloud, she said, "So we don't know anything for sure."

"Not without more information," said Tom. "All I know is that one EMP, at the right altitude and over the geographic center of the U.S., is enough to take out North America."

"*One?*"

"That would account for why there are no planes and why our electronics don't work."

"What could do that?"

Tom looked unhappy. "Two ways I know of. Either a nuclear weapon detonated at high altitude—"

"*Nuclear?*" Alex thought of mushroom clouds on the horizon, firestorms, and radiation sickness. Of ash and smoke. "If it was a nuclear bomb over the Waucamaw, wouldn't there be a cloud?"

"Depends on where it was detonated," Tom said. "If the bomb went off high enough, we wouldn't even see the flash."

"Well, I don't like that," Ellie quavered. "What's the second way?"

"An e-bomb, one *designed* to release an EMP."

Neither alternative sounded good. This was like when Barrett gave her the pros and cons of radiation: *There's a chance of more burn injury or knocking out your brain stem, but at least your bone marrow will be unaffected.* "Which do you think it was?" Alex asked.

Tom shrugged. "Either? Both? I don't know. North Korea's got bombs, Iran's making nuclear weapons, Israel's already got them, and there's Russia. An e-bomb isn't that hard to make either. You can look on the Internet for the schematics. I'm sure our military has them. But you've got the same problem of delivering them to the target as you do with nukes. If you're talking large scale, that means missiles. But then the chances that someone sees you coming are high. They'll counterattack before it's too late. If it's a bad enough attack, they'll lob everything they've got. They call it *mutually assured destruction,* which is just another way of saying the scenario's a no-win situation. You attack us, we'll blast you back to the Stone Age and take the world down with us."

"How do you know so much?" Ellie demanded. "You can't know."

Tom looked suddenly tired. "I know enough. I'm an explosive ordnance disposal expert."

"What's that mean?" asked Ellie.

"It means," Tom Eden said, "that I'm the guy they send out to make sure the bombs don't go off."

"Well then, you did a really sucky job, Tom," said Ellie, and burst into tears.

23

"He's wrong." Ellie's eyes were swollen and the tip of her nose was red, but the rest of her face was pinched and too white in the glare of Alex's flashlight. The tent was warm enough, but Ellie couldn't stop shivering, even with Mina curled alongside her. She bunched the sleeping bag under her chin. "He doesn't *know*."

Alex cast about for something more reassuring to say, unsure if her shakiness was only due to the aftereffects of a concussion. She ended up smoothing Ellie's damp hair from her forehead. "He's just guessing, Ellie."

Privately, she had to admit that what Tom said made some sense, even if an EMP didn't account for everything. *Unless there was more than one, or maybe a lot of EMPs combined with something else—but with what?*

"But what about those kids we saw? Could all those . . . those . . ."

"Electromagnetic pulses?"

"Yeah. Could a lot of them at the same time do that? Make you go crazy and eat people?"

"I don't know, Ellie."

Ellie's eyes shone like twin high beams. "When you were asleep, Tom said it wouldn't be safe to go back home right away, especially to any of the cities. He said that if this was really big, there wouldn't be power or water, and no way to get food because nothing would work. People would be scared and maybe hurting each other."

Alex opened her mouth to reply, but then came the sound of the tent being unzipped, and a moment later, Tom stuck his head in. "How we doing in here?" he asked.

"You're wrong," Ellie said, without a lot of heat.

"We were just talking about you," Alex said.

"I knew my ears were burning." Tom shouldered his way in. The tent was a two-man and a tight fit. Alex felt Tom at her back, and she could smell him, too: the fragrance of wood smoke and musk so potent it made her a little dizzy. "What's up?" he asked.

"We were wondering. . . ," Alex began. When she turned to look over her shoulder, their faces were inches apart. His cinnamon-colored hair, thick and wavy, was mussed and his cheeks rosy, as if he'd just come in from a ski slope—and he smelled so *good*. Her pulse jumped at a powerful tug of attraction. "Ellie said you think we shouldn't go back."

Tom's eyes flicked to Ellie then back. "We can talk about this in the morning. You know, after Ellie gets some rest."

She got the message. "Sure."

"Don't go," Ellie said. She put a hand on Alex's arm. "I don't want to go to sleep."

Tom grinned. "No arguments, kiddo. We got to get an early

start tomorrow. Mina will stay here, and we'll be right outside, okay? We aren't going anywhere, and we've got my Winchester, and I got a Mossberg for Alex here. We'll be fine."

"If we'll be fine, how come you need guns?"

Tom looked so perplexed that Alex almost laughed. "Honestly, Ellie, everything will be okay," she said. "The guns are for just in case."

"Maybe I should have a gun."

"I don't think so. Guns are pretty heavy, and your hands are too little," Alex said, relieved that this was true. "We'll watch out for you."

"Promise?"

"Pinky swear. If you're ever in trouble, all you have to do is yell and we'll hear you."

"I don't have a very big voice," Ellie said.

"I know how to fix that." She dipped a hand under her sweatshirt and fished out her silver whistle, warm from her body heat. "You blow on that and I bet you ten bucks they'll hear it in the next state."

Ellie held up her hair as Alex slipped the chain over the girl's head. The girl cupped the whistle in her hands as carefully as a robin's egg. "Who gave it to you?"

Swallowing was suddenly very, very hard. She felt Tom's eyes on her. "My parents. I was a little younger than you. They gave it to me on my first camping trip."

Ellie said, gravely, "You have very smart parents."

"You know, Tom's right. It's pretty late," Alex said. "Come on. I'll tuck you in."

24

Outside, by the fire, Tom said, "That was pretty good."

Alex tried on a smile that kept slipping from her lips. "She's just scared." She paused. "Me, too."

"Makes three of us," Tom said, and took her hand. The act was so natural and so quiet, not a come-on at all. She didn't flinch, although her heart did that little *thump-bump-a-dump* again. His hand was calloused, but his skin was warm and his grip was strong. It was weird how he was about her age but seemed older somehow. Maybe that happened when you went to war. "Cut yourself some slack," he said. "Ellie would be dead if not for you."

"I don't know if you noticed, but you saved us," she said.

"True. But I had a gun."

"And we got lucky."

"Half the battle. Like Stan and Earl."

"Can you tell me what happened?"

He hesitated, then said, "I still don't get it all. The . . . Zap happened, and Stan dropped dead. Just *dropped*."

"You mean, like Ellie's . . . ?"

Tom was shaking his head. "I don't think so, not like her grand-father. Stan was a healthy guy, in his forties, I think. He might have had a pacer or something else mechanical, but I doubt it. Earl had just turned sixty-five. I know because Jim talked about throwing his dad a big party when he got back from Afghanistan."

"Did he bleed?"

"Jim? Yeah, but so did I. So did Earl."

"How did Earl die?" But she thought she knew. "Was it Jim?"

Sighing, Tom gave her hand a squeeze, then let go. "Jim was okay at first, but then his headache came back, worse than before, and then his memory started to go. Like the second morning he didn't know what a spoon was for. It only lasted a second, but it was really spooky, and then it wasn't just the spoon, it was every-thing. Like his memory was full of holes."

God, this was all too familiar. "How long before he"—she fal-tered over the word—"before he changed?"

"End of the second day is when things went to hell. We'd made camp, mainly because Jim had stopped talking and was just staring, like guys after an IED's gone off, or if they've seen too many other guys get blown up. Combat fatigue, shell shock . . . you know. I went off to get water and then I heard the shots. By the time I made it back, it was over. I got off two shots with the Winchester, for all the good that did."

His voice faded. She waited.

"I think the reason Earl died was because he hesitated, or maybe he was firing wild. Jim was fast when he was sane, and you saw him. He was crazy *and* fast. Earl probably couldn't believe his kid was coming after him. After that, I couldn't just *leave*. I kept hoping Jim'd snap out of it. Tracking him took some time. Whatever else he was, he was still partly *Jim*. He knew how to evade. It was part of our training. Then I started to find animals. You could tell that something had been at them, know what I'm saying?" When she nodded, he said, "Then I heard Ellie and . . ." He spread his hands. "You know the rest."

"I'm sorry you had to shoot your friend," she said.

He looked away, but not before she saw the sudden shine in his eyes. "You know what I don't understand? Why not me or Earl? Why did Stan die? And why, out of all of us, only Jim?"

"But it wasn't just Jim," she said.

"Yeah, Ellie told me about those kids. Still doesn't make sense."

"What if it's got to do with age?"

"How do you figure?"

Since the idea had only just occurred to her, she wasn't sure what she was groping toward. "I'm seventeen, almost eighteen. You're—"

"Twenty. Twenty-one, come December."

"Was Jim older or younger than you?"

He thought about it. "Not too many years older. Maybe . . . twenty-four, twenty-five?"

"So what if being *older* means the change happens later?"

"Maybe." He scratched his head. "That doesn't explain why Stan died. You and I are younger than Jim, but those brain-zapped kids you saw were also about our age. Only it can't be just age, because we're okay. So is Ellie."

So far. He didn't say that, but he might as well have. She said nothing for a moment. The fire popped. A shower of sparks flared, then died. Tom's scent—that complex, musky spice—touched something deep in her chest. And that made her think of something else.

The dogs smelled Jim, and so did I. I smelled those kids, but Ellie didn't. But what does that mean?

"What about smell?" she asked.

Tom looked confused. "Smell?"

"Yeah. Did Jim . . . did he complain of a weird smell before he, you know, *changed*?"

"No," Tom said. "I don't believe he did."

That night, the moon was green.

25

The sound reached them two days later, while they were still several miles from the station. At first, Alex thought the sound might be a woodpecker—likely a big pileated thwacking some tree. As they got closer, though, she realized that what they were hearing was not an animal at all. The sound came very fast, a trip-hammer stutter: *putta-putta-putta-putta-putta.*

Now the dog was alert, balanced on its three good legs. "What is that?" Ellie asked. She'd tired some miles back, but Tom had insisted they go on. When she refused to budge, he'd swept her into his arms and labored up the nearly vertical corkscrew of a trail without complaint. Now Ellie squirmed out of his arms, and her face broke into a smile that stretched from ear to ear. "It's a *machine*. Tom, it's an *engine!*"

"Shh." Tom cocked his head, listening hard. "I think . . ."

"She's right," Alex said. Her breath thinned. She stood stock-still, every nerve quivering like a hound on point, and her fatigue—these last six miles had been all uphill—vanished. "Oh my God, that sounds like a generator. Tom, maybe they fixed things somehow, not just here but everywhere."

"See, see?" Ellie beamed in triumph. "You're wrong."

"I don't like it." Tom did not smile. "First off, not every generator uses a computer, which means that someone had to throw the transfer switch manually. But it's been too long: eight days since the Zap."

"So what?" asked Ellie.

"So that means the generator's been running for a really long time, and most generators can't, not without refueling about every four hours."

"Maybe they're really prepared and have lots of fuel. Or maybe the generator wasn't started until only a couple days ago, or they've run it only once in a while. Who cares?" asked Alex.

"There's still plenty of daylight," Tom said. "Why run a generator if you don't need to?"

She couldn't come up with a good answer. "Look, whoever's there has power. That's—" She saw the sudden, intent expression on Tom's face. "What?"

"Don't you hear it?"

Ellie frowned. "Hear what?"

"Listen hard, behind the engine sound." Tom closed his eyes. "There it is again."

Alex shut her eyes and concentrated, and then she caught it: something low and hollow and rhythmic. Not mechanical, but—

"A song." Ellie gasped. "It's *music*."

Okay, Alex had to admit, *that* was very strange. Limited resources, four hours of power at a pop, and you waste it playing records? If Tom's EMP theory was right, it would have to be a record, too; a CD player wouldn't work, but an old turntable would. Would a tape deck?

But Tom might be wrong, or maybe they grounded the players somehow.

"If they can play music," Ellie said, "that means you're wrong, Tom."

"I hope I am, Ellie," Tom said patiently. "I really do. But here's what's bothering me, honey. You're in the middle of the woods. As far as you know, there's no power—and you advertise that you've got it? You waste power playing music?"

"Tom," Alex said, "they're *rangers*. Maybe they're *trying* to attract attention. You know, tell people that they're open for business."

"But what if they're not?" asked Tom. "What if whoever's there is trying to attract attention for the wrong reasons?"

They all stared at one another. Then Ellie said, "You mean, like a trap?" at the same time that Alex said, "That's ridiculous." But Alex was thinking: *If Jim could remember his training, would a ranger remember how to work a record player? A tape deck? A generator?*

Tom said nothing.

All of them, Mina included, listened to the *putta-putta* of the generator and, in the silences between, that unrecognizable line of music. Ellie fidgeted, then said, "Aren't we going?"

"Yeah," Tom said finally. He thumbed the carrying strap of his Winchester, shrugging from a cross-carry to his right shoulder where he could get at the weapon in a hurry. "You'll have to walk the rest of the way, okay? I know you're tired and it's all uphill, so we'll go slow. But I need my hands free."

"It'll be fine," Alex said to Ellie as they followed. She made the girl get between them with the dog, though, and when Ellie wasn't looking, she draped the Mossberg over her right shoulder and rechecked the safety. Just in case.

Hours later, Alex inched closer to Tom and said, "Now what?"

Tom only shook his head. The night had slammed down, a hazy galaxy of stars like sequins in black velvet. The moon would not rise for several more hours—a good thing, because that uneasy green color was like an old bruise and it really freaked her out. No moon also meant that they could be fairly certain of near invisibility, although they crouched not sixty yards from the hulking skeleton of a fire lookout tower to their right. The tower was dark.

The station was not. Set upon a rocky plateau, the station shone, each and every window of the low rectangle fired with light. Elongated buttery-yellow rectangles spilled over the ground, and Alex could see the corner of an armchair butted against one window and a tower of books on a low coffee table. Music seeped through the open windows, and they had listened as Mick Jagger vented over his lack of satisfaction only to give way to Robert Plant's screaming about eyes shining bright red. There was so much light, the panes of a nearby structure to the far right sparkled. A garage, probably: Alex picked out a twist of gravel.

"Look at the dog," Tom said into her ear.

She did. Mina was staring at the station with what seemed like curiosity but not alarm. *Not like the reaction those wild dogs showed when they smelled Jim,* Alex thought. Then, feeling a little stupid—hoping that Tom wouldn't notice—Alex took a cautious, experimental sniff. The only aroma she detected was wood smoke mixed with creosote. Fireplace, or maybe an outdoor fire pit, but that was all. No dead smell, which might not mean a thing. What, she'd turned into a bloodhound?

"If the dog's not worried, then it's probably okay," Tom said. "Let me just check it out."

"Wait." Alex put a restraining hand on his arm. "I should go with you."

"I'll be fine. I've done plenty of recon."

"Don't you always have someone watching your back? If I stay up here, I'm too far away to hit anything with the Mossberg."

"Believe me, if you have to go shooting at people, I'm just as happy to keep you as far away from *me* as possible."

She bristled. "Hey, don't diss me. It's not like I've never handled a gun before."

"I'm only saying the odds are against there being anything to shoot at."

"If the odds are so against that, why are we having this discussion?"

"Are you *always* this difficult?"

Ellie piped up. "Yes, she is."

"Hey," said Alex.

Tom said, "This isn't Iraq or Afghanistan. I'm just checking things out. Besides, someone needs to stay with Ellie."

"Well, at least take the dog."

Ellie: "Alex is right, Tom. Mina searched for bombs."

"You guys watch too many movies. There won't be any bombs," Tom grumbled. But he took the dog.

They watched as the darkness swallowed up first Mina and then Tom. Robert Plant had finished screaming about his dreams only for the music to segue into a bluesy guitar and something about a boss man. Alex didn't know the song. She was straining so hard to pick up any sign of movement—outside, in the house—that her eyes felt as if they were going to pop right out of their sockets.

"Alex?"

She kept her eyes trained on Tom as he darted right, well away from the tidal wave of yellow light washing over the rock, and headed for the garage. "What?"

"I'm sorry."

"What for?"

"For saying you're a pain. I mean, you *are* a pain sometimes."

"Look who's calling the kettle black."

"What?"

"Never mind." She twisted around to flash the girl a grin she probably couldn't see in the gloom. "It's okay."

"I just didn't want to be alone . . . Oh, look, there he is, there he is!"

Tom peeled out of the darkness to their left. He was crouched very low, his head well below window level. Mina was only a dark slink, briefly visible as the two cut beneath the far left window, and then were gone. Alex watched as Tom eased his head up for a peek and then ducked down again before duckwalking to the front door. Alex saw him dart quickly from left to right, and she tensed, waiting for the boom of a shotgun. None came. A moment later, Tom and the dog wheeled into the house. She could see him clearly now, passing into the room on his left, stopping for a moment to stare at the books. He reached for something, and a second later, Billy Joel cut out, and then there was nothing but the sputter of the generator. After another minute—it felt like twenty—Tom and Mina reappeared as dark silhouettes in the doorway. Tom waved an arm.

"Let's go," she said to Ellie, then grabbed at the girl's waist as she started to spurt forward. "Me first."

"Why?"

Alex could hear the eye-roll, but she didn't smile. "Because I'm a pain, and in case Tom missed anything, they can't get to you unless they go through me."

The station was deserted and frigid. "Whoever was here left in a hurry," Tom said. He pointed to the coffee table. Alongside the books were two plates crusted with petrified spaghetti and three mugs still half-full of scummy coffee. A red wooden clothes tree with two sheepskin jackets—one men's medium, one woman's small—and a khaki ranger's hat was snugged into one corner. A braided rug lay in front of a stone fireplace, the charred remnants of several logs resting in gray ash.

"Boy, they were messy," Ellie said.

"Where would they go? Why? I don't get this," Alex said. She was uneasy, her skin prickling with anxiety. The cabin was a jumble of odors: rotting food, gray ash, dish soap, the metallic sting of tracked-in dirt, even a spike of peppermint chewing gum probably squirreled in one of those jackets. But no roadkill, none of that dead-meat stink, so that was good. Still, the setup was freaky. Her eyes flitted over a bookcase filled with paperbacks and, beside that, a vintage-looking cassette-and-speaker system balanced on a rickety pine table strewn with tapes. Probably mixes, she thought, judging from the cassette still lodged in the now-silenced player. After so many days with nothing more than a few flashlights and firelight, the artificial light was too bright, more like an assault, and hurt her eyes. The sound of the generator had receded to a muted stutter. "This food is old, but the generator's still going. Other than the lights, what's the generator powering?"

"Not much," said Tom. When he turned to gesture behind him, the wood floor squalled. "Refrigerator, as far as I can tell. The record player. There's a television in the kitchen, so there's probably a satellite dish on the roof. Doesn't matter, though; it wouldn't work now anyway. There's a woodstove in the kitchen—one of those really old cast-iron jobs with an oven—and a hand pump for water. No toilets or showers. There must be an outhouse."

"No shower?" Ellie asked, clearly dismayed.

"Just a wood tub in the kitchen next to the stove and a big old sponge. Cheer up, kiddo. The Amish do it. Betcha those folks up near Oren are doing that right now."

"Well, I'm not Amish and we're not in Oren," Ellie grumbled.

"What about heat?" Alex said. "Heaters draw a lot of power."

"Yeah, that's a good thought. No fireplaces in the bedrooms, but there are outlets. So there must be portable heaters some-where. No washer or dryer, for that matter."

"You mean, they did their clothes by hand?" Ellie said. "By *hand?*"

"Must've." Tom scratched his head. "This is all kind of weird. I mean, this station is pretty barebones."

"Not even a radio? Like, you know, to call for help?" When Tom shook his head, Alex wanted to point out that this was some piss-poor excuse for a ranger station, but only said, "So why keep the generator on if you're leaving?"

"Maybe they wanted to find their way back," Ellie said. "It's really dark."

"They'd know the way, honey," Tom said.

"So maybe they left the lights on to make sure people like us knew how to find them, so we'd come inside."

Tom and Alex shared startled glances. "Jesus, I never thought of that," Tom said.

Alex had visions of a sudden flash and then the boom of an explosion. *Relax, this isn't Afghanistan.* "You cleared it, right? There's nothing here? Nothing outside?"

"As far as I can tell."

"What about the garage?"

"I only looked for a second. There are a bunch of tools, maybe a snowmobile or two, but I definitely saw a Jeep and . . . come to think of it . . ."

"What?"

Tom gave her a queer look. "There's a pretty old truck in there."

"Wait a second. Didn't you say that older trucks and cars might work?" When Tom nodded, she said, "So why didn't they take it?"

"Maybe it's out of gas," said Ellie.

"No, there's an inground pump by the garage."

"So? Maybe they couldn't fill the tank."

"Or it might not be as old as I think. I only saw it for a moment." Tom debated another half second, then said, "Look, if it was a trap, whatever was supposed to happen would've by now. Most booby traps are set with trip wires, and we already know that a cell phone signal wouldn't work here anyway. Now I opened every door and every closet, the pantry. On the other hand . . ."

"What?"

Tom inclined his head at the open windows. "You want to light up a target, that's the way to do it. Only my guess is they'd have shot us by now."

Alex didn't think that was such a comfort. "There's no one out there."

"That we saw."

"Maybe they're only gone for now," Ellie said. She was sitting cross-legged on the floor, with Mina at her side.

"Mina would've known," Alex said. *And maybe me, too.*

Ellie shrugged. "Maybe they check back to see if someone's taken the bait."

"She's got a point," Tom said. He ran a hand through his hair. "For all we know, turning off the generator is some kind of signal."

"Maybe the generator will blow up if you turn it off," Ellie suggested.

"Can you check for that?" Alex asked Tom.

Tom nodded. "But I'm wondering if maybe we should stay at all."

"You mean, go back? *Outside?*" Ellie said. The bright, brassy light had washed her skin yellow and the dirt smudging her cheeks, neck, and ears pewter gray. Her blonde hair was lusterless and clotted with trail rubbish, and her Hello Kitty parka was nearly black. Alex thought she probably looked just as bad, and suddenly, the idea of a long hot soak made her nearly faint with anticipation. "I don't want to go back into the woods," Ellie said.

"We wouldn't have to go far. We could even stay on the lookout towe—" Tom's eyes widened. "Oh, shit."

This time, Alex insisted on taking the Winchester: *"It's not like the dog can climb up with you, and the Winchester has a scope." "Yeah, but by the time you see the muzzle flash, I'm dead."* But Tom didn't have any better ideas, and in the end, he found that the tower was little more than a platform with a roof, and deserted.

They all agreed then. They were psyching themselves out. The only precaution they took was to cut the generator, which Tom did as Alex, Ellie, and the dog waited at a safe distance. There was no *ka-boom*, and after doing so long without electricity, getting rid of the racket and that brassy artificial light was a relief.

As tired as they were, they were all too keyed up to sleep and so set about putting the station to rights. Alex scrounged up lanterns, and Tom brought in armfuls of wood from one of two piles laid out neatly beneath a lean-to at the back of the station and got a fire going in the woodstove. Flopping alongside, the dog promptly dozed off. After Alex pumped water into several large pots, she set those on the woodstove to heat, and then she and Ellie gathered up dirty dishes to add to those already piled in the sink. While Ellie explored the bedrooms, Alex took a quick inventory of the refrigerator and pantry. There was fruit in the refrigerator—oranges and apples—as well as eggs, a carton of milk, butter, a variety of vegetables, and a bonus: two packages of ground beef, still fresh, and a string of sausages. Steaks and a roast, and two cartons of ice cream—chocolate and rocky road— in the freezer. The pantry was as well stocked as the woodpile, stuffed to overflowing with canned goods; boxes of dried fruit, powdered milk, and instant eggs; packets of beef jerky; bags of sugar and flour and baking soda, as well as tins of baking powder; cartons of oatmeal, grits, and barley; dried beans; two sacks of potatoes; onions and garlic; and, of course, MREs. There was so much food—and so much variety—Alex got a little giddy.

She was perched on a step stool, riffling through a shelf packed with candles and matches, when Ellie came to the door. "I found a whole bunch of clothes and soap and shampoo and tow—" The girl's eyes widened as her flashlight swept over the pantry's shelves. "Wow. We could live here forever."

"Maybe not that long," Alex said. "But it sure looks like they were set for the winter."

"Hey, hey!" Ellie swooped on something on a bottom shelf. She came up with a bag of chocolate chips. "Can we make cookies?"

The girl's face shone with so much excitement that Alex laughed. "Sure, but not tonight, okay? Let's get cleaned up and then we'll scare up something to eat. Tomorrow we can see about cookies. Show me what you found."

"Ooo, ooo, I almost forgot," Ellie said as they left the kitchen and the still-sleeping Mina. In the common room, they passed by Tom, who was scooping the clog of ash from the fireplace. "I found the basement."

Tom paused, shovel in one hand, broom in the other. "What basement? Where? I didn't find a basement."

"In the *bedroom*," Ellie said, all but adding *duh*. She tugged on Alex's hand. "Come on, I'll show you."

"Okay, that's a weird place for a cellar," said Tom. They were in the smaller of the two bedrooms, clustered around a small rug doubled over on itself to reveal a hinged cellar door cut out of the floor. Ellie had dragged the door open by pulling on a metal ring set flush to the wood. "And you found it how?"

"I heard it," Ellie said. "When I walked on it, the wood squeaked, and then when I pulled back the rug, there it was."

"I can't believe I missed this," Tom said.

"Maybe I have better ears," Ellie said.

"You're heavier," Alex said to Tom. "Everything squeaks. Honestly, you'd almost have to know it was there." She aimed her flashlight into the dark maw. The light rippled over a set of narrow wooden stairs and brick walls. At the very bottom, she saw that the floor was poured concrete. This close, she could feel cold air feathering up from underground, and then she smelled it: wet rock, moist earth, and—

She sucked in a sudden breath.

"What?" Tom asked.

The stink was almost nonexistent but absolutely unmistakable. *Probably nobody down there now, though; it's too faint.* Still, she didn't like it. "I'm not sure we should go down there."

Tom's forehead creased in a frown. "Why not?"

"I've been down already," Ellie said.

Tom rounded on the girl. "You went down without—"

"Guys, it's just a great big room with a couple boxes and a big metal, you know, *box*." At Tom's look of consternation, Ellie sighed. "I just *looked*. I didn't touch anything. Come on, I'll show you."

"Ellie!" Tom and Alex said in unison as Ellie backed down the stairs. "Wait, Ellie," Tom said. "Let me get—"

"And you said *I'm* stubborn," Alex said.

"No, I said you were difficult." Tom turned on his heel and started for the hall. "Go down with her. I'm getting the shotgun. Don't touch anything."

"I'm not *stupid*," Alex muttered, but he was already gone.

And the smell was still there.

Ellie was waiting at the base of the stairs. "See?" she said as Alex backed down. "It's empty except for the boxes."

Well, not quite empty. Her light glided over a workbench running along the near right wall. A rusted iron vise was clamped to one end, and there was a mousetrap atop the work space, but no tools and only a thin rat's coil of wire hanging from the pegboard.

A haphazard stack of cardboard boxes were piled against the brick to the right of the workbench. *Christmas Ornaments* was scrawled in black Sharpie on one. Another was labeled *Fishing Gear*. One stood open, and Alex saw a tongue of black cloth. The dead-meat stink was no stronger down there, though, and she thought Ellie would've mentioned a dead body or two.

She heard the creak of Tom's footsteps overhead, and a spear of light pierced the darkness as he shone his flashlight down the stairs. "What do you see?" he called.

"It's like I said," Ellie called back.

"Workbench, boxes." Aiming her light, Alex strafed the darkness to her left—and froze.

The metal cabinet was dark green, wide, almost directly opposite the stairs, and the door was open. Not much, maybe six inches, but enough so that when she moved a little to her left, her flashlight picked up a glint of metal, the twinkle of a scope.

"Alex?"

"Tom," she said, and smiled. "Tom, it's a gun safe!"

"What?" She heard Tom clattering down the steps, fast. "Wait—"

"So there are more guns?" Ellie asked. "That's good, isn't it?"

"I think so." She started forward, reaching for the safe, wrapping her hand around the metal latch. "Good thing it's open, too. Otherwise, we'd have to find the combina—"

From behind, Tom cried, "Alex, no, *stop!*"

Something slammed against her back as a bright orange flash erupted out of the dark, and a shotgun boomed.

26

The blast was deafening, loud enough that Alex thought her head would burst. Her ears shrieked with pain. The air split with the whirr of a slug where she'd been standing just a second before. Her throat closed on the choke of burnt gunpowder, scorched cloth, and hot metal, and her mouth was watering, her eyes streaming. She could feel the icy cold of the concrete against her hips. She thought Ellie was screaming, but the sound was muffled in cotton; she was virtually deaf and could barely breathe. Tom had hit her from behind, knocking her to the ground, but now his body lay draped over her. He was not moving.

"Tom?" She couldn't hear herself, but felt the word in her throat. Still half-stunned by the blast, she tried turning over. *God, please, let him not be dead.* "Tom?" A moment later, his hand closed on hers and relief flooded her chest. She heard the low drone of his voice, but couldn't make out the words. "What?"

"Booby trap." His mouth was against her ear. "Are you okay?"

"Yes, I think so. What about you?"

"I'm fine." Tom's weight eased. The ringing in her ears had

thinned to a high whine, enough so she could hear the dog barking from the bedroom overhead. Her head was killing her, and
when she sat up, the darkness spun.

Tom aimed his flashlight at her. "You sure you're all right?"

"Yeah." She put up a hand to shield her eyes from the light, then
spotted Ellie crouched a few feet away, mouthing hanging open,
tears flooding her cheeks.

"Alex, are you okay?" The girl was crying and screaming at the
same time. "Are you *okay?*"

"She's okay." Tom wrapped up Ellie in his arms and pressed her
against his chest. "Honey, shh, calm down."

"But she almost got *killed!*" Ellie shrieked. She grabbed fistfuls
of Tom's shirt and bawled, "I almost got her *killed!* If I hadn't been
so nosy, if I'd waited for you, she wouldn't have—"

"This is not your fault, Ellie," Tom said. "You didn't touch the
safe. Alex did. You didn't do anything. And see? Alex is fine."

What she'd been, Alex decided, was lucky. Clearly visible now
that the concussive blast had knocked the blanket askew, the shotgun was wedged between two boxes, its barrel aimed at the safe.
The muzzle flash had ignited the cloth, which still gave off a stink
of burning wool. Now that she knew what she was looking for,
she picked out the wire attached to the trigger easily enough and
followed that to the mousetrap. A separate wire, cut from the
same coil on the pegboard, snaked from the now-sprung trap, up
the brick wall, over exposed beams in the ceiling, and then down
to the top hinge of the safe's door. When she'd dragged the safe
open the rest of the way, the wire wrapped around the hinge had

tightened, the holding bar on the trap had disengaged, and the force of the hammer snapping shut had taken up enough slack to pull the trigger.

She felt Tom's hand on her shoulder and turned.

"How about we all go upstairs and celebrate being alive?" he said.

By the time Alex returned to the kitchen with Ellie, Tom had prepared a feast: panfried hamburgers with all the trimmings, a huge salad, and fried potatoes. "Wow," Alex said, "I thought all you knew how to do was raccoon. Where'd you learn to cook?"

"For your information, I love cooking." He grinned. "My mom's a fantastic cook, and so's my dad."

"I don't suppose you've figured out dessert."

"As a matter of fact." Tom produced a box of Oreos from behind his back. "Ta-da. I liberated them from behind a sack of dog food. There's one more box and a package of Mallomars, too. Somebody didn't want to share."

"They had a dog?" Alex asked, and wondered, *What happened to it?*

"This is very nice of you, Tom," Ellie said in a small voice. She was quite pale. No amount of reassurance from Alex had worked; the little girl blamed herself for what had happened down in the cellar. She'd been virtually mute as Alex stripped her out of her clothes, scrubbed her clean in the wood tub they'd dragged to a back bedroom, and then dressed her in a woman's flannel shirt and jeans rolled up to her calves. "But I don't think I'm very hungry."

"Well, I'm starved." Dropping into a chair, Alex grabbed up a hamburger bun and spooned out a huge dollop of mayonnaise.

Tom grinned. "Nothing like a little near-death experience to work up an appetite. Ellie, you want something, feel free."

"I'm not hungry," Ellie repeated. She looked uncertainly at Mina, who'd scrambled for the bowl Tom plunked on the floor and was now practically inhaling kibble. "I should maybe just go lie down."

"That's fine, honey." Laycring his burger with lettuce and tomato, Tom squirted a spiral of ketchup. "You do whatever you want. Pass the mayo, would you, Alex?"

"Sure," Alex replied, although her mouth kept trying to twitch into a smile. She caught Tom's warning look and rearranged her features to as bland a deadpan as she could manage. Alex understood reverse psychology when she saw it; she hadn't spent all that time staring at her shrink's carpet for nothing. As Alex forked a burger onto a mound of lettuce, she saw Ellie slide into a chair.

"Mustard," Ellie said in a very tiny voice. "And relish. Please."

"One spoonful or two?" asked Tom.

"Two."

Tom doled out relish. "And let me give you some of this tomato here . . . There, that's good. Try that. There's more where that came from."

They ate in a silence that was comfortable and almost heartbreaking because it was so normal, and Alex thought that Tom was right. Food was fundamental. After so long a time of eating only in memory, feasting in actual fact—with all its aromas and tongue-popping tastes—was a celebration.

The silence also gave her a chance to think about that cellar.

Leaving aside how dumb she'd been—the promise of more guns had swept away every particle of good sense—that dead-meat stink, however faint, meant one of two things. Either the rangers had changed, or maybe some other brain-zapped crazy had been rummaging around down there. Either would account for why the rangers had cleared out in a hurry.

But why set a trap? She bit into her burger and slowly chewed as she thought the problem through. A booby trap like that would only work if you knew where the gun safe was. Tom had missed it; Ellie had found the cellar by chance. So, presumably, only another ranger would know where the safe was, or that a cellar even existed.

Say, hypothetically, there'd been two rangers. Say one had changed, and the other hadn't. Had the normal one set the trap, hoping to kill the ranger who'd changed? Or—

Wait a second. Tom said Jim was still partly Jim after he went crazy. What if the ranger who'd changed set it to take out the one who was still normal?

"That burger okay?" Tom asked.

"What?" Alex looked up and realized she'd stopped chewing. "It's great," she said around burger, and swallowed.

But she thought, *Those brain-zapped kids changed the very first day. Jim was older and he changed on the second day and ended up just like those kids. And now, maybe, there's a ranger, and that would make four people who changed.*

Well, actually, there were five. Because she had changed, too— just not in the same way as the others.

Not yet.

27

Tom looked up from the farmer's sink where he stood doing the dishes. Perched on a windowsill over the sink, a Coleman lantern hissed out brilliant, harsh white light. "She asleep?"

"About thirty seconds after she told me how she'd never sleep again," Alex said. Fingering up a dish towel, she accepted a dripping plate and began to dry. "Actually, I don't think she would've settled down without Mina and if you hadn't dragged out the mattresses and made up beds in front of the fireplace. How'd you get so experienced in dealing with kids?"

"Twelve years of four little sisters." Tom fished a handful of forks from the soapy water, scrubbed, dunked them in rinse water.

"Four? Ouch. What did you do wrong?"

Tom handed over the cutlery for her to dry. "My parents split when I was eight. Then my dad got remarried and he and my stepmom started cranking out babies. It was okay. Kids are cute."

"Where's your family now?" she asked.

"Nowhere good."

"What do you mean?"

"They live in Maryland, right outside D.C." In the Coleman's light, his features were flattened and void of color, all except the darkling shadows beneath his eyes. "That's about as ground zero as you can get."

"And you say I watch too many movies. Tom, you're making an awful lot of assumptions. We have no idea what's going on."

"You're right." Tom huffed out a breath. "Hang around a war zone long enough, you begin to always assume the worst. Sorry. So . . . what about your parents?"

She didn't stop to think about sugarcoating it. "My parents are dead."

His face fell. "I'm sorry."

"Don't be. You didn't know."

"How long have you been alone?"

That surprised her. After the initial shock and embarrassment— why people were embarrassed she never did understand, unless it was one of those *better you than me* moments—people asked *how* her parents died. The way they asked always bothered her, as if they had this, well, *hunger* for bad news. Like when people slowed down to look at an accident or gathered to watch lions feed at the zoo.

"Couple years, but I'm not really alone. I live with my aunt near Chicago." She paused. "You really think the cities aren't safe?"

"Depends." He was silent a moment, still staring into the dirty dishwater, and then he said, "I think I know a way we can find out."

★   ★   ★

The icy wind was a steady nor'wester from Canada, soughing through the lookout tower's struts with enough power to make the metal hum. Wrapped in the ranger's heavy sheepskin coat, Alex shivered as much from the metal's moan as the cold. The deeply emerald light of a waning three-quarter moon bathed the landscape in a dank gray-green. The color reminded Alex of a pond at high summer when the algae bloomed.

At the very top of the tower, seventy feet above the ground, a walkway ran on all four sides of a square cab. Inside the cab was a waist high table, and on the table squatted two pieces of equipment, one protected by a plastic sheath and the other by a dark metal, vaguely military-looking rectangular box with six metal clasps. Beneath the plastic sheath was a digital, battery-powered CB just as dead as all their electronics. She aimed the flashlight at the metal box as Tom forced the squalling clasps spotted with rust.

"I didn't want to say anything around Ellie," he said, levering the last clasp. "I'd half decided to wait until tomorrow when it's light. Nearly everything looks better during the day, but now's as good a time as any."

"What is it?" The main body of the unit was light gray, but the face was a darker gray-green, like the moonlight, and studded with controls, some lever-type dual controls that could be clicked from one setting to another and others like the round knobs Alex knew from Aunt Hannah's gas stove. There was a very large control knob in the center that controlled a black dial scored with white numbers and hash marks. Alex read the bold, silvered letters—HEATHKIT—and above that, in a much smaller inset, SB–101.

"Old ham radio receiver is my guess. I've seen guys who use these in hunting cabins." Tom pointed to a coil of wires spooling off the table to a car battery. "All you need is the inverter here to make sure you don't fry the radio, and you're set."

"Will it work?"

"It should. This is old, which means pre-solid-state. The guts are tubes, not transistors. Of course, that presupposes there's someone transmitting."

"Well, we can't be the only normal people left on earth," she said. "There have got to be other old radios like this out there, and if the cars don't work, there are still plenty of batteries. Besides, worst case scenario—if you're right and it's all of North America—there are other countries. Someone's got to be *somewhere*."

The radio worked. Tom zeroed out the frequency and then slowly goosed the large dial, moving with exquisite care like a safecracker listening for the telltale click of a tumbler. There were no speakers, and they shared the one headphone, Tom turning up the volume loud enough that the crackle of static sounded like a hard rain on tin. There was a great deal of static, in fact; too much, Tom said, especially for a cloudless night, which meant there must be a lot of atmospheric interference.

"But what does that mean?" she asked.

"Shh." He fiddled with the large dial, feathering it with two fingers. "I think . . ."

Through the static sizzle, Alex heard a soft murmur and then a single word: . . . *control* . . .

"Wait, wait!" she cried. "Right there!"

"I got it, I got it—hang on." The radio let out a sudden saw-tooth crackle of static. "Here," Tom said. "I think—"

"... *firestorms* ... ," the radio spat. "... *lantic seaboard* ..."

"What?" Alex said.

"... *system failures* ... *ground-based* ... *secondary nuclear events* ..."

"Oh Jesus," said Tom.

"What? Nuclear? What does that mean?" Alex asked. "Do you understand what he's saying?"

"I think so."

"Well, *what?*"

"In a bit." Tom's free hand found her icy palm and held on. "I know you want it all right this second, but let's see how much we can get out of this, okay? If one guy's broadcasting, there's got to be another, and there are people in other countries, and then we'll have a better picture."

Picture? Of what? How could doomsday get any better? She didn't want to wait; she wanted the answer now. But instead she gritted her teeth and concentrated on parsing words from the static: "... *under the age of* ... *children* ... *panic* ..."

More words, broken by sputters of static, dribbled from the headphones, words that were phantoms woven from thin air, spinning a nightmare. When that signal faded, they got another, this time from England, and then another from somewhere in Africa.

By the end of it all, her eyes were still dry, but Tom's hand gripped hers hard enough to hurt.

★　★　★

"So that's why the moon is green." In the kitchen, next to the woodstove, Alex hugged a mug of tea from which all the heat had long since gone. Two hours ago, they'd been scarfing Oreos, and now the world was in flames. Well, half the country, which was enough. "I remember now. We studied Krakatau in world history. After that blew, the sunsets were bloody and the moon was blue and green because of all the ash in the air. Our teacher said that the sky in that scream painting by Munch? He painted it that way because he'd actually seen it, right after Krakatau." She looked across at Tom. "It's the same, isn't it?"

"Maybe." Tom hesitated. "If what we heard is right. It might not be, though."

"Tom, we've heard it a couple times over from different people in different countries, so there has to be some truth to it."

"Unless they're just repeating a story."

"But the story makes sense, doesn't it? You wipe out power and communications with a bunch of those e-bombs. Boom. No power, nothing works. That guy from England said there were enough all over the world to knock out just about every country."

"But it might be only rumors. People panic. They can't know for sure without satellites."

"Which are *gone*. You're the one who said that would happen. You know that means there's no Space Station either. Without computers, they can't come back here, and nothing works up there. So they either suffocated or froze, and now they're orbiting in that big, dead tin can; they'll be up there until the orbit decays and they burn up."

"It still might not be everywhere," Tom said stubbornly. "We only picked up five broadcasts."

"We were lucky to get those. Besides, *you* thought of this days ago. What did you call it? Mutually assured destruction? Well, you were right; good for you."

"You know, I didn't *want* to be right about this."

"Maybe not, but hey." Alex let out a bitter laugh. "You called it."

"Not all of it." Tom's face was bone-white in the Coleman's light. His mouth was a black gash. "I didn't think about e-bombs *and* targeting nuclear waste storage facilities."

"More bang for the buck."

"No, the facilities wouldn't explode like an atomic bomb."

"Same diff. You're not the only geek in the universe; I had a very weird physics teacher who really got into doomsday, especially after that earthquake in Japan when those reactors in Fukushima started going critical. Besides, it's not that hard to understand. You set off bombs over the facilities, the water cooling the waste rods vaporizes, the rods melt and release radioactive steam, and then *boom*! Just like back in the eighties, with Chernobyl. Do you know how fast the core overheated there?"

"No."

"Only a few seconds after they tried to scram the reactor." Her eyes stung, and she could feel the bright burn of panic in her chest. "Like I said, he was a real geek. We spent two whole days on Chernobyl. It took something like forty seconds for the temperature to spike and radioactive steam to build up to the point where that first boiler blew. Forty *seconds*. The fires went on for weeks, and that released even more radiation. That's what's happening out there, over and over and over again, only it's a thousand times more destructive because the facilities are bigger. Come on. You're the explosions guy; you know about firestorms and pressure waves from nuclear explosions. Everything melts or vaporizes, and that's just the first *day*."

"Alex—"

"Because without power, there's no way to cool any of the remaining reactors, or the rods in the facilities that weren't hit—"

"Alex, calm down."

"Which means they blow up, too: every plant and every storage facility in the country, around the world, *everywhere*."

"Hey. Stop." He was out of his chair now. "This isn't doing any good."

"I don't care! The moon is green, Tom. It's *green!*" She thought she was shouting—the words cut like knives in her throat—but all that came out of her mouth was a tortured, watery wheeze. "The world's over! There's crap and dust and debris in the air and people are dead; they just dropped *dead* when the e-bombs went off, and the ones who didn't will die. They'll starve or get radiation sickness or kill each other—and what about those kids? And Jim? We still don't know what happened to them, or if other people have changed, or when *we* will—"

"But we haven't. We're not dead, we haven't changed, and we're not going to."

"You don't *know* that."

"Yes, I do." Kneeling, he captured her hands. "Look at me, listen to me. I don't believe in God, but I do believe in fate."

"What does that—"

"Shut up and listen. I've lived through firefights you wouldn't believe. You don't know how often I thought I was toast; that I thought, *This is it, I'm going to die.* But I made it home. I made it *here.*" He reached up to cup the back of her neck. "I made it in time to save you and Ellie."

"That was luck."

"It was fate. I was *exactly* where I needed to be at *exactly* the right moment. I refuse to believe that we've gone through all this just to die," he said fiercely. "Now we are alive. We are safe. I am not going to let anything happen to you or Ellie, and that's a promise."

Fate or not, that's not the kind of promise you can keep. I've got a monster in my head that might have other ideas. Oh, but she wanted to believe him. She was shaking all over, a deep and visceral shudder so strong she was afraid she would blow apart. "B-but where are we going to g-go? W-we can't go back. Wh-where?"

"We don't have to go anywhere right now. We'll think of something. Come on, I've got you, ease down." Somehow he'd pulled her from her chair and they were on the floor, and she was clinging to him, every muscle tight as a coiled spring, and then he had clasped her to his chest the way he had Ellie, and they were rocking back and forth. "It's okay, I've got you," he said, holding her tight. "Ease down. I've got you, Alex, I've got you."

She wept then: for Jack and Ellie and poor loyal Mina and her own dead parents, lost forever; for her aunt, whom she would never see again. She cried for Tom and especially his little sisters who lived near D.C., which really was nowhere good. She even wept for the astronauts riding a doomed orbit beneath an alien moon.

And Alex wept for fear, too. As bad as things were, she thought things were going to get a lot worse.

Because where there was one Jim, one Ponytail Blonde, one Basketball Boy, there might be others—and no telling if one of *them* might be next.

28

A week passed, then two, and then three. They rested, inventoried their supplies, and ate well—even the dog. They passed the time reading from the rangers' considerable selection of books, taking short hikes around the station, and throwing a Frisbee for Mina, whose bum leg was clearly on the mend. They didn't power up the generator at all; the noise made them nervous, and the rangers had left hurricane lamps and a lot of candles. After that first night, they'd told Ellie what they knew, and Alex was surprised at how calmly the little girl took in the information. Maybe not having any family to go back to made the world going up in flames a little easier to take. Or, maybe, Ellie figured *they* were a family now, which wasn't far from the truth.

They slept before the fireplace in the front room, with Ellie sandwiched between Alex and Tom, who took turns keeping watch at night. Tom didn't sleep much, though, either because he couldn't or wouldn't. More often than not, Alex would awaken hours into her shift, look over, and see Tom propped on cushions by the front window, still awake, with the dog by his side. Every now and again, the dark silhouette of his head would turn as he looked over at them, his scent steady and sure, and she knew he would keep them safe, no matter what. Yet he sat up often and that made her think of stories she'd heard about guys who went to war and came back with their minds choked by nightmares. She didn't pry. She liked to think that she was only respecting his privacy.

But that was a lie. Once, when Tom and Ellie were outside, she opened her soft-sided black case to stare at the plastic baggies, the Bible, that unopened letter. She had no idea what she was going to do now with all that stuff. At this rate, she might be lugging that case around for the rest of her life, which might not be a whole lot longer. She could tell Tom about the tumor, and probably should. She trusted him, and they depended on each other. She thought that a guy who'd been to war—who'd defused bombs—would understand about nightmares and monsters. Yet every time she considered telling him, she felt that familiar prick of fear. Once people knew about the tumor, they changed. They were awkward, their eyes darted away, and she could feel their relief when they escaped. Worse, she knew exactly what they thought: *Better her than me.*

Fear held her back, but there was something else. True, Tom had been in the right place at the right time, but his family was in Maryland. He had said that he was due to deploy again in December. So why come all the way to Michigan for a camping trip with his team leader? Because Tom hadn't seen him enough in Afghanistan? It didn't make sense. Wouldn't someone heading off to combat again want to spend time with his family?

And why couldn't Tom sleep? Was it because of what he saw when he closed his eyes? She didn't ask, but she sensed from the way he looked at her, how he sometimes took her hand or touched her arm, or how he treated Ellie with such care and patience, that Tom was afraid. Of losing them? Maybe. Or maybe the fear went much deeper, to something he'd already lost. As strong and capable and brave as he was, Tom had his secrets, too.

Still, there were other times: when their eyes met and his scent deepened to a complex spice and then her heart gave this little jump. Sometimes, she let herself think about how his lips might feel against hers. Sometimes, she thought about more—what it might be like to really let herself go—and wondered if he had the same thoughts.

But she did nothing about that. Said nothing. Didn't ask. There was a monster in her head. Not telling wasn't fair or right, but then no guy would want her if he knew, not even Tom.

So she zipped up the case and stowed it away again in her fanny pack and decided not to think about it.

By the end of the first week of November—six weeks after the Zap—they still had not changed, but the weather had. Tom stomped in with an armload of firewood to break the news, which Alex confirmed by simply stepping outside and looking north. The day was gray and the wind was up, so she got a good whiff—that edge of chilled aluminum—and eyed the dense blanket of clouds, potbellied and slate gray.

No need for her special spidey-sense this time. "Snow."

"Uh-huh. And probably sooner rather than later," Tom said. "We need to decide."

"Go or stay." Beyond the kitchen, she could hear Ellie folding laundry and talking to Mina in the front room. "Tom, I don't know. What if we stayed? No one's bothered us, and we know it's not safe to go to a city yet."

Every night, she and Tom clustered around the ancient radio atop the lookout tower, trying to glean as much information as they could. More often than not, all they got was static, but from the few broadcasts they'd picked up, they knew that both coasts were virtual dead zones, either burning or radioactive or both. Everywhere else was chaos, and there didn't seem to be much of a government, at least in the U.S. They'd heard enough to understand that Stan hadn't been the only one to drop; a lot of people— tens of millions—had died in those first few moments. They knew something more was going on, too, from the garbled stories of cannibals and crazed zombies and kids going suddenly insane. In fact, kids came up a lot.

"There's plenty of wood," she said now. "We've got water and food."

"Yeah, but that's now. We'll need more food come spring."

"We could hunt. There are a lot of bullets down in the cellar. We've got more guns, and there's the bow."

"But we'll run out of other supplies eventually. Then we either learn to make candles and soap and toothpaste and clothes, or we leave the station and the park and go find supplies. That could take a very, very long time, and then we have the not-so-little problem of gathering enough and getting it back up here. And what if one of us gets really sick?"

"What about all your battlefield medicine stuff?"

"That's not the same as being a doctor and you know it. Even if I were, I'd need supplies. So we have to leave. It's just a question of when. Either we hunker down until spring, or leave now while we still can and before other people start showing up to take what we've got."

"No one's come yet."

"But they might. People are desperate. They might come walking out of those woods just like we did, and then what do we do? Fight them off? Let them in?"

"Tom, once we leave, there's no telling what might happen. There's no government, no one in charge other than maybe the military—and who knows what they're doing?" She had another thought. "Wait a minute, *you're* in the army. Where's the nearest base?"

"South. Wisconsin. There's Sawyer Air Force Base here in the Yooper, but that closed a while ago and got turned into a tiny airport and a pretty dinky museum. Couple planes on static display, mainly. Most of the original buildings are still standing, but there won't be any soldiers based there now."

"Maybe we should try to go south then."

He shook his head. "The military's going to be way more interested in protecting itself than helping us. Trust me on this. They've got a lot of guns, and guys who aren't afraid to use them."

"You're not making a great case for leaving."

"I'm not saying that. I'm thinking we *should* go, but I think we should head"—he hesitated—"north."

"North? Tom, it's going to snow. It's already freezing out there."

"Yes, that's the point. People will move south and west, not north. They'll go where it's warmer."

"Tom, the only thing north of us is Superior."

"Not if we head into Minnesota."

For a second, she was speechless. "Minnesota? You want to go to *Minnesota*? Tom, that's *hundreds* of miles."

"According to the ranger maps, it's about five hundred miles to the border."

"The border. You mean, Canada? That's nuts. You want to go farther north, into Canada, at the beginning of winter?"

"Lot fewer people. More territory for the people who are left to spread out. There'll be fish in the lakes, plenty of game if we stay out of the mountains. Come spring, we can grow things."

"Tom, you're making a lot of assumptions about what we can and can't do. I don't know anything about farming, and I'll bet you don't either."

"We're not talking acres of wheat or corn. I'm saying we find ourselves a safe place and then grow enough to live on. We can do that. People do it all the time. My parents always had a garden. Alex, if things are really as bad as what we've heard, it's not like anyone's going to be driving to the local grocery store anymore. That means we learn to fend for ourselves. I'm not saying it'll be easy. I think it will be more difficult than we can imagine. But not facing up to that won't help us."

"I know that," she said, a little irritated now. "Okay, say you're right. Even if this was a good idea—and I'm not sure that it is— we've got Ellie to think about. You and I might make it, but you can't expect Ellie to hike that kind of distance, sleep out in the snow. The rangers only left two pairs of snowshoes and cross country skis, and none fit Ellie. That means we'll have to carry her or figure out some kind of sled. Best case scenario, we wouldn't make it for almost two months—and that's if it doesn't snow. No way we won't run out of food."

"An awful lot of people are dead, Alex," he said quietly. "They died weeks ago, in the first few minutes."

"Assuming you can trust rumors."

He pushed through her objection. "That means a lot of abandoned houses and plenty of supplies, provided no one's gotten there first."

"It's still really far. Think of how long it took us to make it here." She saw how his face had changed. "What?"

"We might have wheels."

Her mouth unhinged. "What?"

"That truck in the garage. It's pretty old. I think it might actually work. I just haven't . . ." He punctuated with a shrug.

"Oh my God," she said. "You mean, we could *drive*? Why didn't you say anything?"

"A couple reasons. Once the snow flies and it gets more than eight inches, a foot, we'll be dead in the water, even with chains, and there won't be snowplows. There's also fuel to worry about. We've got some here, but inground tanks work on electric pumps. No electricity, no way to get gas."

"But there'll be a lot of abandoned trucks and cars, right? We'll siphon off what we need. Tom, in a truck, five hundred miles is almost nothing. We could be there in ten or twelve hours. We could go anywhere."

"Under normal circumstances. But how much you want to bet that the roads are parking lots? Everything stopped moving, all at once. If what we heard on the radio is right, then a lot of people flat-out died, just like Stan. That means bodies, lots of them. Where there are bodies, there are going to be scavengers, and I'm not just talking wild dogs. There'll be raccoons, opossums, foxes, wolves, maybe bears. All those cars mean we'll be spending half our time just trying to clear the road. Eventually we'll run into something too big to move and then we walk."

"What if we stay away from major roads?"

"Yeah, but remember that Spielberg movie *War of the Worlds*? Remember what happens when they try driving past all those people without wheels? They nearly get killed, and then they lose the van and end up with nothing. That's how the real world is, Alex; that's what'll happen if we take the truck. There is nothing near what you think of as civilized out there. Everything is different."

She saw his point, she really did. She had, after all, seen the same movie. "If we're too freaked out to leave, then this isn't any better than a prison."

He was quiet a few moments. "What if we run into more of *them*?"

She knew what he meant. "Maybe they're all dead by now. It's *cold*. They've probably frozen to death." Then she thought, *Yeah, but if a brain-zapped ranger did set that booby trap, they might be a lot smarter than they look.* This assumed there *were* more brain-zapped kids out there. Panicky radio broadcasts, fueled by rumors, weren't facts. Although they believed everything else. So why not that?

"Jim," he reminded her, "gave me the slip for more than two days. If there are more of those zapped kids or adults, I wouldn't count them all out."

"Well," she said, "maybe we shouldn't count us out either."

"Maybe not," he said, "but those radio guys made it sound like the people who survived are scared of kids, of *us.* That means we're the enemy. We're the threat. We'll be lucky they don't shoot us on sight."

Ellie was not as unhappy as Alex had expected her to be, even when Tom sat the girl down and explained how things might be very different once they ran into other people. To Ellie, Tom was a soldier, as her father had been. Tom had saved them once before and would save them again.

Over the next two days, Alex re-inventoried their supplies, decided what they should bring, and, if it came down to it—if they lost the truck or got bogged down in snow—who would carry what. Tom worked on the truck, and Ellie stuck close, shadowing Tom, handing over tools. When Tom cranked the starter, they were rewarded with a series of heavy metallic clatters and coughs before the truck settled down to a throaty rattle. Tom and Ellie gave each other high fives, and Ellie crowed to Alex, "And now we got wheels!"

That night, after grilled steaks and baked potatoes, Tom asked, "What do you know about hunting, setting traps, that kind of thing?"

She handed him a plate to dry. "Well, I know how to shoot. I've done skeet. I know how to make a deadfall."

He made a face. "That's okay if you don't mind hamburger. How about bow-hunting?" When she shook her head, he said, "Tomorrow, we go out with the bow. You know how to change a tire? Or drive a stick?"

"Why are we talking about this?"

"Because." Opening the cupboard, he replaced the dried plates. "If something happens to me, or we get separated somehow, you need to know these things."

She stared at him for a long moment. "Nothing's going to happen to you." It was, in fact, much more likely that something would happen to her. She wondered again when she would tell him.

"Believe me, I'd just as soon not go anywhere either, but I want you guys to have the best shot at making it."

"With that logic, you ought to be teaching Ellie how to handle a gun. If something can happen to you, it can happen to both of us. Then she'd be all alone." She could tell he wasn't thrilled with the idea, and added, "She doesn't have to carry one, but she should know."

"Okay. There's a Browning Buck Mark. That'd be good to start with. So." He carefully folded his dish towel. "Leave in two days?"

She nodded. "Sounds like a plan."

29

"But I've already got a knife," Alex said. It was early morning, two days later. The sky was still very dark, almost cobalt blue to the north where the snow must be falling. They were in the front room, their gear and provisions already packed onto the Ford's flatbed. Alex looked down at the top of Tom's head as he fiddled with her boot. "I'll never remember it."

"The beauty of a boot knife is that no one thinks to look for it unless you blouse your pants or tuck the cuffs into your boots, which you don't." Tom gave the right leg of her hiking pants a stiff tug. "How's it feel?"

"Like I've got something clipped onto my boot. Tom, I've got the Mossberg, and there's the Beretta from the safe. You've got your Winchester and a Sig, and there's the Browning, and we've got the bow."

"Which you did very well with, by the way."

"Like Uryū," said Ellie, appearing at the door. Her arms were full of green wool: blankets for the dog.

"What?" asked Tom.

"Who," said Alex. "It's a Quincy. Anime?"

"And manga," Ellie added.

"Oh. Well, I know Hellsing," said Tom.

"You would," said Ellie. "They all use guns. Except for Alucard. He likes guns *and* rips people's heads off."

"What can I say? My kind of guy."

"Great." Alex rolled her eyes. "Tom, I don't know how to fight with a knife."

"And with any luck, you won't have to. In fact, you'll probably just end up getting yourself killed, so I wouldn't recommend it."

"So what good is it?"

"Ask the bad guy you stab when he least expects it."

"You just said I'll get myself killed."

"Not if the first stab's so good you don't have to do it again." He pushed to his feet. "Come on, relax. I was joking."

"She's not laughing," said Ellie.

"This is for just in case," said Tom.

"You say that a lot," Alex said.

"Because I mean it." He ran a critical eye over her body and then shook his head. "There's still something missing," he said, patting around his pockets. "Just give me a sec . . . ah . . ." He pulled out a holstered handgun. "I knew I had this on me for a reason."

She knew what it was before her shaking fingers pulled the Glock free. The magazine was missing, but there was no mistake. "My dad's . . . Tom, where . . . how . . . ?"

"Hey, cool, you fixed it!" said Ellie. "Tom made me promise not to say anything. We went back for it the morning after . . . you know. Tom said you wouldn't wake up and Mina would protect you, so I showed him where I dropped it."

"You went into the water?" Alex asked, incredulous.

"Not me," said Ellie. "It was way deep and really cold. Tom got it, though. It only took him four tries."

"I didn't want to say anything until I had a chance to take it apart, clean it, get it back in working order. Ellie told me it was your dad's. I figured you would want to have it, and it's a perfectly fine weapon. Here." He held up the Glock's magazine. "The extra's still in your fanny pack, and I tossed a couple bricks into our gear, too."

"Thank you." She carefully butted the magazine into place. "I mean that, Tom."

"I know." He held her gaze for a long moment, then said, "Best jack a round into the chamber before you safety that thing."

"Just in case," she said.

"So do I get a knife?" Ellie asked.

Tom and Alex looked at each other, and then Alex said, "You started this."

"Okay, okay," Tom said. "You can have a knife, Ellie, only yours is going to be a regular old knife-knife."

"What?" Ellie cried. "That's not fair. How come *she* gets a boot knife and I don't?"

"And I want it on your belt, in the sheath, thumb guard on, at all times."

"I can't even use it?" Ellie looked unhappy. "Then what good is it?"

"If you need to skin a rabbit or whittle a fishhook, I'll show you. It's like when I showed you how to work the gun. It's just in case."

"Yeah, yeah," Ellie grumbled. "If it's for just in case, how come you guys look like you're going to war?"

No one had a good answer for that.

They piled into the truck, with Ellie between Alex and Tom. Tom slotted the ignition key and paused. "Not too late to change our minds."

"No, let's go." Ellie twisted around to peer out the cab's rear window. "You sure Mina will be okay? Even with the crate, it's awfully cold."

"With all those blankets and a fur coat to boot? She'll be fine."

"Okay. Should we maybe lock the front door?"

"Let's leave it," Alex said, her eyes rising to brush over Tom's. "Someone else might find their way up here and need a place to stay."

"Or maybe the rangers will come back," Ellie said.

"Maybe."

"Let's do this," Tom said, and cranked the ignition. The truck's engine caught with a throaty bellow, and then he dropped the truck into first. "Say good-bye, house."

"Good-bye, house," Ellie said. She waited a beat, then added, "Soooo . . . are we there yet?"

Alex and Tom both looked at Ellie and then at each other, and burst into laughter.

That was the last good time.

PART THREE: THE CHANGE

30

The gravel fire road was riddled with ruts, and the truck lurched and dipped, the rough stone crunching beneath the tires and pocking against the undercarriage. Their speed was pitiful, and after an hour, they'd only covered ten miles. Three miles farther on, they hit the paved access road and then made better time, the tires humming over asphalt as they headed due east. After twenty miles, Tom said, "Parking lot coming up. That where you left your car?" When she nodded, he said, "You want to stop? Might be something you want."

It was on the tip of her tongue to say that there was nothing of her old life that she wanted at all, other than her aunt. She'd briefly considered asking Tom to head south, not north. He might do that for her, but given the little they'd gleaned, venturing out of the park was dangerous enough. Heading for a major city in a state loaded with nuclear power plants and storage facilities was probably suicidal. They didn't call it "Nuclear Illinois" for nothing; the first chain reactor ever constructed was squirreled away in squash courts beneath the bleachers of the University of

Chicago's Stagg Field. That was where Fermi coined the word *scram*.

Now, she only nodded. "Sure."

"Wow," said Ellie as Tom doglegged left past the park entrance booth. The booth was stone with a large picture window in front and a sliding-glass window on the side, like a serving window at McDonald's. The picture window was smashed, the door hung open, and both the American and state flags puddled on the grass at the base of a large flagpole. The ropes were gone. "Someone was pissed."

"Or looking for something they could use." As they pulled around the bend and into the lot, Tom said, "I was afraid of that."

This late in the season, there wouldn't have been many cars to begin with, and there were only six now in litters of pebbly glass. All the cars had been sacked: broken windows, open doors, gaping glove compartments, battered trunks, dented fenders.

"There may not be much left," Tom said. "Which one's yours?"

Alex pointed. Her Toyota stood on the left, in a corner of the lot, near a freestanding shelter with a trio of smashed vending machines. The Toyota was a wreck, and the trunk had been popped, the spare tire left leaning against the rear fender.

"Hey," said Ellie suddenly, and pointed to the right. "Over at the bathrooms. Look!"

A tall, slight man, with a froth of white hair, slipped from the side entrance marked WOMEN, which would've struck Alex as strange in any other setting. The guy was old, about Jack's age, and clad in dirty jeans and a smeary olive-green parka. One fist gripped a baseball bat. He looked oddly familiar, but Alex didn't recognize him until he pushed a pair of glasses back up the bridge of his nose.

"Hey, I know him," she said, leaning forward for a better look. She told Tom about the school bus. "He was one of the teachers. I'm almost positive." She saw the guy raise a tentative hand. "Do we stop?"

Before Tom could answer, Ellie said, "Of *course* we do. He's stranded." When Tom and Alex exchanged looks, Ellie continued, "We have to help him."

"No, we don't," said Tom. "We already went through this, Ellie. We're bound to see a lot of people who will want what we've got. We can't share with everybody."

"Still," said Ellie.

Tom thought about it another second, then braked, threw the truck into neutral, and said to Ellie, "You wait here." When she opened her mouth to argue, he added, "One word, and I'm driving away."

"Fine," Ellie said grudgingly, then clapped a hand over her mouth with exaggerated drama. "Oops."

Tom tried to keep a straight face but failed. Then his gaze shifted to Alex, his eyes clicking down to her waist. She read his meaning and thumbed away the Glock's retention strap.

It wasn't until she popped the car door that she caught that unmistakable stink of dead meat. The small hairs bristled on the back of her neck. From the flatbed, she heard Mina's anxious whine. "Tom, hold up," she said.

Tom was already half out of the car, his Winchester in one hand. "What?"

"Mina smells something. There's . . ." She sniffed the air again, not caring how she must look. The roadkill stink was definitely there—not strong, but she thought it was close. "Don't you smell that?"

"Smell wh—"

"I'll be damned." A man's voice. She turned to see the teacher hurrying over, his long white hair drifting behind like an Old Testament prophet's. A pair of wire-rimmed glasses perched precariously on the bridge of his nose, the right lens riding higher than the left, and gave the old man the look of an absentminded professor. He said, "Jesus, you're . . . you're *kids*. Oh my God, I don't believe it. When I heard the truck, I thought I was hallucinating." He stuck out a grimy hand. His knuckles, swollen and gnarled, were scraped raw, and crescents of black rimmed his nails. There was ash on his neck, and to Alex, he smelled of smoke and desperation and something she couldn't quite place. The roadkill stink wasn't coming from him, but she smelled the man's fear, no question, and something else, a sharp solvent nip.

He's hiding something. The thought simply popped into her head. *He's worried about something.*

Why would she think that?

"Larry Mathis." The old man's eyes drifted to Tom's Winchester and her Glock before fluttering back to their faces. "You don't know how happy I am to see you. Got yourselves a dog, I see. Smart, real smart. I knew it couldn't be every kid, I tried telling Marlene, but she . . ."

"Whoa, whoa," said Tom. "Slow down. What are you talking about, every kid? What do you mean, having a dog is smart?"

"Listen to me." Larry clamped his mouth shut, rubbed a horny palm over his cracked lips. "Sorry. It's just I've been alone, except for people passing through. I haven't seen another soul for, God, maybe two weeks?"

"How long have you been here?" Tom asked.

"What's the date?" asked Larry.

"November tenth," Alex said.

"And the attack happened on the first of October, so that's how long I've been here." Larry waved the bat at the bathrooms, and for the first time, Alex saw what could only be a large stain of dried blood that had seeped into the wood. "I've been hanging in the ladies' room. Cleaner than the men's, and I found a nice couple tents, sleeping bags. There's a caretaker's shed about a quarter mile in, though, and now that it's getting colder, I was thinking of moving, but . . ." He shrugged. "Haven't been able to make up my mind."

The choice between bedding down in the ladies' room or a tent didn't seem much of a contest to Alex, and she noticed that the nip of that scent had sharpened. What was that odor? A mix of gun oil and cleaning solvent, she thought.

He's lying about something. She couldn't shake the association; for whatever reason, this combination of scents set off a bunch of alarms. *Or maybe he's just omitting some detail. But what?*

"You said there'd been an attack," Tom said. "You know this for sure? What kind?"

"All I got for sure is what my eyes tell me and what other people say, know what I mean? EMPs is what I heard, and then I guess the cities got nuked, but some people say it was just the EMPs and then all the nuclear power plants and storage sites went up on their own. I don't think anyone knows for sure, but I guarantee you it's a mess out there. I've been too scared to make a move out of here."

"What have you been living on?" Alex asked.

"What I scrounge. I had some supplies left in my pack, and there was vending machine crap in the beginning. Lucky I made it here when I did before older folks started straggling out of the woods, or there'd have been nothing left. Found this in the booth." He held up the bat. "One of the rangers must've fished, too, because there was a rod. So, fish and, well, like I said, there's a campsite maybe two miles west. I've been there a couple times. Bunch of tents and sleeping bags and supplies to pick through, as long as you don't mind the bodies, and scavengers have pretty much taken care of those. I've been getting by."

"Bodies?" Tom said.

"Yeah. You know, most looked to be in their thirties, forties on up. Not a lot of folks, because it's off-season, but—"

Alex interrupted. "No, we don't know. What are you talking about?"

"Jesus." Larry's myopic gaze clicked from Alex to Tom. "You kids really don't know?"

"For God's sake, just say it, Larry," Tom said.

So he told them. When Larry was done, Alex felt as if she'd

stepped into a kind of breathless pause. Through the roar in her ears, she heard Tom: "That can't be right. *Everyone?* No exceptions?"

"Well, you two are, so there must be some. Son, I'm only telling you what I've heard. The rumors might be wrong, but if they are, they're all the *same* wrong coming from everybody who's been through. Now, that's no more than thirty people, so take it with a grain of salt. But based on what I've seen and heard, I believe it. The people who dropped right away were, mostly, adults in their early twenties on up. There seems to be some kind of cutoff around sixty, sixty-five, but I'll bet some really old people dropped, too. But other than me, you two, and that little girl in your truck, the youngest person I've seen come through here so far was sixty-six. Her husband was younger, fifty-nine, and he keeled over in the first couple of minutes." Larry snapped his fingers. "Gone. Just like that."

"How old are you?" Tom asked.

"Sixty-two, and still ticking, thank God." Larry eyed Tom. "You with anyone older when it happened?"

"Two guys." Tom swallowed. "One died right away. He was maybe forty. The other one, he'd just turned sixty-five, and he was fine after the attack. But my friend . . ." His voice faded.

"Young like you?"

"A few years older."

"Close enough." Larry's eyes narrowed. "He changed, didn't he? Started losing track, looking lost?"

Tom gave a reluctant nod. "Then he got . . . he went crazy."

"He went wild," Larry said flatly. "I'll tell you what. You're

lucky he didn't change in the first couple of minutes, or you probably wouldn't be standing here. From what I heard, all those people
passing through, kids your age and younger, they change fast."

"But that's just it. I haven't changed. Alex is fine, and so is—"
Tom broke off. "People panic. Those are just rumors."

"No, wait. Larry was with a bunch of kids," Alex said. To the
older man: "I saw you at a Quik-Mart right across the Michigan
border."

"That was us," Larry said. "I teach . . . taught bio. We're on our
fall and winter ecology unit: me, my daughter, eight kids from the
class, and three other chaperones." Larry's gaze slewed sideways
to fix on a spot on the ground. "Marlene, she taught chemistry.
About my age. She was the only other chaperone to make it out."

"What happened to everybody else?" asked Tom.

Larry's eyes watered, and he swallowed, the knob of his Adam's
apple bobbing. "I just told you. You look like a smart young man.
Why you think I got the bat?"

"All the kids changed," Alex said. Her voice sounded thin and
strained in her ears.

"Yeah." Larry was blinking rapidly. "Well, not all of them at
once."

"Really?" Alex and Tom looked at each other, and then Alex
said, "How many didn't?"

"Three. A couple kids changed right away and then the others
started maybe half a day later. One kid didn't show signs for almost
two days."

"Was there any pattern?" asked Alex. "Like age or—"

"No. The first two killed Harriet . . . she taught advanced bio. She was early sixties, I think. Her husband, Frank, was already dead."

"What happened then?" Tom asked.

Larry looked almost angry. "What do you think? We ran like hell, me and Marlene and the other kids. Took us a couple days to get out of the woods. The wild ones followed us and got one of the kids who hadn't turned that very first night. It was awful, and we couldn't . . . there wasn't anything we could do." Larry's voice cracked. "My daughter, Deidre, was the only kid to make it out, but once we got to the bus, Marlene took off. Just scrambled on, locked the door, and drove out." He shook his head. "That bus was so old, I probably rode it when *I* was a kid. That's the only reason she was able to drive off, too. And she always said district budget cuts never did anyone a lick of good."

"And she just left you?"

"She wouldn't take Dee, and I wouldn't leave without her, so." He spread his hands. "Here I am. You're the first young people I've seen pass through. I knew there had to be some left. There was just too much variability in who changed when."

"Does anyone know why it's happening at all?" asked Tom.

"I teach high school biology. I sure as hell don't know. Maybe brain chemistry, or something about hormones." Larry's eyes slid away again, but not before Alex caught another surge of that solvent nip.

Then she had it: what he was hiding. "Larry, where's your daughter?"

For a moment, she thought Larry would try to lie. In the end, he just looked defeated.

"This way." Larry inclined his head toward the bathrooms. "You should probably make sure the little girl stays put."

Well, Alex thought as her gaze roved over the handicapped stall, *at least we know who took the rope from those flagpoles.*

Larry had used the handicapped stall for obvious reasons. It was bigger, and there were the rails, which were handy for restraining someone. Either the girl was asleep or, more likely, unconscious, judging from the crust of blood caking the left side of the girl's head. Her hands were bound behind her back, and more rope was looped around her middle, which Larry had then tied off around a rail.

The dead meat stink was very strong now.

"Deidre," said Larry. His lips trembled, and he rubbed at them with one shaking hand. "She's only thirteen. I don't blame Marlene, I really don't. Not after what we saw. But I couldn't leave Dee. I only hit her the one time, when she came after me. That was enough, though. I know I can't . . ." His voice firmed. "The change might not be permanent."

Tom touched the old man's shoulder. "How long has she been like this, Larry?"

"Out of control? Only the last four, five days, but the change started about two, three weeks ago, I guess. She started complaining about not feeling right. Lost her appetite and her mood changed and then . . . well, she's a little bit of a late bloomer. That's all I thought it was."

The confusion was clear on Tom's face, but Alex understood. *Late bloomer.* Her eyes found a battered white napkin dispenser hung from one wall, its cover open to reveal a stack of small, gray cardboard boxes. Larry must've broken it open. "She started her period."

"First time. She got worse about three days after, and that was maybe a week ago." Slow tears trickled into the deep rills on either side of Larry's nose. "Now she's only getting weaker. She'll drink, but anything solid I get into her mouth, she spits out. The last couple times I got close, she's tried to bite . . ." He skimmed tears from his face with the back of his hand. "Breaks my heart, you know? In some ways, she's still kind of a typical teenager. Like always waking up just when I'm ready to sleep. She'll stay up all night and only nod off again a couple hours after sunrise."

Hormonal changes. Puberty? Alex stared down at the unconscious girl. *Her* periods had completely stopped over a year ago. A side effect of her many rounds of chemo, or the monster itself—Barrett didn't know which.

And how did hormones or puberty explain Tom? He was her age, way past puberty. And what about boys in general? Since boys and girls were different, hormones couldn't be the only reason—could they?

"Larry," Tom said, "I'm sorry, but we can't take her with us." He wasn't brutal about it, just factual. "Even if this might turn itself around, we don't know that."

"I know. I wasn't going to ask. Everyone who comes through

takes one look and then it's"—Larry wiped the air with one hand—"*adiós, muchachos.*"

"You could come with us," Alex said.

"I'm not leaving my daughter. The hell of it is she might not die if I let her go, but that would mean she'd go after—" Larry swallowed. "I can't do that either."

Tom asked, "What do you want, Larry?"

"I can't . . ." Larry took a weak swipe at the air with the bat. "I can't do that. But you have guns. I'm not asking you to, you understand, but I only need two."

"Two what?" asked Alex.

"Larry," said Tom, "there's no need for you to do this. I could—"

"Two *what?*" Alex repeated, and then she got it. "No, Tom, you can't give him—"

"No." Larry put a hand on Tom's shoulder and gave it a squeeze. "You seem like a fine young man, and I appreciate it, I do. But there are some things you're still too young for. She's my daughter. If anyone does this, it should be me." After a brief silence, Larry added, "Please don't make me beg."

Tom studied Larry a moment longer, then reached around for the Sig and withdrew it from its holster.

"*Tom,*" Alex said.

Tom did not reply. Instead, he quickly jacked out the magazine, popped out every bullet except one, then reseated the clip.

"What are you *doing?*" Alex asked.

Tom checked the safety and then proffered the pistol, grip first. "Careful. There's already one in the chamber."

"Thank you." Larry wrapped his hand around the butt. "I'll take it from here."

Tom didn't let go of the pistol. "You don't have to do this. All it would take would be the one."

"But I'd always remember. No parent should have to live with that." Larry gave a slow, sad smile. "A word of advice. You two and the little girl? There's a lot of anger out there, and fear. People'll either shoot you, or decide you're worth your weight in gold."

"What do you mean?"

"I mean, you're an endangered species. I don't know about the rest of the world, but we had eight kids in our group when we started and not one survived. So you be very careful." Larry clapped Tom on the shoulder again. "Go on now. I'll wait until you're gone."

"That took a long time," Ellie said as they piled into the truck. "Isn't he coming with us?"

"No, honey." Tom cranked the truck's starter, and the engine caught with a roar. "He decided to stay behind."

"*Why?*" Then her eyes fell to Tom's waist and narrowed in suspicion. "Where's your gun?"

"We better go," Alex said.

Ellie looked from Tom to Alex and then back to Tom, and Alex saw the moment the lightbulb went off. A look of betrayal replaced the confusion, and Ellie's lower lip began to tremble. "My daddy would never have done that."

Alex put a hand on the girl's arm. "Ellie, that's not fair."

The little girl shook her off. "Don't stick up for him just because he's your *boyfriend*."

Alex's cheeks flamed. "He's not—"

"You're supposed to help," the little girl said to Tom. "You're supposed to save people. That's your *job*."

"I *did* help him, Ellie," said Tom, with an effort. "It's just not as simple as you think. Everything's different. Nothing's simple anymore."

"That's not true. Good guys don't help people die. My daddy would never—"

Tom rounded on her. "Well, I'm not your dad, all right? Your dad is dead, and I'm doing the best I can. Now I'm sorry if that's not good enough for you, but give me a break already! I didn't ask for this, and I didn't ask for *you*—" He clamped his mouth shut, but the damage was done.

Ellie's face went as still as polished marble. "Okay." She didn't cry or shout, and every word cut the air as cleanly as a razor. "Fine."

Tom was gray. "Ellie, honey, I'm sor—"

"Don't call me that," Ellie said in her new, deadly voice. "Don't ever call me honey again. Only my daddy called me that, and like you said, you're not my daddy."

Alex was almost afraid to breathe. Ellie turned away and stared straight ahead.

Without another word, Tom butted the truck into first, and they left.

31

After Larry's warning, they decided to stick to forested country roads. This also meant that they couldn't go very quickly either; the roads weren't in great shape and tended to swerve and curl, so they weren't able to lay down many miles. The only saving grace was that the snow held off. Alex drove while Tom literally rode shotgun, ready to blast anyone who might come roaring out of the woods to steal the truck or kill them or both. But no one came, and they saw no brain-zapped kids either. Alex kept her window cracked—for air, she said—but she didn't catch a scent that raised any alarms. They passed by a few mailboxes at the end of narrow dirt roads. Presumably there were houses back there, but they saw no one.

They did come to a single farm, but the house was dark and looked deserted, and in the air, big black birds wheeled. The sight set off a fluttery feeling in Alex's chest, and then she got a big noseful of rot—but it was real rot this time. She spotted lumps of soggy wool in a muddy, enclosed paddock—sheep that had died of starvation—and as they rolled past a fenced-in field, the chug of the truck made the crows whirl up in a cloud. In another moment, they'd settled back to feed on the cows, most so bloated they looked like balloons about to burst. Vultures quarreled over the bodies, and Alex spotted two sleek gray foxes playing tug-of-war with a tangle of guts. The only animal still standing in the field was a tired-looking, old dray horse calmly munching on a clump of weeds. The horse's head lifted as they passed.

"Hold up." Hopping from the truck, Tom unlatched the fence's gate, then climbed back in. "For when it runs out of grass. It'll be okay."

"Why didn't you just shoot it?" Ellie muttered, but Tom didn't answer.

When night fell, they'd managed a little under ninety miles, the last twenty on a snaky scratch of earth no wider than the truck. The ranger map was useless; the thin red squiggle marking the fire road had changed over to hyphens, a polite topographical symbol for an unimproved road. If the tall switches of dead grass sprouting in a Mohawk down the very center were to be believed, no one had been on this road—really, nothing more than a cut in the dirt—in years. The truck bounced and jounced in a squall of worn shocks as their speed dropped from thirty to twenty to ten and night leaked into the dense clouds, inking them black.

"We need to stop," Alex said. "Even with headlights, this is impossible."

"I know. Over there." Tom gestured to the right. "Looks like part of an old fence."

In the dimming light, Alex spotted a jagged post listing like the Tower of Pisa. Beyond, the ground was level, open, and over-grown, probably part of an old pasture gone to seed. She braked, jockeyed the stick into neutral, then killed the engine. "I think this takes being off the beaten path to a whole new level."

"Yeah." Tom popped his door and swung out. "Come on, let's set up the tent. Ellie, Mina needs to be let out."

Ellie said nothing, but when Alex slid from the cab, the girl scooted out, waited until Tom had dropped the tailgate, and clam-bered onto the flatbed.

"Careful where you step," Tom said. He held out a flashlight. "They might have used barbed wire for the fence."

"I'm not talking to you," said Ellie, digging into her Hello Kitty backpack. "And I have my own flashlight."

"Best thing is to leave her alone." Alex watched the bob of Ellie's torch and saw the dog weaving in and out of the light, its nose to the ground.

"Yeah." Tom stood, arms akimbo, looking after Ellie as she waded through the field. "I really screwed up."

"Hey, you're always talking about cutting myself a break. What about you? She's just a kid. Come on, let's set up the tents and get a fire going. We'll all feel better after we eat something."

As they pitched the tent, she said, "I know you don't want to hear this and I know I wasn't much help back there, but now I think you did the right thing for Larry."

Tom was pounding in a stake, so his face was hidden. "I'm having a hard time believing that."

"Did you ever . . . I mean, over in Afghanistan, did you . . . ?"

"Kill someone because he asked me to? A mercy killing?" Now Tom looked up. "No. I know this will sound stupid, but there's killing the enemy and then there's flat-out murder. There was this one guy in my squad, name was Crowe. He was all torn up. This EFP—explosively formed penetrator—blasted right through the Humvee and his helmet. Took out most of his face and half his skull. Didn't kill him, and when I got to him, he was conscious. So I was holding his hand, you know, telling him to hang on, and Crowe looked right at me—well, with the one eye that was left— and he said, clear as a bell, 'Kill me.' I heard him okay, but I pretended I didn't, so Crowe said it again and kept on until he passed out. One of his buddies went to see him later, and Crowe said, 'You tell that son of a bitch Eden he fucked up.' "

"He survived?"

"Oh yeah. Haven't you heard? The war's been great training for those brain surgeons. The upside is you live. The downside is you won't want to spend a lot of time around mirrors—assuming you're not a vegetable. Why do you think he wanted me to kill him?"

"But he *is* alive. He might not think that way now, Tom."

"Alex, he was our age." Tom gave the stake a final, savage whack. "If Larry's right, I'll give you three guesses what Crowe's like now."

Ellie spent the evening not eating, and avoided them both. When Tom tried talking to her, the girl resolutely stared at the ground and hugged the dog until Tom gave up. Shortly thereafter, Ellie took Mina and ducked into the tent. For the next hour, Tom and Alex huddled over a road atlas they'd found at the ranger station.

"Maybe we should double back," Alex said.

"I hate doing that. It's just a waste of gas and time. Look, the map says this levels out, and we already know this is farmland, right? So there will be other houses along the way, which means that the roads have to get better. We keep on this, eventually it'll feed into that fire road, and that'll take us northwest, up around Oren."

"Big town."

"Yeah, and a lot of people."

"How far?"

"Forty, fifty miles, give or take."

"And the other choice?"

"We head southwest and then cut west. There's an old mine there and a pretty small town about thirty miles north of the mine. Actually, it doesn't look like more than a village." He squinted close to read the name. "Rule."

"So that might be better. Fewer people, anyway."

"Maybe. I just wish I'd thought to stop at that farm. Might have been a truck or car and some gas." He shook his head, his breath pluming. "Man, I'm not thinking straight."

"You're doing way better than I could. I couldn't shoot anyone I know, and you cared about Jim."

"No." Staring into the fire, he sighed and let his hands dangle between his knees. "I mean, yeah, I did, but that's not all of it. Remember I said that I tracked him? Well, I had Jim twice before.

I could've taken him out and probably should've. But I didn't. I was like Larry; it was like Crowe all over again. I kept thinking what if I was wrong; maybe he'd snap out of it and be Jim again. I just couldn't do it, and then it was almost too late. If Ellie hadn't screamed . . ."

"But she did, and then you saved us."

Their eyes locked, and then he reached over and cupped her face with one hand. "Maybe we saved each other," he said.

Alex took the first watch. "Go on. I'll wake you up around one, I promise."

"Mmm." Tom glanced toward the tent into which Ellie had disappeared an hour or two before. "I'm thinking I'd just as soon not risk waking her up. I'll put up the pup tent against the truck and sleep there."

Midnight came. There were no stars and no moon, for which Alex was grateful. As she fed the fire, she wondered, dreamily, how long it would take for the moon to go back to the way it had been. Years? She yawned. The fire's warmth toasted her face and hands. Her back was cold, but the cold helped keep her alert.

She thought about Tom, too. She wasn't sure what was happening, or what all this meant. Her whole body hummed, hungry for his touch. It wasn't lust; it was the desire to be close, to be held by him.

She'd never had a boyfriend, never been kissed. There'd been one guy, very hot, a moony sophomore with long eyelashes named Shane. They'd gone out as part of a pack and swapped shy glances, but never hooked up. Then her parents died, and it was like she became radioactive, as if her friends weren't sure if having a good time was allowed, so they stayed away. Then she'd moved in with her aunt, changed schools, got to be the new kid in midstream. Then came the diagnosis, and her world became an endless round of therapy and hospitals and doctors.

She glanced over at Tom's pup tent. Had he thought about her before he fell asleep? Actually, knowing Tom, he might still be awake. So . . . what would happen if she slipped into his tent?

Or what if *nothing* happened?

God, she could see it now. Tom trying to let her down easy, telling her that they're under a lot of stress and this isn't the best way to start a relationship . . .

Leave it, she decided. She didn't want to know.

The hour mitten on Ellie's Mickey Mouse watch hit one. Alex decided to let Tom sleep another hour, which became two, and slipped into three, and then—

A prod at her back. "Alex?"

"What?" She jammed awake, stiff and very cold. Fumbling with the Mossberg, trying to turn at the same time, she almost fell from her perch.

"Whoa, it's just me," Ellie said. Mina was by her side, grinning, her tail whisking in the chill air. The night was nearly over and dawn showed as a dull pewter smudge on the horizon. Snow sifted down in a fine salt.

"Ellie." She huffed out in relief, her breath coming in a cloud. "Don't *do* that."

"I'm sorry, but you wouldn't wake up." Ellie pointed. "The fire's out. I would've started it, but I was afraid I'd burn you."

"Oh." Now she saw that the little girl was cradling a stack of kindling. She glanced at Ellie's watch: seven o'clock. Beyond, she saw that Tom's tent was still sealed up tight—unusual, for him. "I guess I was tired."

"Can I go ahead and—"

"Sure." She crouched alongside the dead fire as the girl slid her kindling onto the frosted grass. Mina came to press against Alex's side and moaned as Alex ruffled the dog's ears. "You want me to help?" Alex asked.

"No, I got it," Ellie said. She worked in silence, sweeping away dead, cold ash and then mounding fuel.

Alex watched as Ellie touched a match to shredded wood and what looked like milkweed. "Where'd you find the fluff?"

"Over by the woods," Ellie said, not looking up. She blew a slow, even breath, and a tiny, orange bloom flared as the tinder caught with a crackle. Ellie carefully fed thin twigs to the flames. "I didn't go alone. I took Mina, and I've got the whistle."

"I wasn't criticizing. You're doing great."

"Oh." Eyes still on the fire, Ellie chewed on her lower lip. "I'm sorry about yesterday. I shouldn't have yelled."

Ellie's pigtails were crooked, hair corkscrewing out in unruly tufts. Reaching over, Alex hooked an errant blonde curl behind the girl's left ear. "You were upset with Tom. Me, too."

Ellie cut a quick, sidelong glance. "You were?"

"Yeah. I didn't think what he did was right."

"What about now?"

"I understand better. I think Tom's doing the best he can. We all are."

"I don't want him to hate me." Ellie's eyes pooled. "I don't want anything to happen to you guys."

She wanted to promise that nothing would. Instead, she opened her arms. "Come here."

Face knotted against a sob, the girl slid into her embrace, pressing her face to Alex's neck as Alex gathered her up and held her tight. Whining, Mina danced back then came to lean against Alex. After a few moments, Alex felt the girl relax and her muscles soften, and then Ellie's scent became fuller: nutmeg and warm vanilla. No one moved or said anything, except for the dog, which sighed and nosed Ellie's hair.

Beyond the orange rose of the fire, Alex saw Tom's tent shiver, heard the smooth zip as he opened the front flap, and then he was pushing his way out. His thick hair was mussed, and his face was still creased with sleep. "Alex, why—" He stopped when he spotted them and stood, uncertain.

Wordlessly, Ellie left Alex and made a beeline for Tom, who knelt as the girl flung herself against his chest. "I'm sorry," Ellie said, her voice muffled by Tom's shirt. "Please don't hate me, Tom."

"I could never hate you, honey," Tom said. His arms hugged Ellie, but his eyes were on Alex. "I'm so sorry. I'll try really hard never to hurt you again."

"Me, too." Arming away tears, Ellie gave him a shaky smile. "I made the fire."

"By yourself?"

"All by herself." Alex swallowed against a sudden tightness in her throat. "Why don't you get cleaned up? I'll get breakfast going."

"Can I take Mina for a walk?" Ellie asked. When Tom hesitated, she continued, "I'll be careful. I went out yesterday and it was fine. And I had to get stuff for the fire this morning."

"Sure." He chucked her under the chin. "Don't go too far, okay?"

"Okay," and then Ellie darted in and startled him with a swift, hard kiss on the cheek. "Come on, Mina," she called, dancing away.

The dog took three steps, paused, and then, tail wagging, looked back at Alex. "Don't look at me," Alex said to the dog. "I have to make breakfast."

"Mina!" Ellie stood in a thicket of brown meadow grass so high it brushed the girl's waist. Snow billowed around her shoulders in a soft, fine curtain. "Come on!"

"Go on, girl," Alex said, puzzled. She watched as the dog gave her a reproachful look before bounding after Ellie. She turned to look up at Tom as he came to stand alongside. "Well, that was weird. The dog, I mean."

"Probably just hungry," Tom said absently, staring after the pair, already partially obscured behind a veil of swirling snow.

"She really cares about you."

"And I care about both of you," he said, still staring after Ellie, although there was nothing to see now but snow. "I meant what I said, too. I would never hurt her, or you. I'd rather . . ." He shook his head.

"Hey." Close up, she saw that his cheeks were hectic with color; his smell was warm and lush. She wished she could be like Ellie and simply go to him, no questions asked. "I feel the same way."

He looked down at her, the snow clinging in delicate, perfect flakes to his hair. "You mean that?"

They were close enough that she saw the throb of his pulse in his neck. "Yes," she said. "I mean it."

"Then I want you to promise me something," he said.

She heard the wild, hard drum of her heart. "What?"

"Promise me that if I change," Tom said, "you'll kill me."

32

"What?" She stared, openmouthed. "Are you crazy? I'm not going to promise anything like that!"

"Alex, you *have* to." His eyes blazed. "This isn't a game. We don't know what's going to happen. I could change; I could hurt you or Ellie. I might not be able to help myself. So you can't hesitate. If I start to change, you have to do it."

"Why are we *talking* about this?" She stumbled back a half step. "I'm not having this conversation."

His hand flashed and hooked onto her arm. "Running away won't help. We have to talk about this *now*, while we still can."

"Tom, it's been *weeks*."

"We don't know if that means we're safe."

She knew that. "Why are you assuming it might be you? It could be all of us. It could be me or Ellie."

He was shaking his head. "Not Ellie; I think she's too young. You said it yourself; Larry's kid got her period. Her hormones . . ."

"I know what I said." She wrenched her arm free. "Hormones can't be all of it. Girls and boys aren't the same that way, and then there's Jim. He changed, but only after a couple days, while the kids I saw changed the very first day, after six or seven hours. Larry said some kids in their group changed right away. So it's got to be way more complicated than just hormones or age." When his face set, she said, "Tom, if I changed, would you shoot me? Without knowing if the change is permanent?"

An arrow of indecision flicked through his eyes, there and then gone in a second, but a sharp nip she'd first caught from Larry, the mingled scent of cleaning solvent and gun oil, leaked from his skin. He pulled himself straighter. "Yes, I would. I'm not saying it would be easy, but—"

Even without the scent to give him away, she knew the truth. "You're a liar. Your friend *begged* you, and you couldn't do it. I know you're a soldier, Tom, but you're not a killer, and neither am I."

"But I did kill Jim."

"That was different."

"No, it wasn't. It came down to deciding who should die." His tone was steely, almost angry. "Don't ever tell me I can't do what needs to be done."

"I'm not saying that," she said, with less heat than before. "But aren't you the one who said this was fate? That you refused to give up?"

"I'm not giving up. I'm trying to think ahead. Look, if *you* changed—if there was the slightest chance that you'd hurt me or Ellie—would you want me to do nothing? Just . . . let it happen?"

"No." All the fight dribbled out of her, and she felt her shoulders slump. "I don't want to hurt anybody." *You, least of all.*

"Well, me neither. So we have to promise each other." Stepping closer, he reached for her hands, cradling them in his. "Please, Alex, I need to know you'll do whatever it takes to keep you and Ellie safe."

She wanted to promise; she really did. But there was something he'd said last night that made her pause: *Maybe we saved each other.* Why would Tom need saving? From what? Whom? She thought of all those endless nights when Tom, brave and now so ready to sacrifice himself, had not slept. Last night, though, he *had*, and straight through. So what had changed?

Maybe we saved each other.

Was that it? What could she save Tom from? Going back to war? Maybe. He'd thought of Canada, knew how far away the border was. Was that it? Or had he come here looking for some sign? For his *fate*?

Had he been saved from *himself*?

"Tom," she said, "why did you come here? You don't live here; you don't belong here. You said finding Ellie and me, being there at the moment you were needed most, was fate. Is fate what you came here to find? Or are you looking for something else?" She reached a hand to his cheek. Her fingers were icy, but his skin was hot. "Tom . . . did you come here to die?"

They were questions she could've asked herself. His scent altered, and then she heard his sharp intake of breath, felt his shock beneath her hand—and knew her words had found their mark. His face twisted with some strong emotion, and then he was pressing her hand against his cheek.

"Alex," he said hoarsely, "you can't imagine what I . . . what I've don—"

A shrill note, sharp and clear, pierced the air. Alex gasped, her breath balling in her throat. She knew that sound. It was the whistle she'd given Ellie: *You blow on that, they'll hear it in the next state.*

"Tom," she said urgently. "Ellie—"

"I know." Tom was already moving, darting toward his tent, reaching in and coming up with the Winchester. The whistle came again, its call as crisp and distinct as a bolt of bright light in an otherwise darkened room—and now she could hear the dog barking, faint but unmistakable. Tom started for the weedy field. "Come on!"

Grabbing the Mossberg, she held it over her head as she thrashed through the overgrowth after Tom, who was taller, with longer legs, and would've outdistanced her on level ground. Running on asphalt or a track was much different than wading through high grass, and her boots felt heavy and clumsy in weeds that seemed to have grown long, sinewy fingers to wrap and tug at her ankles. Farther ahead, Tom was at the edge of the woods, but he paused to look back.

"Go!" Alex waved him on. She could hear the dog barking again. "I'll be right there!"

Tom nodded, turned, disappeared into the trees. A minute later, Alex struggled out of the field, but Tom was already out of sight. The line of demarcation between field and forest was abrupt, the grass immediately giving way to a tangle of brush edging the trees and then, farther in, a deadening carpet of pine needles already dusted with snow. Somewhere ahead, she heard the dog.

"Ellie?" She began to run again. The woods were duller than the field, the light not penetrating well this early in the morning, and the air smelled dank and cold. There were too many contrasting odors; she couldn't pull Ellie's, Tom's, or even Mina's out of the mix. The whistle came again, and the dog's barks had grown frantic, high-pitched, almost continuous.

Something wrong. Her boots thudded on frozen earth. *Something's wrong, something's not right.*

Straight ahead, through the trees, she caught a glimpse of broken sky—a clearing—and then, just a little farther on, a flash of rust-red that was Tom's parka. The dog was a sable blur, dancing around Tom's legs before bolting away again. She opened her mouth to call out, but something about Tom's posture made her voice die in her chest. She heard Tom call Mina and then make a grab for the dog's collar. Why? She slowed—

And then her nose wrinkled against a sudden, musty mélange: fried onions, dirty socks, and rotten teeth.

Behind her.

With a muffled gasp, she pivoted, her thumb already pushing against the safety—

The woman was sallow and pinched with a frizz of gray hair. Maybe in another life and before this nightmare, she'd baked chocolate chip cookies for the grandkids, but not now.

She sighted her rifle on Alex's chest. "Don't."

33

"Is she dead?" asked Ellie.

"I can't tell." They'd backed Alex and Ellie away from the truck, and Alex had to crane her head to peer into the high grass. She could just make out the dog sprawled on the snow-dusted ground and wished she'd known the command for *shut up*. Unfortunately, she hadn't, and when the dog wouldn't stop barking, one of the two men—who were both pretty old, about Larry's age, Alex thought—had decided his rifle made for a great baseball bat, too. Maybe that was good. A wallop to the head, the dog stood a chance. A bullet, and it would've been over. Alex saw the dog's chest struggle to rise and then fall, and then rise again. "No, she's breathing. They just knocked her out."

"They made me blow the whistle." Ellie glared up at the woman. "She said they'd shoot Mina if I didn't."

From behind her rifle, the woman said, "I still might, you don't shut up."

"It's okay, Ellie." Alex turned her attention to Tom, who was breaking down the big tent. The older of the two men kept a rifle trained on Tom's back as he worked. The one who'd clocked Mina had already packed up the pup tent and was now rooting around the flatbed. They'd found all the weapons, except the boot knife and her Glock still snugged in its paddle holster at her waist beneath the sheepskin jacket she'd taken from the ranger station. She prayed that no one thought to make her unbutton the jacket. Most of their ammo was in a separate soft pack they'd taken from the gun safe, and she watched now as the younger old guy dug out the ammo pack.

"Found it." The guy had a face that looked as if someone had taken an iron to it when he was a baby. "Gotchyer forty-five cal, gotchyer nine mils, gotchyer twenty-twos for the Buck Mark."

"What about for the rifle and shotgun?" the woman called over her shoulder.

"It's all here." Iron Face zipped up the soft pack. "I get the Winchester. I'm sick of this pissant twenty-two. Like to pitch the thing."

"We're not pitching anything," the older guy rumbled. He was bald, round, and florid, his jowls covered with thick gray stubble and a road map of angry capillaries. "Never can tell when something's gonna come in handy. We take it all, what we carried in and what they got."

"Then you're killing us," Tom said. He cinched up the tent's carry bag. "You take everything—our food, our weapons, the truck—and you're as good as shooting us right here and now."

"You want, we can do that," Iron Face said. "Better off without your kind around anyway."

Tom ignored him. "Please, leave us a gun or the bow and one of our packs," he said to the bald guy. "Man, you think I'm going to shoot out the tires with an arrow? You're taking everything else. At least give us a fighting chance."

Alex saw the indecision in the older guy's face. Iron Face must've sensed this as well, because he said, "Hey, shut the fuck up. Don't listen to him, Brett."

"Please," Tom said.

"I said for you to shut up."

"I'm sorry, but I can't help you," Brett said. "I would if I could, but I can't. There are three of us, and we got a long way to go to get us down south. I heard they got an army refugee camp there. If you're smart, that's where you'll head, too."

"With what? You're taking everything," said Tom.

"You hoof it then, same as we have," Iron Face said. "Plenty of farms, plenty of dead people, thanks to you and your kind."

Ellie's cheeks were flushed. "We didn't do anything. My grandpa *died*. You're just bullies with guns!"

Alex saw the look of shame cross Brett's face, which Tom must also have seen, because he said, "Brett, that little girl's dad was a soldier. KIA in Iraq. He served his country, and you're going to kill his kid?"

"Brett," the woman warned.

"You can't leave her here, Brett," Tom said. "You're not that kind of man."

Brett's face wavered. "We *could* take her. Might be a good thing. Didn't those guys say the army got to let you in if you got a kid who hasn't changed?"

"And there's Rule," said Iron Face. "Remember, we heard they're taking people in, whether you got kids or not. Kids is better, though."

"What?" Ellie cried.

"No," said Tom, inching a step closer. "You know that's not right, Brett. You want the truck, take it. But leave us some supplies. Other than the truck, we'll be no better or worse off than you are right now. Everyone will run out sooner or later, anyway."

Brett shook his head. "That's not what I heard. I heard the government set up these camps. They're bringing in supplies, like they done in New Orleans."

"How? Brett, you've heard stuff, but so have we. There's no government. The East Coast is gone, man. Nothing works."

"Your truck runs."

"Because it's very old. I know the military might have hardened some of its equipment against this kind of attack, but that's all untested, and if you want the honest truth, I don't think it'll stand up. Brett, things are not going back to normal anytime soon."

"Don't tell me what I already know." Brett's face darkened. "When that thing hit, Harlan's wife dropped dead. A day later, I lost my Jenny to one of *your* kind."

"I'm sorry for your loss," Tom said. "But we haven't changed."

"Not yet you haven't. Soon as you do, all this stuff you got won't do you a damn bit of good."

"But what if we don't? It's been weeks. If it's true that they're letting people with kids into camps and towns, then they know not every kid's going to change."

"See, Brett, this is what I'm telling you," said the grandmotherly woman. "Army's got to let you in if you got a kid. These older ones, they're no good; they'll just cause trouble, but the little girl . . ."

"No," Alex said. Ellie was shrinking against her. Larry's words came floating back: *You might be worth your weight in gold.* "You can't have her."

"Brett," Tom said, "I'm Army, and I'm telling you that their first concern is going to be taking care of themselves, not kids and not anyone who isn't one of them."

Now Brett looked uncertain. "You a soldier? You been to Iraq?"

"Afghanistan."

"What are you doing here? Why aren't you over there?"

"I was on leave."

"Yeah?" Iron Face—Harlan—said. "Well, your leave's canceled, soldier. Isn't it when things go to hell you're supposed to be helping? There's no army up north." To Brett: "He's running away is what he's doing."

"I'm trying to keep my people safe," Tom said, but Alex heard a new note in his voice she couldn't decipher, and then she picked up that stinging, sharply chemical scent and thought, *Tom's not just scared. He's* lying.

"Brett," Tom said, "going due south or east isn't safe. There's only one base south of us, and it's going to be overrun with refugees. I've seen when crowds get out of control. You don't want to be in that, man."

"He's just scared," said Harlan. "He's a damn deserter is what he is."

"No," Tom said.

But Alex heard—she smelled—*Yes.*

"How do you know east isn't safe?" asked Brett.

"The radio on the flatbed." Tom gave a hurried summary, then said, "Going east would be the worst thing to do. Brett, the moon is *blue.* It's *green.* That can only happen when there's crap in the air."

"When was the last time you heard anything?"

"About two weeks ago."

"Well, hell," said Harlan, "a lot can happen in two weeks. You said you heard people from Europe? Well, how would anyone way the hell in France know what's going on over here? Remember what those bastards did when it come to Iraq. Saved their own sorry butts."

"Harlan's got a point," said the woman.

"Brett." Tom took another step toward the older man. "Come on, man, you're not a kill—"

The crack of the rifle sent a bolt of fear racing up Alex's throat. Ellie let out a little yip. Tom stopped dead in his tracks. From his place on the flatbed, Harlan said, "Next time I tell you to shut up, Tom, you'll shut up, or I won't be wasting a bullet."

For a moment, Alex thought Tom might defy him, but then Tom shook his head, and her heart fell. If *Tom* couldn't save them . . .

"Now that's settled," Harlan said, "bring me the damn tent." When Tom tossed the tent onto the flatbed, Harlan grinned through a jostle of stained teeth that Alex could smell from twenty feet away: years of chewing tobacco and Jim Beam. "Keys."

They're really going to leave us here. With a kind of detached disbelief, Alex watched as Tom let the truck's keys fall with a muted, metallic tinkle to the thin snow. *They're going to strand us in the snow, in the middle of nowhere. We've got to do something.*

"Whose dog is that?" When Alex didn't answer, the old woman nudged her head back with the rifle. "I'm not going to ask again. It yours?"

"No, she's mine," said Ellie. "She was my dad's and then my grandpa's, but she's really mine."

"All right then," the woman said. She smiled up at Harlan. "Twofers."

Harlan was nodding. "Yeah. Taking 'em both's the best thing."

"*What?*" Alex cried.

"I don't know, Marjorie," Brett said.

"Brett, if we take the dog, there won't be as many questions, right? Everyone's got dogs," Marjorie said. "Dogs and kids is good."

"Why?" asked Tom. "What are you talking about?"

Brett hunched a shoulder. "Couple guys we run into said dogs can tell who's going to change."

"Did you rob them, too?" Ellie spat.

Brett flushed, and Alex thought maybe Ellie nailed it. "We don't know that's true," he said to Tom. "Just what we heard. There's all kind of talk."

"A dog and a kid," Marjorie pressed. "We got them, they'll have to take us in, too."

"No." Tom started toward Alex and Ellie, who was cringing against Alex's hip. "You can't have either of them."

"Hold up, Tom," said Harlan.

"I won't help you," Ellie said to Marjorie. "I'll tell Mina to *kill* you."

"Fine," said Marjorie, sighting along her rifle. "Then I'll just kill the dog now and we still got—"

"No!" Tom and Alex cried at the same moment, and then Tom lunged. Marjorie saw him coming, tried bringing the gun around, but Tom ducked under and crowded in, got his hands out, got his hand around the barrel. He gave the rifle a vicious jerk. Gasping, Alex tumbled into Ellie, pushing her into the snow as Marjorie squeezed the trigger. The rifle cracked, the bullet whizzing over their heads, and then Marjorie was backpedaling, off-balance, and Tom had the rifle and he was slotting it against his shoulder, already swinging, bringing the rifle up just as Alex saw Harlan, on the flatbed, pivot—

"Tom!" she screamed.

34

Three days later, Alex eased up until her eyes just cleared the ridge of freshly fallen snow mantled over a high stack of firewood. A gust of wind flung snow into her face, and her eyes watered with the sting. Blinking away tears, she peered across an expanse of asphalt parking lot and past a trio of gas pumps. Slotted next to one pump was some flavor of Toyota sedan, abandoned when the power to the gas pump had died and the sedan refused to start. The driver's-side door was open, as were, inexplicably, both the driver and passenger side windows in the front. A drift of snow feathered the front seat and dashboard. Another vehicle—a Dodge Caravan—had cut out as the driver was making a turn into the station, both front doors standing open like giant ears. From her vantage point, Alex could see that the panel doors had been slid back on their tracks. There was an empty child's safety seat, and Alex saw the limp, furry red leg of an Elmo doll dragging from the footwell. Her chest hurt at the sight, and she thought, again, of Ellie.

"What do you see?"

"No bodies." She looked down at Tom, his back propped against the woodpile. He'd looked worse this morning, feverish and ill, and she didn't think the beads of moisture on his face were snowmelt. Harlan's twenty-two really had been pretty pissant. The bullet hadn't shattered bone, but it hadn't exited either, and was still lodged deep in Tom's right thigh. She saw with dismay that the strip of flannel shirt she'd used to bind his wound was dark. "You're bleeding again."

"Yeah." Tom's face was drawn and white, but his eyes were too bright. His tongue skimmed his upper lip. "Can we get inside?"

"I think so." Her eyes skipped from the van to the building, a tired-looking combination gas station/convenience store/bait shop deal with a corrugated tin roof piled with snow and polarized windows so dark she couldn't see inside. The front door was shut tight, though, and the windows were intact, which might mean there was someone home. The snow in the parking lot was unbroken except for animal tracks, probably deer. She took a tentative, experimental sniff, got nothing but the scent of motor oil and gasoline.

Her eyes flicked to her left wrist. Mickey said it was five minutes to four. "Going to be dark soon, and it feels empty," she said. "I'm going to take a look around back."

"Okay. Might want to have that Glock handy, though. We may not be the only people looking for a place to spend the night."

He was right. She dug under her coat, pulled the gun from its holster, then unfolded to a stand. Even that small movement made her head swirl with vertigo, and she put a hand on the woodpile to steady herself.

"You all right?" Tom's voice rose with concern.

"Fine," she lied. Her hands were jittery, and she felt water-weak and nauseated. Her stomach was a raw, empty pit. A person could theoretically survive on nothing but water for a week or so, and while they'd found some food, Alex wasn't sure how much longer she could manage on a theory. They had come across seven houses since losing Ellie, and each had already been picked almost completely clean—and that included the bodies. At the very last house, they'd been lucky, but only because they'd cut across a field and Tom had spotted a glint of glass far back in the woods. The glass turned out to be the only window left in an otherwise ramshackle hunting cabin. The door was so old that the boards had contracted, leaving wide gaps, and snow had blown in through the ruined windows. There wasn't much in the way of furniture—just a tattered, mouse-eaten couch and two broken straight-back chairs—but Alex had dug out a ratty knapsack from one of the bedrooms.

They'd hit the mother lode in the kitchen: some twine; a stub of candle; an old, battered aluminum saucepan; a can of Sterno; a jug of bleach (nearly gone); three empty water bottles; four tins of sardines; a third of a jar of mixed nuts; a half jar of chicken-flavored bouillon cubes; and four pouches of beef jerky that had somehow escaped the mice.

That had been two days ago, and they were down to one tin of sardines, four bouillon cubes, and three pouches of jerky. She'd kept the empty nut jar for the bleach and used a drop whenever they needed to purify more drinking water. She'd supplemented their starvation rations with a handful of tiny minnows yester-day, using Tom's undershirt as a net to fish them up from a small stream. Otherwise, Tom wasn't eating much, mostly drinking chicken broth and water, and his face, already thin, was gaunt. Their only weapons were Alex's boot knife and Glock, and neither wanted to waste bullets hunting game. Things might have been different if they'd stayed in one place, had a cozy cabin or tent, set up deadfalls, and, oh yes, had bait. But Tom was getting worse, and their progress was very slow, much worse than when she'd been with Ellie, because Tom could only hobble and needed to rest often as they moved southwest, going by memory and dead reckoning.

Tom hoped that Brett had listened and gone west. If so, they would have to go past Rule. If Harlan was right, maybe the people there had let them all in, so when Tom and Alex showed, Ellie would be there.

Maybe. The only thing Alex was interested in now was finding help for Tom.

She just hoped she found it in time.

She cautiously wound her way behind the shop. She spotted a cor-roded truck on blocks and an open Dumpster, piled with collapsed cardboard boxes, backed against a stand of hardwood. At the base of the Dumpster, a trio of rusty paint cans was arranged in a little pyramid alongside a quartet of snow-covered tires piled like dis-carded Tiddlywinks.

There was a back door, with an unsecured screen held open by snow that had filtered in through the mesh. The screen protested with a loud, grating squall that made Alex wince. When she tried the knob, it turned, and she nudged the door open with the toe of her boot. She tensed, waiting for the boom of a shotgun, but nothing happened.

She stepped into a small back hall. A pegboard with hooks was tacked to the wall from which a jacket still hung. The jacket was light blue, with darker blue stretchy cuffs and NED embroidered in black thread over the left breast pocket. A pair of boots rested on the floor.

Another door opened to a short, narrow hall. There was a stinking bathroom to the left; the toilet had been used since the power went out and had overflowed in a foul, reeking mess. Alex could see, farther on down the hall, the front door and one wing of a Krispy Kreme case.

Then the smell, more powerful than the shit stink from the toilet, hit her: gassy as a sewer and bad enough to make her stomach crawl into her throat. She knew what she'd find.

The store was a mess: bare shelves, empty boxes, burst juice boxes, a squashed doughnut that had tumbled from an otherwise empty Krispy Kreme display case. Someone had dropped a carton of eggs in front of the dead coolers. Smashed shells and exploded yolk mingled with a lake of milk desiccated to a snot-colored crust. The coolers were empty. To the right of the front door were shelves of fan belts, quarts of oil, and jugs of antifreeze and windshield wiper fluid that looked relatively untouched.

The same, however, could not be said of the dead guy.

The corpse lay in a pool of dried blood near the front of the store. Most of his face was gone. Without lips or most of his gums, his teeth—stained yellow from cigarettes, with some half-rotted—tilted like tent pegs about to blow over in a storm. The back of his shirt and his jeans were chewed to ruins, the muscles and skin of his limbs stripped off the bone neatly, as if he were fried chicken.

Three weeks ago, a month, six weeks . . . Alex probably would've thrown up. Or run screaming. Or both. Now, she studied the floor. There had been a few animals—wolves, she thought, or maybe a couple dogs—and several people. The floor was a stencil of rusty shoe prints. The prints were all old, the outlines not even tacky, but then as her eyes swept across the tracks, she paused.

Someone had been barefoot.

They'd read *Robinson Crusoe* in fourth grade. As she remembered it, when Crusoe finds Friday's footprint, he's terrified, believing that the Devil might be on the island. But then what surprises Crusoe more is the discovery that after being alone for so long, the idea of other people scares the hell out of him.

Looking down at those footprints, she thought of Crusoe. They had not seen any brain-zapped kids, or even signs that they'd been anywhere around the houses or farms. Frankly, she hoped they were all dead. She hoped that with only half a brain, a cannibal kid was too stupid to come in out of the cold.

She butted open the front door and then moved the body, dragging the dead man by his feet, hoping they wouldn't come off. It wasn't as bad as she thought it might be, or maybe she was getting numb to the whole thing. Anyway, it had to be done, because there was no way she was spending the night under the same roof as a corpse. After the relative respite offered by the store, the cold was a shock. The wind had picked up, and icy snow needled her face, but she was relieved to breathe air that didn't smell like decaying Ned. She thought about getting the work shirt from the back room before dark to cover the dead man's face, and then decided that they had more use for it. She felt an urge to apologize to Ned, but didn't.

Tom was shuddering with cold by the time she went back for him. She half-supported, half-dragged him inside, eased him to the floor, and then combed the entire store. There was no food, although Alex discovered an unopened water bottle that had rolled under the Krispy Kreme case. Near the front door, she unearthed a package of AA batteries behind an overturned magazine rack. Whoever had ransacked the place hadn't cared if he caught a cold and had left fistfuls of aspirin and Tylenol and cold remedies in those little foil packets, as well as packages of Kleenex and tins of throat lozenges.

Behind the checkout counter, the register's cash drawer was open and empty. Not surprisingly, there were no cigarettes or tins of chewing tobacco, but what did amaze Alex was that the plastic lottery-ticket dispensers were also empty. Like there would ever be another multi-gazillion dollar Powerball jackpot in the very near future.

There was a back office behind the counter. The door was

locked, but the keys still hung on a nail next to the cash regis-ter. Inside the office was a plain metal desk and a swivel chair on squeaky casters. In the desk, she found a few pens, two pencils, three paper clips, rubber bands, and—in a bottom drawer—a bottle of Maker's Mark, half-full.

She left the jugs of windshield-wiper fluid and antifreeze, but crammed the rest into their knapsack. She lingered over the cans of WD-40 and deicer, the quarts of oil; thought that of them all, the oil might be good. Soak some rags in the oil and throw them in a plastic bag, in case they couldn't find tinder for a fire.

Then she tore open a packet of Tylenol, made Tom swallow back the medicine and then the rest of the water. It was very cold inside the store, but Tom's face glistened with perspiration. His hair was damp, but when she put her hand against his forehead, his skin was very hot. "You've got a fever," she said.

"In-in-infection." He was shaking so badly she heard the click of his teeth. "I c-can sm-smell it."

So could she, even without her spidey-sense. When she took down the bandage, she had to clamp back on a moan. The wound was very bad. The bullet had gone in a little left of center, about six inches below Tom's hip. His thigh was swollen and tight, the skin flushed, shiny, and hot to the touch. The edges of the wound were black, and when he moved, a thick worm of blood-streaked green pus bubbled up and ran down the side of his leg. The bandages were oozy and sopping with a mixture of blood and more pus.

"I don't th-think I can wa-walk much more," he said.

"You walked today."

"T-Too s-slow."

"So what? It's fine. I'm not leaving you behind."

"You h-have to." He let his head fall back, his eyes half-shuttered. His lips were split and bleeding.

"You would never leave me, or Ellie. You'd carry us if you had to."

"D-don't be too sure about th-that."

"I could make a stretcher."

His head moved in a weak negative. "J-just slow you d-d-down. We're n-not getting anywhere f-fast this way. You'll be a lot f-faster on your own."

She would be; she knew that. Alone, she could cover twice as much ground in half the time, and if she kept heading southwest, she would run into Rule. If Larry was right—if Marjorie and Brett and Harlan were to be believed—whoever was there would want to help Tom.

Or, maybe, something else that Larry had said would be true: *They'll shoot you on sight.*

"We don't have to decide anything right now. Come on." She gave him a little shake. "You know medical stuff. Think. Would it help if, I don't know, we got that gunk out of there?"

He gave a sluggish nod. "C-couldn't hurt."

"Okay, just give me a few minutes. I want to check out the cars. At the very least, we can use the mats. Better for you than lying on the floor."

The Toyota was closest to the front door, and she searched it first. The car was barren and cold as a freezer. Her breath came in clouds as she hurriedly piled floor mats on the front seat, and then she thought, *Trunk.* Reaching in, she found the right button, popped the release, heard the trunk click open.

Jackpot. Inside the truck were a collapsible shovel and three signal flares. They could use the flares for fires, if they had to. Was there a way to reuse the striker? Tom might know.

The shovel was for camping, with a triangular steel head and a removable handle that unscrewed to reveal a six-inch blade saw. She pulled the shovel out to its full length, felt the heft in her hand. From the condition of the head, she didn't think the shovel had ever been used.

Backing out with the trunk mat, her eye fell on a corner of white and red protruding from beneath the spare tire. Putting aside the mat, she reached for the bit of color. Was that . . . ?

She felt a little squirt of adrenaline, which she tried to quash, but she knew as soon as her shaking fingers touched the cardboard, and then she was carefully prying the Marlboro box free. Interesting place to keep a stash, but she'd heard of people squirreling away drugs in spare tires, so maybe not so strange if you didn't want your wife or husband to know you couldn't quite kick the habit. The Marlboro box rattled and smelled like cold tar. She didn't care about the cigarettes. But if someone had stashed the pack into the trunk for a rainy day, he'd need a light.

She was almost afraid to look, but she did. Inside the box were three cigarettes—

She let her breath go.

A matchbook. The book had once been white but was now

gray. She could still make out the words beneath a stylized martini glass—EDDIE MARTINI'S—and, in much smaller letters below that, the restaurant's address and phone number. She held the matchbox between her fingers for several seconds, thinking, *You just watch. There won't be any matches left. There won't.*

But there were: a half dozen.

She let out a whoop. "Tom!" Elated, she ducked out of the trunk, shovel in one hand and the matchbox held high in the other—and then the stink of rotted flesh cut right through the lingering aroma of stale tobacco.

Later, she would wonder if things might have turned out differently if she hadn't just inhaled a snootful of Marlboro. But that would be later.

Now she saw not just one kid, or two.

She saw three.

35

Two boys and a girl, and they were very close, no more than twenty feet away, and between her and the front door of the station. Judging from the snarl of leaves and debris in the girl's hair, they must have come from the woods behind the gas station. They were filthy and dressed in a motley assortment of clothes that couldn't be their own. The boys were older, maybe in their early twenties. The oldest, lanky with a flop of black hair, wore a woman's pink, fur-trimmed parka. The other boy was very fat and wore the remnants of a tattered black poncho so thoroughly used that he looked like a Batman blimp passed through a shredder.

The girl was her age, Alex thought. Somewhere along the way, the girl had picked up a man's torn camouflage pants and a too-small smeary gray peacoat that rode midway up her arms. Every inch of skin not covered by clothing was a swirl of dirt and blood and what was either engine oil or feces—probably both. The left sleeve was mangled, as if the girl had caught her arm on a branch and simply yanked until the wool ripped. The girl shifted, and Alex saw, peeking beneath her pants' tattered cuffs, a single sneaker on the girl's right foot. The girl's left foot was bare save for an anklet of bloodied sock. Alex thought back to the blood-prints in the store and, with a sudden, sickening twist, realized that the footprint Robinson Crusoe had seen did not belong to Friday. The print had been made by a cannibal.

This cannibal—the girl—had a club: a polished length of what looked like very stout, very heavy wood, probably an ax handle.

The car. She could dive in, lock the doors. But she was afraid to move. Her knees were wobbly. The Toyota's open back door looked a million miles away. Anyway, she couldn't just wait them out. The front door to the store was open, and so was the back, and if they got in, they would find Tom—

The girl rushed her. She was absolutely silent and insanely fast. Her wiry arms lashed out in a blur, her left hand hooked into a claw, the right swinging the club. Almost too late, Alex ducked. She heard the club whir through the space where her head had been a second before. Then she screamed as a starburst of pain tore into her scalp. The girl had her by the hair, and now Alex was lurching forward, being pulled and dragged off her feet. Off balance, her boots tangling, she stumbled to the icy asphalt, still clutching the shovel in her left hand. The matchbook went flying as she tumbled onto her back. She saw the blur of the club again as the girl cocked her elbow, and Alex jerked left just as the club axed down, crashing against the concrete with a solid *thunk*, so hard that the club splintered. A huge, ripping laser burned fire into her scalp, and she felt a stinging jolt; then she was free, rolling away onto her hands and knees.

Left with nothing but a bloody knot of Alex's hair and a tooth-pick of a club, the girl bawled in frustration. The boys had not moved; Alex didn't have time to wonder if maybe they took turns or simply thought the girl could handle her. Scrambling, Alex was just getting her feet under her when the girl charged again.

What happened next was pure instinct. Still crouched on the ground, Alex saw the girl coming, heard the slap of that bare foot, felt her fingers fist around the shovel. Her brain detached, and her body simply took over, because then she was unfurling, driving forward, closing the gap.

She feinted low, then aimed high. The shovel cut the air, blade on, in a vicious chop. The sturdy metal edge sank into the soft exposed flesh of the girl's neck. There was a great jet of spurt-ing blood burning into the snow like red sprinkles on white icing, and then the girl was falling away, the momentum wrenching the shovel out of Alex's grasp. The girl sprawled, hands wrapped around her throat, gargling as blood pumped between her fingers. The shovel clattered to the ground.

Her own momentum spun Alex almost completely around. Disoriented, she looked up, realized she was staring at the stalled Caravan half-in, half-out of the gas station's driveway, and thought, *Oh God, they're* behind . . .

She caught a papery flutter, the thud of boots against thick snow, and as she turned, a black rippling blur swooped in from her right.

The gun, she thought suddenly. In her terror, she'd forgotten all about it. She fumbled the coat open, wrapped her fingers around the grip. *The gun, the gun, the gun, the gun . . .*

Blimp Boy plowed into her. The Glock went flying; she saw it cartwheeling through the air, heard the *thunk* as it hit the Toyota, and then she was on the ground again, the boy using his weight to pin her down. The tattered plastic of the boy's poncho dragged at her arms like tentacles, and she thrashed, trying to bat her way free. Gasping, she looked up to see the kid's lips twitching back from teeth that were stained and slimy with gore.

"No!" she screamed as the boy's teeth flashed—

Tom slammed into the boy. The blow knocked Blimp Boy onto his back, and then he and Tom were rolling, thrashing, grunting. The pudgy boy was snapping at Tom's face, his teeth clashing together. Tom rammed the heel of one hand into the boy's lower jaw. The pudgy boy let out a gurgling howl as his teeth drove into the soft flesh of his tongue. Rearing up, mouth drizzling blood, the boy let loose with a vicious backhand to Tom's jaw: a solid *crack* loud as a gunshot. Tom's hold slackened for just an instant, and then there was a flash of bloodied teeth as the pudgy boy's jaws battened down on Tom's neck, just above his right shoulder.

Tom screamed.

No, no, no, no! Frantic, Alex clawed her way to her knees. Tom and Blimp Boy were still struggling, but even if Tom hadn't been sick and weak, the boy was much heavier and he was astride Tom. Tom's shirt was saturated with blood. Blimp Boy brought his cocked fist down. There was a sound like eggshells being crushed by a heavy boot as the blow connected with Tom's nose, and then Tom went limp.

Screaming, not even aware that she was moving, Alex grabbed

up the fallen shovel, wound up, and then swung it with all her might. The shovel hit with a hollow *thunk*; she felt the jump and sting of metal against her hands and the force of the impact shiver up her arms. Howling, Blimp Boy went sprawling, but he was still conscious, already rolling onto his hands and knees.

That's when she spied the butt of the Glock sticking out from behind the rear tire of the Toyota. Out of the corner of her eye, she saw Blimp Boy on all fours, shaking his head like a dog, and she whirled, grabbing for the gun . . .

The third boy—whom she had forgotten about—rammed her at a dead run. The blow drove Alex back against the unyielding metal of the Toyota. Alex felt a lightning surge of pain as the car's rear fender jammed her spine. Gagging, Alex sagged, and then she was on her back, the boy slashing with a claw-fist. Alex's face fired white-hot as the boy's nails scored her flesh from the corner of her left eye to the angle of her jaw. Alex tried twisting away, but the boy brought his balled fist down like a hammer, catching her just above her ear. Her head banged the asphalt, and then a burst of wet copper filled her mouth—and she lost the shovel.

Dimly, her head singing with pain, Alex heard the boy screech again, felt his hands close around her throat, and then her air was gone. Her fingers scrambled over his, but he had her tight and he was shaking her now, pounding her head against the snowy asphalt. The edges of her vision went red and then black, and then the margins began to contract, grow smaller and tighter. Her lungs screamed, and her pulse thundered in her oxygen-starved brain. She fought, but his grip tightened; his thumbs crushed her throat, and the pain was huge: not just a burn, but a sensation of something breaking in two like a dry twig. Her arms and legs were no longer listening to her, and her hands began to loosen as her hold on consciousness started to slip-slide away. She was going numb, the strength flowing from her like blood, and the pain, too. The bitter cold was no more substantial now than smoke, and her vision was nearly gone, her consciousness fading, and there was nothing she could do—

And then, her mind gasped a single thought, so crisp and clear it was like a word scissored out of black paper: *KNIFE.*

Against every instinct, she made herself let go of the boy's hands and reach for her boot. Her fingers brushed fabric and then curled in a sudden convulsive spasm, bunching her pant leg, not because she was thinking anymore but because she was dying.

Her hand closed on hard plastic.

With the last of her strength, she jerked the knife from its holder and drove the blade into the boy's left flank. The knife was very sharp and she felt just an instant's hesitation as the tip met fabric, and then the nothing as it sliced cleanly all the way through the parka and the shirt beneath and buried itself to the hilt in the meat of the boy's back.

Arching, the boy shrieked. His hands flew away, and then she was gawping like a fish, pulling air in great, wheezy gasps that cut her throat. Tumbling from her body, the boy was shrieking, his fingers closing over the knife handle, tugging, trying to work the blade free.

Get up. The fog over her mind bled away. Gagging, she rolled onto her stomach—and spotted the Glock, six inches away.

Snatching up the gun, she twisted, crabbing onto her back. She saw the boy, on his knees, two feet away. Her knife, smeary with his blood, was in his hand now, and his raging eyes locked onto hers and he bellowed—

She squeezed the trigger.

The shot was very loud. The Glock bucked. The boy's chest bloomed red, and the warm, wet blowback of his blood misted her face. The boy flopped onto his back without a sound.

She had time for nothing, not even relief. In the next instant, she heard that familiar papery rustle, turned, and saw Blimp Boy surging forward, Tom's blood smeared over his mouth in an obscene leer. And then the fat boy loomed, huge and horrible, only five feet away; he was there, he was right *there*!

She shoved the gun at his face, and fired.

36

Tom bled a long time, soaking through a balled-up shirt and his own flannel before the flow finally slackened. Then he told her to use the bourbon. She didn't want to—she knew the alcohol would burn like hell—but she did what he said. As soon as the bourbon hit the raw, macerated tissue, Tom's whole body went rigid, the cords standing out like wires on his neck, his teeth bared in a grimace.

"I'm sorry, I'm sorry," she said helplessly. The last thing she wanted was to hurt him even more. Already dark amber, the bourbon turned a muddy brownish-purple as it mingled with Tom's blood. She used a scrap of torn shirt to wipe away the sweat from his face.

"It's okay," he said, his voice rusty with pain. There was a crust of blood under his shattered nose, and his eyes were beginning to puff. "You're doing f-fine."

"I don't *know* what I'm doing," she said. She felt sick, not with fear now or hunger, but dread. The wound was very deep, enough to expose tendon and muscle and a glimmer of bone. The blood

welling up wasn't pumping, and she dared to hope that he wouldn't bleed much more. But she knew she could never move him now. Tom was too weak, too drained. He already had one infection, and she was pretty sure that human bites were as bad as an animal's, maybe worse. "What about your leg? Should I wash—"

"Cut it."

She froze, unable—unwilling—to believe her ears. "What?"

"Cut it," Tom whispered in that same pain-roughened voice. "T-too much pus . . . has to d-drain."

"I can't," she said, horrified. "Tom, I can't—"

"Please. Alex . . . I can't . . . can't do it m-myself." He paused, his chest heaving, his face oily with sweat. When he spoke again, his words broke with airy gasps. "The knife . . . use a fl-flare . . . st-sterilize . . ."

"But I'll burn you."

Tom actually laughed, a faint splutter that quickly died. "Least of my p-problems. Skin's dead anyway, but the . . . the tissue underneath . . . m-might be okay. But you have . . . have to d-drain it. A-Alex . . . Alex, d-do it, *please*." His glittery, fever-bright eyes locked on hers, and she read his desperation and fear. "Before I l-lose my n-nerve . . ."

This was like his story about Crowe. For Tom to ask her to do something like this, he must know he didn't have many options left, or much time. But what if he was wrong? What if she did more harm than good?

Outside, she retrieved her boot knife, prizing it from the dead boy's clutching fingers. Plunging the knife into deep snow got rid

of much of the gore, and then she used bourbon and water to wash away the rest. At the convenience store's front door, she twisted off the cap of one of the flares and scraped the tip against the striker. The flare caught, the crimson flame spitting fiercely. The knife's handle was a hard black polymer, so she was able to hold it without burning herself as she heated the blade, watching as the color changed from silver to a dull gold to a bright lava-red.

"Tom," she said, kneeling over him. The knife had cooled to a dull orange, but she could feel the heat radiating in waves and knew the steel was still plenty hot. "You're absolutely sure there isn't another way."

"C-cut it fast as you c-can. I'll try n-not to move. Once you're through skin, you'll have to . . . have to maybe c-cut deeper. H-heat will help with th-the bleeding. When the pus starts coming, st stop. You'll . . . you'll kn-know when," he panted. Turning his face away, he pulled in another gasping sob. His eyes screwed shut and his hands balled to fists, but a deep shudder was running through him now, a trembling he couldn't control. "I'll t-try to stay on . . . on t-top of it, but no matter what I s-say . . . don't stop, Alex. Finish the j-job. . . ."

Oh please, God, she thought, staring down at Tom's thigh and the blackened, angry eye of his wound. *Please save him; please help me.*

She had seen movies: scenes where men dug around for bullets with bare hands. In movies, people passed out when the pain was too much.

But this wasn't a movie or a book.

This was, in fact, much, much worse because Tom did not pass out, and he lasted only three seconds before he began to scream.

"That's the best I can do." She thumbed his tears away. His pain-ravaged face was dead-white, his eyes sunken into purple-black hollows. The fleshy lips of his wound gaped, and his thigh was streaked with thin rivulets of bright-red blood, but there seemed to be very little pus left. The air reeked with the stink of dead meat, boiled pus, and cooked blood. The mats under his leg had gone soupy with the muck, and she'd dragged them out, pitching them into the snow before retrieving the floor mats from the abandoned van. She'd used straight bourbon on the raw flesh of his thigh, but now she used a wad of torn shirt, stuffed with snow, to mop sweat from his forehead. "You smell like a bar."

"Yeah." His weary gaze fixed on her neck. "L-lot of b-bruises."

Her throat still felt broken. "You should see the other guy."

"Not . . . not a joke. That was t-too close. C-can't l-lose you . . ."

"I'm not going anywhere," she said, knowing deep down that she would be forced to. She sponged away dried blood from his chest. His torso was stippled with other, older wounds, shiny with scar tissue.

"Sh-shrapnel," he whispered, feeling the question in her fingers. "Got myself fr-fragged six months ago. You ought to s-see me l-light up metal detectors at an air-airport."

"And this?" She touched what looked like small burn marks just under his left armpit. Then she peered closer and made out letters:

EDEN
Thomas A.

A series of numbers. *Social security number,* Alex thought. The line below read **O POS**, and, beneath that, **Catholic.**

"A tattoo?" she said.

"Yeah. We call them m-meat t-tags. Sometimes there's not a lot l-left after . . ." He swallowed. "You know."

"Tom." She reached up to stroke the damp hair from his forehead. His lips were pale, as transparent as glass. "What are we going to do?"

"St-stick to the p-plan." He tried a smile that quickly faded. "We . . . we leave in the m-morning. All I n-need is a little r-rest."

He needed a lot more, and she knew it. They spent the night on a mound of car mats in the convenience store's back room. A few hours before dawn, Tom either passed out or fell asleep—she couldn't tell which. Stretching out along his left side, she hugged his body to hers, so close she heard his heart. She was exhausted but afraid to sleep, worried that he would be dead when she woke up. But eventually, her thoughts thinned and she spiraled down and—

The dream, again: the one where she saw the chopper, the one carrying her mother and father, take off in that snowstorm. The helicopter rose like a helium-filled balloon, higher and higher, until at the very limit of the sky and the edge of night, it exploded in a fireball.

Alex hadn't been there. She'd waited at home, alone, as the storm raged, while her mom did her doctor thing, accompanying a patient on an emergency evac. The only reason her dad was even aboard was that the med tech, freaked by the storm, chickened out and her dad, trained in ACLS because all cops are first responders, took his place.

The chopper had not bloomed into a fireball either. After delivering the patient safe and sound, the helicopter took off for home—and simply crashed into a hillside. No drama, no Fourth of July, although the fire had been so intense that they'd identified the pilot and her parents by their teeth.

She was fourteen. She'd felt nothing when her parents died: no premonition, no seismic shudder, no chasm opening beneath her feet. She had been awake, watching the snow swirl in a golden nimbus around the streetlight at the end of the block, waiting for her father's patrol car to turn the corner. She'd even pictured how that would look: first his lights and then the cruiser itself pulling together out of the snow like something from a dream.

And then a cruiser *had* appeared, although she'd known, immediately, that it wasn't her father's. His was a newer model white-and-black. The one that pulled into the driveway was older, all black. Still, she didn't think anything of it; even when she saw the officers unfold and flounder toward the front porch—even when she recognized her father's old partner—she still didn't understand what was happening. Leaving her seat by the window, padding to the front door in her slippers, she didn't get it. Throwing open the deadbolt, opening the door, feeling the gust of cold air push in . . .

she didn't get it. She never got it; it just never dawned on her that anything horrible had happened—until she recognized the minister from their church.

Then she got it.

A month later, the nightmare started. A year later, when the smoke smell started and Aunt Hannah sent her to that shrink, *she'd* spun some crap about Alex being Dorothy and her parents flying away to Oz, blah, blah, blah. For the shrink, the dream was all about Alex's fantasy that her parents were still alive somewhere.

Alex thought the shrink was full of shit. Her parents were dead. She knew that. The dream was all about her life jumping the rails, blowing up in her face, leaving her with nothing but ashes.

Which was happening now, with Tom, all over again.

When she awoke, Tom's skin was clammy. His fever raged and his heart was rabbiting in his chest, and she knew she couldn't wait any longer. She had to bring help, or Tom would die. He might die before she returned, but she couldn't just sit and wait either.

Tom wanted her to take the gun. "You might need it." His skin was whiter than salt, so translucent she saw the faint blue worm of tiny veins under his eyes. At least the shakes had vanished, if only temporarily. "I'm not going anywhere."

"That's not what I'm worried about. If anyone gets in here, the gun's all you'll have."

"If someone breaks in—if it's a couple of those things . . . a few bullets won't make any difference. Besides, I don't think they're smart enough to do that. They're too one dimensional."

She wasn't so sure the brain-zapped kids were as dumb as all that—they knew enough to stay warm—but she saw what he meant. While the kids could easily have overwhelmed them both if they'd planned their attack and acted together, they hadn't. *The girl had a club, and that kid I stabbed figured out the knife pretty quick, but they worked separately. What if that changes?*

Tom lifted a hand to touch her face. His fingers were ice. "Please, take it. If something happens to you, then it won't matter about me."

Privately, she thought she stood a much better chance of being shot if she advertised the gun. Given her age, she might be shot on sight anyway.

"All right," she said. Then she surprised herself, and leaned down and kissed him. She meant to pull back, but his other hand snaked into her hair to cup the back of her head, and the kiss turned into something she didn't want to end, that she worried might never happen again. Her heart filled and her blood warmed, and Tom's scent—spicy and strange—bloomed, nearly over-powering the choke of sickness and decay. Whatever Tom's secrets, this was no lie.

When she finally broke away, he said, weakly, "At last. Something to live for."

His face splintered into shimmery prisms, and she knew she would never leave if she started crying. "Don't you dare die on me."

"I'm not gone yet." But then that twist of emotion, furtive and fleet, chased through his face again. "Alex, what happened before we lost Ellie . . . I need to tell you—"

"No." She put a hand to his lips. If he told her, would he die? Isn't that what happened when people made confessions in books and movies? "Don't. It doesn't matter now. Tell me when I see you again."

He captured her hand. "But it *does* matter. I *need* you to know. Please, just listen." He paused, shutting his eyes against some other, hidden pain.

"I'm here," she said. "I'm listening."

"You were right." A single tear trickled from the corner of one eye to disappear into his hair. "About me looking for my fate. I won't . . . can't tell you everything now. It's not the right time. But I want you to know." He opened his eyes, his feverish gaze holding her fast. "I found it. I found my fate."

"Me, too," she said, and meant it. For the first time in what felt like forever, she wanted a future, and she wanted Tom in it. She kissed him again, memorizing the feel and the taste and his scent.

Then she shut the door and locked it and left him there.

37

She wasn't an idiot. If she kept to main roads, kept moving west and south, she would run into people way before she got to Rule. This might be good and bad: bad because the survivors were much more likely to shoot first and ask questions later, but maybe good because all the brain-zapped kids she'd seen hung close to the woods. If she paid attention, maybe she'd smell them coming, too.

She slogged steadily southwest through a good two feet of snow, keeping to the road, her eyes always scanning, searching: for movement, for brain-zapped kids, for grandmothers with rifles who thought she might be a meal ticket. There were billboards, too, advertising gas stations and mine tours and gift shops. She spotted a sign for Northern Light—GOD'S LIGHT IN DARK TIMES—and a few others suggested that people stop in at Martha's Diner: BREAKFAST 24/7.

The day was fine, sunny and very bright, and not as cold. If the way had been level and the road clear, cross-country skis or snowshoes would've been nice. Sunglasses, too. As welcome as the sun was, her eyes streamed against the wink and dazzle of glare bouncing off snow.

The road was clogged with cars and vans and trucks hunkering beneath a mantle of snow. Most were wrecks, with smashed windows or doors that yawned like mouths. She kept her eyes peeled for *their* truck, half-hoping she wouldn't find it because she was afraid to know what that really meant. Clouds of birds circled in the sky, while crows lined the trees and perched on icy wires and studied her passage in absolute silence. She felt as if she'd stumbled onto a movie set, the kind where the camera pans back to reveal destruction and devastation all the way to the horizon, with no end in sight, and then her—the only thing moving other than the birds.

Away from the woods, the air was sullen with smells: engine oil, gasoline, rubber and death. The stink was so thick and cloying that she gagged, and she wished she had something to tie around her mouth and nose.

There were a lot of bodies, all in various stages of decomposition. Many had died in their cars. Others—men and women who'd stumbled from their cars only to collapse on the road that first day—wore shrouds of snow. Even with the cold to slow down the rot, the corpses were hideous, as bloated as those dead cows she, Tom, and Ellie had seen. There were many animals, too: fat raccoons with paws full of meat, mangy foxes, and opossums, their white snouts clogged with gore, braving the daylight for the feast. And of course, there were always the birds, jabbing and pecking and stripping away frozen niblets of flesh right down to the bone.

One pair of very large crows squabbled over something in the snow. At her approach, they fluttered off, and she spotted what she thought was a fat drop of blood—only to realize that she was staring down at a woman's disarticulated big toe, the nail still painted a bright, cheery, fire-engine red.

All the dead were adults. Most looked old enough to be parents but not grandparents. There were empty car seats and discarded lunch pails and book bags, but no kids. No bodies of anyone close to her age, or Tom's.

Then she saw something that made her blood ice. The farther down the road she went, the more prints she found from the people who'd survived: boots, sneakers, everyday shoes. Even some flip-flops.

And footprints.

Not socks.

Bare feet.

That gave her pause.

Deer laid down trails, taking the same path to and from streams and meadows. Ducks and geese flew routes they'd taken before. All a hunter had to do was either hunker down and wait or follow his prey.

People took roads. Honestly, they might as well have been wearing cowbells, because it looked to her like those brain-zapped kids weren't simply sticking to the woods now. They might *live* there, but they'd figured out that if they wanted to eat, they had to go where the food was.

Then she noticed something else.

Some of the dead people were very old. They had died because they'd been shot: in the back, some in the chest, and many in the back of the head. Their clothing had not been tattered or ripped by animals, but, it seemed, simply taken. These bodies were fresher, too, and lay in bunches in a scatter of discarded, empty knapsacks and duffel bags and suitcases.

These people had survived only to be robbed and then killed by their own kind: the Harlans, the Bretts, the Marjories.

And that's when she finally understood that Larry had been right.

Those brain-zapped kids weren't the only—or maybe even the worst—enemy.

As she passed by a panel truck—doors open, two ravaged and nearly skeletonized bodies dragging from shoulder harnesses— she heard something that was not the harsh caw of a bird. The sound was pathetic, a whimper, almost like the cry of a baby. She looked down and saw an old man and an even older woman, sprawled facedown near the truck in a scatter of pilfered duffels. They'd been shot in the back of the head, and not too long ago, judging from the lack of snow cover. The woman's coat was bunched up, so Alex could see the spread of her fleshy thighs, ropy with bulging, green varicose veins, above her support stockings. The woman was flat on her face, her arms flung out in a reverse snow angel. Alex spotted a loop of leather around the woman's right wrist and more leather snaking beneath the truck.

Then she caught the scent, something very familiar.

"Oh my God," she said out loud. Dropping to her knees, Alex searched the shadows under the truck.

Cowering next to the right front tire was a shivering gray puppy.

She had no idea what the puppy was, though it looked like a cross between some kind of hound and a Labrador. When it saw her, it whined, then scooted toward her, just an inch, on its belly. The stub of its tail moved in a hopeful wag.

All of a sudden, rescuing the dog felt important. If she could save the dog, it would be a good sign, like an omen. If she saved the dog, she'd save Tom, too. Later, she'd think about how illogical this was, but that didn't make the feeling any less strong at the time.

She tore open a packet of beef jerky and offered a piece to the pup. At the smell, the puppy inched forward again, its nose brushing her fingers, and then it wolfed down the meaty bit, only to spit it out a few seconds later. Whimpering, the pup pushed the jerky with its nose, and she understood that the meat was too tough for the dog to chew. She shoved another piece into her mouth, working it into mush. The rich flavor of spicy, smoked beef was so good her stomach cramped, and it took all her self-control not to swallow. When she spat out the meat, she heard herself groan.

This time, though, the dog snapped the food up right away, then scooched forward for more. Three more pieces of jerky and the puppy squirted out from beneath the truck, grunting like a little pig and squiggling and wagging the cropped, gray pencil stub of its tail.

Unclipping the leash from its collar, she gathered the dog in her arms. "So what's your name?"

The puppy let go of a little yap. The dog's coat was short and silvery-gray, and it—he—had very blue eyes and big paws, and must weigh a good ten pounds. She fed the puppy the rest of the jerky, then scrounged in the discarded duffels and came up with three cans of puppy food, a foil packet of puppy kibbles, and a small aluminum water bowl into which she poured a scant two inches from her bottle.

Afterward, she buttoned the dog up in her jacket, cinching the belt around her waist so the puppy couldn't slip out. When she was done, she looked either a little bit pregnant or in need of a very large bra. The puppy was very warm. When it poked its head out to watch the sights, she started laughing.

"I got you," she said as the puppy waggled all over and kissed her fingers. "I got you. Don't you wor—"

That was when she smelled the wolves.

38

No mistake. The wolves were behind her. That she didn't need to see them to know *what* they were freaked her out even more. She didn't know how *many* might be there, but their scent was indescribable—not like *dog* at all. Some primitive part of her brain set off a complete total-body alarm that dried her mouth and made her muscles seize. Her heart was a fist pounding the wall of her chest.

The puppy sensed them now, too. She felt it go rigid, and then the puppy was hunkering down and shivering all over, trying to make itself very, very small. She kept her left hand under the puppy but let her right drift to her hip. Her fingers curled around the butt of her father's Glock.

Then she pivoted—slowly, carefully—to face them.

There were three.

She didn't know anything about wolves, other than what every hiker knew: you didn't want to run into them, despite the fact that wolves were supposed to be as freaked out by people as people were by them. She'd heard wolves off and on throughout her time in the Waucamaw. Back when things were normal, their plaintive cries were eerily soothing. Of course, that was then and this was the end of the world.

These wolves were big and charcoal gray, like something out of *National Geographic*, and clustered on a small rise at the edge of the woods, perhaps a hundred feet away. The alpha male—she knew it by its smell, which was more acrid and quite strong—was very tall with rangy legs, a broad chest, and golden-yellow eyes: alien eyes for an alien world. It wouldn't have surprised her at all if that rogue moon had risen.

A stationary target, at this distance, was no problem. But wolves were very fast. She could never outrun them, and if they charged, she would probably empty her magazine and not hit one.

She left the Glock in its holster. Instead, she held her right hand, palm out, hoping that the wolves would know *empty* when they saw it. Locking eyes with any animal was a very bad idea, but the alpha male's gold eyes grabbed hers, and she couldn't look away.

The wolves stared. She remembered to breathe.

The alpha male moved first. It settled onto its haunches and then sank to its belly, like a dog settling down for a nap, and began to pant. The sense she got was that the wolf was not necessarily *comfortable*, but it was ready to wait until something changed. As if by silent command, the other two sank down as well. The smallest squirmed on its belly to lick the alpha male's jaw. The alpha's scent—all their scents—had changed, too: still *wolf*, but now mingled with something a little less sour. Another one of those weird flashbulb moments flared in her mind: Mina, lying by the fire, pressing against her thigh. This was not *exactly* the same, but the scent was calmer somehow, like . . . *friend?* The tense spring of her guts uncoiled just a smidge. Well, perhaps not *friend* so much as *no threat.*

"I'm leaving," she said. Maybe she should say something else? She couldn't think of anything else. What did you say to a wolf? She eased back a single step and waited. The alpha male was a sphinx. She took another small sliding step back, felt the heel of her boot butt against the dead woman's leg, and realized she would have to turn around.

She didn't want to do that. But she had no choice. All the tiny hairs on her arms and neck spiked with fear, and her skin was so jumpy she thought it might just tear itself from her bones and go screaming down the road.

Heart pounding, she turned on her heel and began to walk, not too fast, not too slow. Every jangling nerve told her to bolt like a bunny rabbit, but she thought that would make the wolves chase her, maybe change her smell from *no-threat* to *dinner.*

After thirty feet, she was still alive. The wolves' scent remained unchanged; no one was storming after her, and she decided to chance it. She craned her head over her shoulder for a look back.

The wolves were standing now, watching her go, their breaths wreathing them in smoke. After a moment, the smallest wolf turned and glided back into the woods. A second later, the third followed, leaving the alpha alone on the rise.

For reasons she didn't understand, she stopped and turned to face him. She was too far away to make out its face, but she felt its eyes. Nothing wordless passed between them, no deeper under-standing; no telepathic, paranormal stuff. But when the alpha male reared onto its back legs like a playful shepherd before pivot-ing and melting back into the forest . . . when that happened, she thought maybe there'd been yet another change.

In her.

39

By mid-afternoon, when a sign told her she was twenty miles from Rule, she'd noticed three things.

The closer she got to the village, the fewer dead bodies she saw.

She had yet to run into anyone who wasn't dead.

And she smelled smoke.

The smoke was very strange and very familiar, and it made her heart thump a little harder. She'd smelled this kind of smoke before, only then it had been a phantom, the first sign of the monster in her head.

God, no, not now. Don't let me die here. Please, just a little longer. Get me through to Rule so they can save Tom, and then if I've got to die—

The puppy sneezed, pawed at its nose, then sneezed again.

Her relief was like splashing into a pool on a very hot day. If the puppy could smell the smoke, she wasn't hallucinating. This wasn't a symptom. It was *real.*

She got a good snootful, trying to sort out the components: wood char mixed with a chemical sting, like the fluid her father used to spritz over charcoal briquettes, and something almost sweet and juicy like the pork roast her mother made on Sundays. But there was something sooty and unsettling about the odor, nothing that made her mouth water.

Shielding her eyes against the sun's glare, she aimed a squint at the sky. At first, she saw nothing—just an impression of white from the sun burning her retinas—but then she spotted just the faintest wispy tail, a thin dreadlock of very dark smoke. Not leaves, she knew, which burned white or gray—and not wood. A chemical fire?

Dropping her gaze to the snow, she eyed the by-now familiar scuff of boots and shoes and flip-flops and bare feet—and then spotted deep, straight cuts and the stamp of horses' hooves: wagons.

Interesting. North, up by Oren, was Amish country. With its proximity to the mine, she didn't think Rule was, but maybe even the Amish had decided to come south. Or . . .

Of course. They'd come out with wagons to gather up all those bodies. The people in Rule must've decided to establish some kind of perimeter. That made perfect sense. No one would want heaps of rotting corpses piled outside town.

But why no people on the road? Where was everyone? Hiding? Waiting until dark, hoping to avoid those brain-zapped kids? No, that didn't make sense. All her run-ins with those kids had been either in the early morning or at dusk. Come to think of it, she had never seen one in broad daylight. Something Larry said popped into her head: *In some ways, she's still kind of a typical teenager. Like always waking up just when I'm ready to sleep.*

Well, that was interesting. *Before* the monster, when her parents were still alive, she'd been the same way. Staying awake in morning classes was an act of will. Everyone her age was chronically sleep-deprived, downing Red Bulls and Mountain Dews and coffee to stay alert.

The monster had taken that away. When she really stopped to think, smelling that phantom smoke hadn't been the first monster-sign but the second. The first sign had been the change in her sleeping patterns: frequent awakenings in the middle of the night, bizarre and fractured dreams, a feeling of restlessness as if she'd drunk two pots of coffee. The monster in her head had made her very different from her friends. Maybe very different from other kids her age. Before stealing her sense of smell and eating her memories, it had taken her sleep. And of course, there'd been her parents and that recurring nightmare, a trauma she relived over and over that blasted her sleep.

And Tom hadn't slept much either. When he did, he always seemed to pop awake just a few hours later, and he kept that up all night. From bio, she knew most people slipped into REM sleep—dream sleep—a couple hours after falling asleep, and normal people went through three or four REM cycles every night. Other than that one night—before he'd come close to telling her what weighed on him so much—Tom never slept for long stretches, maybe because he couldn't help it. Maybe Afghanistan had changed Tom and altered his brain somehow. She thought again of post-traumatic stress and nightmares that stormed in Technicolor across the black screen of Tom's mind: horrors from the past Tom could not outrun.

Horrors—nightmares—that might have saved him.

Messed-up hormones might not be the only things that had saved her from changing so far. Maybe, as with Tom, altered sleep and nightmares were important, too. More to the point, maybe it was her whole screwed-up brain.

Maybe the monster had saved her life.

40

At dusk, she caught their scent: faded and musty. Most old people smelled like used underwear, and she could tell from the rich clog of odors that there were a lot of them, all bunched together. She was downwind, and she thought they were still fairly distant, but she sensed their exhaustion and the sharp sting of their panic. That made sense. These old people must know that the brain-zapped kids woke up just as it got dark, and they'd want to be off the road and somewhere safe. She could envision the road ahead: a solid whip of humanity stretching from Rule for miles.

She felt a prick of anxiety. It was one thing to find Rule; it was another to try battling her way through a crush of fellow refugees to get help for one person, even if he was young. And how would these old people react to her?

Judging from the frowsy reek, there were also dogs and—she closed her eyes, concentrated, caught the aroma of sunshine and warm hay—*horses*.

Something more, too. She inhaled again and then her nose twitched with the bite of gun oil and singed metal.

Guns. A lot of those, too.

When she first picked up the puppy, she'd taken the Glock from its holster and slipped it into the right-hand pocket of her jacket. She debated simply taking out the weapon, more as a deterrent than because she wanted to pick a fight, then thought better of it. If someone started shooting, it would be over fast, and there was only one of her. So she left the gun where it was.

On her right, a small green sign flashed out of the darkness:

RULE 6

Beyond, there was another billboard for the hospice and a sign urging visitors to stop in at Harvest Church: TRUST IN THE HEALING HAND OF GOD.

A few more hours, Tom, she thought. *Hang on. Just a few more.*

Two hours later, she heard them: a muted, confused gabble. Then she spotted the yellow bob of flashlights and silver edged silhouettes. Not a throng, but easily several hundred bathed in the sickly green light of that surreal moon. She smelled them much better now: a great stinking ball of old men and women at the end of their tethers, and not a few dogs. People and animals were streaming and bunching around her, but either they hadn't noticed her in the dark, or didn't care. The puppy was awake, too, and she could feel it begin to shiver with fear.

"It's okay," she murmured, hugging it close, praying that it wouldn't start to bark. The last thing she needed was attention. She'd already done up her hair in a long braid and shoved it beneath her watch cap, but she still felt exposed. One good look at her face, and these oldsters would know she was a teenager. She jammed on a John Deere ball cap she'd found on the road, pulling the bill as far down as she could. She turned up the collar on her coat, too, hoping that would mask her silhouette.

No one was moving forward; that was the thing. Instead, the crowd milled uncertainly before a huge eighteen-wheeler, lying on its side like a beached orca. The forest hugged the road on either side, but no one made a move toward the woods to go around the roadblock and then she saw why. Among the trees, ranging on either side of the overturned semi, and perched on top of the truck, were other people and many, many dogs. She heard a hollow clop coming from behind the trailer, the jingle of traces, and knew she'd been right about horses.

Far ahead, one of the men at the roadblock was shouting into an old-fashioned bullhorn: "We will get to everyone. We know you're tired, but you'll just have to wait your turn. You'll be safe here. The Changed don't come this way, so everyone just calm down."

The Changed. So that's what people were calling them now? How could they be sure those brain-zapped kids wouldn't come? She slowed, hanging back, teetering on the very edge of the crowd, trying to decide what she should do. She was afraid to slip into the woods, and those guys on the truck had rifles. Duck and weave through the crowd? Man, that was a big risk. If she bumped anyone, if someone got a good look . . .

Just ahead, a trio—one man and two women—bunched with a Labrador tagging behind. Its tail drooped, and it smelled of dog and salt—and another smell that made her flash to a bowl of slimy cold oatmeal her aunt tried to make her eat the day after the helicopter exploded. *Sad*, she thought. *The dog's sad*.

But then the lab's ears pricked. She scented its sudden surprise as the pop of an electrical outlet, a burnt fizz sizzling in the air, and then it was pivoting, straining at the end of its leash, its tail whisking back and forth. And it started to bark.

At her.

41

Shut up, she thought. Her knees began to shake, and she felt her legs go rubbery as the dog continued to bark. *Shut up, shut up, shut up.*

"Watson." A gangly elderly man in a fur-trimmed parka sounded both exasperated and exhausted. "Come on, what are you—" He turned, his flashlight scything through the dark, cutting across her body before continuing on. As soon as the light passed, she ducked, tried turning away, but then the torch swept back like the beam of a lighthouse and caught her. She heard him gasp: "Oh, Jesus."

"What?" said one of the women. Alex thought her scent was very sour, the combination of days without washing and annoyance rolling off in a cloying fug. Turning, the woman got a good look at Alex, pinned in the light like a bug to cardboard. "Holy shit," she said, and then Alex heard the metallic *ga-thunk-chunk* of a shotgun pump.

"Wait," Alex said. The puppy was whimpering now. Hugging the dog with one hand, she held up the other, palm out. "I'm not one of them."

"Not yet you aren't," said the woman. To her left, another, much older woman with a beaky nose had drawn an ancient-looking Luger. "Or maybe you're just moving up the fucking evolutionary ladder."

"Please." Alex sidled back a step. "I'm just trying to make it to—"

"Not with us, girlie, no way." The older, hawkish woman with the Luger tugged the toggle joint and then let it snap forward.

"Hold up, Em," the elderly man said. "She seems okay. Look, she's got a dog. Let's just take a second here."

"Look at your dog," Alex said. The lab was still barking, but its tail whisked the air in a frantic semaphore and now she could hear more dogs beginning to bark. Beyond, heads were turning, flashlights stabbing through the dark. The pool of light around her body widened and got brighter as more and more people shone their torches her way. "Your dog's not afraid."

"Because you haven't turned yet," said the woman with the shotgun.

"I say we shoot her now." The beaky woman squinted down the Luger's barrel. Her bony hands had tightened to claws. "Get it over with. Better yet, hang the little bitch."

"Wait a minute," the man said. "We *need* her. We have her, they'll let us in."

"I got no use for one of them," the Luger Lady spat. "Remember the last one we run across? Went to sleep a little angel, woke up an animal."

"But the dogs know, don't they?" Alex said. The lab, Watson, was straining at its leash,, and beyond, Alex could hear other dogs whining and a general murmur rippling down the line as more and more people became aware of her presence. There was the sound of handguns being drawn and the rack of rifle bolts and shotgun pumps. "Isn't that why you have them?"

"She's right," the man said. "We didn't have Watson then."

"It's just a damn dog," Luger Lady said. "What the hell does it know? Did it know that little bitch that got my Cody? I *told* him to kill her, but she was just a kid, just a sweet little innocent monster *killer*."

"Hell, you don't want her, I'll take her." This from another man dressed in hunter's camouflage. He held what looked like a stubby machine gun, maybe an Uzi, in one hand, and two ammunition belts crisscrossed his chest. He had very white, very square teeth that were too perfect and probably false, but his grin was wide and maniacal and menacing. "I'd like to see one of them try to come after me; I'd just dare them to try."

"No one's taking me," Alex said, working to keep her voice steady, but her heart was trying to punch its way from her chest. The puppy had gone silent and was trying to melt into her body. She saw Uzi pushing past the others, and she took a step back, then another. "Please, I just want to—"

"Hey, wait a minute!" Another voice, very angry, coming from the crowd. "Who says she's yours?"

"I said she's *mine*!" Uzi clamped a beefy hand around her left wrist just as someone else—she couldn't see who—grabbed at her from the right. She felt the puppy clawing at her shirt, and then the dogs began to bark, not snarling or foaming, but in a prancing, jabbering frenzy, and then it seemed that these were not people anymore but plucking, grasping hands and angry mouths and shattered, ancient faces full of desperation and hatred and despair. They weren't really seeing her at all, only what she represented: the cause of the disaster—a symptom and the disease itself.

The puppy was crying, trying to squirm its way out of her jacket. "Careful!" she pleaded. "Please. Stop, you're going to hurt him, st—"

"Calm down!" From the front of the crowd and far away, the man with the bullhorn was shouting. "What's the trouble here? Everyone, calm down, just stay calm!"

The ripping roar of bullets, a stuttering flash of light, split the night. "I'm telling you, back off!" Uzi brandished his weapon. "Just back the fu—"

Another shot, this time from behind, and Uzi jerked, a look of stupid surprise on his face, and then he was falling in a rattling heap.

"Get her!" someone shouted.

And then they were running, the crowd boiling around, pushing her back and forth in a tug-of-war. Hands tore at her clothes, tangled in her hair. Her jacket burst open, and the puppy was suddenly gone in the crush, although she heard it yelping. The man with the bullhorn was shouting, and there were more shots, and then she screamed as fingers stripped off her coat.

Someone sang, "She's got a gun, she's got a gun!"

A chaos of dogs thrashed and twisted on their leashes, the

clamor of their barking and yawping redoubling in the general roar, and now the people were shouting: *Kill her! Get her! Get—*

Quite suddenly, she was airborne, her feet swept away from under her. She screamed again as the night sky—and that sinister moon—spun in a drunken whorl. They were passing her from hand to hand like a crowd in a gigantic mosh pit. She couldn't see where they were taking her, what they meant to do, but then she was pinned to the ground, staring up as if from the bottom of a very deep well.

"Little *bitch!*" The old woman with the Luger darted one gnarly claw-fist at her face. Shrieking, Alex wrenched her right foot free and kicked; feeling the solid thump all the way to her knee and the moment the woman's beaky nose crumpled. Flailing, the old woman staggered back as a great spume of blood gushed down her face.

Alex kicked again, but more hands caught her, and then she felt her head being pulled back and the skin of her neck exposed, and she thought, *Oh, God, they're going to* cut—

Instead of a knife, she felt the rough bite of rope. Her scream choked off, and then they were dragging her by the neck over the cold, hard earth. This was like the nightmare at the gas station all over again, but there were so many of them, and she had no chance. Still, she fought, twisting, digging in with her heels. She clawed at the rope, felt her fingernails tear as she scrabbled for a handhold, but then they were hoisting her up, hands catching at her to keep her from falling, and her air choked off as the rope tightened.

The woman whose nose she'd broken—Luger Lady—was back. Her mouth hung wide open in a bloody, ravenous snarl, and this time, she clutched a knife. "Gonna cut your little head off!" Luger Lady shrilled. She exhaled a cloud that reeked of iron and rage. "Gonna cut your little—"

The sudden crackle of gunfire was crisp and sharp and glassy. Then a voice, very clear, cut through the din and the thundering roar of blood in her ears: "Go, Jet, *go!*"

Someone screamed as a German shepherd bulleted out of the crowd. The shepherd was black as coal and very large, and as Luger Lady half-turned, the dog sprang. Luger Lady had time to get her hands up, but then the dog barreled into the old woman. She tumbled to the ground, her knife flashing away, and then the old woman was shrieking, "Get it off me, get it off me!"

"Jesus Christ," someone said.

"Don't shoot it!" a man shouted. "It's one of theirs, don't shoot it!"

Around her neck, the bite of the rope suddenly eased, and then Alex was on her knees. Her chest was on fire, and her throat felt as if someone had taken a razor blade to it and slashed. Gasping, she hung on all fours, trying not to be sick.

Luger Lady was still screaming, but no one moved to help her and, incredibly, no one tried to shoot the dog. Alex couldn't really see what was happening, but she heard the voice again, closer now: "Jet! Off, boy, off!"

And she had a single, stunned thought: *That voice . . . he's not old.*

The shepherd instantly obeyed, dancing away from the old woman, but it did not leave. Instead, the dog turned toward Alex, its black lips curling back, and Alex waited, helpless, for the jaws to snap at her flesh, tear her skin.

Instead, the dog nosed her: a single playful nudge. The scent that came from the animal was like a splash of cool water on a hot day. She thought of the morning Mina had broken out of the underbrush to save them from the wild dogs, the intense relief that had melted the icy sludge of fear in her veins. She remembered how, all of a sudden, Mina had been reluctant to leave her to follow after Ellie.

She thought of the wolf: *no threat.*

All around, dogs bristled and snarled—but not at her.

They were growling at their owners.

The voices in the crowd fell instantly, deathly silent, and people let go of the dogs. Surging forward, the animals ranged around Alex in a tight, protective circle. Some licked her face. Others nosed at her as she dragged the rope from her neck. The big black shepherd pressed against her, as if daring someone to cross it, and then something very small spurted from the crowd and into her lap. It was the puppy, wriggling all over, so frantic with relief that it tried to climb on top of her head.

"Good boy," Alex said, still stupid with amazement, and then looked up as the crowd wavered and broke. She saw old men with rifles and shotguns parting the crowd like Moses at the Red Sea, wading into the dogs.

Looking up, Jet let out a soft whine, his black tail whisking the air in greeting. Following the dog's gaze, Alex pulled in a sudden, startled gasp.

"Are you all right?" He knelt on one knee and reached a hand to steady her. His eyes were as jet-black as his dog, his cheekbones were high and sharp as ax heads, and his scent was a complex mix of the darkness itself: cold mist and black shadows.

With a little yelp, the puppy jumped to lick at his hand, and the boy smiled.

"Hey, you," he said, ruffling the dog's ears. "That's a good pup."

42

The dark-eyed boy's name was Chris Prentiss, but his friend, Peter, was in charge of men who were, with few exceptions, old enough to be grandparents.

"I don't care about the damn dogs. We don't know that it's not a trap." Peter didn't look much older than Tom and had a tumble of wheat-brown hair that fell to his muscular shoulders. "She could be luring us, man."

"I'm not," she said. They'd marched her back, under guard, behind the semi, and she now sat cross-legged in a wagon. They'd taken her pack, and one of them might have her Glock, but she wasn't sure. The puppy curled in her lap, its ears lifting anxiously as Chris and Peter argued. When they'd nudged her into the wagon, the shepherd had sprung up after to lie quietly by her side, as Mina had done. "Aren't the dogs supposed to know?"

Peter's face flashed with annoyance. "Could be early yet. You still might change. Anyway, the dogs won't know if you're telling the truth about this other guy. We go out there, you've got an ambush set up, and there go a wagon, horses, weapons . . ."

"I think the risk is worth it," Chris said. He was the quiet one, the observer, and Alex thought he was about her age, maybe a year older. "We need someone like him. He's a soldier; he knows *bombs*. You're always saying—"

"I know what I'm always saying." Fuming, Peter planted his hands on his hips. "Okay. But we wait until morning."

"That's too long," she said.

Peter fired a warning glance. "I don't think I'm asking you. But if you want to march on out of here, fine by me."

"Peter," said Chris in his calm, patient way. "You know we can't let her leave."

Alex wasn't sure she liked the sound of that. On the other hand, she wasn't particularly anxious to face that mob again. "Look," she said to Peter, "I've been out there all day. We're not talking zombie hordes."

"I'm sorry, but you don't know *what* you're talking about," said Chris. His tone didn't change, but she heard the rebuke. "You're lucky to be alive. Three attacked you, and you said one had a club. That's new. Even though they didn't coordinate their attack, they've never really *hunted* together before either." Chris looked at Peter. "Could be a first step toward them getting organized."

"All the more reason to get Tom now," she said.

"If he isn't dead yet," Peter said.

"You keep saying that, he will be. Is that what you want?"

Peter scowled. "Of course not. I'm not an asshole. I'm just saying that you're really lucky. If you'd been caught farther out from town when it got dark, you might not be sitting here."

In case they hadn't noticed, a bunch of old people had nearly lynched her, so she hadn't exactly been safe close to town either. "Is that why you've got the roadblocks? To keep out those brain-zapped kids?"

"Brain-zapped." Peter barked a humorless laugh. "I like that. We call them the Changed. But yeah, that perimeter's one of the reasons they're not walking down Main Street."

But a perimeter couldn't be the only reason, Alex figured. Short of building a fence, how did you secure an entire village?

"What sucks," Peter continued, "is that they've figured out how to survive. They know to get warm, they know to find shelter; they follow people. From what you said, it sounds like they're learning how to really hunt."

"So maybe they'll kill each other," Alex said.

Peter shook his head. "They don't, which completely blows. Right now, they're not organized enough to overrun the town. They might get there, though, and then we're screwed. There are way more of them than we got bullets for."

She wasn't giving up on Tom. "You have all these people. You've got guns. With the horses, you could get to Tom in a couple of hours. If one of you were hurt, you'd go after him, wouldn't you?"

"I'm not doing hypotheticals," said Peter. "Look, I understand. You care about this guy. I get that. He sounds like he was a pretty good guy."

"He is," she said, her eyes filling. "He *is*."

"Peter," Chris said quietly, "I say we go after him. It's not like there are a lot of us. If we don't fight for each other, who will? If he's Spared, then it's worth the risk."

Alex heard the emphasis: *Spared*. Like *Changed*. These people didn't see Tom or her or even themselves as *survivors*. They were *Spared*, like people who'd escaped some sort of wrath-of-God thing.

"Damn it," said Peter. He scuffed snow with the heel of his boot, and Alex smelled the peppery edge of his resistance ease. "All right. But you stay behind, Chris."

Alex didn't like the sound of that either—not because Chris was such an ally, but because Peter already didn't like her. So if there was a little accident . . .

Chris apparently felt the same way. "I don't think that's a good idea."

"Yeah, yeah, yeah, that's just it. You're not *thinking*," Peter snapped. "But I *am*, and I do not want to explain to the Rev or the Council why the hell you're dead and I'm not."

A splinter of ice stabbed the dark mist of Chris's scent. No hint of anger crossed his face; there was nothing to betray him except his scent. Chris may have been only a little older than Alex, but he was very calm, a lot like Tom in some ways, and Alex thought she understood why Chris's scent was so . . . what was the word? *Dark*. Not evil, but shadowy, as if Chris knew how to hide. Maybe he'd dealt with people about to go nuclear his whole life.

"My grandfather is not here," Chris said evenly. "The Council of Five is not here. It's just us, Peter, and the deal is we watch each other's back. So I'm coming."

The two stared at each other a long moment, and then Peter gave a curt nod. "Fine. If we're lucky, we can be there a couple hours before dawn. Now excuse me while I go sell the others on this crazy scheme."

After he'd stomped off, she said to Chris, "Thank you."

"You're welcome," he said, but he did not smile and his scent thickened, folding him in darkness again. "But I didn't do it for you."

"And if Peter told you to put a bullet in my head?"

"I don't think you want to go there," he said.

43

They were eight altogether. Two men on horseback flanked either side of the wagon, Peter rode point, and another man brought up the rear. Chris handled the wagon, and Alex sat between him and Jet. The puppy curled in a knot in her lap.

"Nice pup," Chris said.

"What?" Everything was so *loud*: the creak of the wagon, the jangle of traces, the heavy clop of horses' hooves. After days of skulking around, hiding in the woods, and nearly jumping out of her skin every time a branch cracked, she was a little freaked out by the noise.

"Your pup. Don't see too many Weimies around here."

"Weimies?"

"Weimaraners. He's going to be one big dog when he grows up. If I'm not wrong, he's going to be a ghost, too." At her confused look, one corner of his mouth lifted in a half-grin. "You don't know much about dogs, do you?"

Other than that they suddenly like me? "Never had one."

"It's the color of his coat. They call those kind of Weimies 'gray ghosts.' He got a name?"

"I haven't had time." She looked down at the dog. "I like Ghost."

"Good a name as any. You'll have to let our vet give him the once-over before we can let you keep him, though."

"You've got a vet?"

"Yeah, and we could use a couple more. We've got a lot of live-stock and, of course, all the dogs. We get a lot of people headed this way, so a vet'll eventually come through."

She remembered the argument about Tom: *We need him.* "That what you were doing back at the roadblock? Weeding people out?"

"Uh-huh."

"You don't sound sorry about it."

Even in that queer moonlight, Chris's eyes and hair were as dark as his scent. "It's necessary."

"How can you turn people away?"

"We do what we have to. We don't have unlimited supplies. Whether you get to stay depends on what you bring to the table."

"That's pretty harsh."

"Yes, it is. But there's only so much food to go around, and we have to balance who we bring in with what we need. Right now, we need people for labor, tending to the animals, and general upkeep. We need guys to man the perimeter. Come spring, there will be fields to till and plant, so we might let in more—if people are still coming, that is."

"Who decides? Peter?"

"No. The Council of Five."

"Like"—she frowned—"a town council?"

He shook his head. "More like, you know, elders."

She almost laughed. "Nearly everybody's an elder."

"Except for us, yeah. But these guys have family ties that go way, way back. The Reverend's family—the Yeagers—pretty much started Rule from the ground up, and a Yeager's always been the head of the Council. As I understand it, the Council of Five has been in charge of Rule for a long time."

Something dinged. "Peter said the Reverend is your grandfather. But your last name is Prentiss."

"That's right. Growing up, I never saw my grandfather."

"So you didn't live here before?"

She sensed a sudden wariness, a reserve that reeked of secrets and shame, and his scent got even darker. "No. I'm from Merton, about sixty miles southeast. You?"

"Evanston, Illinois. A couple blocks from Northwestern."

A flicker of something like amusement. "I'd just applied to Northwestern. Wasn't my first choice."

Okay, so he was a senior, either seventeen or, more likely, eighteen. "What was?"

"Doesn't really matter now, does it?"

Ouch. She felt the barrier slam down and decided there was no answer to that. Instead, she watched a knot of clouds scud over the face of that alien moon. Snuffling, the puppy burrowed deeper into her lap.

Chris said, "Sorry. It's just that I don't like looking back. No point. It's all dead anyway."

"How do you know that?"

"We scrounged up an old radio, the kind that still works."

Her pulse skipped. Harlan and Brett had taken the ranger radio when they'd stolen the truck. "Where did you find it?"

Maybe he heard something in her tone, because he flicked a curious glance. "Farm about ten miles out of town."

"Oh." She worked at keeping the disappointment out of her voice. "Have you heard a lot of broadcasts?"

"Not tons, and even less as time's gone on. Enough to know it's a mess out there." He paused. "Where were you when it happened?"

She gave him the bare minimum: the mountain, Jack, Ellie. He didn't ask why she was in the Waucamaw or about her parents, and she saw no reason to volunteer the information. "What about you?" she asked.

"School. I was outside, helping the chemistry teacher set off a smoke bomb for the sophomores. She just dropped. I thought at first she'd fainted, but she was gone."

"What did you do?"

"Before or after the plane crashed in the football field?"

"After."

"I nearly beat a kid to death with a textbook. It was either that or he was going to take my face off. There was this other girl in the group. She was still okay—not Changed—only she freaked out and took off for the playground where there were all these kids. Most of them hadn't Changed. Some had, though, and they were going after the others."

"Oh my God." She didn't even want to imagine that.

"Then these five football jocks spotted her. Plowed right into that playground and tore that girl apart, and after that, they started in on the little ones." He paused again. "I still see it sometimes when I close my eyes. Hear it. The whole freaking mess."

"What did you do?"

"Not what I thought I would," he said. "I ran."

They rode in silence for a while and then she asked, "How did you end up in Rule? Because of your grandfather?"

He shook his head. "My car wouldn't start. Home was twenty-five miles away, and Merton's a big town. After what I saw at the school, I figured it would be five hundred times worse there. All those people dead or getting killed or going crazy. No point."

"But it was still home."

"There was just me and my dad." The shadows in Chris's scent thickened, and Alex thought that his father was someone Chris didn't like thinking about. "Now that we understand more—how old the people who dropped were—I know there wouldn't have been any point. He was fifty."

"But you couldn't have known that then, and there have to be exceptions. Look at us."

"We only prove the rule. As near as we can tell, the majority of normal people walking around are either really young or pushing sixty-five or seventy on up."

"Oh." She cast about for something to say. "Well, your father would want you to save yourself. He wouldn't want you dead."

The corner of his mouth lifted again. "You didn't know my dad."

She didn't know what to say to that either. "How many of *us* are there?"

"In Rule? Well, we've got about five hundred people total. Out of those, sixty-three are Spared."

"Sixty-three kids out of five hundred people?"

"That's right. Only twenty-five kids are our age: twelve guys, thirteen girls." He measured her with a look. "Fourteen, now."

"Only *twenty-five*?"

"Uh-huh. Peter's the oldest Spared; he's twenty-four." He hesitated. "He's actually a pretty good guy once you get to know him."

She'd reserve judgment on that. "How does anyone know we won't change? Maybe it's just a matter of time, like Peter said." She thought about Deidre. "Have any of the younger kids Changed since the Zap?"

"Never quite gotten that far."

She didn't understand. "What do you mean?"

"I mean, we don't let things get that far." In the moonlight, his face was nothing more than a glimmer. "Why do you think we have the dogs?"

An early warning system, she realized: like canaries in a mine, the dogs must sense the change before it happened. Still, she couldn't believe it. "You decide about a kid on the basis of what a *dog* thinks?"

"They haven't been wrong yet."

Meaning these people had experience. My God, had they locked the kids up and watched them change? Like an experiment, just to make sure? They must have, or else they wouldn't have such faith in the dogs.

A wave of unreality washed over her, leaving her shaky and ill. *The dogs finger kids, and then these people . . . what do they do? Kick the kids out of town? Kill them?* She thought back to those three kids, the girl with her club and those two boys. Until that moment, she hadn't dwelled on them much. She'd been too busy trying to keep Tom alive and then fending off a mob, and there really was no point, to borrow a phrase. What she'd done had been self-defense. She'd had no choice.

"We do what we have to in order to survive," Chris said quietly. "When you've been here awhile, you'll understand."

The hell of it was: in a way, she already did.

44

The bodies of the three kids still lay where they'd fallen—where she'd killed them—in the parking lot of the convenience store. Which begged another interesting question: why weren't the Changed lunch for run-of-the-mill scavengers? Scavengers had clearly visited. Ned was still dead, but headless now, and something else had wandered away with Ned's left hand. But the Changed hadn't been touched.

And someone else had been there.

The back door of the convenience store had been forced from the outside. In the office, there was only a pile of car mats and the reek of bourbon and infection—and nothing more.

Tom was gone.

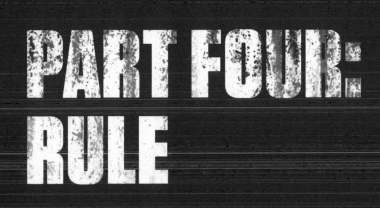

PART FOUR: RULE

45

The pop of distant gunfire jolted Alex from yet another fitful night's sleep. She registered the slash of morning sun in an already too-bright and very cold room, the soft bed, and the comforting, oh-so-normal aromas of sausage and eggs and fried potatoes and . . . yes . . . *coffee*. Yet what she felt was not hunger or gratitude but a horrible sinking sensation, like when you go to sleep hoping the world will change only to wake up and find that it hasn't. Yes, she was safe and warm and fed and clean for the first time since leaving the ranger station, but Tom was gone and she had failed.

More shots. Not many. After three days—almost Thanksgiving now—she was getting used to the gunfire, which was sometimes more, sometimes less.

She pulled the pillow over her head to blot out the noise and light. She had nothing to be thankful for. She had failed. Tom would never have failed her. She should never have left him. God, this was so unfair. First her parents, then the monster and her life and school and friends, then Aunt Hannah, then Ellie and Mina, and now *Tom* . . .

She had to get out of here; she had to find Tom, and then Ellie, too. Gather supplies; she could get a pack, a map, a gun. But then what?

There was a quick rap on the door, more a formality than anything else. The knob turned and Jess poked her head into the room. "I thought I heard you moving around," she said. "Time for you to come downstairs. Matt's here to take you to meet the Reverend."

"Why?" Three days, and her body still felt like one big bruise; her back ached, her throat was raw, and her hands were a quilt of healing cuts and scrapes. "It's not like it changes anything."

"Now, none of that self-pity, girl." Jess had the look of a spinster librarian: dry and efficient, with steel-gray hair pinned in a bun. All she needed was a pencil behind one ear and cat's-eye glasses on a keep chain. "Corinthians says, *God is faithful, and with the temptation He will also provide the way of escape, that you may be able to endure it.*"

"Yeah?"

"Yeah. It means stop feeling sorry for yourself. God is testing you."

"How do you figure that?" Alex said, feeling very sorry for herself.

"How do you think?" Jess counted off on her fingers. "Let me see. You survive the attack. You don't change. You rescue a child. You nearly get eaten by wild dogs. You nearly get eaten by the Changed. And you're almost lynched. Oh, and the dogs like you. Did I miss something?"

Yeah, I failed the one person who would've died rather than hurt me. "I don't see how those are tests. They just happened."

"Then you are very blind, and it's high time you woke up. You're not the only one with problems. Every single person here in Rule has lost someone they cared about, and some of us more than one. I watched my girls drop dead in front of my eyes, but I thank God my grandson was spared. Our lives are a ruin, but you don't see us all dragging around with long faces, feeling sorry for ourselves. Everyone works, and that includes you, young lady. Now get your little butt out of bed before I drag it out."

"You're not my mother," Alex said, and then thought, *Oh boy, did that sound like Ellie or what?*

"And thank our Lord for that," Jess retorted. "I am not a bully, Alex, but neither you nor I, nor anyone else here, has time for a pity party. There's a puppy downstairs going crazy because he wants to see you and there is work to be done."

"I don't have to listen to you."

"Under my roof, you do." When Alex didn't reply, Jess lowered herself to the bed with a sigh. "Look. I don't enjoy this. I'd much rather we just get along."

Alex thought that was probably true, but Jess was hard to read. As straightforward as she appeared to be, her scent was . . . well, what Alex imagined *white* smelled like. Not mist; nothing shadowy like Chris. Jess's scent was a blank. "You can start by leaving me alone," Alex said.

"I can't do that. I know this sounds trite, but if Tom meant this much to you, then he wouldn't want to see you like this. He sounds like he was a very fine, very brave young man, and he saw something in you worth saving—not once but several times over.

You can try telling yourself that it was a reflex, that he would've done it for anyone, that he didn't have a choice, but remember one thing: in the end, dear, he chose you over his friend. He chose *you*." Jess brushed a hank of hair from Alex's forehead. "Scripture says, *By faith he still speaks, even though he is dead*."

"What does that mean?" she asked miserably.

"It means you must honor Tom's sacrifice. You must honor *him*. He would want you to live."

"Living feels like a punishment." Tears streamed down her cheeks. "Everyone I care about is gone."

"As long as you're alive, there is hope," Jess said. "Hope is saying that I will live one more day, and that is a blessing, too."

"Where's that from?"

"The Book of Jess," she said. "Now get up. Don't make Tom's suffering all for nothing."

In the kitchen, Jess was puttering over a skillet as Alex's house-mates—a plump, cheery sixteen-year-old named Tori, and Lena, an arrogant-looking brunette Alex's age—washed and dried. A much older man, weather-beaten and craggy as a cowboy, slouched at a white, farm-style kitchen table. Chewing, he looked up from a mug of coffee and half-eaten muffin, then swallowed and said, "Well, good morning, sunshine. How'd you sleep?"

"Fine, thank you, Doc," Alex said. Kincaid had told her the very first day that it was either Matt or Doc, and Alex just couldn't wrap her head around being on a first-name basis with a guy pushing seventy-five. After her icy room, the kitchen—warmed by an old-fashioned cast-iron stove and filled with the intoxicating aromas of cinnamon, nutmeg, and apples—was a relief. Alex's mouth watered, and her stomach growled.

The kitchen's side door opened, and Ghost crowded in. Spying Alex, the puppy let out a happy yawp, scampered over, and, in general, made a fuss. Grinning, Alex bent to give the squirming puppy a tummy rub. "How you doing, big boy?"

"More like *fat* boy," said a third girl, who'd come in with the dog. Sarah was tiny, with very dark eyes and bones as delicate as a porcelain doll. Dragging off a rose-pink knit cap, she shook out a tumble of blonde ringlets. "He practically rolls down the steps."

Lena said to Alex, "Yeah, now that you're done sulking, *you* can go out in the cold for a change."

"I don't mind walking him." Kneeling, Sarah scratched Ghost's stomach, then giggled as the puppy dissolved into helpless squiggles. Her face turned wistful. "My brother had a dog this really cute little cocker spaniel—only he got hit by a car."

"Well, since there are no cars, you won't have to worry about that anymore," Lena said.

"I'd love your help, Sarah," Alex said, ignoring Lena's eye-roll.

"Alex, I made up a plate for you." Tori turned from the sink, wiping her hands on a dish towel. Her cheeks were dotted with color and her hair had frizzed from the steam. "Why don't you sit down and I'll—"

"You know, she's not a cripple." Lena dropped a dried plate onto a stack with a clatter. "Stop being such a suck-up."

Alex pushed to her feet. "It's okay, Tori. I can get it."

Tori's eyebrows crinkled and her mouth formed a tiny, hurt O. "I'm *not* sucking up," she said to Lena.

Lena snorted. "Yeah, right. Just because Chris keeps hanging around doesn't mean that Peter—"

"Lena," Jess warned.

"What? I'm just *saying*. I don't get why you're all treating *her* like she's any different from *us*."

"Well," Sarah began timidly, "I *did* hear that the dogs—"

"The dogs, the dogs, the dogs." Lena did another wildly exaggerated eye-roll. "They don't know everything. What if the animals change? Has anyone thought about that? It's not like the animals didn't go apeshit that first day."

"Thank you for that stunningly precise scientific observation, Lena," Jess said, expertly flipping an egg. "When you get your degree in veterinary medicine, I'll be sure to ask your opinion. Now, the last time I looked, those dishes weren't drying themselves."

Lena gave a mug a half-hearted swipe. "When does *she* start? You would never let us get away with this shit."

"Oh, my ears," said Kincaid.

"Lena Christina Stoltz." Jess hacked off two thick slices of brown bread. "I will not tolerate abusiveness in my house. One more trashy word out of that sewer mouth and I will speak to the Reverend."

"You're bluffing." Lena threw her towel aside. "You won't do it, and the Council won't turn me out, because you need us; we're just so *Spared*, we're so *valuable*."

"Lena, they just want to protect us," said Tori.

"Protect us? We're prisoners. They won't let us leave."

"But it's for our own good."

"Just because the adults say that doesn't make it true." Lena glared at Jess. "You can keep me here a million years, but you'll *never* make me agree with you."

"I don't care if you agree," Jess said, calmly pouring coffee into a silver thermos. "But let's be clear. When you are Chosen—"

"I'll kill myself first."

"When you are Chosen, you may do what you wish under your own roof. But so long as you remain here, you will follow the rules, or I *will* ask the Reverend to reconsider. I don't think you want to test me on that." Jess capped the thermos. "Is that understood?"

The kitchen had gone very quiet. Even Ghost was still. Tori looked on the verge of tears, and Sarah was milky-white. Alex's eyes kept sliding from Lena's pale face to the floor, but her mind whirled.

Chosen? What's that? And Lena tried to leave, but they wouldn't let her? Wait just a minute. . . .

"Yes, ma'am." Lena's voice was small, but Alex could smell the hot, peppery sting of her fury.

"Excellent." Jess tucked the thermos under one arm and picked up the wrapped sandwich. "Now, if you'll excuse me, that poor guard's waited long enough in the cold for his breakfast." The door closed behind her with a decisive snick.

No one moved for a moment, and then Sarah crossed to Lena and touched her arm. "It'll be okay," she said. "I miss my mom, too."

Lena shook her off. "I don't miss that bitch," she hissed, and rushed from the room. In another moment, Alex heard her storm up the stairs.

Kincaid broke the silence. "Tori, I would dearly love another muffin, if you wouldn't mind."

46

Kincaid had brought a gentle, swaybacked pinto named Honey for her, but Alex balked. "I've never ridden a horse," she said, ignoring the guard who lounged against the front gate, looking amused. His dog, a fawn-colored pit, capered up to Alex for a pat. "Why can't we walk?"

"Because it's faster to ride," Kincaid said. "Believe me, if you end up assigned to one of the farms, you'll be happy to have a horse."

"Yeah," the guard drawled. He sucked back steaming coffee. "Otherwise, you'll be getting up before you go to sleep."

"Come on, Alex," said Kincaid. "And leave off with that dog."

"Yeah, yeah, I'm coming," said Alex, but she was grinning. Sensing that Alex's attention was wandering, the dog had rolled onto its back and was plaintively pedaling air. Alex stooped to scratch the dog's ruff as the pit bull groaned. "It's not my fault."

"Looks like we got ourselves our own little dog whisperer," the guard said, shaking his head. "Lucy doesn't like anybody, but seeing is believing, I guess. Lucy, come on now, heel!"

With an almost human sigh, the pit rolled to its feet and gave Alex a reproachful look: *Do something*. Then, head hanging, the dog walked slowly back to the guard and settled onto its haunches with an audible harrumph.

It took her a few tries before she could boost herself onto the saddle, and some more time for Kincaid to fuss with the stirrups and go over what the reins were for, how to sit, what to do. Then they headed for town, the pit woofing encouragement.

"That's good. You're getting the hang of it," Kincaid said. He was astride a lean, leopard-spotted Appaloosa. "Couple of days and you'll be cantering with the best of them."

"Mmm." She was thinking, *Yeah, maybe canter right on out of here.* Unfortunately, Honey seemed happy to take all of life at a walk. Even so, the animal's easy motion was pleasant. Every dog they passed—and they went by quite a few—let out a friendly bark and tugged at its leash, tail frantically whisking back and forth.

Kincaid eyed her. "Dogs always this friendly?"

"Not with me."

"Uh-huh." Kincaid watched a guard wrestle a chocolate lab to a sit. "Well, you keep this up, you'll never be lonely."

Jess's house was a little west of the village center, perhaps less than half a mile away. As they rode, Kincaid gave her a rough idea of Rule's layout. The village itself had always been a small, virtually closed community, a stopover between the now-defunct mine and other towns that catered to the men who worked there. After the attack, however, Rule had expanded to protect nearby assets, principally forest, outlying farms, and livestock. All the major roads were barricaded at one-mile intervals beginning five miles from town and guarded twenty-four hours a day. More foot patrols, with their dogs, roamed the woods. The only road into the village was northeast. Anyone not allowed to stay was escorted to the southwest corner thirty miles north of the mine.

"You got pretty much free rein in town, though you always got to have an escort if you want to go anywhere outside the village center," Kincaid said. "Tempers still run a bit high when it comes to the Spared. We don't want anything happening to you."

The way he and everyone else said *Spared* and *Changed* made her very uncomfortable. That *Chosen* thing, too—what was that about? The whole scene felt way too religious, what with this reverend in charge and his Council of Five. Maybe these people all belonged to some kind of cult, like Jonestown or Waco or something. Look at Jess, spouting Bible quotes. They seemed pretty organized, too, like they had a set of rules in place from way before. "Is that why I need to meet this reverend and the Council? So they can figure out what to do with me?"

"Sort of. The Rev's pretty hands-on, and the Council runs things and decides who goes where and does what on the basis of need."

"Did you elect them or something?"

Kincaid shook his head. "The Five Families have been running Rule since the village got started. The Reverend's family—the Yeagers—are the most important. They're the richest, the first of the Five Families to settle Rule going on over a hundred and fifty years now. Owned the mine, built the village, started the church. The Rev and his brother took over the mine after their father died.

Mine pretty much tapped out twenty years ago, but you got men here worked that mine their whole lives. That kind of loyalty and sense of family carries through in times like these. The Yeagers took care of people before, and people figure they will now."

"So everyone listens to Pastor Yeager?"

"Reverend. Yeah. Let's just say he's the final arbiter."

"What if everyone else on the Council disagrees with him?"

"Never happened yet."

Everyone always agreed, always came around to one guy's way of thinking? That didn't sound good. They couldn't *always* see eye to eye, could they? "But what if I want to leave? Ellie's out there, and Tom—"

"Well, as I get it, you have no idea where they are. That right?"

"No, but that doesn't mean I shouldn't be looking for them."

"You got some bright ideas where you should start?"

She bit back a snarky retort. "No."

"Then, until you do, might be best if you find a way to fit in here."

"But Rule's not my home," she said. Lena's words ghosted through her mind, and she was starting to get a very bad feeling about this. "You're not my family."

"Well, let's see what we can do about that," he said.

The village center wasn't much. A large white church and rectory stood on the northwest corner. To the west was a sprawling, two-story village hall with high, arched windows and a clock tower made of old-fashioned brownstone. Due south, the square was lined by an ancient five-and-ten, a bakery next door to a small grocery called Murphy's, Martha's Diner—BREAKFAST 24/7— and, at the end of the block, a combination Christian bookstore/ coffeehouse: Higher Grounds. Directly across the square from the coffeehouse was a shuttered bar, which from the looks of the vintage ads for Blatz and Ballantine beer festooning the brick face, hadn't done business since the dinosaurs. Guards patrolled the sidewalk in front of the grocery, five-and-ten, and coffeehouse. Martha's was also open, judging from the lacy scent of brewing coffee, maple syrup, and pancakes. Men in camo gear hunched over tables ranged along a steamy front window. Spying Alex, their dogs scrambled to their feet.

Definitely getting worse. She saw more dogs butting their noses against the diner's plate glass, and she smelled how much rounder and more fecund their scents grew when they spotted her. *Mina wasn't nearly this bad, and it's only been, what, a week? Ten days?*

She felt eyes on her and turned to see Kincaid studying her. She didn't know him, but she didn't sense anything bad rolling off him either. He smelled like a comfortable leather coat, something her dad might have worn, edged with a hint of something lightly floral. Powder? She said, "Do you know why they're doing that? I've heard that the dogs don't like people who are going to . . . you know. But me . . ."

"But you, they love." Kincaid's shoulders moved in a small shrug. "Dunno yet. Let me think on it."

The church's front door opened, and a gaggle of children spilled out. They were all young—none were older than ten or eleven—and they tumbled over one another, racing for a playground just off the rectory. Seeing the children, listening to their shrieks and laughter, hearing the joyous barking of the dogs—all this brought an unexpected crush of grief to her chest, and she had to look away.

Belatedly, she realized that she'd pulled back on the reins and now Honey stood, her breath smoking, patiently waiting for Alex to make up her mind. Kincaid had also pulled up and was watching her. When their eyes met, Kincaid said, "Still gets to me."

"It seems so normal," she said.

"That's because it is. We try to make things as normal as we can."

Yeah, right, normal little things like gunfire and guards. She'd heard no other shots since awakening, but she wondered who they were shooting—and where. And why.

"We don't want them to grow up dumb either," Kincaid said. "School's one thing they all have in common. Gives them a routine. We got a guy used to be principal over at Merton Elementary. You'll meet him when you start class tomorrow."

"I'm going to school?"

"Oh yeah. Just because it's the end of the world doesn't mean you get to cut."

"That is so not fair."

"Cheer up. We got some good teachers that have come out of retirement. Kind of ironic, you think about it. We do our time and get put out to pasture and now we're the ones left picking up the pieces."

Put out to pasture? She opened her mouth, but then turned at the rapid clop of horse hooves. A hay wagon bounced down a snaky cut that jagged through the woods. This time, Peter was driving; Jet was perched on the driver's seat alongside Peter, and Chris trotted behind on a muscular blood bay. Instead of hay, the wagon was crammed with people—all blindfolded. More refugees who might be just valuable enough to keep, she figured. When Jet caught her scent, the black shepherd barked a greeting, and Chris turned, spied them, and lifted a hand before continuing on. She watched as the wagon rolled to a halt in front of the village hall.

"What goes on in there?" she asked.

"That, young lady," said Kincaid, "is what you are about to find out."

47

The village hall's main corridor was lined with offices, some open, others shut tight. Fear curdled the air. A clog of guards and more dogs kept watch over a long line of bedraggled, elderly refugees. Alex fixed her eyes on Kincaid's back, but she heard the resentful whispers as they passed. Then one man said, quite distinctly, "Leave me alone with her, I'll show you how it's done."

A burst of mean, raucous laughter. The dogs whined anxiously. Alex half-expected Kincaid to say something, but he kept walking.

Behind came the clatter of dishes, and Alex turned to see two women pushing a metal food cart, like the kind they used in hospitals to bring patients their meals. No need for spidey-sense either: bacon was bacon.

Someone in line groaned at the aroma. All the refugees watched, hollow-eyed, as the women trundled up to a thick wooden door with a push bar and reinforced glass. One woman knocked, and a few seconds later, the door was pushed open from the inside. Alex saw the back of yet another guard, and as the women disappeared, she caught the thinnest finger of a scent coming from beyond the door. Not the dead-meat stink. She thought she would've caught that as soon as she entered, anyway. This was different. It was familiar, a scent she'd picked up before: tobacco and rotted teeth and old whiskey.

I know this. Who—

A loud, piercing scream came from the end of the corridor, and Alex gasped, her thoughts instantly derailed. The refugees fell silent, but the dogs in the hall began to whimper, and a few barked. The scream came again, and then two guards rounded the corner, dragging a sobbing, struggling old man between them.

"No, no, you can't!" the man wailed. He was very old, almost withered, with arms like twigs and a knot of twine around his waist to keep his pants from falling down. With a sudden burst of strength, the old man spurted free of the guards and scurried for an office door. At that, the dogs strained at their leashes, yapping and pawing at the air. The old man grabbed the knob and yanked, but the door was locked. A look of utter despair broke over his weathered face, and as the two guards approached, the old man began to weep. He crumpled to his knees, his gnarled fingers still wrapped around unyielding metal.

"You can't send me back out there! I got no one; I got nowhere to go!" he pleaded as the guards tried to pull him free. The old man hung on with the grim tenacity of a leech; terror had lent him a furious strength, and the wasted muscles of his arms went as taut as rubber bands. "I can still work; I'm still good for something—please, *don't!*"

Amid a chorus of excited barks from the dogs, another guard

hurried to help. Between the three, they pried the old man's hands free and then carried him, still thrashing and screaming, down that long corridor and finally, mercifully, out of sight.

"Jesus," said the man who wouldn't have minded showing the others how things were done with her. He flashed Alex a hostile glare. To Kincaid, he snarled, "You ought to be ashamed. He's one of us, and you're saving *them*. What the hell makes her so special?"

"Well, for one," Kincaid said mildly, "she knows how to keep her mouth shut."

At the end of the T corridor, they hung a right. The windows here faced south, and the hall was much brighter. There were more guards—she was starting to get used to seeing old men in camouflage with rifles—and then Kincaid led her to a set of closed double doors on the right. A plaque to the left of the doors said COURTROOM.

"We'll wait out here a few minutes," said Kincaid. He dropped into a straight-back chair with a little sigh.

She remained standing. Her mouth was dry, but her palms were wet. "Why is it so important that I see this Council and the Reverend? I mean, they can't decide where *everyone* goes. There are too many people."

"Five hundred, give or take, yeah. And no, they don't eyeball everyone. Wardens—men who've been given the keys—do that."

"Keys? You mean, like, to unlock doors?"

"Not physical ones, no. It's, ah, a biblical reference. Matthew: *And I will give unto thee the keys of the kingdom of heaven: and*

whatsoever thou shalt bind on earth shall be bound in heaven: and what-
soever thou shalt loose on earth shall be loosed in heaven. Same concept
as the Mormon priesthood, although we're not Mormons. What it
boils down to is that the Council awards certain men the authority
to make decisions in certain areas: the farms, the armory, supplies,
sanitation, for example. Peter, he's an Ernst, and they're one of
the Five Families, so he's warden of the militia. He decides which
missions get carried out, how many men'll be needed, things like
that. He'll see newcomers, too; decide if they're suitable for guard
duty or good in a fight."

"So the people in the hall are waiting to see the wardens?"

"Or their representatives and lieutenants—people like Chris—
yeah."

Her eyebrows drew together in a frown. "But Chris is the
Reverend's grandson, right? So why doesn't he have a key? How
come he's not a warden?"

Kincaid's lips screwed to a rosebud. "Well," he said carefully,
"there's the fact that Chris isn't pure Rule, born and bred. He's got
some of the bloodline, but his parents weren't, uh, *of* the village.
They left, and their history is a little . . . murky. Peter is Rule-bred,
older, has more experience with these matters. There are other
reasons, but those are good as any."

Rule-bred? Bloodlines? Rule sounded a lot more closed and reg-
imented than she'd originally thought. "So who does the Council
see?"

"The Spared—kids like you—and the borderline cases: people
who might do well here, but the wardens aren't quite sure. So they

send them on to the Council for final judgment. The Council also sees people who might not be, well, *adjusting* very well."

She recalled Jess's threat. "Is that what Jess meant when she said she'd ask the Reverend to reconsider?"

Kincaid bobbed his head. "The Reverend always has the final say when it comes to the Ban."

"Ban?" The fingers of a chill walked her spine. "Like, banishment?"

"Something like that." Kincaid put a hand on her shoulder. "Look, that's not your worry right now, okay? Best thing you can do is concentrate on putting your best foot forward, and don't lie. The Rev will know if you do."

Okay, that was interesting. "If you lie, do they, uh, ban you?"

"Not as a first choice, no. But some kids can't adapt. They don't settle down."

"Like Lena?"

"She's a handful, that's for sure."

"So why not let her leave?"

"We're, ah . . . we try to hang on to the Spared. Safer, all the way around."

"But isn't that her choice?" *Isn't it* mine? "What about free will?"

"Free will's okay," said Kincaid. "Only look where it got Adam."

One of the courtroom doors opened, and a rickety old guy, who looked to be about a hundred and ninety, stuck his head out. "Rev'll see you now," he said mushily.

"Just as I was getting comfortable," Kincaid grumbled, then

grimaced as he stood and his knees crackled. "I shoulda got these replaced when I had the chance."

"Don't talk to me about your damn knees," said the rickety guy. He worked his jaws, and Alex heard the clack of dentures. "What I want to know is who we gonna get to fix my damned teeth?"

48

The courtroom looked like something out of *Judge Judy*: wood-paneled and small, with a three-row gallery for spectators, a rail—the bar—with a swinging gate, and two rectangular tables, one to either side of the gate. A jury box was snugged along the right-hand wall. The judge's bench was front and center, and behind the bench sat five men, all in black robes, all with stolid faces seamed by wrinkles. Two, who bracketed the rest on either side like matching bookends, were ancient, so withered a strong breeze might knock them over. She couldn't guess the ages of the other three. Old was . . . old.

She knew which one was Yeager, though. Kincaid had said that the Reverend always sat dead center, and she studied him now. He was completely bald, with a nose like a squashed tomato and wattles hanging from his neck that wobbled when he moved, like those of a turkey vulture. His dark eyes were alive and bird-bright, and they fixed on her now with a coldly speculative look, the way a crow eyed roadkill to decide if it was worth the effort.

"So, you're Alexandra." Yeager's voice was surprisingly even and deep, almost booming, perfect for belting out a sermon. "Come on in. Don't be shy. Just walk through the bar there."

She threw a quick, furtive glance at the other four men, but they were silent and expressionless. What was their job? To observe? Ask questions? Their skin exhaled the mingled funk she'd come to associate with the old: peppermint and papery skin, dirty socks and old farts, and a general fusty decrepitude. Nothing menacing, at least.

Yeager was different. He smelled opaque and chilly, like cloudy glass or fog. A little like Jess, she decided: a blank. She couldn't sense his intent at all, or what he felt.

"Well." Yeager peered down from the bench. From that angle, he looked more like a vulture than before. "Finally, we meet. My grandson's told me about you."

What had Chris said? "Yes, sir."

"I like to meet all the Spared. You are our future, and I want to feel that when the time comes, we've chosen well. Come here. I'd like to see you eye to eye." Yeager beckoned her closer, and now Alex saw a small step stool set up before the bench. As she mounted the steps, her eyes brushed over narrow brass nameplates, one squared before each of the old men. The first two, starting from her left, read BORN and ERNST. Front and center was YEAGER, and then came STIEMKE and, finally, to her far right, PRIGGE.

Now, she also saw something else she hadn't before: a sixth chair, set off by itself, beyond Prigge. There was no nameplate, nothing to indicate to whom the chair belonged. It might be simply a spare, but she didn't think so. She eyed the bench and, for the first time, noticed that the way the Council was arranged seemed . . . unbalanced. Like there was someone missing.

Six chairs, but only five men and it's the Council of Five . . . unless it hasn't always been that way.

Yeager extended his hands, palms up. "If I may."

She hesitated, flustered, then remembered Kincaid's quip: *He's very hands-on.* She slid her palms onto his, her skin jumping at the contact. Yeager's hands were gnarled, the knuckles swollen, the skin dry as old parchment and spotted with age, but his grip was strong.

"Warm hands," said Yeager.

"Yes, sir." She expected him to let go then, but he didn't. She wanted to tear her hands from his grasp, but forced herself to remain still. She felt the eyes of the others, but didn't dare look away.

"One thing I would like to understand, Alex," said Yeager. "I'm not clear how it is that you ended up in the Waucamaw. Tell me about that."

"I . . . um . . . I cut school." Really, she figured it didn't much matter now. But she decided to keep her answers short and to the point.

Now the man to her right rumbled, "Was that a habit of yours?"

Caught off guard, she cut a look his way: STIEMKE. "No," she said.

Yeager said nothing, only rubbed his horny thumbs over her palms. Stiemke continued: "So why then?"

"I wanted to think some things through." When Stiemke only stared, she added, "College, things like that."

"Ah," Yeager said. "The future, what you were going to do with your life?"

Close enough. "Yes."

To the far left, one of the withered guys—Born—piped up in a reedy quaver, "What did you decide?"

"I didn't have a chance, sir," she said. It helped that this was true—but then, feeling the Reverend's grip shift, she had a sudden flash of intuition. What had Kincaid said?

Don't lie. The Rev will know if you do.

And *hands-on* . . . My God, was Yeager like *her*? She'd never considered that other people might have changed as she had. Larry, who'd seen more survivors than she or Tom, hadn't said anything about it. Maybe because that kind of change wasn't common, or the people who *had* developed a super-sense kept it a secret. She had, even from Tom; then again, she had a lot of secrets. Given how paranoid everyone was now, not telling about a super-sense might be smart.

So, could Yeager sense whether she was telling the truth—not by smell but through touch? Like a human lie detector?

How would that work? She knew that people flushed when they were nervous, so there were temperature changes. A person's skin also carried an electrical charge; that was how a computer touch pad worked, by sensing the electrical gradient. That was why a fingertip worked but a pencil, which carried no charge, wouldn't.

Yeager might've had a natural-born knack to begin with. He was a pastor, after all. She remembered the sign for Harvest Church: TRUST IN THE HEALING HAND OF GOD. Maybe not far from the truth: Yeager might not heal, but perhaps he could *feel*—an innate ability augmented by the Zap. But why Yeager and not all the other people who'd survived, some of whom were very old indeed?

Why her?

"A penny for your thoughts," Yeager said. He smiled his vulture's grin, but his grip did not change.

"My father always said they weren't worth that much." It was all right to mention her father, she decided; all parents were dead, pretty much, so that made her no different from anyone else. And if she could steer the conversation . . .

To Yeager's immediate right, Ernst—Peter's grandfather? Great-grandfather?—said, "What did your father do?"

"He was a cop."

"Ah." This seemed to please Prigge, the other bookend. He actually rubbed the knobbed twigs of his hands together. "A man who knew good from evil."

She had never heard her father refer to any of the drunks or wife-beaters or scammers as evil, but she said, "Yes, sir. I guess so."

"Well, that is also what we do here. Tell me"—Yeager cocked his head—"why do the dogs favor you? Why do they . . . *recognize* you?"

"I don't know," she said truthfully. "I'm not a dog."

"But you must have an idea," Ernst said.

She nodded. "Probably the same way I recognize them." *But not Reverend Yeager or Jess—and why is that?*

"And that is?" Yeager asked.

She decided to chance it. "I guess the same way you're able to tell things."

She heard Ernst's sudden, involuntary inhale. Yeager's vulture-eyes slitted. "Meaning?" Yeager asked.

She'd guessed right; she had him, and there was just the smallest crack in his blankness, that cloudy glass: something very wet and a little metallic, an odor that reminded her of the day the dogs had nearly killed her and Ellie.

Water? A river? No, that's not quite it. More like . . . rain.

Rain? She remembered the day this had all begun, and those storm clouds to the southwest and the gray slashes that looked like rain.

Is that why he smells like wet glass? Because he was by a window, watching the rain when it happened?

"Meaning?" Yeager repeated.

She felt the intensity of the other men's gazes burning holes into her brain, but she did not allow her eyes to wander. "Meaning you can tell if what I'm saying is true because you feel it, literally, through your hands."

A beat. No one spoke. Yeager's eyes raked her face and then he abruptly let go of her hands. His gaze clicked to a point over her shoulder. "Matt, wait outside a moment, will you?"

She'd completely forgotten Kincaid was there. "Uh," Kincaid said, clearly surprised. "Okay."

She felt a quick prick of fear. "Why can't he stay?" she asked Yeager.

He ignored her. "Matt?"

"Sure. I'll be right outside, Alex. It'll be okay."

Yeager waited until Kincaid was gone, and then he turned his searchlight gaze onto Alex once more. "Yours isn't touch."

"Why couldn't he stay?"

"Because there are some things better kept behind closed doors," Ernst said. Of all the others, he seemed to be the one closest to Yeager in authority. On Yeager's right hand, she realized: pretty biblical. She wondered if Ernst's first name was Michael. "The fewer who know, the safer for everyone," Ernst said.

"What is it that you sense?" Yeager asked. His eyes pinned her. "Is yours touch?"

"No. But I can tell things like you can."

"Such as?"

"I know what people are feeling sometimes." She paused. "I know when *they*—the Changed—are around."

"What?" Ernst said, startled. "You can *do* that?"

"Yes," she said, but she kept her gaze on Yeager.

"How?" Yeager asked.

"The same way I know there's a murderer in this building," she said. "Because I smell him."

49

He'd lost weight and grown a beard. His hair was much longer, too, well past his shoulders. Yet the smell she'd caught in the front hall when the ladies were let in with their food trolley was the same as on the day he'd shot Tom: stale tobacco, rotten teeth, and Jim Beam.

"I don't know what you're talking about." Glaring, Harlan balled a grimy rag in one ham-fist. On top of his normal reek, he also smelled of the bleach and ammonia he used to mop the floors of the jail cells. As the village hall janitor, Harlan had, Alex decided, found his true calling. Harlan jammed the rag into a grubby hip pocket. "I've never seen this kid before in my life."

"Why would she lie?" asked Yeager. The others were still at their places on the bench, but he had descended, coming to stand alongside her. Yeager was smaller than she'd imagined, nearly half a head shorter than she. He had not taken Harlan's hands, however, which Alex thought must be a test of some kind.

Not of Harlan, though. Yeager was testing *her*.

Harlan glowered. "Because she's a kid, and she's got some kind of ax to grind. But I'm telling the truth. I never seen her before just now."

"Liar. What happened to Ellie?" Alex asked.

"I'm sorry. Who's that? Relative of yours? A dog, maybe?"

From the bench, Ernst said, "This isn't getting us anywhere."

"Let's wait until—" Yeager broke off as the courtroom door opened and Peter hurried in, a bulging knapsack in his arms. Chris and Jet followed close behind.

"Sorry." Peter's hair was windblown, and his cheeks were ruddy with cold. He plunked the knapsack onto one of the courtroom's long attorney tables as Chris dumped a second. "There was a lot of crap to gather up."

"Hey," said Harlan, "that's my stuff. You got no right to go through my stuff."

"On the contrary," said Yeager, and nodded at Chris and Peter. "Open them."

What tumbled out were clothes, mostly: underwear, jeans, sweaters, flannel shirts, long johns, socks. Peter had gathered up toiletries, shoes, two watch caps, a set of mittens, and several ratty magazines. "And a Bible," he said, pulling the leather-bound volume from the knapsack.

"Anything you recognize?" Yeager asked her.

Alex shook her head. She'd felt a flare of hope, but a single glance told her that the Bible was not Aunt Hannah's.

"See?" Harlan folded his arms over his chest. "You got the wrong guy."

"No, I don't," Alex said. She looked at Chris. "There's nothing else?"

"Just this," Peter said, and reached into one of the knapsack's side pouches. "Heavy sucker."

Alex had to bite her lip to keep from crying out. "That's my fanny pack."

"That's crap," said Harlan, although Alex caught a thin stiletto of sour milk now. Harlan was worried. "I've had that thing for years."

"No, I packed it myself," Alex said.

"A fanny pack's a fanny pack," Harlan said. "She's gonna guess some of it."

"Yeah." Peter unzipped the pack. "So that's why we'll let you tell us first. What's inside?"

Harlan visibly relaxed, and Alex thought with dismay, *He emptied it.* "Sure," Harlan said. "Lessee, there's a pack of tissues, some old gum, knife . . ." He rattled off a list of items as Peter pulled each from the pack.

"Yeah," said Peter when Harlan was done. "That's all of it, except this." He pulled out Alex's soft-shell black case. "This thing weighs a good ten pounds. What's inside?"

Harlan opened his mouth, but Yeager said, "Just a minute." He took the case from Peter, studied its contents, then raised his searching, bird-bright eyes to Alex. "Tell us what this is."

"Hey, it's my pack," said Harlan.

"Then she won't have the slightest idea, will she?" Yeager nodded at Alex. "Go on. Tell me. What are these?"

Later, she would wonder why Harlan had kept them. The pack, she could understand, but not the rest. Maybe, when he saw the Bible, he realized what he'd done and was just superstitious enough to think that keeping *them* would somehow undo all the rest. In the end, all that mattered was this: if the pack was still heavy, she knew exactly what—who—was inside.

"My parents," she said.

50

Her parents' ashes were there, but Aunt Hannah's Bible—and her mother's letter—were gone.

"The little kid musta done it," said Harlan miserably. He was slouched in a hardback chair, looking as shriveled as a deflated balloon. Once Kincaid looked through the bags to confirm that they contained cremated remains—teeth survive cremation— Harlan had dropped the bluffing tough-guy routine. Now he stared at his hands and sighed. "She said the stuff was important to *her*." He jerked his head at Alex. "Once Marjorie got killed, I had my hands full just keeping us alive. Couldn't be watching the kid every five seconds."

"Where is she?" Alex demanded. It was all she could do to keep from screaming and scratching Harlan's eyes out.

Harlan hunched a shoulder. "I don't know. Like I said, she run off maybe a day south of here." He let out a grunt of disgust. "Brett was so sure the army was gonna let us in . . . only we never got that far. I told Brett we ought to keep off the interstate, and Marjorie wanted to go west—to come here, is what she wanted—but he just had to check on his sister, who lived in Watersmeet. . . . Anyway, that's where we lost the truck . . . you know, in an ambush. Buncha guys watching the town, outnumbered us by about twenty. Shot Marjorie before we knew what was happening."

"Yeah," Alex said, "I know how getting ambushed and shot at feels." Chris put a warning hand on her arm, and she bit back the rest.

"What happened after that?" Peter asked.

Harlan shrugged again. "What the hell you think? We couldn't go south on account of we heard they wasn't letting people across the border into Wisconsin, and we sure as hell wasn't staying in Watersmeet. Outside *that* town, they don't even give you a chance to explain, not like here; they just start shooting. So we walked."

"You still had the little girl and the dog?" asked Yeager.

Harlan nodded. "The dog saved our ass a bunch of times. It knew way ahead of us when there was one of those *things* out there. The dog and the kid was with us right up until we was east of the mine, and then the dog went crazy. Just wouldn't go any farther. Even the girl couldn't get it to mind. The dog kept wanting to get away from here. Probably we should've listened to it, because that's the night five of them kids . . . you know, the Changed . . . they got to us."

"The dog didn't warn you?" asked Peter.

"Well, I think it tried and we wouldn't listen. I don't know, man," Harlan said. "Brett was standing watch. One minute I'm sleeping and the next the dog . . . it never did settle down, pacing all night long and whining. It started going crazy, and next thing I know, Brett starts in blasting away. His rifle jammed and I couldn't draw a bead fast enough."

No, this was a lie; Alex smelled it. But whether Harlan had dozed off or accidentally shot Brett wasn't important. Yeager must've sensed something, too, because he said, "Now why do I think that's a lie?"

The skin of Harlan's neck flushed a mottled scarlet. He said, "What are you going to do to me?"

"You left a little girl out there to *die*," Peter said. His voice snapped like an angry whip. "What do you *think*?"

Harlan's Adam's apple bobbled. His gaze skittered away from Peter's angry face to the blank faces of the men on the bench and then finally to Yeager. "But you can't shoot me."

"True, but you cannot stay," said Yeager. "Your sin stains us all."

There were murmurs of assent from the men on the bench. Peter was nodding, but Chris's face was impassive, the scent of his darkness very strong.

"Banned?" Harlan's eyes filled. "Man, please, don't make me go back out there. Those *things* . . ."

Peter, for whom most solutions seemed to involve a gun, said, "Hey, man, no skin off my nose. I'm happy to put a bullet in you right now."

Yeager put up a restraining hand. "You'll be no worse off than that little girl, and a fair sight better. You will have the same three days' rations we give any person to whom we refuse sanctuary."

"But I been a good worker," Harlan whined. "I done nothing wrong since I got here."

"*Do not share in the sins of others. Keep yourself pure,*" Yeager recited. "You bear Azazel's mark. We will not be pure again until you are gone. From this time forward, you are Banned."

"No. Please. At least let me stay the night," Harlan said hoarsely. "For God's sake, it's already late afternoon. It'll be dark soon!"

"Then I suggest," said Yeager, "that you run very quickly."

51

"We need to find her," Alex demanded. Kincaid and Chris sat with her in Jess's kitchen. A golden slant of late-afternoon sun sliced through a window as Jess silently doled out cups of hot tea. Lena, Tori, and Sarah were out at their respective jobs, for which Alex was grateful. The last thing she needed was more of Lena's mouth; she was tense enough already.

Peter had elected to escort Harlan out personally, and from the look on his face, she thought that Harlan would be very lucky to make it through the next hour. She wished she felt sorry for Harlan, but she didn't. "You heard him, Chris. They were a day south. That's what . . . twenty, thirty miles?"

"A day south two weeks ago. We didn't have the manpower to search for Tom, and that was nearly the same distance. It's not a straight line, Alex. It's twenty miles and who knows which direction," said Chris.

"You guys go out all the time."

"Yes, but that's with specific objectives in mind. We know where we're going. A search is very different."

"But she's only *eight*."

"I'm sorry, Alex," said Chris. "We can't."

"You mean, you won't. She's Spared, but she's not *valuable* enough."

Chris opened his mouth to reply, but Kincaid broke in. "Alex, Chris is on your side. He's the one who got Peter to go out after your friend. He can't change what his grandfather decides, or Peter. It doesn't work that way."

"What makes Yeager so right? You make it sound like he's some miracle guy. Why's he in charge, anyway? Don't you guys ever decide anything for yourselves?"

That got to Chris; she could smell that sliver of ice splinter his darkness. "Listen," he said, "you don't know everything. You just got—"

"Chris." Kincaid put a warning hand around Chris's wrist. "Let's not get ahead of ourselves, okay? Maybe it's best you head on home now."

Chris wanted to argue; Alex could see that in the set of his jaw. But all Chris did was give a curt nod before sliding out of his chair. Shrugging into his coat, he said, "I'll be by for you tomorrow."

"What? Why?" she said.

"You need an escort," said Chris.

Before leaving the village hall, Yeager had suggested she work with Kincaid at the hospice, a suggestion that was an order. *Probably to keep an eye on me*, she thought now. "I can escort myself."

"That's not the way things work here, girl," Jess said.

"But I don't *need* him," she said.

"Sometimes you don't know what you need until it's gone," said Kincaid.

She felt a twinge of disquiet. Chris didn't seem to be a bad guy, but all these stupid rules, a guard outside the house, and now an escort? Were they going to watch her around the clock? What had she gotten herself into? "Look, it's nothing personal," she said to Chris. "It's just that I—"

"No, it's fine." The skin around Chris's mouth was white. "I'll get someone else to do it. I wouldn't be able to do it every day anyway."

"But I don't want anyone."

"It's not my call," said Chris.

"Well, he's your grandfather. Talk to him."

"It's not that simple. The rules are the rules. You have to follow them."

"Or what? You're going to kick me out?" She pushed back from the table. "Fine. That's what I want anyway. I'll leave now. Just give me back my gun and a pack, and I'm out—"

"Oh, for pity's sake, put a plug in your jug, Alex," said Jess. "I've aged five years just listening to you."

Alex felt her neck heat. "I'm just *saying*—"

"Jess," Chris began at the same moment, "if she doesn't want me—"

"Be quiet, both of you. Honestly, you two are like cats in a gunnysack. Alex doesn't know what she wants."

"Wait a minute," Alex flared.

"You only want to brawl. You want a fight. Fighting tricks you into believing you can change the past, even when the past is dead and gone and all of it ashes," said Jess.

Alex felt the hot burn in her chest dim. Jess was right, damn her. Fighting back had been drilled into her from day one of her diagnosis. For her, accepting the monster meant giving up, succumbing. If you didn't fight, you died. Had that changed when she walked away, cut school, and headed for the Waucamaw? No. She'd fought back in a different way, that was all: pushing back at the doctors and the tests and the treatments in favor of calling the shots herself. Since the Zap, she'd been fighting to stay alive every day.

So, now what? Accept what was happening here? No. She hadn't chosen this life; this wasn't her home. These were not *her* people. They were nice enough, but they had their reasons for keeping her here—she was sure of it—and by God, she wasn't going to stop fighting now. She *was* getting out of here, and she *would* find Tom and Ellie. She just had to figure out a way.

Aloud, she settled for something that was also true. "I'm just mad about . . . you know. Everything."

"I know that," said Jess. "You're only human, but you need to start thinking about the greater good. As for you, Christopher, you need to get over yourself and lighten up. Now, you're young, you've been thrust into a position of responsibility well before your time, and you're scared. But sticking to rules just because they're there does not make them right. You need to learn when the rules should be broken."

"Yes, ma'am," Chris said. If anything, his dark scent grew even blacker—not anger, Alex thought, but embarrassment. Chris's eyes bounced from Jess to Alex and then to the table. "An escort's probably overkill."

Yes. Alex squashed a quick spurt of triumph, afraid it would show on her face. *Now, if I can get them to loosen up a little more . . .*

But Kincaid was shaking his head. "You let her go without an escort, you're gonna have to change the rule for everybody then. Not sure you want to go there without a lot of thought. Gonna have to go up against Peter on that one, and probably the Council. I don't think you'll win."

Chris threw up his hands. "There's no satisfying you guys. First, Alex fights me, then Jess tells me I should break rules, and then *you* turn around and tell me I shouldn't. I mean, *Jesus.*"

"Language, young man," said Jess. "Matt is right. If you want to make an exception, you'll need a good reason. Charting your own course isn't the same as being impetuous. Right now, Alex is just complaining. She could be Lena all over again."

"Hey," said Alex. The fact that she was trying to figure out a way to escape didn't make her any less pissed. She was *so* not Lena.

"So this is what's going to happen," Jess continued. "Christopher, you will take her when you can and if your duties permit. Get to know Alex. If you feel that she can be trusted to come and go on her own, then let her. Tell Peter why. Heavens, if it's a question of protection, let her prove that she can take care of herself."

"And how am I supposed to do that?" asked Chris. His pale skin was a patchwork of white and scarlet, and his dark eyes were glittery with anger. "Give her a gun? Let her get in some target practice? *Ride* with us?"

"Yes," said Alex. "I'll bet I can shoot just as well as you guys."

"For so is the will of God, that with well doing you may put to silence the ignorance of foolish men." Jess threw Alex a look. "And foolish girls. Until you know what you're about, Alex, hold your tongue." To Chris: "You are a very smart boy. Figure out what is right and then do it."

"Jess, it's not as easy as that," said Chris.

"Nonsense. You want to be a man? Start acting like one."

"Jess," Kincaid said, "the boy's doing the best he—"

"I can defend myself," Chris snapped. That icy edge was more pronounced now, cleaving his shadows in two. Alex felt a squirt of sympathy. She could handle Chris, but she didn't really want to watch him getting hammered by a woman old enough to be his grandmother.

Jess said, "Chris, you have survived this long by being both very lucky and very smart, but eventually, you must follow your own path, however frightening."

"I am," said Chris. His face was ashen. "I *am*."

"No, you're not. Obeying orders just to obey is the mark of a person who has ceased to think. Remember, it is better to suffer for doing what is right than for doing what is wrong. Don't fool yourself, Christopher. Peace comes with a price."

What was going on? Alex had the feeling that they—Jess and Chris and even Kincaid—were talking over her head somehow. This was not about Chris's playing bodyguard, but an argument over a question she hadn't yet asked. She thought Chris would say something, but his hands fisted, grabbing back whatever had been on the tip of his tongue. Then he stalked out, flinging the kitchen door shut with a resounding clap that made the glass chatter.

"That went well," said Kincaid.

"Sow the seeds of righteousness," Jess murmured.

"That what you were doing? Felt like you were ripping the boy a new one."

"Watch your language, Matt." She shot Alex a warning glare. "He is not the only young person who has ceded his free will."

"Wait a minute," Alex said. "Why are you getting on my case? I *want* to be free."

"Freedom has a price, too, girl. For all your bravery, you do not—" She broke off as the kitchen door opened again and Sarah appeared, shaking a salting of snow from her hair.

"What's wrong with Chris?" Sarah asked. "Is he all right?"

"Never you mind," said Jess, and then she turned to Alex: "You are an ungrateful and very foolish young woman. While you are here, you will be quiet and follow the rules."

What, *what?* Follow the rules? Alex's shock flashed to anger. "Five seconds ago, you said the rules—"

"Don't presume to correct me!" Jess cut her off with a vicious swipe of her hand. "You will be *quiet*, young woman. Stop spouting about things you know nothing about. Is that understood?"

Sarah's eyes were round as pie plates. Alex was mortified. If the floor had opened up to swallow her, that would've been fine. "Yes, ma'am."

"Excellent." Jess favored Alex with a frosty glare. "I'm so glad we cleared that up. Now, I'm sure there's something useful needs doing somewhere." She swept from the room.

"Wow," Kincaid said after a moment. "Bet you really *could* hear a pin drop."

52

Kincaid waved off Sarah's offer of more tea. "Thank you, no. I got to get back. Alex, walk with me a second, okay?"

Alex said nothing until they were outside and heading for the front walk. Then she looked up at Kincaid. "What was that all—"

"Hush." Kincaid put up a warning hand, and then she saw their house guard straightening from his slouch. Kincaid hooked a thumb over his shoulder. "I got her, Greg. You want, there's hot tea inside. Jess or Sarah'll give you a cup."

"How about Tori?" Greg's breath chugged like a steam engine. He was younger than Alex, maybe fourteen, with a halo of muddy brown curls fringing a watch cap. His cheeks were red as beets from windburn. "She inside?"

"No, but she should be back soon. Sure she'd love to see you." Kincaid clapped the boy on the shoulder. "Bet she could scrounge up a sandwich or two."

"Yeah, that'd be good. If you think it's okay. If you don't think Chris'll be back. He looked mad enough to spit nails."

"Oh, I think Chris is done for the day."

"Okay." Greg gestured toward his golden, whose bushy tail and fluffy ruff were chunky with ice and snow. "Daisy needs a little time to defrost, anyway."

"Then go on in before you catch your death," Kincaid said. They'd already taken Alex's horse, Honey, to a three-car garage down the block that had been converted into a stable. Kincaid's horse was tethered to a tree at the curb, and as he unclipped the lead, he glanced over his shoulder, saw Greg and Daisy disappear into the house, and said to Alex, "You okay?"

"Yeah," she said. "But that was so embarrassing."

"That's what happens when you behave like an ass."

"Thanks."

"You'll get over it."

"But what was that all about? One second Jess is chewing Chris out for not breaking rules and then she's yelling at me to follow them."

He flicked another look over his shoulder. "Look, it's too much to explain right now, but I would watch what I say around the house."

"What for?"

"Let's just say that there are . . . factions. People taking sides. Not everybody's happy with the way things are going, and you don't want the wrong people talking to the *other* wrong people."

Factions? Wrong people? "What is this place? Are you a cult or, you know, one of those really religious . . ." She groped for the right word. "You said you're not Mormons or something, but like the Amish? Some kind of weird sect? Things seem so *decided*."

That wasn't exactly the word she was looking for either, and then, too late, she realized that if Kincaid was a believer, she'd probably just managed to insult him. She thought about apologizing, but figured it wouldn't do any good.

Kincaid studied her for a long few seconds. "Considering some of my best friends are Amish, I might take offense. They're not weird, or a cult. They're gentle, good people."

"You know what I mean."

"Yeah, I do." But he didn't smile. "I don't pretend to understand everything. As a doc, though, I've seen what happens when people are under a lot of stress. Doesn't always bring out their best. When people are scared, they get angry. They'll do things they never thought they would. They'll bargain and compromise in order to survive; they'll chase after miracle cures and believe just about anything so long as it gives them hope. When hope fails, then watch out. Some people get brutal. They'll turn on each other; they'll become their own worst enemies."

He could've been talking about her life. How many specialists had Aunt Hannah insisted on? What were the PEBBLES, those little rocks in her brain, but a last-ditch effort? When her parents had died, Alex refused to believe it until she saw their bodies. Her aunt hadn't wanted her to, which was understandable; between the impact and the fireball, her parents were reduced to a charred jumble of blackened limbs and too-white teeth. Her grief—such a small word for such a monstrous feeling—was almost too much to bear, and Alex had lashed out at everyone with a sort of desperate fury.

It was, she thought now, exactly what Jess had just said: anger was easier to bear than grief. Rage tricked her into thinking she might still change something. That acceptance was defeat.

"So when it's the end of the world," Kincaid was saying, "people who didn't give a darn before suddenly become believers. If there was a core of believers to begin with, then they take control. This village has always been . . . well, *conservative*'s a good word, and then some. The Council's only the tip of the iceberg."

"Are you? A believer, I mean?"

"I believe in living, and I'm old enough to take the bad with the good. Maybe I'm only rationalizing things, but I like to think I'm doing some good here. And to be honest, living here beats the alternative."

"What about Jess?"

"She would"—Kincaid chose his words with care—"*change* a few things. Like she said, the price for us being left alone is a bit steep. People are scared, though. No one wants to make waves, especially not now. You live long enough, comes a time when it's easier to just go along to get along. I agree with her in principle, but I'm not sure we can afford the alternative."

Meaning . . . what? That these old people were tired out? That they were looking to people like Chris? Her? Maybe. If Rule was owned by the Council but a Yeager was always the final arbiter, then Jess would press *Chris*, hoping that Chris would command the respect that his grandfather did. But to change what? "Why can't Jess say something? Or get together a committee or . . . whatever?"

Kincaid looked like he'd sucked on a lemon. "No power. Majority rules, and the majority's with the Council and the Rev."

Yeah, meaning majority men. "Are you with Reverend Yeager?"

"I'm not against him on principle. I see the logic of it. If we're going to survive this, we need to maintain order. I disagree with the execution."

And adults say we're *evasive.* "So change it."

"Not as simple as you think, kiddo. Besides, it's one thing to criticize. It's another to have a better idea. I don't know that I do. Even if I did, I'm not the man for that."

"But Chris is?" She shook her head. "Lena was right. Why are you waiting around for us to clean up your mess? You guys are cowards."

"Yeah," said Kincaid. "That's fair."

"One thing I gotta know," said Kincaid. He threw the Appaloosa's reins over its head. "What happened between you and the Rev? After he threw me out, that is."

She remembered Ernst's admonition: *Some secrets are best kept behind closed doors.* "Why?"

"Alex, I've seen a lot of Spared with the Rev, and this is the first time I ever saw a Spared nail it. You *knew* what was going on with him."

"I just guessed."

"Bull. How did you know? Only me and the Council and a couple others know about him and that . . . *touch* thing he's got going."

"Um . . . well, I guess it was the only thing that made sense."

"Don't give me that crap. Look, I'm not the enemy here. I just want to understand what's going on."

"Weren't you the one who just told me to watch my mouth around the wrong people?"

"Yes, but in case you haven't noticed, I'm one of those *right* people." Kincaid's eyes shifted toward the house. Alex followed his gaze and saw Jess staring from a window. When she saw them looking, the older woman inclined her head in a small nod, then twitched the curtains closed. Kincaid said, "You trust me?"

Despite what Ernst had said, she trusted Kincaid about as much as she trusted anyone in this place, maybe because his scent reminded her so much of her father. During their conversation, that smell had not changed; there was none of the bite she associated with a lie. And he seemed to be going out of his way to help her. So she said, "I guess."

"Then trust me now. How did you know about his . . . well, I call it a super-sense. His is touch. And yours?"

She licked her lips. "I smelled him."

Kincaid's eyebrows crawled for his hairline. "Smell? As in a scent?"

She nodded. "It was the same way I figured out that Harlan was there. Harlan has . . . had a certain scent I recognized."

"You saying Yeager has a scent? You *smell* him?"

"Well, when you say it like that, it sounds like he's got BO, but . . . yeah. Everyone has a scent. Some are more"—she searched for the word—"*concentrated* than other people. A lot of the times I think what I smell is how they feel." She explained about her sudden flashes of memory. "Like I associate the scent with a memory that gives me a certain feeling, and then I know what they're feeling. It doesn't always work, because there are some things I just can't put a name to. Like . . . you know, a squirrel smell is a squirrel smell."

"Do I got one?"

"Yeah. You smell like leather and"—she thought about it—"baby powder."

"Well, leather's good. If I weren't such a manly man, I might have trouble with baby powder, though." He grinned. "What about the Rev?"

"Opaque. Like really dense fog, or, you know, how cloudy glass has that cold smell. I couldn't really get a read on him, and then when I guessed about his, you know, *touch*, I could tell he was surprised because it was like something suddenly opened up and then I smelled rain. I think that means it was raining when it happened for him."

"That," said Kincaid, "is true. It *was* raining here that day. The glass smell is interesting, too. What do you make of it?"

"I think he was staring out of a window."

A smile flirted with Kincaid's mouth. "Yeah, that's true, too."

"How do you know?"

"Because I was sitting next to him when it happened."

"Where?"

"Where we were living, along with all the other Awakened," Kincaid said. "In the Alzheimer's wing of the hospice."

53

Alex gaped. "You were a patient? You had *Alzheimer's?*"

"Yeah. Why do you think we're called the Awakened? I wasn't terminal, but I was close. Stage six. Believe me, no one was more surprised than me to wake up in diapers. Thank God, I was dry."

"How can you *joke* about something like that?" All she could think of was Kincaid, crapping in his pants and drooling. "I don't think that's very funny."

Kincaid hunched his shoulders in a shrug. "At my age? You learn not to take things so seriously. Anyway, I woke up in front of the picture window strapped to a wheelchair, and the tech—young fella, maybe thirty—he's dead as a doornail. Try working your way out of those straps without help. Those things are geriatric straitjackets. Take a Houdini to get out of one. Near about strangled myself." He looked at her and laughed. "You know, you don't shut that mouth of yours, you're going to be catching flies."

"How many of you are there?"

"Awakened? Just five, including me and the Rev."

"So, do you . . . can you sense . . . ?"

"Nope. I'm just me. Besides the Rev, there's only one other person has something similar. Hears stuff a long way off, kind of like a bat, I guess, but with nuance, which can come in handy. You're the only one can sense *them*, though. You're like the dogs that way, when they catch a whiff of the Changed." He favored her with that one-eyed squint. "But you, they see you as a friend. More than that, they'll *protect* you. So you must have changed another way, too. Pheromones, probably."

The word was familiar. Something from biology . . . "What are those?"

"Chemicals made by the body that produce certain odors that trigger certain responses. As far as I know, all animals make them. So do a lot of insects. That's how bees and ants communicate, for example." Kincaid's lips turned in a regretful grin. "I always thought my wife smelled like lilies. After she died, I hung on to her clothes for the longest time. Walking into her closet was like getting wrapped up in a hug."

She remembered how Tom had smelled, that complex spice that made her dizzy and hungry for his touch, and a hollow ache that she recognized as grief settled in her chest.

Kincaid saw the look on her face, and misinterpreted. "Thanks, kiddo. You never quite get over losing someone you love, but I'm okay." He squeezed her shoulder. "Now, there's nothing we can do about the dogs deciding you're their new best friend, but we can spin the Harlan thing pretty easy. We'll just say you recognized him, okay? The Rev is right about keeping this super-smell thing under wraps. Don't even tell Chris."

"Don't worry about that." She wasn't tempted to tell Chris anything. That Kincaid assumed she might confide in him was a little alarming. *Maybe they're already seeing us as a couple. Maybe that's why Jess badgered him into being my escort when he wanted to bail.* "Would people really try to hurt me?"

"It's a possibility. They might think you got some agenda. This super-sense-of-smell thing you got going . . . it's a blessing and a curse. Good for us because you might catch kids the dogs don't— and they have missed a few."

A vision of children being paraded past for her inspection floated into her mind. "I don't want to do that."

Kincaid gave her a hard look. "You're a smart girl, so don't make me spell this out for you. We need to use every advantage we got—and that includes you. But that's also where it could be a problem, because then it's your word against theirs. You can't see or touch a smell."

"You guys always believe Yeager."

"Yeager's one of the Five Families. He's head of the Council now."

Yeah, *now* . . . but she couldn't believe they'd let some demented guy decide policy. So who had called the shots before Yeager Awakened? "I wouldn't lie."

"You know that, and I know that. Yeager and the Council would know, but why would regular folks trust you? If what you can do gets out, then somebody else just might decide they've got a super-sense, too. In other words, they *would* lie. Even with the Council and the Rev to say otherwise, things could get pretty nasty. See what I'm saying? We could have our little version of the Salem Witch Trials, and we got no time for that kind of crap."

She had never considered this, but she could see the logic. In school, your reputation could rest on a rumor. "Okay."

"Good. Now if you *do* sense something off, you tell me or the Rev, period. You got that?"

And not any of the other Council members . . . That was interesting. "What are you going to do if someone else pops up with a super-sense?"

"We'll deal with it then. I don't think it's as common as all that, anyway." That one-eyed squint again. "You got any ideas why this might have happened to you?"

She felt a small flutter of alarm. "No." When he said nothing, she added, "Really."

"Mmm." Kincaid's mouth screwed to a pucker. "You know, I'm not like Yeager, but I do believe that's the first lie you've told me, Alex, and here's why. All the survivors—us older people—our brains are different even from people who are in their forties, fifties. Sleep patterns are way different, for one; we don't dream as much as younger people."

She thought about Tom and his broken sleep, as well as her monster and that nightmare. "Would it only be sleep then? Dreams?"

"A magic bullet? No, probably a combination of things that tip the balance. Older people's brains just aren't as spry as they used to be. Our brains don't make as many neurochemicals. Now, that's not uniform; there are some very sharp ninety-year-olds. I knew one, in fact, but the hell of it is, he died right away, too. Like he was forty instead of ninety."

"Meaning what?"

"Well, let's just think about it for a second. This . . . *Zap*, as you call it, was a whole bunch of high-intensity EMPs, right? Well, what are those but electrical discharges, and what is the brain but an organ that relies on what is, in essence, electricity to function? A brain is like a hive of bees; all the cells have to be firing in the right order, or you've got chaos: a bunch of bees going every which way and nothing getting done."

She thought she saw where he was going. "So if you zap the brain with enough of a charge, you'd create chaos? Release a flood of neurochemicals? Why would that matter?"

"Alex, what do you think a seizure is? It's that chaos thing again: a bunch of brain cells firing in an uncoordinated manner. Plus, seizures can kill you. The brain can seize up and stop working, and the person will die. So what I'm thinking is that older people, whose brains already don't work as well as when they were younger, were protected. They got knocked for a loop when the Zap hit, but they didn't die. Those of us who were bad off—the Awakened—our brains were like little raisins. So, for us, the Zap kind of woke us up, primed our brains to make chemicals we'd been missing. I think it's probably more complicated than that, but you get the general idea."

She did, but that still didn't answer why Tom had lived. Or her—unless she was right about the monster having done enough damage to save her. "But then what about kids?"

"Don't know. Kids' brains aren't set in stone. They're still growing

and developing. I know for a fact that kids can survive brain inju-
ries, like cold-water drownings, that would kill or cripple an adult.
The older you get, the less able your brain is to absorb an injury and
adapt. I guess there's just a natural cutoff where the injury gets to
be too much for the brain to handle. In the context of the Zap, that
means the majority of adults couldn't absorb the trauma and they
flat-out died."

"What about the Change?"

"Based on what we've seen, I think it's got to do with brain
development and hormones."

"Tom and I wondered the same thing." She told Kincaid about
meeting Larry and Deidre.

Kincaid bobbed his head in a nod. "That fits. Hormones would
also explain why kids are still Changing as they get older."

Her thoughts darted to Ellie. "You mean, every little kid is going
to Change?"

"Maybe. So far, that looks to be true. On the other hand, it's only
been a couple of months, and so maybe whatever changed in their
brains will repair itself. The really young ones—babies and toddlers,
kindergartners—they might have a chance. But maybe not."

A whole generation of kids Changing? The thought sent a shiver
down her spine. "But then why have some of *us* Changed and not
others?"

"The Spared? I don't know what's going on with you all; why
you and people like Chris and Peter and this Tom of yours didn't
change. Your brains are probably different somehow, but I'll be
damned if I know."

She hesitated a moment. "You said that old people's sleep and dreams are different. I think something bad happened to Tom in Afghanistan—enough so he . . . he didn't sleep much and never for very long."

Kincaid's eyebrows arched. "Post-traumatic stress? Hmm. I never thought of that. Could be, though."

"Why?"

"Because the brains of people with PTSD show permanent changes, and the symptoms reinforce the damage, and then the damage means more symptoms. That's why PTSD is so hard to treat. People can learn to function, but it's an injury the brain just never recovers from." Kincaid huffed out a silent laugh, like a dog. "If I wasn't just a country doctor and got a big enough sample of kids and had a fancy laboratory and could do all kinds of tests, maybe I'd figure it out, but that's not ever happening. One thing I do know, though: all of us Awakened, we got some kind of brain damage, by definition, and now I'm thinking that some of the older kids who should've changed didn't because their brains and hormones were somehow different." He paused. "You see where I'm going with this, right?"

Her stomach tightened in a sudden twist of fear. "Not really."

"Alex, I may not be the sharpest knife in the drawer, but I am a doctor and I can put two and two together. The Rev had bad brain damage, and he's got a super-sense. We got another Awakened with super-hearing. But you are the only kid I know who's both Spared *and* got a super-sense. So, Alex, I got to know," Kincaid said, with his best one-eyed squint, "what *exactly* is living in that head of yours?"

54

"Are you okay?" Sarah said. She halted as Ghost snuffled around a tree. "You've been really quiet all night."

"Just tired." Alex hunched her shoulders as the wind forked up a fistful of icy snow and sent it whirling in a sparkling arabesque in the light of their torch. She could see the bulky silhouette of their guard a few steps ahead and the flash of snow splintering the harsh white light of his lantern.

"I'm really sorry about what happened," Sarah said.

"Happened?"

"Yes. At the courthouse? That's all over town—about how you recognized that man, Harlan? Peter told me that Harlan left that little girl alone out there."

"Ellie. Yeah," Alex said, a little ashamed now, because she'd not been thinking about Ellie but Kincaid. He might call himself a country doctor, but he was sharp enough to guess about the monster. She supposed she could've lied; there was no way Kincaid could look inside her brain, after all. But telling him had been kind of a relief.

What he'd said about the monster was interesting, too: *You don't know that the tumor's gone or dead or dormant. Maybe the Zap shorted it out. Or maybe all those EMPs organized it somehow, made it functional instead of destructive, like another lobe of your brain.*

Or maybe both. She recalled how sick—chemo-sick—she'd felt right after the attacks. She'd assumed the Zap caused that, but her brain was chock-full of PEBBLES loaded with a new and experimental drug. Barrett hadn't been able to get the PEBBLES to dump their payload; the light probes hadn't worked. But light was just a visible form of electromagnetic radiation—a different kind of EMP. So maybe the Zap—from all those EMPs—was strong enough to trigger the PEBBLES. The monster had either died or altered in some way, and so had she.

She could share none of this with Sarah. "It's okay. I mean, it's not. I understand why Chris didn't want to go after Ellie, but . . ." She let out a breath that the wind stole. "Doesn't make it feel any better."

Sarah was quiet as they waited for Ghost to finish. "I think they're doing the best they can," she said finally. "You know, to give us homes and stuff."

"That's not the same as being happy or free."

"People did try to kill you," Sarah pointed out. "I'll bet a bunch of them would kill all of us if they could."

Larry: *You're an endangered species.* "Yeah, but then who'd be left? Lena's right. They need us. I mean, have you seen some of these guys? They're *really* old. Eventually, they're going to, you know, break down. They need us to take care of them."

"Well," said Sarah, "I don't know if that's the only—"

There came the sudden distant stutter of gunfire. The shots were very quick, nearly overlapping. *Rifles*, Alex thought. Ghost flinched, tried to scurry between Alex's legs, and only succeeded in winding his leash around her calves. At the end of the block, she saw their guard hurrying back to them.

"You girls about done?" he asked. His own dog—a long-haired mutt—swished around Alex and then stood patiently as the puppy nipped at the other dog's neck and did the *I'm-so-thrilled-to-see-you* squiggle.

"Who are they shooting at?" asked Alex.

The guard simultaneously shrugged his shoulders and shook his head. "Could be some Changed, but they don't bother us much anymore. Ten to one, it's raiders. Night's when they try to come in through the woods. Stupid, you ask me."

"Why?" asked Alex.

"Because *they* come out at night, too," Sarah said.

"Double the risk, double your fun," said the guard, doing the cold man's two-step. "We got our perimeter, which means they got to make it through the Zone, avoid the Changed, and slip in through the perimeter without us catching them. Only way to do that is come out by day, hunker down in the Zone, and wait. Ones we don't get at night, we get come daylight."

Well, that answered the question of the shots Alex had heard that morning. The image of Rule's guards combing the woods to pick off strays bothered her. She bet Peter wouldn't have a problem with it. Would Chris? Was he out there now?

So what if he is? She felt a nip of impatience. *Who cares what Chris thinks or where he is?*

Still, the thought nagged at her, and what made her even angrier was what she felt when she pictured Chris taking risks out there in the dark.

Worried.

Back at the house, Jess was sewing by candlelight, and seemed unconcerned. Alex figured she was probably used to the nightly gunfight at the O.K. Corral. She and Sarah said good night to Jess and the guard, who seemed happy enough to thaw out by the woodstove.

"That dog stays downstairs," Jess said when Ghost tried following Alex. She handed Alex and Sarah red rubber hot-water bottles and a lit candle, then bent to scoop up the puppy. "Oh, aren't you a brute?" she scolded, and then laughed as the puppy's tongue darted for her chin. "He'll be fine in his bed down here. If you girls want to double up, though, you might be warmer."

"Uh," said Alex, and glanced at Sarah, who shrugged. "It's okay with me," said Sarah.

"Good. You should both stay in Alex's room then. It's right over the kitchen," said Jess.

Pushing through the anvil of cold air solidly wedged on the stairs was an act of will. It was so cold, their breath steamed in the light of the single candle Jess had given them. Tori's bedroom door was closed. A towel-covered tray of food was still squared before Lena's door. When she'd come back after her job at the laundry—Alex didn't envy Lena one bit—Lena had gone straight upstairs and refused to come down.

Crouching, Sarah peeked under the towel. "She hasn't touched it," she whispered.

"She'll just bite your head off. Come on, she'll eat when she's hungry," Alex hissed back, thinking only of diving beneath the covers. Even with the hot water bottle tucked around her feet, there was no way she was sleeping without socks and long johns.

Sarah lingered a moment longer, then followed. After they'd washed—the icy water gave Alex brain freeze when she brushed her teeth—then swiftly changed and crawled under a double feather quilt, Sarah whispered, "She's really not so bad, you know."

"What?" Being in bed with Sarah had dredged up thoughts of Ellie, and Alex had to think a second. "Who, Lena? Only if you don't mind permanent PMS."

"She had it really rough before. She doesn't talk about it much."

"Did she really run away from here?"

"Yeah, about three weeks after she got here. She was trying to go back up north. I think she's still got family up near Oren."

Amish country, she thought, remembering the sign she'd seen months ago at that Quik-Mart. "Wow. Like, how old?"

"Old enough to be dead, young enough to be Changed. Her mom's dead, for sure. I think her dad died years ago. She said that she, her mom, and a couple brothers were living with her grandparents. They might be alive."

"Then how'd she end up here if she still had family?"

"I never asked, but I don't think she liked home much. Anyway, when she ran, she only got about a mile into the Zone—"

"Zone?" The guard had said that, too.

"Yeah, like 'buffer zone,' the cushion between Rule and everybody else. The dogs caught her. That's another reason she hates them so much."

"A mile's still pretty far. That means she had to slip an escort, too."

"Well, she got pretty friendly with the guards. I think she bribed one by, you know . . ."

"No, I—" And then she got it. "Oh, that's just gross."

"Some of these guys are gross," Sarah said matter-of-factly. "They only *look* like grandpas. Anyway, that's why Jess always has to be around when the older guys come in. If a guy our age visits, though, she leaves so we can, you know, talk and stuff. They want us to get to know those guys."

"What happened to the guard that Lena . . . you know . . ."

"They Banned him, like they did with that guy you recognized."

"And people just nicely decide not to sneak back in?"

"I guess when they know they'll be shot, they decide not to."

"No way."

"Way. Reverend Yeager's really strict about it. Like, once he's decided you're Banned, that's it. There are a lot of guards in the woods."

"Like, walking around?" She wasn't sure she'd want to be out there after dark, even with a rifle.

Sarah shook her head. "Tree stands. You have to know where

to look. Even then, they move around, so you can't predict where they'll be."

"You know a lot about this."

"Oh. Well . . . Peter and I are . . . we talk." The way Sarah said that, Alex thought they maybe did a lot more than just talk—in which case, Tori was in for a major disappointment.

"So what do you have to do to get permission to leave?" asked Alex.

"Why would anyone want to?"

"Well," Alex said, momentarily flustered, "what if you want to try and find family or something? I mean, if I wanted to."

"Oh, we'll never get permission. They got us, they're going to keep us."

Rule, Alex thought, was like a commercial for an insecticide: roaches check in, but they don't check out. "And you're okay with that?"

"Well, sure," said Sarah. "I mean, it's not like we've got a ton of choices."

That made her think of something Lena had mentioned that made no sense. "Is that what they mean by Chosen? Like, is it the same as Spared?"

"No. Chosen means that someone picks you."

"Picks you?"

"Yeah." A pause. "A guy."

"A guy?"

"Yeah. A guy, you know, decides . . . that he wants . . . you know . . ."

"What?" Alex said, much louder than she intended. "They *give* us to a guy? To go live with him?"

"Yeah, but not with any of the old ones," Sarah said reasonably. "They give us to guys our age. One of them picks one of us, and if the Council says it's okay, then we go live with him. We get our own house, which is way better than here. Anyway, the idea is we live together and get to know each other." She paused. "It's like that old Amish thing. You know, bundling? Only we get to live together, not just get in the same bed."

Neither sounded good. "Are you serious? You're serious. Are we . . . if a guy picks us, do they expect us to, you know, *sleep* with him?"

"If we want to, I guess. It would be normal. Not right away, of course . . ." Sarah faltered. "No one's supposed to force us. But . . . sure. I mean, that's what people living together do."

No, that's what people in love do. Even if they lock you in some guy's house, they can't make you feel that way. "And they've done this to some girls already? It's only been a couple of months."

She felt Sarah nod. "I think they were doing it before for a real long time. All I know is no one's asked to go back. The Council says you can if you want to, but no one has. I mean, think about it. You get your own house. You make up your own rules . . . well, pretty much. It's not like you get to go wherever you want, but it's not safe outside Rule anyway, so who cares?"

My God, no matter what Kincaid said, it was *like a cult.* "So no one has ever refused."

"Well, I think Lena was worried that this one guy was going to ask." Sarah sighed. "It was Peter, okay?"

"I thought Tori liked Peter."

"Tori." A snort. "Peter is *so* not interested. Greg's got this complete crush on her, though. It's kind of embarrassing, you know? Like a seventh grader asking out a senior."

"So what happened with Lena and Peter?"

"He started hanging around a lot and asking to walk her places . . . you know."

"Like a date?"

"About as close as you get to one in Rule, yeah. I think that's how she figured out which guard was working where. After they brought her back, Peter was so mad, he wanted her Banned, but you'd have to pretty much murder someone for that to happen to one of us, and even then I'm not sure the Reverend would do it. We're really valuable."

"What if we say no?"

"Well, I wouldn't say no to Peter," Sarah said. "And if you're smart, you won't say no to Chris either."

55

Sarah fell asleep soon after. Alex stared into the shadows on the ceiling, her brain going like a runaway train.

She had been so stupid. How could she not have seen this? This was why people kept saying that she—and every other girl—was so valuable: because a girl could be paired up with a guy. Hell, the way things were going, maybe a girl would end up paired with more than one.

Because they were valuable. Because they could make babies.

It really was the end of the world as she had known it.

Rule wasn't a sanctuary.

It was a prison.

But Sarah was wrong. Alex had not one, not two, but *three* choices.

One: She could go along with the rules and hope that some guy who wasn't totally gross picked her. Maybe Chris, for that matter.

Two: She could make some noise. Her father had trained her well. She was easily as good a shot as any of the guys on patrol and maybe better than some. Riding couldn't be that tough. So she could get herself assigned to a patrol. She did have something to offer, after all, and her super-sense—if, say, she told Chris or Peter—would come in handy. She wasn't exactly sure what she'd do if she actually had to shoot someone who wasn't Changed. On the other hand, if she ran into another Harlan, that might not be such a problem. Anyway, the point was to get out of Rule. So, once she'd been on a couple patrols and they loosened up, she could just ride on out—and not come back.

Three: She could grab her parents' ashes and run like hell. Which would, as it happened, be pretty much coming full circle, picking up where she'd left off when this whole nightmare started.

The first option completely creeped her out. She didn't want to be given away to anyone. And making babies? She couldn't think about that without her skin getting all crawly. And where it would stop? There was no guarantee she'd end up with anyone she even liked. Men made the decisions in Rule. Jess was a strong woman; for all Alex knew, these were some of the things Jess wanted Chris to change. Yet, despite all her bluster, Jess bowed to the will of the men.

Either way, option one was a complete nonstarter.

The second option was a possibility.

If she got herself assigned to a patrol, she could figure the best way to get the hell out of here. They couldn't keep her glued to one of them forever. Eventually, they would have to trust her. She could picture it: out on horseback, and one of them—Chris—would say, *You check over there; I'll check here.* By the time he thought to look for her, she would be gone.

So how to get on patrol? She had to talk to someone. Peter? Yeah, Peter would like that she knew guns. Maybe she could even tell him about her spidey-sense? Yeah, but how would she demonstrate something like that? Kincaid had believed her because he was one of the Awakened, and he knew about Yeager's supersense. But if no one else knew . . . Kincaid had said it was subjective: no way to prove that what she said was the truth, unless she fingered someone.

Chris . . . she didn't know about him. She might be able to work on him, but it wasn't like she was all that experienced. And playing up to Chris made her uneasy, and not just because she didn't want to encourage this whole Tarzan-Jane thing. With Peter, what you saw was what you got; Chris lived too much in the shadows, and she had this sense that he was always watching her—watching *for* her—trying to figure her out.

And what would Chris do if he knew about her? Bad enough that Kincaid had guessed about the monster. Not even Yeager had put that together; the Rev seemed to accept her ability as an Act of God kind of thing.

Wow, wait a minute. If Chris or Peter found out about the monster, she bet either—both—would figure they could trade her for someone who might, you know, *live*. They'd drop-kick her out of town if they knew about the monster. . . . And wasn't that what she wanted?

Well, yeah, but not like that. When she left, she wanted it to be on her terms, when she was ready. For that, she would need supplies—enough for a month, she figured, and that meant MREs mostly. Three days' worth of trail mix and an egg-salad sandwich just wouldn't cut it. She'd need bleach to purify water, or tablets. A sleeping bag, a tarp, water bottles. Her busy mind ticked over the items: flint, waterproof matches, snare wire, lint for tinder. . . . She would have to make a list.

She still had the boot knife Tom had given her. In all the fuss, they'd overlooked that. She'd squirreled the knife beneath her mattress first, then thought that was too obvious. So she hid the knife where she thought no one would think to look: in Ghost's bag of dog food, all the way at the bottom. Just so long as she kept an eye on his kibbles, she was golden. But she would need a gun. Her Glock, if she could find it again, and a rifle would be good. Ammunition, several bricks, if she could find out where they kept all that. Maybe a bow? No, too big. Same thing with a rifle, but a gun for sure. Without question. And a place to hide everything until she got herself on a patrol . . .

But which way to run?

Lena.

Lena had tried. Lena would know. Would have a rough idea anyway. Yeah, but Lena wasn't stupid. If Alex started nosing around, asking questions, Lena would put it together. Lena would want in, and that was a recipe for disaster.

Once she ran, how long would they try to find her? Maybe only as long as they figured she was worth keeping . . . which brought her around to full disclosure about the monster, and that was no good.

Bringing her around to Door Number Three.

Just cut and run. *Soon.*

If she could lie low for a couple weeks, play along while she got stuff together, she might pull it off. No need to get herself put on patrol. In fact, it might be better if she hung around town, figured out its rhythms and who went where. Get people to trust her and see her as a familiar figure. The familiar was usually invisible; how many people really noticed everything they saw?

Plus, Rule needed supplies. For that, they would need Chris and Peter and a bunch of guys. A bunch of horses, a bunch of wagons, and men to ride as escort, like the old wagon trains. That might be the time to boogie: when a lot of the guys were out of town and everyone else was covering their butts.

Carefully, she eased out of bed, wincing at every squeak of the bedsprings, but Sarah was deep asleep and didn't stir. Crossing to the window, she slid a finger between the curtains and peered out. She heard the soft patter of snow against glass but saw nothing. The night was deep and dark and vast. With no streetlights or bob of a flashlight or even a helpful cigarette, she could only guess where the guard kept himself, and he probably moved around, if only to stay warm. It occurred to her that she didn't know if they had a kind of shelter or guard-box, which would make the most sense. Hanging out in a snowstorm couldn't be good for any person, even a younger guy her age, and she couldn't imagine some poor schnook hunkering down all night on the porch with a rifle in his lap. It was more likely that there were mounted patrols, like cops in New York City. She would have to find out.

And what about the dogs?

Crap.

If she happened to pass by—and she *would*, there was no help for that—they would give her away. She was every dog's best friend. Taking Ghost with her was one thing, but having an entire pack . . . Yeah, but could she use that somehow? She flashed to an image of assembling an army of dogs: *Go, fetch, play dead!* Not bloody likely, as Aunt Hannah would say.

The cold seeped through the glass and broke over her face. She thought of herself out there, alone, struggling through drifts. Even with snowshoes and skis, it would be hard going. Her window of opportunity was closing, and fast. Winter would only get worse.

So, how to avoid getting caught—or, worse, being mistaken for a raider and shot? Maybe duck out the southwest corner, hightail it for the old mine, then loop back north and head . . . where?

Minnesota. The border. Canada. If Tom was still alive, that's where he'd go. A lot of ground to cover and a big country besides, but if Tom was alive . . .

If Tom was alive . . .

"Tom." She exhaled his name in a soft whisper, watching as her breath fogged the window and then slowly cleared, leaving only a memory that there'd been anything there at all.

Saying his name brought on that hollow ache again. If Tom wasn't dead, where was he? What had happened to him? Was he looking for her? No, he'd have gotten here by now; he knew she was going to Rule. But if he was alive and he was thinking about her at the same moment she was thinking about him, maybe . . .

She closed her eyes. She forced herself to be very still, wrestled her thoughts to gray, and yet opened her memory to his smell, that strange and spicy scent that was Tom.

She saw and felt him in flashes: Tom in the light of the fire, Tom as he held her the night they found the radio, Tom as a silhouette keeping watch over her. Tom's lips. Tom's hand in her hair. His taste . . .

She didn't know if the tightness in her throat or the fullness in her heart meant that he was there; that they were connected somehow. Maybe all that she saw and felt was the sensual fullness of memory: that which abided and was nothing but the ghost of a touch, the whisper of a word, the lingering of a scent.

But she felt him just the same, and thought that, maybe, this was why some people didn't mind being haunted.

56

By morning, she'd decided that for the time being, she would follow the rules. *Recon*—that's what Tom would've called it. Work with Kincaid at the hospice, which doubled as Rule's hospital. Learn who went where. Get her bearings, gather supplies, and then, when the time was right, get herself gone.

School was a joke. She was way more advanced than her teachers could handle, and by lunchtime of the first day, the principal figured she might as well spend all her time with Kincaid.

Chris was waiting in the hall outside the principal's office to escort her to the hospice. He and the principal exchanged greetings, and then the principal said, "Chris, think you can scare up a few more copies of *Robinson Crusoe*? Say, ten? Oh, also *Island of the Blue Dolphins*, anything by Cleary or Dahl . . ."

As they headed for the front door of the church, Alex said, "You can really find those?"

"Probably not." Chris held the door, then followed her out into the cold. The sun was shining for a change. Squinting, he rooted around in a breast pocket, pulled out a pair of aviator sunglasses, and slid them on. Alex felt a quick sting of envy. The sun was bright enough to hurt, and she put up a hand to block the glare. He said, "You don't have sunglasses?"

"I did," she said, with faint annoyance. She wasn't stupid. "They were in my pack."

"Sorry," he said. "I wasn't criticizing."

"No big deal." *Recon*, she thought. "So where *do* you get books?"

"Some in town, but the closest library's three, four days out, so that's not really an option. Too many men and wagons tied up to make it worthwhile. Most of the houses for twenty miles around have been cleaned out already, if they haven't gone up in flames."

She unclipped Honey's lead, then swung into the saddle. The snow came halfway to Honey's knees. She would have to trade up for a larger horse soon. Either that or just ski to the hospice. Which might be a way of getting skis, come to think of it, and maybe a pair of snowshoes. "Yeah, I saw that. Burned-out houses. I don't get it."

Chris guided his blood bay, Night, and fell in alongside as they crossed the village green before taking a side street north toward the hospice. "Raiders, mostly. People who take what they can, then torch the rest. They're not as organized or big as we are, or they'd have taken over Rule by now. But what they're doing is kind of an interesting strategy."

"Why?"

He regarded her from behind his dark glasses. "Burn out more people. They head here. Word gets around. The more people we take in, the farther out we're forced to go to find things. The farther from Rule we have to go, the easier we are to pick off. That's why we limit who we take in, but even so, we're taking more risks now than before, traveling days sometimes to find what we need. Things might get easier once we can plant again, but until then we're as dependent as everyone else on what we can scavenge."

"Is that what happened last night? Raiders tried to get into town?"

He nodded. "We lost three men."

"What about the raiders?"

"Got two, but two got away. Next time, I'm following them. I don't care what Peter says. If we could follow them to their camp or town or wherever, we could finish them off and take what they've found. One less group to worry about, and more for us."

"But they're not Changed. They're just people trying to survive, Chris."

"Who are trying to take what we've got."

"If you talked to them, maybe cooperated . . ."

"There's no talking with these guys."

"How do you know that? Have you tried?" When he didn't reply, she pressed: "Chris, you can't just go around killing people and taking what they have."

"Why not?" He kept his shuttered eyes on the road. "They'd kill us if they got the chance."

The hospice was small: four wings, sixty beds, and only twenty of those occupied by true hospice patients. Most were in the terminal stages of cancer or lung disease. "Miners, a lot of them,"

Kincaid said as they stopped outside a dayroom. "We're just trying to make them comfortable."

She swept her eyes over the scatter of patients—old men, mostly, with portable green oxygen tanks—slumped in overstuffed chairs. Most were dozing, although some played checkers or chess. A few shuffled greasy cards for games of solitaire. The sight depressed her, and the smell of antiseptic soap brought back too many memories, all of them bad.

She turned to see Kincaid's eyes on her. "You won't be working here much," he said. "We got dedicated hospice staff still around for this."

"It's okay," she said, although she was relieved. She could too easily see herself here. Back when the only thing she'd had to worry about was, oh, imminent death, she'd visited a few hospices for people her age and thought that waiting around to die with strangers was even nuttier than waiting around to die at Aunt Hannah's. "How are you getting your tanks?"

"The way we get everything." He started off down the hall, motioning for her to follow. "Either the guys out foraging bring 'em back, or they don't. Right now, mostly they don't. If it's a choice between our guys grabbing a wagonload of antibiotics and bandages versus a couple oxygen tanks . . . it's not a contest."

"What are you going to do when you run out of supplies?" Alex asked. Foraging was all well and good, but there had to be limits to what they could stockpile. Judging from the nightly rifle fire, Kincaid must see his share of wounded.

"Triage," Kincaid said briefly, like that explained something. She knew the word; her mother had worked the emergency room. But sorting the wounded by category didn't answer anything unless . . .

She stared up at Kincaid. "What happens when someone's really, you know, shot up pretty bad?" She didn't want to say *when someone can't be saved* or *when someone's going to die.*

Kincaid held her eyes a moment. "If you're smart enough to ask that question, you already know the answer."

She did. Chris had said it. When there was only so much to go around, you did the math. Treat the ones who were either most likely to survive or valuable in some way. The rest? You had to hope the end came fast. She wondered if Kincaid helped those people along. Given the situation, she thought he just might.

Kincaid had two other assistants, both older men in their late sixties who'd been nurses but in retirement before. There were six techs, a fancy name for people like her who did things like mop up blood, change sheets, empty bedpans, bring meals. When he saw the look on her face, Kincaid laughed. "Don't worry. When the patrols start coming back, someone's usually hurt. That's where you're gonna cut your teeth."

True to his word, Kincaid had her assist when a farmer hobbled in a few hours later. The farmer had laid his thigh open almost to his knee: *Damn saw jumped and bit me.* The wound was very deep, and Kincaid kept her busy irrigating away blood as he worked. Halfway through, when the bleeding was mostly under control and he'd put in the first few stitches, he handed her the Kelly clamp and tissue forceps and said, "You been watching? Good. Now, I want you to throw a couple stitches in that muscle there.

Don't be shy; just do it." He watched as she threw in and tied off the first stitch, and then he nodded. "That was good. You done this before?"

"My mom was a doctor." She could hear her mother's voice in her head: *Roll your wrist, sweetie; don't be afraid to take a big bite.* "We practiced on chicken legs. She said it was closest to what sewing up people was like."

"Jeez, remind me not to come over for dinner," said the farmer.

She tagged after Kincaid until well past dark, and when she walked out of the building, Chris was there with Honey. Which was only a little freaky. How had he known? It wasn't as if someone could just pick up a cell. Was he keeping tabs on her? If so, that wasn't good.

Compared to that morning, they didn't talk much, nothing more than *hi, how are you, just peachy, that's good.* That was fine. Once they were on Jess's street—a cul-de-sac—he dismounted, waited while she stabled Honey in the garage at the end of the block, and then walked her to Jess's house. She said good night and thanks, he nodded and said nothing, and that was that.

Which was fine.

Chris showed up the second day, but not the third, fourth, fifth, or sixth. Instead, Greg escorted her and pumped her about Tori. Unlike Chris, Greg was both chatty and sloppy. Which was how she figured out that supplies—backpacks, food, clothes—were cached back in the village. And also, that the southwest corner was the least heavily patrolled. "We even got a couple gas depots,"

Greg said. "We've been siphoning gas from cars and trucks and stuff. Figure to use it for the tractors, chain saws, stuff like that come spring."

"Why not use the gas now?" she asked. "Wouldn't some snow-mobiles work?"

"Sure, and we would, in an emergency. But no one's going to be making any more gasoline for a long, long time. Once we use up our stockpiles, that's it. We might figure a way to pump gas up from the tanks under stations, but we need an engineer to help us with that. Even if we can get at the gas, we still have the problem of eventually running out, and it's kind of spooky anyway, you know? The noise? Anyway, the Council's into us being self-sufficient and simpler, like the Amish. Which we already kind of were before the . . . you know. That's why so many of the houses have hand pumps and stuff for water. Without those, we'd have been completely screwed."

With that logic, Alex thought, Peter and Chris and everyone else ought to wear deerskins, give up guns, and take up bows and arrows. Or clubs. "What about the people you turn away? You don't just throw them out with nothing, do you?"

Greg's forehead crinkled in alarm. "Oh no, that would be like . . . *wrong.* They get, you know, a backpack and some supplies. Couple days' worth of food, water."

"What about guns? They'd need those, too, won't they?"

"Yeah, but . . ." Greg scrunched up his nose. "They'd probably shoot us, right?"

"Good point." She inclined her head at his rifle. "Nice. It's a

Henry, isn't it?"

Greg beamed. "Yeah, it's sweet. Big Boy .44 Magnum. The scope is completely awesome. I also got me a Bushmaster M4 for patrol. We got, like, this arsenal."

"Cool. Where?"

"Well, we all got a couple guns at home, but most we lock up in the village hall, down in the basement below the jail. Keep the ammo there, too. It's about the safest place in town."

Well, that wasn't good. She couldn't think of a decent excuse that would get her into the basement so she could steal some ammo— or past a locked door, for that matter. So that meant she would have to steal a weapon from someone's house. Did Jess have a gun? No, being a *girl*, probably not. One of the guys then, or maybe Kincaid . . .

She'd figure it out. She had to.

Sunday was church. The Council sat in tall chairs ranged on the pulpit while the Rev led worship, early and mid-morning, and everyone attended one service or the other. Of course, Jess had Alex and the other girls go to both, which was a drag. The service was pretty much what she expected: a couple readings, a bunch of songs, a sermon, more songs, and then *go-forth-and-be-numbered-among-the-righteous*. Yeager's was mostly brave-new-world stuff, about how much darker than darkness the world could be and how God could permit such suffering, blah, blah. Along with Revelations and gall and Star Wormwood, the Rev also seemed overly fond of brother stories: Jacob and Esau, Ishmael and Isaac,

Cain and Abel. For the Rev, the Changed bore the mark of Cain, the wickedness of Ishmael, the hard primitiveness of Esau. Cain was a no-brainer, but from what she remembered, Jacob tricked his dad, and Abraham couldn't keep his pants zipped. How any of that reflected on either Esau, who was just a hairy, hardworking farmer looking for a meal, or poor Ishmael—whose only crime seemed to have been being born—she didn't know. Judging from the stony look Jess gave the Rev when he started in on his brother rant—the way her scent, so white and blank, swelled—there was something about brother stories that touched a nerve in her, too.

Anyway, Alex tuned out. God and religion had ceased to have much relevance for her a long time back. No one had to tell her about darker than dark. Been there, done that, bought the T-shirt.

It wasn't until nearly two weeks later, on a Wednesday, that she pushed out of Jess's house to find Chris waiting with Honey.

"Hi," she said, genuinely surprised. "I thought Greg was going to be my escort from now on." Too late, she realized how that sounded and added, "I mean, I thought you were busy—"

"I was," he said, handing her Honey's reins. The slight smile he'd worn dribbled away. Turning, he jammed on his sunglasses, then swung up onto his blood bay. He peered down at her. "Now I'm back. That okay with you?"

"It's fine." Her cheeks heated, but whether from anger or embarrassment, she wasn't sure. He said nothing more as she mounted and they started off, the horses' hooves thudding dully on fresh-fallen snow. She waited until they'd turned out of Jess's street before trying again. "So . . . where were you? Out finding supplies?"

"Uh-huh."

"Uh . . . where?"

"Around." He kept his gaze fixed on the road ahead. "Up by Oren."

"Oh." She cast about for something to say. "Isn't that pretty far?"

His shoulders rose and fell in a quick hunch. "Not bad. Only a few miles north."

She knew Oren, and it was way more than a few miles. "You couldn't find what you wanted any closer?"

He hesitated before answering; she could almost see the wheels turning. "I remembered that Oren had this bookmobile."

She was confused for a moment, then recalled Chris's conversation with the principal. "You went all that way for books?"

"Well, not just books. There was other stuff."

"Did you find the bookmobile? How many books were left?"

"Everything, as far as I could tell. It was"—Chris's voice took on a wistful note—"kind of peaceful, actually."

She imagined it would be: a nice, quiet, very big van filled with books. "How many books did you bring back?"

"All of them."

"*All* of them? That's a lot of wagons."

"It wasn't so bad. Peter was kind of pissed, but winter's pretty long and there aren't going to be any more books."

"You don't know that," she said. "Maybe we'll write them."

He looked at her then. "You wanted to be a writer?"

"I hadn't thought about the future much." It helped that this was true. The most future she had was an expiration date.

"Doc says you're good. Assisting, I mean."

That didn't sound like a question, so she said nothing.

"You ever thought of being a doctor?" he asked.

"For a while."

"What changed?"

"Oh, you know," she said vaguely. "I was keeping my options open."

They rode in silence the rest of the way. At the hospice door, Chris said, "Hang on a sec." He reached inside his parka and pulled out a slim, rectangular black case. "I thought maybe you could use these."

She opened the case. Inside was a pair of women's sunglasses. The lightweight plastic frame was sage green, and the lenses were amber.

When she looked back up, he'd taken off his own. His dark eyes were suddenly tentative, and his scent was different: still dark and cool, but with just a touch of something sweet and tart at the same time. . . . Apple?

"They're sport glasses," he said. "The lenses are polarized and shatterproof, so they ought to be good for a long time."

They were, she thought, very expensive, very nice sunglasses, and the right thing was to take them. To refuse would be mean, petty. But she didn't want to encourage or like him. All she wanted was to figure out how to get away.

"Thanks," she said, then closed the case and held it out. "But I'm really fine."

A sliver of hurt arrowed across his face but was gone in an instant. The scent of apples faded as he took the case from her.

"Sure," he said. "No problem."

57

She was such a complete shit.

She should've taken the glasses.

What an idiot.

When she gave herself a second to think about it, Chris had ridden into the carnage and chaos beyond Rule, gone for miles to bring back books so a bunch of kids would have something to read. In the middle of all that, he'd thought of her. She could picture him wandering empty streets, weaving around dead bodies and dead cars, keeping one eye open for the Changed or an ambush and the other for the perfect pair of sunglasses for a girl he barely knew and who, with her track record, might just throw them back in his face.

Which she'd done. Even if she hadn't needed him for information, being mean just to be mean . . . that wasn't her at all. *Idiot.*

Kincaid kept her very late, until almost nine, and when she hurried to the front entrance, Chris wasn't there. That was fine. A relief, really. But this was also the first time he hadn't arranged for someone to wait for her. Maybe a sign that he trusted her to find her way back? No, after this morning, more like a big *screw you, honey.*

"Oh, thank goodness." A tech—Loretta—fluttered up. She was a plump woman with no waist and hair that looked like a pudding bowl trimmed around the edges. "Chris wanted me to keep an eye out and let him know when Matt let you go, except I got busy and I forgot."

She felt a little jolt. Relief. She felt *relieved*, and that was even more confusing. It was one thing to feel like a shit; it was another to realize that she cared if he was angry at her. "He's here?"

"Yes, but—" Loretta put a hand on Alex's arm and dropped her voice to a confidential whisper. "He's over in the hospice wing. Let me go get him."

"I'll go." Alex started down the corridor. "Which room?"

"Delmar's." Loretta flitted alongside. "Really, it will only take me a second. You should wait out front."

"It's okay." Alex was studying name tags: *Holter. James. Mitchell.* She spotted the right room. The door—with its glass insert—was halfway open, and candles danced as dim orange flickers reflected on the glass. She felt a warm puff of air from the room's catalytic heater. Okay, good, she could apologize for being an ass, or . . . well, think of *something.* "It's right—"

She fell silent. Her eyes took in the single bed and the man lying there. He was withered and skeletal and looked so dry and desiccated that Alex wouldn't have been surprised if a sudden strong wind was enough to shake his bones to dust. A green nasal cannula snaked over his ears and under his jaw. The only reason Alex knew he was still alive was because he blinked every few seconds like a turtle: slowly and thoroughly.

Chris's back was to the door, but she saw the book and heard the low murmur of his voice as he read.

Something told her to be quiet, to just ease on out of there without Chris noticing, which she did. Loretta waited a few feet from the door and beckoned for her to follow. When they'd tiptoed halfway down the corridor, Loretta leaned in and whispered, "He reads to the very sick ones every night he's in town. It gives them something to look forward to. But you won't tell him I told you now, will you? He doesn't like people to know. He's really very private."

"No problem," said Alex, still dazed. *That's why he's always here when I'm done.* It hit her again that there was a lot more to like—even admire—about Chris than she'd imagined. "We'll just pretend it didn't happen."

"Good." Loretta looked relieved. "Now, here's what we'll do. You go on back and make like you've just gotten out, and *I'll* wait a few moments and go get him. He usually slips out the side door for the horses."

She did what Loretta asked. Perhaps five minutes later, she heard the dull clop of horse hooves, and then Chris was there, on Night, with Honey's reins in one hand.

"Hi," he said, with about as much enthusiasm as she might muster for a cockroach. "Sorry."

"It's okay," she said, swinging into Honey's saddle. They rode in silence for a good ten minutes before she worked up the courage to ask, "So . . . what did you do today?"

It being dark, she couldn't see his face, but she felt his eyes.

"Why," he said, "would you even care?"

Well, that shut her up. They didn't speak again. At Jess's street, Chris waved to the lantern that was the guard and then said to her, "You can get off at Jess's. I'll stable Honey."

"I can stable my own horse," she said.

"Fine," he said. "Whatever."

As they passed Jess's house, she said, "Look, this morning—"

"Don't worry about it," he said.

"No." She reined in Honey and turned toward him. There was no moon, and she couldn't see his face at all. "Please, let me just—"

"Can we not do this, please? There's nothing you have to say that I want to hear."

The words hit like a slap. "Then don't listen, but you can't stop me talking," she said.

"Fine. Knock yourself out."

"God, you're making it so hard for me to apologize."

There was no change in his scent at all. If anything, his shadows got stronger. "It doesn't matter."

"But it *does*," she said, much more loudly than she intended. Her voice must've carried, because she saw the hard white blob of light that was the guard flick their way. She lowered her voice. "I was a real asshole. You were being nice, and I threw it back in your face. You didn't need to get the books at all, but you did. You could've hightailed it back with just a couple, but you didn't. You found a way to bring back the whole stupid bookmobile. And on top of all that, you remembered I didn't have sunglasses and you rode around that whole town, looking for a pair. There are cannibals out there and raiders and people who want to kill *us*, kids like you and me, and you still risked it. So . . . I'm sorry."

"Fine, I accept your apology, all right? Now, can we please stable Honey?"

They did so by the light of a Coleman, but Chris did not, as she'd expected, remove Night's bridle or lead his horse to a stall. Instead, he remounted then held out his hand. When she looked up in surprise, he said, "Come on. I'll give you a ride back."

Without a word, she grabbed his hand and swung up behind him onto the cantle. "Better hang on," he said. The scent of his darkness had not changed, but when she slid her arms around his waist, she felt the warmth of his back against her chest.

They didn't speak during the brief ride back. At Jess's, though, she dismounted and said, "Would you like to come inside for a little while? I didn't have dinner, and I bet Tori put back a plate. She's always doing stuff like that."

"Wouldn't want to eat your food," he said.

"That's okay," she said. "I'm sure there's enough for both of us."

Jess opened the door just as Alex stepped up to the small landing outside the kitchen. "I thought I heard you out there. Come on in, both of you, before you catch your death."

Alex could see the girls were all there, in their robes and slippers. Balls of yarn and a scatter of knitting needles littered the kitchen table. Ghost capered over to weave around Alex's legs and whimper for attention.

"Jess. Hey, Tori, Sarah," Chris said, crowding in after.

"Chris." Alex heard the surprise in Tori's voice and then saw Tori's eyes pinball between her and Chris and then back again. "Jess was just teaching us how to cast on."

"Cool." He nodded at Lena. "Hey."

"Hey," Lena said. Her normally sour scent did not change.

Tori started to rise. "Alex, there's a plate in the oven and—"

"She knows her way around the kitchen," said Jess, gathering up the yarn and needles. "Come on, let's leave these two to their dinner."

"Hello," said Lena, *"obvious."*

"Do you always have to be mean?" asked Sarah.

"Chris, would you like some bread to take back to your place? There are a couple loaves in the pantry." Tori started that way. "Let me—"

"Alex can do it, Tori," Jess said. "As Lena is so fond of pointing out, she's not a cripple. Alex, there's hot water in that kettle, and Tori made a very nice crumble."

"Apple," said Sarah. She was studying Chris. "That's your favorite, isn't it?"

"Yeah," said Chris. "Uh, thanks, Tori."

"Come on, everyone. We'll get that fire back up in the front room," Jess said, shooing the other girls out, closing the connecting door to the front room behind them. Beyond, Alex could make out Lena's muffled complaints and then something sharp from Jess.

Her cheeks warmed. "I'm sorry," she said.

"Don't worry about it. Come on, let's eat," he said.

She got the food—Tori had left enough to feed a small army—while Chris dug out another plate and silverware and then set about making mugs of herbal tea. As she sliced bread, she said, "Chris?"

"Yeah?"

"Thank you for remembering me when you were out there. I . . . it . . ." She turned around, saw from the set of his back that he was listening. "It feels nice that you remembered."

There was nothing for a moment, and then, as he turned, she caught a fleeting scent of apples.

"Actually," he said, "you're kind of hard to forget."

It was déjà vu all over again.

After polishing off dinner and devouring what was left of the crumble, they sipped tea. They sat long enough that Alex heard the creaks overhead and knew that Jess had chased everyone upstairs. She and Chris didn't talk much, which both relieved her and made her crazy. With Tom, conversation just came. Chris was so quiet. Yet this was cozy; it was intimate. . . . It was Tom all over again, but it wasn't, couldn't be. If anything, it was a pale imitation, like a faded Xerox you'd copied about a hundred million times until there was just an impression of the original. Tom was Tom, and Chris was shadows, and no amount of wishing would make Chris into Tom either. And she didn't wish that, not for a second, not in a million years. She needed Chris, pure and simple; she wanted his trust, to make him her ally. That was why she'd invited him in, right? *Right?*

"Can I ask you a question?" he asked, breaking into her thoughts.

"Um . . . sure," she said, pushing out of her slouch. Ghost dozed on her lap, his paws twitching. "What?"

"Why are you carrying your parents' ashes?" When he saw her expression, he said hastily, "I mean, you don't have to tell me if it's too personal."

"No, it's okay," she said. Yeager hadn't even asked that, and of course, Tom hadn't known to begin with. "They died a couple years ago, and they wanted their ashes scattered on Lake Superior, that's all."

And it really *was* all, come to think of it. No big deal. Why oh why hadn't she told Tom when she had the chance? But of course, she knew why.

Because then I would've told him about the monster. Once I got started with Tom, there would've been no holding back, and I just didn't want to risk it. I should've trusted him; I held back too long—

"Oh. Was there something special about now? I mean, you could have done it anytime, right?"

"It just seemed like the right time," she said, and realized the truth of this. If she'd been back at Aunt Hannah's, she would've been trapped in the city—and quite likely very dead by now. It was as Tom had said: the right place at exactly the right moment.

Chris might have heard something in her tone, because his eyes narrowed a bit, but his shadow-scent didn't change and then he shrugged. "Okay. I'm sorry you didn't get the chance, but maybe come spring, we could go up there. If you want. I mean, I would take you."

The fact that she had no intention of being in Rule come spring didn't make her hesitate for a second. If he thought she would be there, he and everyone else might chill out, and then she'd find her chance to get away. "Thanks. That's really nice of you."

She dumped Ghost from her lap, and they gathered up the dishes to wash and dry. More déjà vu. All they needed was a little kid hanging around.

"You're lucky you've got something left," Chris said. "The ashes, I mean. I don't remember my mom at all."

She handed him a plate. "You don't?"

He shook his head. "She's just this big white spot. She left when I was really little. Like only a couple months old. To hear my dad grouse about it, she would've booked right out of the hospital if she'd had the chance. I don't know who she is or where she went, and my dad didn't keep any pictures."

"Do you know why she left?"

"My dad was a drunk." He threw her a tentative glance to gauge her reaction. "He beat her up is what I figure."

Well, that explained the shadows. Any man mean enough to beat his wife probably didn't spare his fists when it came to his kid either. "Is that why you said he wanted you dead? I mean, you didn't say it, but—"

"Yeah, I know what you mean." He sighed. "Probably. He had a couple girlfriends. There was this one, Denise. When I was ten, she picked me up from basketball practice. I don't remember why my dad didn't come, but he was probably passed out or something. She was dead drunk, too. I knew as soon as I got in the backseat. We'd have had better luck if *I'd* been driving. About a mile from our house, she crashed the car. Slammed right into a tree. She wasn't wearing a seat belt. Went through the windshield. Of course, that was my fault, too. I still have nightmares."

There it was again: nightmares, like her and Tom. "That's terrible."

"Yeah. I heard about it every day, dreamed about it every night. My parents are both dead now. Thing is, I'm not sorry about either of them. My dad hated me, and my mom left." His mouth twisted in a sour grimace. "If I could wash my brain and get amnesia, I would. It would be a relief."

"Bet not," she said.

58

More snow fell. The weeks melted away, and then it was only two days before Christmas. Alex watched as her window of opportunity grew smaller and smaller, contracting as her vision and then her mind had when she'd almost died outside that gas station. She didn't give up, not exactly, but with every day that passed, leaving seemed less urgent and more difficult, as if her will were being slowly suffocated under all that snow.

And really, was it so bad here? Five hundred miles was a lot of miles, especially when she didn't know what she was looking for or who was waiting, and with the Changed and desperate people out there, too. No one was really bothering her. Where, exactly, did she think she could run to that was safer than where she was?

She hadn't totally thrown in the towel. She'd gathered things, squirreling them in an old feed bucket that she hung from a joist in the darkest corner of the garage where she stabled Honey. Every item she added—a twist of rope, a book of matches, a jar of peanut butter, a scalpel swiped from the hospice and zipped into the lining of her jacket—felt like a triumph, but for only a moment. A flash in the pan, like the fizzle of a Roman candle. At this rate, she would be here all winter, or until the monster in her brain got tired of playing possum. Well, maybe waiting until spring was a good idea. She didn't want to set out in all this snow, did she? That was just begging for more trouble she didn't need.

Her life fell into a rhythm: work with Kincaid, chores at the house, rides with Chris. They were comfortable with each other. Maybe they were even friendly, though they weren't friends. After that night at Jess's, Chris had turtled back into himself, covering himself in shadows, as if embarrassed, afraid he'd said too much. That was all right. She had a few secrets of her own, and she didn't really want to get to know him better. She even understood why. Tom would, too. It would be like Tom giving the enemy a face. Do that and you'd never squeeze the trigger.

But she was scared. She was starting to forget Ellie and Tom.

At night, as Sarah slept, she would lie still and try to block out the distant crack of rifles and summon up Tom's face, his scent, a flashbulb moment . . . *anything*. Yet the harder she tried grabbing hold, the more her memories were like soap bubbles, bursting with every pop of gunfire. She'd have better luck hanging on to a handful of fog. Ellie was only a pink blur.

The attempts left her sick and weepy, gnawing the inside of her cheek until her mouth tasted of rust. There was something wrong with her that might have nothing to do with the monster. Where was the Alex who'd grabbed the ashes and run? The one who said to Barrett, *I'm calling the shots now.* She sure as hell didn't know.

So, really, maybe Rule was killing her with the promise of safety. She was cowering in the corner just like a bunny rabbit, hoping that no one would notice. Or maybe she was letting Rule infect her: squash her will, who she was and had been, what she could look forward to.

She'd never have let the monster get away with that, and there were many ways to fight. So why wasn't she?

Because something was changing. Again. Inside her. She felt it in this slow, general slide into a kind of numb acceptance.

Just like when I was diagnosed. It was that stages-of-anger thing. I was shocked and then I got pissed and then I fought like hell . . . and then I went numb. They called it acceptance, but it wasn't. It's what happens when you have only two choices: live with the monster, or kill yourself.

Only no one would let you kill yourself. It was a crime, which was stupid. Doctors couldn't help you; they'd get thrown in jail. She knew another girl, also terminal, who'd tried suicide. Pills and Jack Daniels. After they pumped her stomach, they threw the girl in a psych ward because they decided she was depressed.

Well, duh. Try living with a monster in your brain and see if you didn't get, oh, a little depressed.

So there was no choice, none at all. You either lived with the monster, or you did what she'd done: *carpe diem* and run.

She should run now. Winter or not, she should get out before it was too late. Sure, she'd probably die out there on her own, but wait too long and she'd be lulled into the belief that all this—Rule, the life they'd mapped out for her, *Chris*—was her best option. She'd settle for what *they* wanted.

Really, come to think of it, there were two monsters: the one squatting in her brain—and Rule.

Either way, she'd end up just as dead.

Run, she told herself. *Run, you idiot, run.*

But she didn't. She couldn't. She just . . . couldn't.

59

Christmas Eve, raiders swooped into the Zone. Whoever they were, they might've thought everyone in Rule was drinking eggnog and roasting chestnuts (that would be no), but—Peter being Peter and always spoiling for a fight—the patrols were ready. The guards kept Alex and the girls bottled up in the house, where they huddled by the woodstove for most of the night, through an intense battle they only heard: stutters and pops and the ripping roar of what sounded like rifles on full auto. The other girls dozed, but Alex remained awake, raweyed and so anxious her skin crawled. Her thoughts churned and tumbled, each new fear feeding another. Before, she'd had some half-baked idea that she might be able to slip away in the chaos, but now all she could think about was Chris, out there fighting, being shot at. Was he safe? What was happening? God, if they'd only let her *help*.

When the weak glimmer of a cold winter's dawn finally lightened the trees, the woods were quiet and word came that the battle was over.

"How many men lost, Nathan?" Jess asked the guard who

delivered the news. The skin over her knuckles whitened as she clutched a shawl to her throat.

"Ten men lost, about the same number wounded—three pretty bad," Nathan said. He was a grizzled, compact fireplug of a man, but his voice was surprisingly light, almost musical. "Could've been worse."

Alex felt the air leaving her chest. Lena's eyes narrowed to watchful slits, and the color drained from Sarah's cheeks.

"What about the boys?" Jess demanded. "What about Chris?"

"Is Peter all right?" Sarah asked at the same moment. "Is he—"

"He's okay," Nathan said, and then his gaze shifted to Alex. "Chris, too."

She wasn't prepared for the surge of relief, a great wash that flooded her veins and made her knees go a little wobbly. Too late, she saw Jess flash a quick measuring glance.

"And Greg?" Tori asked. Her face was pinched with worry.

"Well." Nathan's gray eyes slid sideways. "Greg got clipped—"

"Oh!" Tori gasped, a hand going to her lips. "How bad? Is he . . . will he—"

"Doc says he'll be fine. Just lost some blood, that's all," Nathan said.

"Can I see him?"

"Orders say you got to stay here."

"It's okay, Tori, I'll go. Kincaid will need the help anyway," Alex said, but Nathan was already shaking his head. "Why *not*?"

"Orders," Nathan said again, stolidly. "You'll be safest staying here. Doc wants you, he'll let me know."

From the set of his face, Alex knew arguing would get her nowhere. But why wouldn't Kincaid let her come? Because he didn't want her to see who he was going to let go? Allow to die?

Christmas morning was a subdued affair: no presents other than hand-knitted socks Jess made for each of them, because anything else was wasteful and Jess thought they ought to spend time being thankful they were alive. While that was a little sucky, Alex was glad; what, exactly, would you give someone like Lena? Maybe a muzzle . . .

In all the excitement, church was pushed to the afternoon: one big service held on the town square. Alex looked around for Kincaid, but the doctor wasn't there. Standing on the church steps, Yeager launched into a long sermon about *our men of Rule*, like they were crusaders on some holy mission.

"And our Lord has called on you, my consecrated ones," Yeager said, his breath smoking in the wintery air. He peered down at the rows of men, gathered in front on folding chairs, who'd been in the battle the night before, and now Alex spotted Chris, Peter, Greg—with a bulky bandage around his left bicep—and a clutch of other boys, so easy to pick out from the old men who flanked them. *"I have even called My mighty warriors, My proudly exulting ones, to execute My anger. Is this not a description of our men of Rule? We are the guardians of righteousness! The followers of Satan have become as beasts, they bear the Mark of Cain and the Curse of Ishmael, and yet we endure as the Lord's strong right Hand!"*

This being Michigan, there weren't hallelujahs or anything, but Alex saw heads nod in agreement. When Yeager called the men up for a blessing, her blood warmed as Yeager clamped his hands on Chris's shoulders, and she felt something almost proprietary. A feeling that Chris was hers somehow; that his victory belonged to her, too. Then, when Chris rose and turned, his gaze brushed over the crowd, found hers—and did not falter.

For an instant, it was as if the world had stopped turning; everyone around her simply melted away, the shadows hugging Chris dissolved, and there was only his face and the look they shared. And was it her imagination, or was the scent of sweet, crisp apples that much stronger, so rich it overpowered everything else?

Tearing her eyes away from his was an effort, an act of will that was almost painful—because she didn't want to look away. Her face was suddenly slick with sweat, and her pulse tripped in her neck. What was happening to her? She couldn't have these feelings. Yes, Chris was fine, he was okay, he was a nice guy; but he was not Tom. She couldn't like Chris, shouldn't care about him. If she did, then Tom was gone, really gone—and she wasn't ready to let go.

"Please," she exhaled. "Please, Tom, please don't leave me, please." Her words were no more than a murmur, as insubstantial as the mist rising from her lips, and barely audible to herself, but she felt eyes again—not Chris's. She looked left and met Jess's gaze.

Alex stiffened in alarm. Had Jess heard? No, that was impossible; she'd barely breathed the words. But Jess was studying her with that same calculating look from earlier that morning. The older woman's scent betrayed nothing, and Alex thought once more of how Jess was a little like Yeager that way. Her scent was not like cloudy glass, however: just . . . nothing. Jess's scent was a big zip-zero, like the white spot Chris associated with his mother.

"Hey." Sarah plucked her sleeve. "Are you okay?"

At that, Jess broke her stare and turned to face forward once more. Alex flicked a glance at Sarah. "I'm fine," she said, forcing a quick grin. "Just a little tired."

She heard nothing after that and only mouthed the words to the hymns. Jess did not look at her again, but Alex knew what she'd seen. Jess's scent might be a white blank, but something flashed across the older woman's face just as she looked away that Alex *could* read, loud and clear.

Satisfaction.

And then it was the day before New Year's.

"I'm leaving town this morning. We'll probably—" Chris broke off as Tori slid a plate of biscuits and scrambled eggs onto the table. They were virtually out of baking powder, and the biscuits looked deflated, like miniature hockey pucks. "Thanks."

"Where are you going?" asked Alex.

"Coffee?" Tori held up a pot.

"Uh, sure," said Chris. He watched as Tori poured a dank black liquid that smelled suspiciously tarry to Alex. Even Chris raised an eyebrow. "What's in this?"

"Chicory," said Jess, coming up from the root cellar off the pantry with Sarah close behind. Both dumped an apron of potatoes into the sink. "In New Orleans, that's a delicacy."

Chris gave a noncommittal murmur. "Any butter?"

"I'm afraid not. What little we had we used for Christmas baking," said Jess. "Those milkers need better feed."

"I know." Chris snapped a biscuit in two. "It's on the list."

"Where are you going?" Alex asked again.

"A lot farther than I'd like," Chris said, around biscuit. He swallowed, chased the biscuit with a sip of pseudo-coffee, and grimaced.

"I'm sorry," Tori said. She put a hand on his shoulder. "I had to cut the flour with a little cornmeal. I know they're heavy. You want me to see if I can find some honey?"

"No, no, this is great," said Chris. To Alex: "We're going out a lot farther this time, I think. Most of the towns around here are cleaned out, virtually nothing left. Peter's thinking we should head for Wisconsin."

Tori gasped. "Aren't they guarding the border?"

"We're going to find out. A week there and back, easy, and that's not counting us having to actually *find* something."

"Then you won't be back until after the New Year," Sarah said. She sounded disappointed.

"Nope," said Chris, and then looked up as Lena hip-butted the kitchen door with an armload of firewood. "Probably not."

"Probably not what?" asked Lena.

"Chris and Peter won't be here for New Year's," Tori said. "They may have to cross over into Wisconsin for supplies, if they can get across the border. It's not fair they fight on Christmas Eve and now this."

Lena did her usual eye-roll, but this time Alex agreed with her. Life hadn't exactly been fair, in case Tori hadn't noticed.

Chris said, "If you guys want something special, make a list. I can't promise anything, but—"

"Real coffee," Lena said. "Failing that, a one-way ticket out of here would be nice."

"Here we go again," said Sarah.

Alex was tired of that subject already. "I don't understand, Chris. You said there are other towns, right? And there are the various groups of raiders you guys keep fighting, right? So why don't we, I don't know, organize? Or trade? Or maybe just share and share alike? That way, you guys don't have to worry about getting shot all the time and you don't have to travel as far." She remembered the discussion she'd had with Tom about this. "What you're doing is kind of inefficient."

"She has a point," said Jess. She didn't look up from scrubbing potatoes.

Chris looked uncomfortable. "That's really not my call."

"Why not?" Alex persisted.

"Well, first off, we'd have to have something worth trading," Sarah pointed out.

"We've got supplies. We've got tools and weapons and—"

"We're not going to trade weapons or tools," Chris said flatly. "That's like handing them the keys to the front door."

"Well, what about clothes?" Alex persisted. "Or soap or candles or lanterns or—"

"Or us," Lena said. She dumped wood in a loud clatter. "How much you think I'm worth, Chris?"

Chris looked like he'd been slapped. "Lena, it's not like—"

"Oh, bullshit. We're your precious little baby-makers. So what do you think you can buy with me? I guess that depends on when the guy gets tired—"

"You know," Jess interrupted, "we could do with more wood."

"Right. I forgot. Your house, your rules," Lena said, and banged out of the kitchen.

Tori broke the silence first. "More coffee, Chris?"

"No." His cheeks were splashed with scarlet. He wouldn't meet Alex's eyes. "No, I probably shouldn't."

"Chris," Sarah said gently, "she didn't mean that. She's not angry at you."

And Alex thought, *Oh yes, she is.* Lena was rude; she was obnoxious; but she was deliberately baiting Chris, really pushing it.

The question was: why?

Fifteen minutes later, Alex shrugged into her parka and scuffed outside. It was snowing again, big powdery flakes spinning slowly as feathers. The snow was deep, an easy two and a half feet, and hard on Honey. For the past few days, Chris had taken her to and from the hospice in a Portland cutter, and he'd just left the house five minutes before her. Alex expected to see him in the dark blue cutter, but only Nathan was there, holding the reins of a white dray.

"Where's Chris?" she asked as Nathan's border collie pranced up to be petted.

Nathan chinned in the general direction of the backyard. "Headed that way when he come out. Said he'd be right back."

Puzzled, Alex retraced her steps, then ducked around the house. Jess's yard was very large, about an acre before it blended into the woods. She spotted Chris in the far left corner by the woodpile—with Lena.

Whatever she'd been about to say dried up on her tongue. Chris and Lena were facing each other, and Lena's arms jerked in emphatic, angry gestures. Fighting with Chris? Knowing Lena, that was a safe bet, but after that little scene in the kitchen, why would Chris go out of his way to talk to her? Alex was too far away to hear, but she saw Chris shake his head and start to turn away. In the next instant, Lena grabbed his arm and flung herself into Chris so hard he staggered, and then she was threading her arms around his neck, pressing against him . . .

I don't want to see this. Stunned, Alex stumbled back, her boots tangling, and she let go of a startled, involuntary yip. Chris's head darted around, and then he was trying to disengage from Lena, pulling at her arms. He might even have called her name, but Alex wasn't waiting around. Floundering back up the walk toward the street, eyes smarting, she couldn't breathe; her chest was tight, like someone had punched all the air from her lungs. Just get Honey and go. But no, she couldn't; Nathan would stop her because she wasn't allowed to go anywhere without an escort. Well, that was all right, that was fine; she didn't care what was going on between Chris and Lena, she didn't *care.* . . .

"You find him?" asked Nathan as she clawed her way onto the cutter.

"Yeah." As she settled herself onto the seat, she saw Chris

wheel around the house. He was moving fast, and she smelled him coming: no apples this time, or shadows, but a roiling, angry storm cloud. She looked away as he clambered aboard, and then, with a crisp snap of the reins, Chris urged the dray to a trot and they glided off. He was silent, a black boiling wall pressing the air between them. Her heart was hammering and her stomach was twisting and fisting like her hands.

"It's not what you think," Chris said tightly.

"I don't care," she said, not daring to look at him. "It's none of my business."

He said nothing. Their sleigh swept past the village hall, where a knot of Rule men were marching a cluster of refugees inside, and then they were heading northeast down the approach road to the hospice. The forest closed in and echoed with the clop of horse hooves. Alex watched the snow fall, felt it melt on her cheeks like tears.

Chris cleared his throat. "Alex . . ."

"It doesn't matter, Chris."

"No," he said. "It does. I just . . . *can't* . . ."

"Can't what? Explain?" She darted a look at his face. His skin was tight and white as snow except for the two hectic stains of color along his high cheekbones. The scent of his shadows was stronger, as if they were closing around, trying to protect him somehow. "What's there to explain, Chris? We had sex ed in sixth grade, so if you need any pointers . . ." She heard the cruelty in her voice and choked back the rest. What the hell was she doing? She didn't *care*.

"You don't understand," he said.

"You don't owe me any explanations."

"But I wish I could," he said. She heard his misery and something more: disgust. "God, this is so messed up."

"Yeah, you *think*?" The frustration was pillowing in her head like hot steam. Any second, the top of her head would pop like a cork. "You're realizing this *now*?"

"Please, I don't want to fight with you."

"You know, it's fine, Chris, really. It's your town. If you want to screw Lena, choose her to go play house with, do it."

"Stop." His eyes closed, and the small muscles of his jaw twitched and jumped. "Please. Alex, I don't *want* Lena. I never have."

"Yeah? Well, you better clue her in."

"Will you shut *up*?" With an abrupt twitch of his wrists, he jerked back on the dray's reins. The sleigh slewed, and she had to grab on to the side to keep from tumbling out, but then he was grabbing her by the arms and shaking her. "Do you think I *want* this? Do you think I want *her*?"

"Don't you? No, don't answer that. I don't *care* what or who you want!" she spat, and then she slapped him across the face, hard and fast, the sound as crisp as the snap of a dried bone. The sound broke something inside her, too, and she felt a sudden, hot rush of shame as he gasped and his hands fell away. The sting in her hand burned like acid. "Chris," she said. "Chris, I'm sorry, I'm—"

"Why can't you like me?" he said, his voice breaking. His scent steamed then, hot and heady with a welter of contradictions: apples and fire and the electric roil of those cold, black shadows. "Why can't you like me just a little?"

She would never know how she might have answered, because he never gave her the chance.

Instead, he kissed her.

60

It was not like Tom at all.

This was more like a bomb.

She felt her body go rigid with surprise and then the quick lurch of her heart and a sudden breathlessness. For an instant, just an instant, she could've pushed him away. But she didn't. A stunning white heat scorched the thought right out of her brain, and then he was pressed against her and her body was tingling and she felt his hunger, his need, and she'd grabbed the lapels of his coat because she was starving for his touch; she couldn't get close enough, and the scent of spiced apples made her feverish and dizzy.

The kiss went on forever. It lasted for a second. She wasn't sure who broke it off. Maybe both of them did at the same time, or neither of them.

He let her go. "I'm sorry. God, I'm so sorry," he said, his voice ragged. "Please don't hate me. I just . . ."

"It's okay," she said. The red splotch of her hand stood out on his cheek like a brand. Her lips felt bruised and swollen. "I shouldn't have egged you on. I was just mad."

"I think . . ." Chris leaned back, his chest still heaving. "I think maybe when I get back I shouldn't be around you anymore. I can't *think*. When I'm out there, all I can think about is *here* and . . . being with you. I just . . . God, Alex, I'm just trying to protect you."

Her automatic rebuttal—*I don't need your protection*—jammed up behind her teeth. He was telling the truth; she could smell it. This was like when he'd given her the sunglasses, only this time she held his feelings in the cup of her hands.

"You know what I worry about? I worry that when I come back, you'll find some loophole, something we've overlooked, and then you'll be gone and I don't think I—" Chris closed his eyes. "Please say something."

"I'm so sorry." She reached for his face, touched the mark she'd left there. "I don't hate you, Chris."

He gave a sad half-laugh. "But you don't like me."

"I kissed you back," she said.

"After I surprised you, after I *forced* you . . ."

"No. You didn't force me. I think . . ." She pulled in a shaking breath. "I think I'm afraid to like you."

His surprise and then the hope on his face were almost painful, and she had to bite her lip to keep from bursting into tears. Her hand was still on his cheek, and he covered it now with his own. "Why?" he asked.

A sob tried to push its way out of her mouth. "Because it means giving up. It means that you've closed up all the loopholes and there's nowhere else for me to go."

"But Alex, the rules exist for a reason. They're there to keep you safe."

"Then why does Jess think they need to change?"

"Alex." He moved closer, and when he gathered her up, she didn't resist. "I want to protect you. I *want* to take care of you. If you stayed, would that be so bad?"

Her hands hooked on to his jacket, and she held on.

"No," she said.

They rode in silence the rest of the way, but she stayed close, their thighs touching, her hand looped through the crook of his elbow. The snow was thicker and beginning to swirl by the time they got to the hospice. When the sleigh had coasted to a stop, however, she did not jump down. Beyond the glass doors, she could see the hospice guard watching, his hand on the push bar to let her in.

She turned to Chris. "How long do you think you'll be gone?"

"Awhile, maybe. Couple weeks." His mouth moved in a tense, uncertain, lopsided smile. Snow clung to his dark hair. "Don't worry. I'll have someone here for you."

"I'm not worried about *me*." She took his hand, and their fingers laced. "When you get back . . ."

"Yeah," he said.

This time, when they kissed, there were only apples: sweet and crisp and right.

That afternoon, one of the nurses dashed out of the treatment room for something or other, and left a clutch of fresh instruments spread on a tray. One was a Gigli saw, a coil of wire that could cut through bone—or a tree, or a man's neck. The saw was sixteen inches long with two handles. Coiled, she could slip it into her jeans. A saw like that would come in handy on the road for a girl on the run.

She left the saw where it was.

61

Two weeks into the New Year, a nurse stuck his head into the treatment room where she and Kincaid were putting the finishing touches on a laceration and said, "Boss, just got word from an advance scout. Hank and them's coming in hot. Found someone in an old barn up by Oren."

"We know how bad?" asked Kincaid.

"Sounds septic. Wound infection, looks like a bite." He paused. "Boss, they say he's a Spared."

At that, she almost gasped. Her first thought was that Tom had been bitten. Could it be? No, it couldn't be Tom; too much time, nearly two months, had passed.

"Get me a gurney for out front, and get a tech in here now. I'll be right there," said Kincaid, and then to her: "Go on, finish up. We don't got all day."

"Sorry." She concentrated on that last stitch, then tied and snipped. She did it all calmly enough, but her heart was trying to break through her ribs. She reached for a packet of gauze bandage, but Kincaid was already stripping off his gloves. "Leave it, leave it," he said. "I need you with me." He snapped his fingers at a tech, pointed at the patient, and was out the door with Alex on his heels.

Dashing down to the lobby, they pushed out through the double doors as first a single rider thundered down the approach road, followed an instant later by a horse-drawn flatbed sleigh. A man she didn't know, but who must be Hank, was handling the horses; Alex spotted two boys in the sled. With a little stab of surprise, she recognized Greg. What was he doing here? He'd gone out with Chris. . . . All thoughts of that vanished when she realized that Greg was doing CPR.

"Whoa, whoa!" Hank shouted, as the horses charged around the breezeway. He pulled back on the reins hard enough that one of the horses reared in protest. "Whoa, easy!"

The two horses stamped and jolted to a shuddering halt, and then Kincaid was dashing for the sleigh, hoisting himself onto a runner. "What do we got? How bad is he?" Then he got a good look and said, "Oh Lord."

Heart jamming into her throat, Alex crowded in beside Kincaid and then didn't know whether to sob with relief or fury.

It was not Tom. Of course, it wouldn't, couldn't be. The boy was young, no older than eight or nine. And Greg had ripped open the boy's jacket and shirt to do CPR, so she could see the birdcage of his ribs and the knobs of his shoulders. His eyes were closed and sunken, and he was deathly pale, his lips almost blue. The right leg of his jeans was shredded and oozy, and the smell was overpowering. Her breath thinned as she caught his smell: rotting and fetid.

"Found him by his lonesome in a barn. Arrested on the road," Greg said, without breaking stride. He was sodden with sweat, breathless from exertion. "Been at this about . . . four-one-thousand, five . . . go." At his signal, the other boy who'd preceded the sleigh up the road—she thought his name was Evan—squeezed an ambu-bag, forcing air into the unconscious boy's lungs. Greg ducked his head into his shoulder to smear away sweat. "Ten minutes now."

"Ten minutes too long," Kincaid said. He turned as Paul, an elderly male nurse with a permanent beer belly, rattled up with a gurney. "I got this, Paul. I want IVs set up, large bore, and get me a CVP line—"

"I don't know if we got one, Boss. We're so low—"

"Find me a damned line, Paul! Don't you show your face without one—you got that? And get out the crash cart, whatever you can scrounge. Move it!" As Paul hurried back inside, Kincaid wrestled the gurney alongside the wagon, butting it in place with his hips. "All right, people, bells and whistles on this one. Let's—" He paused, a curious expression creasing his weathered features.

Hank, who'd already leapt down to help move the injured boy to the gurney, looked over at Kincaid. "Doc, you okay?"

"Yeah, just a sec. Greg, hold up there, let me check for a pulse." And then Kincaid stared right at her, grabbing her eyes, and she read the question as if he'd spoken it aloud: *Is it safe?*

It was a question she knew would come eventually, one they'd never asked before.

"Is there a pulse?" said Greg.

Kincaid didn't answer. She knew she couldn't afford to be

wrong. The dead-meat stink was unmistakable, but it was also different: gassy and almost sweet.

"Doc?" Hank asked.

Dead meat, yes; that's infection, not the Change. She gave Kincaid the barest of nods.

"I'm not getting anything. Greg, keep on those compressions. All right, let's go," Kincaid said. "Move him on three. One, two . . ."

Straddling the gurney, Greg continued CPR all the way to the treatment room as Evan trotted alongside with the ambu-bag. She and Paul started the IVs, and Paul had found a CVP line somewhere that Kincaid now threaded into the boy's subclavian vein.

"This is the last of the bicarb," Paul said, handing Kincaid a syringe. "You sure you want to—"

"Can't think of a better time. Push that on in there. . . . We got atropine? All right, hold on. . . . Greg, stop compressions." Eyes closed, Kincaid listened through his stethoscope, then said, "Hold on, I think . . . Paul, push that atropine in."

They waited. Greg was panting, the sweat running in rivulets down his neck. Paul glanced at a stopwatch. "Fifteen minutes, twenty seconds, Boss."

"I got something," said Kincaid, glancing at his watch now and counting under his breath. "Paul, get me a BP."

"Sixty over thirty, Boss."

"All right, that's not great, but it's not terrible. This boy might make it after all." Kincaid snapped on a pair of gloves. "Let's see what we got. Alex, I need your hands—glove up."

The stink that pillowed from the boy's left thigh smelled of rot and was bad enough that even Kincaid winced. Someone had tried to bandage the wound, but the wrappings were soggy and stained green and yellow with pus. Alex felt her stomach turn over as Kincaid peeled away the oozy gauze wraps. Pus, yellow-green as snot, puddled in the open wound, and the shredded flesh along the wound's margins was black. Thin red streaks coursed the length of the boy's thigh to his knee and radiated to his crotch.

"Seventy-five over forty."

"All right," Kincaid said as he began sponging away the mess with gauze pads. On the gurney, the corners of the boy's eyes twitched, and then he let out a low moan. "I know," Kincaid murmured as he worked. "I know it's bad, son. I'm sorry, I know. You just hold on there."

"That's good, right, Doc? His pressure?" asked Greg, arming away sweat.

"Well, it's not bad. You boys catch a name before you hightailed it outta there?"

"Naw. Like I said, he's been out of it."

"Okay. Alex, draw up a couple fifty-cc syringes of saline and irrigate the hell out of this, would you?"

Alex was glad for something to do. As she pulled up the fluid, Greg said, "You can save him, right?"

"We are certainly going to try. He might lose that leg, but one thing at a time. Greg, get yourself into some dry clothes before you catch your death. How's that arm of yours? Either you boys hurt?"

"Naw, everyone got out okay, Doc," said Greg, flexing the arm where he'd been wounded three weeks before.

"Good, I didn't want to be patching you up again. What about the others?"

"They're about a day behind."

"All right. Now you two get on out of here and let me work. Paul, get me a surg kit; we're going to be doing some cutting here, and I want some Cipro in him right now."

Paul pulled a small glass vial from a mostly empty med cart. "Boss, that's the last of—"

"The last of the Cipro, I know. Just do it, Paul. Alex, you can stop irrigating. Cut away the rest of his clothes, so I can see what I'm doing." Kincaid glanced at her over his mask. "Let's just hope this poor boy stays out."

As Kincaid cleaned and debrided the wound, she worked a pair of heavy surgical scissors through the boy's pants, cut those away, and then attacked what was left of his shirt. Slicing through flannel, she suddenly recoiled. "Oh, gross."

"What?" asked Kincaid.

"I think . . ." The boy had another large bite wound, raw and weeping and filled with what looked like white rice—and then the rice *moved*. "I think they're maggots."

"Really?" Kincaid took a long look and then nodded. "Excellent."

"Excellent?" Alex goggled at him. "What's good about maggots?"

"Because they eat the dead stuff and leave healthy tissue behind," said Kincaid. "See the margins there? That's all viable tissue. Alex, see if you can scoop a couple dozen of those little guys onto some gauze."

"Sure," she said faintly, not at all sure she wouldn't pass out.

She couldn't get rid of the image of flies buzzing over the boy's wounds, landing and laying eggs.

And then she thought, *Hey, wait a minute.*

"You want some help?" asked Paul, although he sounded like he'd be just as happy if she refused.

She did not disappoint. "No, I'm good."

"Oh, we are going to give you bad boys a regular feast," Kincaid said. "Warm you maggies right up."

"They look pretty warm to me," said Alex. "They're moving all over the place."

"He is the only person I know who would get excited over a bowl of maggots," Paul observed as he pumped up the blood pressure cuff again. "Ninety-five over sixty-two."

"I like the sound of that," Kincaid said. "Paul, get us another catalytic heater in here and then see if you can scrounge us up a plastic container and an apple."

"You want to eat?" asked Alex. *"Now?"*

"Eventually." He winked at her over his mask. "Apple's for the maggies. Old fishing trick. The maggies'll keep somewhere cool and dark for a couple weeks."

"We could start our own maggot farm," said Paul.

"That is a very good idea," said Kincaid. "We find somewhere warm enough. Flies'll die otherwise."

"I was joking." Paul rolled his eyes. "Be right back. Boss, I hope you and your maggies will be very happy."

"Oh, we will," Kincaid said, "we will."

Great, now she'd be babying maggots for the foreseeable future.

Alex thought it would be a really long time before she looked at rice the same way again.

Presuming, of course, she ever saw rice again.

"That's it," said Kincaid. After peeling out of his gloves, he dragged the mask from his face and sighed. "Wish I hadn't had to cut away so much tissue to find healthy muscle, but can't be helped. Between me and the maggots, though, those wounds might just granulate in. They won't be pretty, but if he's lucky, he won't lose the leg."

"Is he going to make it?" asked Alex.

Kincaid's mouth set in a grimace. "If things were even halfway normal, I'd say only fifty-fifty. He's already arrested once, and he's septic. Fluids'll help, but we only got a couple more bags and no more antibiotic. If his blood pressure falls again, I got nothing left to give him."

"Maybe it won't," said Alex. "Maybe you got to him in time."

"Maybe. Be a damn shame, all this effort and risk for nothing. Just got to hope for the best." He looked behind Alex. "Greg, take this girl home before she passes out."

"Just waiting on you, Doc," said Greg from the door.

Night had fallen hours before. Now she glanced at Ellie's watch and saw that Mickey said it was pushing ten. Untying her mask, Alex said, "Have you been there the whole time?"

"All"—Greg checked his pocket watch—"six hours and twenty minutes."

"And it's way past my bedtime," said Kincaid. He looked as if he was going to fall down, and when he dropped into a chair, he let out a long groan. "Many more nights like this, and I'm going to be old before my time."

"You need to rest," Paul said. A huge butterfly splotch stained the chest of his scrub top, and a sheen of sweat glistened on his ruddy scalp. "We're not kids anymore."

"I heard that," said Kincaid.

"You should get some sleep," Alex said. She was dead tired and she could smell herself. "I can watch him for a while. All I need to do is wash up a little bit." When Kincaid opened his mouth to protest, she said, "Come on, if something bad happens to you, we're screwed."

"She's got a point," said Paul.

Kincaid grumbled some more but eventually gave in. "I'll bed down here. You come get me in four hours," he said as Paul ushered him out. "Don't you forget."

"I won't," she said, and then after he was gone: "Maybe."

"You really do look beat," said Greg, who looked only marginally better than she felt. "You want company?"

"I'm fine," she said, and then ruined it by yawning. "Look on the bright side. You won't have to come get me in the morning."

"I'll bring you a change of clothes. Chances are Doc is going to let you knock off tomorrow, though."

"Yeah, well." She glanced at their patient, whose color was only a little less white than his sheets. His dark hair looked artificial, like something penned in with a Magic Marker. Then she began to gather up soiled instruments. The plastic garbage bags were overflowing with soiled and bloodied gauze and the remnants of the boy's clothes. "Let's see what happens. You should go home."

"I'm gone." Greg tipped her a wave. "Just don't tell Chris."

Now what, she thought, as she began tidying up the treatment room, *would I tell Chris exactly? Oh, bad Greg left me all by my widdle wonesome?*

She *had* thought of Chris, too, and often. Not obsessively, not the way she had with Tom—but that had been different, hadn't it? She wasn't sure now what she'd felt with Tom, but they'd fought together and he'd been hurt, maybe dying, and she'd been on a mission to save him.

Yeah, like, *fail.*

She took the boy's blood pressure, noted his pulse, checked his IVs. Then, gathering up a tray of soiled instruments, she dumped them in alcohol before crossing the hall to retrieve their makeshift steam sterilizer. She carried the sterilizer outside, set it on a small propane stove, and lit the stove. While she waited for the steam to build, she washed the instruments, then placed them in the sterilizer. It would take about twenty minutes of steam to disinfect the instruments, heat being their only . . .

Heat.

Heat.

Staring down at the tiny ring of blue flame, huddled in her scrubs and a thin yellow nurse's gown, she frowned. Something about heat had been bothering her for hours. But why?

Kincaid's words came back: *Flies'll die in the cold.*

That was right. Flies died in the cold. Leave a dead *anything* out in the cold, and there would not be blowflies, not in winter. She had seen no flies in Honey's stable at all, not even four weeks ago. She'd seen more than a few dead bodies on the road, but no flies. And at the gas station, dead Ned . . .

"No flies," she murmured. But the boy had maggots. Maggots could only come from flies, but if they'd found him in an abandoned barn, how had he stayed warm? What would've warmed up the barn enough so flies could live in winter?

Okay, maybe the boy had started a fire. No, that couldn't be it. That boy was out cold when they brought him in; he was just the other side of dead. Hell, he *had* been dead.

Which meant that someone else started the fire. Someone else kept the boy warm. There had been someone else, maybe more than one person.

But Greg had said, *Found him by his lonesome in a barn.*

No, Greg. Not hardly. And they'd been nearer *Oren* . . . what were they doing there? They'd been on their way to Wisconsin, unless there'd been a change in plans. Hadn't Chris been up to Oren already? Right; that's where he'd gotten the books. So Chris had been there not long ago.

Kincaid: *Either you boys hurt? You boys get a name?*

If Kincaid was worried about that, he must've figured there was a fight. Getting a *name*, though, suggested not only other people but . . . a conversation? Or—oh my God—a *trade*? Something worse?

Because Kincaid *knew*: they hadn't just found this kid; they hadn't *rescued* him.

They'd taken him.

62

Almost every kid she'd ever known, herself included, squirreled crap away in their pockets. Before she'd discovered Swiss Army knives, Alex's favorites had been rocks and chewing gum. She had no idea why, and her mother was always grousing about chewing gum that melted in the dryer.

But there was nothing in the boy's pockets.

What kid carried nothing? Alex stared in disbelief at the jumble of tattered clothing she'd retrieved from the trash. The stink was terrible: blood and pus and months' worth of dirt. The boy's name was penned into his sneakers but too smeary from sweat and dirt for her to make out more than a *J* and an *N*. Or maybe *M*. His flannel shirt had only one ripped pocket, and his jeans pockets were riddled with holes.

She picked up a limp tongue of the boy's olive-green jacket in one gloved hand. The jacket had faux-fur along the hood and a sagging, quilted, blaze-orange, zip-in lining. She hefted the jacket. Couldn't tell a thing from the weight. But that was the beauty of a zippered lining. Since coming to Rule she'd certainly used hers to sneak supplies for her Great Escape. So she unzipped and then pulled the lining completely from the jacket.

Something metallic chinked to the floor. When she saw what it was, she clapped a hand to her mouth to stifle the scream.

Not a knife. Not a gun.

Her whistle.

63

She did not wake Kincaid.

Instead, dryeyed, she huddled by the boy, trying to will him back to consciousness. When that didn't work, she checked his blood pressure, fiddled with his IVs, listened to his too-rapid heart, and felt his fingertips, which were cold. That, she knew, was bad, and she might have to get Kincaid soon, but not quite yet. All she needed were a few minutes alone with the boy. If he would just wake *up* . . .

She'd slipped the whistle around her neck and tucked it under her scrubs, and now she touched it just to make sure it was still there. Of course it was. She was not dreaming. This wasn't like her parents slipping away into the night. This was real and tangible and she ought to be able to put this together. All the pieces were there, she knew; she just didn't know how they fit together.

Think.

They'd left the ranger station on November 10. Ellie had been taken the very next day, on the eleventh. By Harlan's estimate, he'd last laid eyes on her a week or ten days after that. Harlan had been banished from Rule before Thanksgiving, so she couldn't ask him, but hadn't he said that they'd been attacked south of Rule? She thought that was right. But the boy had come from Oren, which was northwest and over fifty miles away.

That meant one of two things. Either Ellie had made it to Oren, or someone else had taken the whistle from her—maybe while she was still down south—and then found his or her way to Oren. Either the boy had actually seen Ellie and she had given him the whistle, or someone else had. Any way you cut it, someone had laid eyes on Ellie, maybe as recently as *six* weeks ago, when Chris had returned from Oren with books and those sunglasses.

And Lena. Angry, sullen, furious Lena was from Oren, and she'd tried to get *back*. Why? Because there were other people there? Yes, Lena had brothers who might still be alive. So . . . another enclave of survivors? Had to be.

An image of Lena spitting something at Chris and then grabbing him, flinging herself into his arms . . .

And Chris: *It's not what you think.*

Well, she knew that already, didn't she? Alex had tasted the truth in his lips, felt it in their embrace. Knew it from his scent.

So if not that—if this was not about Lena and Chris as a couple—then what? She went over the sequence again and recognized now not only anger but desperation in Lena's body language. Lena had been frantic about something. But what? What could Chris possibly be in a position to do—

Oh, my God. Alex gasped as the pieces clicked into place, the solution to a puzzle she'd only now realized had been there from the start.

No, not desperate over *what*.

Desperate over *whom*.

Alex thought it might work like this.

Going on patrol must have more than one meaning. There was patrol, as in patrolling their perimeter, keeping out all kinds of bad guys. But there was also riding out of Rule in search of supplies— meaning that they would almost certainly run into other survivors. There were raiders, so she knew there were other enclaves, doubtless many other Rules. She'd been the one to suggest that they band together. Chris had dismissed that, saying that she didn't understand.

But what if the men of Rule were not, in fact, the Armies of Light at all—but those of Darkness?

Now that she allowed herself the thought, she realized its logic. Of course, the men of Rule must raid other settlements. Look what happened in New Orleans after Katrina, in Baghdad when the troops invaded, or in the days when you could go to a grocery store right before a big old storm—a blizzard, say. The shelves got cleaned out in a heartbeat. People fought over bottled water in the aisles and slugged each other in the checkout lines. People stole. They looted. Sometimes, they killed to get what they wanted.

Things were a little different now, but maybe not by much. A lot of people were dead—not young enough to be Spared and not old enough either. But it was a safe bet that the Changed weren't heading out for a loaf of Wonder Bread. That left an awful lot of people—and maybe a fair number of Spared—wandering around, looking for the basics of survival: warmth, water, food, shelter. She just bet those stores got cleaned out pretty quick. Hell, she'd seen enough on the road herself to realize this was true. She'd found a *lot* of bodies—but no food. So why did she ever swallow that Chris or Peter or any of the other patrols just happened to come upon a nice little grocery store somewhere that no one had thought to check out?

Because she'd wanted to believe them. No, that wasn't quite right. She couldn't afford not to. She just hadn't wanted to think, period, because she was grateful to be safe and warm and fed and protected. But if they—*she*—had food and medicine, someone else went without. That was the way the world—brave and new, or not—worked.

So, you're Chris or Peter, armed to the teeth, and you raid and take what you need. But way back, Marjorie had said that towns let in people with kids—because kids were valuable.

So what if you're carrying out a special mandate, following an order that only a few, select people know?

Jess had said it: *Following orders doesn't make you a man.*

So what if the orders were to find the Spared?

And not just that. Maybe the new rule was to find and then *bring* the Spared back, whatever it takes.

And kill anyone who stands in your way.

64

An hour later, the boy's blood pressure fell. Alex woke Kincaid. They pushed fluids and Kincaid used the last of the dopamine to try and bring the boy's pressure back up. By the end, the boy's face was so swollen he looked like one of those good-luck Buddhas.

He died well before dawn and never once opened his eyes.

65

She had to get out, Chris or no Chris; whatever was happening between them didn't matter. She had to get out.

Greg said that the others were a day behind. That meant that Chris and Peter would be back very soon.

She had to get out before Chris returned, though she wasn't exactly clear on why that was so important. Remembering that sudden heat and their hunger for each other made her stomach fluttery with anxiety. Would she lose her nerve if she saw him again? No, no, that was crazy. *She* was crazy if she didn't take the chance and run, *now*. Whatever was happening between them . . . well, she wasn't sure what it was and she didn't want to find out.

Run. *Run.*

Kincaid was done in and not thinking straight or he'd never have agreed to let her take his horse back to town alone. Dawn was two hours away yet, and the night was still heavy and deeply cold, with a green thumbnail of a moon. As she left the hospice, she gave a cheerful wave to the guard hunkered in a puff of polar-weight sleeping bag inside the lobby's double doors. The guard, a retired miner not as debilitated and old as his sicker friends, hollered something she didn't hear but that she thought might be *see you later.*

"You bet!" she shouted back, thinking, *Not bloody likely.*

If there was a time to go, it was now, before Chris and the others made it back. The guards would still change over at seven, but that shouldn't be a problem. Kincaid's horse was much larger and stronger than Honey, and she thought that this horse was probably pretty fast. But she had to be smart. Galloping out of town with nothing was just flat-out dumb, and she needed to gather up what she could.

She touched her jacket, felt the knot of the Gigli saw she'd liberated right before she got Kincaid, and the slender line of a heavy-duty scalpel. Unless she planned on strangling someone, the Gigli wasn't much of a weapon, but you could take off someone's nose with the scalpel. She still had the boot knife. Kincaid had a gun, but it was in his office. Where could she go, right now, to find another? Nowhere. She wasn't about to try breaking into the jail, and she knew only a limited number of streets in Rule, and where a few people lived. Come to think of it, she didn't know where Chris lived either—and that *was* a shame, because she knew he was gone. Greg said all the guys had a couple of guns, so no telling what Chris had at his place. Well, no use worrying about what she couldn't change.

Riding at night was not as hard as she thought it might be. The snow shimmered like a silver ribbon, and the light ghosted through the forest well enough that she could make out individual trees. She'd have to be careful, though. No telling what was under the snow—fallen trees, tangles of brambles. The last thing she needed was a horse with a broken leg.

The southwest corner was her best option. Greg had said there were not as many guards, although Sarah said there were guards in the woods, some in the trees. Yes, but *she* had an advantage. She ought to be able to smell the guards and avoid them. If they had dogs, she might be in trouble, but she couldn't think how a dog would be of any use in a tree stand.

Yeah, but then maybe she shouldn't bring the horse. A horse made a lot of noise, and this night was very quiet, no gunfire at all. Even raiders didn't want to freeze their asses off.

There would be the Changed, though, and they weren't stupid. Yeager could call them beasts all he wanted, but they knew what clothes were for; they'd be out there. She wondered if they'd learned about fire yet. Sure, why not? Jim, Tom's friend, remembered how to evade, and that girl at the gas station had a *club*. And if one of them figured out how to use a *gun* . . .

Stop, you're overthinking it. One disaster at a time.

When she turned into the village square, there were more men, and they all gave her a very long look as she passed. She screwed on the cheerful, chipper, just-minding-my-business look and kept moving. . . .

"Hold up there a sec."

Shit. For a split second, she thought about kicking the horse to a wild gallop, but she pulled up and waited as another rider came alongside. He was squat, with arms like Popeye and no neck. She knew him, had seen him around the village hall, but couldn't dredge up a name.

"You shouldn't be out alone," he said. He even sounded a little bit like Popeye. "That's Doc's horse."

"Yeah, but don't tell anyone, please?" She gave what she hoped was a tired, grateful smile. "Doc let me take him. We've been up all night, and I just needed to get out of there." It helped that this was true.

"That boy they found up by Oren?" He gave her a one-eyed Popeye squint. "Yeah, heard about that. How's he doing?"

"He's dead." She was so tired that her eyes began to well, and then she was crying for real. "We were up all night. It was . . . pretty bad."

"Hey, wow, it's okay." He tried giving her an awkward pat on the shoulder but didn't seem to want to touch her and only ended up patting air. "You're a good kid. It's okay, you're just all done in."

"I'm really tired," she said, backhanding tears from her cheeks. "I just need to lie down, I think."

"Sure, sure." He pulled up in his saddle, looked over his shoulder and then back at her. "Look, I'd take you home myself, but I got to head out, meet up with the guys coming back. . . . You going to be okay going by yourself the rest of the way?"

"Yeah," she said, and snuffled. She used her jacket to wipe her nose. "I'm okay. I should sleep."

"Yeah, that's a good idea. You do that." Then he wheeled around and let her go on her way.

Hurrying back to Jess's, she considered the problem of Lena.

Lena was the only person she knew who'd gotten anywhere close to leaving Rule, and Lena was also from Oren. She would know the quickest way and what they ought to avoid. Hell, for all she knew, that dead boy might be related to Lena somehow.

But taking Lena, even trying to talk to her, made her queasy. Even if she hadn't seen her with Chris—and Lena had avoided her since—Alex didn't know her well enough. What she did know of Lena, she really, really didn't like. The last thing she needed was someone along she'd rather kill than have watching her back, and there was the little problem of trying to sneak back into the house, which was a complete nonstarter. . . .

Ghost.

A small moan pushed out in a steamy cloud. She would have to leave Ghost behind. The thought made her heart knot. There had to be a way to retrieve her dog. It was so unfair. Why was she always losing—

She pulled in a breath. *Oh shit,* shit.

The ashes.

The ashes were upstairs, in their case, on the desk in her bedroom. No way to get at them. No way to take them.

No, no, no, not again, not again, not again.

Mom. Her throat convulsed, and then she was crying again, only soundlessly, like a very small child. *Dad . . . Daddy . . .*

* * *

She'd completely forgotten about the stupid guard.

Nathan's dog fawned over Alex like a long-lost relative. She gave the same story to Nathan about Kincaid, then said she wanted to take the horse down to the garage at the end of the cul-de-sac where she stabled Honey. If he suspected anything, Nathan didn't give any indication; he just dragged off his dog and waved her on her way.

As a precaution, she crossed the street, hugging the sidewalk where the snow was deep enough to muffle the sound of the Appaloosa's hooves. Jess's house looked quiet enough, curtains drawn tight. All the bedrooms were at the back, anyway. No one would be up quite yet, not even Jess.

Honey nickered when she led the Appaloosa into the garage. "I'm glad to see you, too," she whispered, stroking Honey's nose. "But you can't come, girl."

Climbing a stack of boxes, she reached up, patted around until she found the feed bag, and then pulled it down from the ceiling joists. Her stash was miserably small and she hadn't managed to find any food other than peanut butter and a few energy bars and four petrified rolls she'd wrapped in napkins and snuck out of the kitchen the week before. She scooped some oats into saddlebags, threw the bags behind the cantle, then tied them off.

Then her eye fell on a wooden dowel protruding from a bale of hay, and she felt a surge of elation: *Yes!* She twisted out the hay hook. The point was wicked and the hook itself was high-grade. She could smell it: white and icy, the cold-rolled steel as thick as her thumb. The white, clean smell of the steel was nearly overpowering and—

White?

Wait, she thought, *that's not right; steel doesn't smell white. Steel smells like metal. Steel doesn't smell like glare-white ice.*

Only one thing, one person, smelled like that.

She wouldn't go back without a fight. Her fingers curled around the hook's wooden dowel. No way, no *way* she was going back.

Fight. She turned, hay hook in hand, thinking, *Fight, fight.*

"Well," said Jess. She racked her shotgun. "It's about time."

66

"Why," asked Alex, "are you helping me?"

"I've been trying to help you all along, girl," said Jess. Beneath her parka, she still wore a white flannel nightgown, but her hood was thrown back and her hair was loose, flowing over her shoulders in a river of steel. She wore her shotgun—a Remington—slung over her back in a cross-carry. "You had to come to this yourself. Besides, I had to make sure that—" She broke off as Nathan slid out of the darkness with two horses. "Well?"

"Maybe fifteen minutes, Jess . . . Not now, Vi, heel!" Nathan rapped at his dog, which had spurted over to greet Alex. Nathan jerked his head to the left. "They're coming. We going to do this, we got to do it now."

"Fifteen minutes before what? Who's coming?" asked Alex.

"All right then." Jess jerked her head at Alex. "Come on. Bring Matt's horse. We don't have much time."

"Fifteen minutes before what?" Alex asked again as she led the horse out of the makeshift stable. She saw that the night was bleeding away. The sky was still a deep cobalt directly overhead, but fading to slate, fast. It would be dawn in another half hour, maybe less.

"You'll need this." Jess handed over a medium-size backpack. A pair of lightweight Tubbs snowshoes was lashed to the pack. "Supplies, enough to last two weeks. Clothes from your room, and a nice sweater. I'm sorry, I couldn't risk a larger pack or a sleeping bag, but there's an emergency blanket in there, a plastic tarp, waterproof matches, a knife, and a flint."

"Thank you," said Alex. She unzipped the backpack to peer inside. If Jess had been in her room, maybe she'd taken the case? But no, she saw at a glance that her parents weren't there. She'd actually already known that; the pack was too light. Zipping the pack, hefting it to her shoulders, she looked up to find Jess studying her.

"Best you shake the dust off your sandals, girl," Jess said. "The past is past."

She didn't ask Jess how she'd known. It was a moot point anyway. "I could use a gun. That Remington would be nice."

Jess shook her head. "That, I cannot do. You won't need it anyway."

"How do you figure?"

"Trust me."

That, Alex did not. But did she have other options? What would happen if she refused to go? Would Jess shoot her?

"Why can't I have a gun?" Alex asked. "I'm no threat to you. I want to leave." When Jess didn't reply, Alex persisted: "You know what it's like out there, Jess. I'll go, but give me a fighting chance."

Jess studied her for a long moment, then said to Nathan, "Give her your rifle."

Nathan's eyes widened. "Jess, I'm not sure—"

"But I am." Turning, Jess boosted herself onto her horse. "Give her the rifle."

Nathan's jaw tightened, and for a second, Alex thought he would refuse, but then he thumbed off his carrying strap. "You know how to use a bolt-action?" he asked Alex.

"Yes," she said, trying to hide her elation. The rifle was a scoped Browning X-Bolt, with a stainless-steel barrel and dark walnut stock: a very good weapon. "What's the pull?"

She couldn't tell if Nathan was contemptuous or amused. "Medium. Three and a half pounds, no take-up or creep. You got a detachable box mag here." He unlocked the floor plate and swung it open. "Holds five two-hundred-seventy Magnum shorts, and there's one in the chamber now, so you're loaded for bear. Safety's here on the tang, and there's a separate unlocking button where the bolt and the body meet up, so you can open the rifle on safe and unload, okay? She's a real good gun."

That was an understatement. Not only did she have a rifle *and* a scope, a Magnum short meant higher velocity and more power for the same amount of bang. She slung the rifle to a cross-carry, then tucked a box of cartridges Nathan handed over into her parka pocket and zipped that. "Thank you," she said to them both.

"Depending on what you find, you may not have cause to thank us," Jess said. Her scent had not changed, but that didn't mean much. Alex thought Jess was as good at hiding as Chris. Better, actually. In the months that she'd lived in Jess's house, Jess had remained a cipher. But the rifle convinced her.

Jess wants me gone, she thought. *But why now?*

As if she'd read her thoughts, Jess said, "Now or never, girl. This is a onetime offer."

Alex hopped onto the Appaloosa's back without another word and followed Nathan, already plowing into the woods at the end of the cul-de-sac. In two minutes, the three of them were deep into the woods, and Alex could no longer see any houses at all.

"Now, listen very carefully," Jess said. They were moving fast, the horses high-stepping through the snow. "The Zone in this direction extends for two miles. After that, there are no guards."

No more guards? And Kincaid had implied that the Zone went on for five miles, not two. Unless there was something different about the terrain? "How are we going to get—"

"Hold your tongue and listen. We will get you through, but once we reach the edge of the Zone, I can no longer help you, and I can't send anyone with you either. The trail is plain as day. A mile further on, the trail forks, and from there, you'll have to go on foot."

"Why?"

Ducking beneath a low-hanging branch, Jess flashed a look of impatience. "The trail's only a footpath and too narrow for the horse. You want to go *left*, not right, you understand? Right will loop you back to Rule. So you must dismount and send the horse back. It will find its way."

With no horse and no skies, slogging through snow in the

woods, even with the snowshoes, would be rough. "How long before I hit anything like a road?"

"Ten miles. From there, you can go anywhere you want. There's a map in the zipper pocket of the backpack. But remember, take the *left* fork—you understand?"

She nodded. "But why are you helping me? Why me, and not Lena?"

"Peter wanted Lena," said Jess, kicking her horse to a fast trot. "But Peter isn't the one who has to decide."

Alex urged her horse after. "Decide? Decide what?"

"Whether to break the rules or not."

Then she got it. "This is about Chris?"

"Let's just say I'm taking advantage of an opportunity to speed things up a bit," said Jess. "You had to be ready, too. Now you are."

"Ready for what?"

"For the same mission that led Isaac to sacrifice. Abraham was called by God to choose, and he chose righteousness. In the end, he was rewarded and Isaac was saved."

Great, a Bible story. Just what she needed. "That doesn't make any sense. That was a test."

"And so is this," said Jess. "Christopher cares for you. He wants you. He's Chosen, whether he knows it or not."

She felt the flush start in her neck. "I don't know about that."

"Young lady, I may be old, but I'm not senile." Her mouth curled. "Much. I heard it in his voice. I hear it in yours."

"You can't hear something like that," Alex said, then remembered what Kincaid had said: *Hearing like a bat, but with nuance.*

And she remembered all those times she'd caught Jess looking at her: through windows, across a crowd.

Looking, because she'd heard every word, even ones Alex barely gave voice to.

Jess was an Awakened.

67

They were well into the woods now. Nathan's dog bounded alongside, surging through the snow. It was very cold, but there was no wind. The air was gray and still as the trees pulled together out of the shadows and into the coming dawn. Alex caught just a whiff of wood smoke from somewhere far ahead; that, and Nathan's sweat and the dog, and Jess, immutable, as regal as a queen on her horse.

Nathan. Alex's eyes narrowed. The guard was clearly following Jess's orders. Did that mean there were other people in Rule willing to do the same? If so, then Jess didn't need Chris to break any rules; she was doing it herself already, wasn't she?

Unless there was a limit to how much she could do, how many people were willing to follow. Jess and Kincaid were tight; they were Awakened, just like the Rev, but only Chris was a Yeager. Well, not quite: his last name was Prentiss, so that meant that Chris's mother had Yeager blood, but she'd run away. Still, in Rule, that might count for a lot. Pitting Chris against his grandfather might be the only way for things to change. But what things? Turning away refugees? Doling out girls? What was Jess after? What did she want done that only Chris could do? Was challenging Yeager such a risk? Maybe so. Jess clearly thought so, and Chris had always balked, maybe because that meant challenging Peter, too—and Peter was an Ernst, one of the Five Families. So, for Chris to challenge his grandfather *and* Peter, he would have to want something badly enough to risk everything.

If Jess was right, and Chris wanted Alex, then *she* was the bait.

Hell, she was the prize.

"Wait a minute," she said, pulling up on her reins. Kincaid's horse stomped to a halt. "You *want* Chris to come after me."

"Of course," said Jess, but she might as well have said *duh*. "Wanting is sweet, and a person desperately wants what he cannot have. If Christopher wants you, he will have to fight for you."

"But you're using me," she said, trembling with a sudden blast of anger. Beyond, she saw Nathan turn. "How do I know this isn't just window dressing, something to make me think I'm going to get away, so it can't be faked?"

"*You* have a gun."

"So do you."

"I'm not going to shoot you, Alex. You will have to trust me."

"Jess," Nathan called. "Jess, we got to go."

"*Trust* you?" Alex's fists balled in fury. Beneath her legs, the Appaloosa reacted, snorting and prancing. "Why should I? You're making it sound like this challenge is some big deal, like civil war or something."

"It is," Jess said.

Yes, Kincaid had said *factions*, hadn't he? The Ernsts against the Yeagers? Or were there others? She remembered that extra chair, how unbalanced the Council had seemed. Because there was someone else? A sixth family?

"What if Chris gets hurt? What if his grandfather—"

"We won't let that happen," said Jess. "I know you have no reason to trust me, but we won't."

The image of Chris riding into town, finding out she was gone, stole her breath away. He would come after her—and God, in another time and place, she might even want that. "If there are so many of you, why don't *you* do it then? Why don't you break a few rules?"

Jess's voice was as icy as her scent. "And what, exactly, would you call this, Alex?"

Nathan: *"Jess."*

"This is *Rule*, girl, and the best I can do. If there is to be change— a *challenge*—it must come from Chris," Jess said. "If he wants to be a man and blood of my blood, he must be tested. *Test everything, but hold fast to what is good.*"

"Blood of my blood?" said Alex, and then remembered what she had heard but not really understood.

Jess had said it, plain and simple: *I thank God my grandson was spared.*

Not spared as in saved from seeing how the world had ended, or seeing his mother die—but *Spared.*

Jess was Chris's grandmother.

Did Chris know? She didn't think so. He had never said—

Nathan let out a shrill, warbling whistle, and Alex jumped in surprise. "What is it?" she asked.

"There," said Jess. "On the trail and in the trees. We're almost there."

Alex looked. Maybe three hundred feet farther on, there was movement on either side of the trail, and then she spotted two snow-white horses in the woods and their riders, in camouflage white with only the dark ovals of their faces to betray that they were there at all. A bit farther on, in the high, spreading branches of a large oak, a man, armed with a crossbow, nestled in a wooden tree stand.

"All right," said Jess. "Remember: at the fork, take the *left*—"

Someone shouted Alex's name, faint but unmistakable, and as she turned in her saddle, she knew.

Chris, on Night, charging down the trail, bulleting through the woods at a dead gallop. He was still just a little too far away for her to make out his face, but she heard him just the same.

"Alex!" Chris screamed. "Alex, no, stop! *Stop!*"

68

"Go!" Jess shouted. When Alex hesitated, Jess swatted the Appaloosa's haunch. "Hiyah! Go, *go!*"

Startled, the Appaloosa shied and then spurted down the trail, surging with a mighty heave of its legs, and then Jess was right there alongside, and they were hurtling toward the edge of the Zone. Gasping, Alex had to fight not to pull back on the reins; if she did that, she would be thrown in an instant. Ahead, she saw Nathan's dog dance out of the way as Nathan's horse kicked off the trail and they thundered past.

"Keep going!" Nathan shouted. He waved them on. "Go, g—"

"Alex!" Chris shouted, and now his panic was unmistakable. *"Alex!"*

"Go!" Jess slashed the Appaloosa with her reins, whipping the animal to a frenzy, and now it was all Alex could do just to hold on. Hunching down in the saddle, she grabbed for the pommel, tightening her thighs around the horse's middle, feeling the horse's power jolt up her spine with every pounding step. She and Jess were dead even, their horses blazing through the woods. The trees were a blur, a flash of whippy branches that grabbed at her arms and her hair, and she felt the sting as one scored her cheek.

"Alex!" Closer now. She risked a quick peek back, saw that Chris was chewing up the distance between them; saw that he was gaining, would catch them, catch *her*. "Alex, *stop!*"

"Let her *through!*" Jess shouted, and then she gave the Appaloosa one final, vicious cut of her reins.

Kincaid's horse screamed, a braying screech, and then it rocketed through the snow, bearing down on the mounted guards, and then they were there and gone in a flash, and she was past them and still going. Streaking beneath the archer in his stand, she broke through and then she was out of the Zone, she was out of Rule, she was out of reach and gone, and Chris—

A shotgun *boomed*, a blast that sounded like the earth was breaking in two—and Alex just had time to think, *God, no*, Chris!

With a high, bawling cry, Kincaid's horse reared. Alex shrieked and flung herself at the horse's neck, knotting her fists into its mane. The horse reared again, its neck popping back. It hit Alex's forehead, and for a dizzying moment, she thought she would be thrown for sure. There was blood in her mouth, and her vision tilted as the horse stabbed down, but she held on.

They were turned around now, the horse dancing beneath her, and she was looking back down the trail, back toward Rule. She saw the shotgun in Jess's hands, saw that Night was still rearing, saw that the guards had converged and were now wrestling Chris from his horse. Chris tumbled to the ground, but he was flailing, fighting them, clawing his way back to his feet. She saw one guard slip and fall, and then Chris was free, and he was churning through the snow, trying to get to her.

"Alex!" He was close enough now that she could read his despair, and then she suddenly caught the keener edge of another scent she knew: horror. He shouted, "Please, Alex, you don't know what you're—"

Jess clubbed him with the Remington. The blow was short and precise and caught Chris behind his right ear. Chris dropped to the snow in mid-stride and was still.

"No!" Alex cried. She tightened her knees, and the Appaloosa started back toward Rule. "What are you do—"

"Stop." Jess racked the Remington and pointed it at Alex. In the tree stand, the archer leveled his bow, his arrow ready to fly into her chest. "Not another step."

"But Chris . . ."

"Will be fine. *Shake thyself of dust and loose thyself, o' captive daughter of Zion*. Go, Alex," said Jess, "and do not look back."

She did as she was told.

PART FIVE:
MONSTER

69

Four miles on, she was on foot, having dismounted and then slapped the Appaloosa's rump to send it on its way back. The horse hadn't seemed to need much convincing and cantered away toward Rule. The correct trail was marked with a blood-red kerchief, and was so narrow and twisting that she thought it had once been a deer path, something a hunter might follow to find game. In a way, it was like the footpath that had led her and Ellie, in what seemed like another century, to the river and then to those dogs and poor crazy Jim—and, finally, to Tom. Which made her wonder if she was doomed to spend the rest of her life blundering down one path after another, searching for God knows what.

The snow was deep and heavy and sucked at her boots. Her thighs were starting to burn, and her head ached. Her mouth hurt from where she'd bitten her tongue. When she swallowed, she tasted old blood, and her body was sore and bruised and shaken from her mad, wild dash through the woods, like she'd been stuck in a blender while Jess hit "frappe."

A test. This was all a test for Chris. She was free, but Chris couldn't be, not until he broke the rules of Rule . . . whatever they were. Frankly, she thought that all of Jess's spouting was about as nutty as Yeager's.

Her eyes snagged on something blue protruding on a stick from the snow about ten feet ahead, to the right of the trail at the base of a spindly pine. The color was startling and very clear, like a daub of turquoise paint on a perfectly white canvas. At first, she thought it was an old nylon trail blaze, the kind hiking clubs tied around tree branches.

But when she got closer, she saw that this something was the remains of a sleeve.

And the stick was a bone.

She went absolutely still. Her mind blanked. She froze in mid-step, and for a second, she could only stare, waiting for the white grip of stunned horror squeezing her brain to let go.

She thought the bone was an ulna, not that it really mattered. The small bones of the hand and fingers were gone, so either the rest of the body was buried under the snow, or the arm had been dragged here by whatever scavenger had claimed it before stripping off the meat.

Okay, this is like the road. It's not like you haven't seen a body before. There are scavengers. You're outside of Rule's protection now, so of course you're going to find bodies. People dropped dead in their tracks, remember?

She took a cautious sniff, but smelled nothing more than the forest. No wolves, no raccoons. The bone wasn't that old and it was not as white as the snow, but it wasn't fresh either.

It's okay. Thumbing the rifle's carry strap, she checked the safety, and then she stripped off her glove and snaked her right hand to her back, her fingers slipping around the wooden dowel of the hay hook where it dangled from a belt loop. She had the rifle, the hay hook, a knife. She'd be fi—

She wasn't sure what she sensed first: the long furl of something obscenely pink hanging from an oak to her left, or the rot.

The smell made the tiny hairs on her forearms stand on end. She knew the stink was dead meat but not *them*, not the Changed. But there were bodies here—a lot of them—and she knew that things would not be fine.

The thing dangling from the tree was a body, but it was not human. The fur was completely gone, peeled from the flesh like a glove. The animal's muscles were intact, not so much as a scrap missing, which was very strange, considering all that meat. And come to think of it—she listened over the thrum of her heart—no birds here. No crows. Nothing.

The thing hung from a noose like some weird imitation of a scarecrow. She recognized what it was from the shape of its head and the curve of its teeth.

A wolf.

There were more wolf bodies now, on either side of the trail, marking the way like flags down the avenue of a parade. In less than an eighth of a mile, she came to a small clearing, a circle where the snow was tamped down like a dinner plate. Which was, when she stopped to think of it, pretty apt.

Actually, if you didn't know about the bones, you'd have thought that the clothes had all gotten dumped out of several, very large laundry bags. There was a jumble of mismatched shoes and tightly laced boots, several with splintered leg bones poking from stockinged feet that had rotted—*that* she could smell, very easily, even in the cold—as if clawing away the laces had been just too much trouble. The clearing was a riot of color and deflated sacks of clothing filled with bones; she even spotted the black tarantula of a toupee and a silver wig of tight, permed curls. A golden puddle of chain nestled in a swath of shimmery black fabric.

Because you can't eat the jewelry, she thought, a little crazily. The ruby-red frames of a pair of sunglasses stared up from the snow, the right lens broken into a starburst. *You can't eat glasses.*

This wasn't just a clearing.

It was a feeding ground.

And maybe one of several, because now her numbed brain registered more color in the trees to her left, and then farther on to her right again. Each area was marked by more wolf carcasses as well.

Her gaze crawled from the clearing back to the trail. Ahead, she saw a neat pyramid, a crude trailmarker, maybe—the kind normally made of stones.

Only these were not stones.

They were heads.

No.

Some were leathery and very old, the eyes and noses and ears gone, and the tongues. Others were fresher, with nerves worming from their sockets and half-eaten lips clotted with frozen gore.

No.

A few weren't old at all—were nearly fresh, with blue tongues and noses only slightly gnawed and eyelids that dropped sleepily. But no maggots, no flies—it was too cold; hadn't she just learned that?

She counted, her gaze slowly ticking from one ruined face to the next. The pyramid was twelve heads long, seven deep at the base, and stood maybe four feet hi—

No.

Her breath died in her chest. She went completely and utterly still.

No,

She couldn't tear her eyes away.

No, please, it can't be him.

It took all her will to blink, and then blink again—as if her mind was a camera and she could somehow unsnap that picture so the image she'd just captured would be erased.

But no. Nothing changed.

Harlan was there: second row down, three heads from the left. She could never forget that face, or those teeth.

Her stomach seized. A flood of incredibly vile, intensely bitter liquid rushed from her mouth to spatter and steam in the snow. Her knees unhinged, and then she was sagging, the rifle sinking into the snow as the vomit roared from her mouth. She threw up until her stomach was empty, and then she hung there, groveling in ruined snow, gasping, her nose full of the stink of her own vomit—

And then a fresh wave rolled over her, a stench of something sick and dead that had sweltered and decayed beneath a hot summer sun.

A bloom of black horror squeezed her lungs and choked off her breath, and she finally understood why Jess had talked about Isaac—and sacrifice.

Maybe they had been watching. Maybe they had even enjoyed what they saw. But more likely, they came here out of habit, hunters following the likely path of good game—knowing where to find their next meal.

There were five: three boys, two girls. They wore parkas and boots and gloves. One boy and one girl wore skins, the animal fur pulled down so their eyes peered from a wolf's face.

And they all had weapons. One girl and two of the boys, including Wolf Boy, had rifles. The third boy, maybe a middle-schooler once, had a Beretta, which would be much easier for a young boy with small hands.

The only one without a gun was Wolf Girl, who held a corn knife instead. The blade—very long and very sharp—was stained with rust spiders of dried blood.

And there was one more thing, one last detail that made these kids so very different.

These Changed weren't clean, but they weren't filthy either.
They looked, in fact, very well fed.

The truth hit her like a hammer.
Rule wasn't fighting them.
Rule was feeding them.

ACKNOWLEDGMENTS

The cool thing about acknowledgments is no one gets to change up a single word. So—<cue maniacal laughter>—*bwahahahaha!* Seriously, if you guys embarrass easily . . . better stop reading.

To my fabulous editor, Greg Ferguson: I got to admit that when I first read that cover letter and all your edit notes, I was seized with this overwhelming urge to lie down and maybe drink heavily. Or maybe that was the other way around. Really, I was in the slough of despond. Later, after I woke up, I realized the care that went into each and every question. You made this a much better, more focused and tighter book, and I can not thank you enough for your enthusiasm, perseverance, and patience. Hold on to that fine-toothed flea comb; we got more nits to pick, fella. (Oh, and those packs? God, you are so brilliant.)

More thanks to my eagle-eyed, wizard of a copy editor, Ryan Sullivan, who both forced me to be clearer and knew, exactly, which words deserved a quick and merciless death.

To Katie Halata: thank you for answering every question and keeping my life in order. To Elizabeth Law, who came through with a single word when I most needed it: bless you. A big-shout to the rest of the good folks at Egmont USA: please know that I am so grateful for all your hard work. Go, team!

Many thanks again to my splendid agent, Jennifer Laughran, who never hesitates to give a reality slap whenever appropriate: *Whoa, thanks; I needed that.* Babe, I'll keep you in rock salt and snow shovels forever.

To Dean Wesley Smith, once more, for his knowledge, friendship, and ever-available shoulder: I am so fortunate to know you.

To Erin Coppersmith and all the other ladies at our little library that time forgot and the decades cannot improve: thank you for locating each and every bizarre book I need, needed, or ever will need. Seriously, I could not do this without you guys.

To my daughters, Carolyn and Sarah: yes, it's safe to come into the study now.

Finally, to David: you are a saint, my advocate, my sweetheart. Every woman should be so lucky. Really.